Praise for Christian Ba
The Ice Ben

T0090224

"Impressive. . . . Equal parts *Stripes* and *Apocalypse Now*. . . . Evokes the great soldier-writers Tim O'Brien and Thom Jones."
—Mark Rozzo, *The Los Angeles Times*

"This sterling first novel offers a study in quiet tension and contemporary social malaise. . . . Bauman's style is terse, candid, and on target with both language and circumstances. His close analysis of character motivation lends extra tension to an already suspenseful account. . . . A war story for the new millennium."
—*Publishers Weekly*

"A fresh, straightforward debut that strikes just the right balance between action and recollection."
—*Kirkus Reviews*

"An impressive debut. . . . As with all great war novels, *The Ice Beneath You* is not so much about war itself as the consequences of war."
—*The Tallahassee Democrat*

"Bauman's pure prose suits his naturalist approach. What is striking . . . are the tiny minefields laid along the way, microscopic psychological bombs detonated by the realization that the war is never really over for anyone who has fought it. With unadorned honesty, Bauman has illuminated us."
—Elisa Ludwig, *Philadelphia City Paper*

"An addictive, quick read. . . . Unforgettable characters. . . . Original, timely, and important."

—*Home News Tribune* (E. Brunswick, NJ)

"This year's most riveting return flight into the heart of darkness . . . searingly real."

—Anneli Rufus, *East Bay Express* (Berkeley, CA)

"Darkly comic. . . . Bauman's intercutting is a nervy stylistic that zeroes in on the drab lives of less-than-historical figures. . . . [A] late-night tavern tale of a likeable anti-hero and his dubious comrades in arms."

—*Eugene Weekly* (Eugene, OR)

"One of the finest books on life in the American army."

—Chris Hedges, author of
War Is a Force That Gives Us Meaning

"Beautifully crafted, structured, and simple. . . . It is a pleasure to read the work of a real writer. Thank you, Mr. Bauman."

—Hubert Selby, Jr., author of
Last Exit to Brooklyn and *Requiem for a Dream*

"A remarkable debut . . . a tense, razor-edged, powerful effort. . . . This is a book that will *hold* you."

—Richard Wertime, author of
Citadel on the Mountain

"*The Ice Beneath You* is an important book—a profound meditation on the stark realities of the American male experience. The truths of soldiering are brilliantly examined here from angles previously unexplored, but this is not so much a war novel as it is an exploration of the human heart. The writing is beautiful, deft, and it displays an almost religious devotion to unwavering honesty."
—Don De Grazia, author of *American Skin*

"Bauman renders the true spirit of men at war—not just the frustrations and fear that come with operating over a dangerous landscape, but also the deep bonds that tie men and women together through such experiences. With both humor and compassion, he captures well the deeper wounds that such places can inflict."
—Scott Anderson, author of
The Man Who Tried to Save the World and *Triage*

"Shorn of artifice, probing, moral. . . . A writer to be watched."
—Andrew Huebner, author of *American by Blood*

VOODOO LOUNGE

a novel

CHRISTIAN BAUMAN

A TOUCHSTONE BOOK
Published by Simon & Schuster
NEW YORK LONDON TORONTO SYDNEY

TOUCHSTONE
Rockefeller Center
1230 Avenue of the Americas
New York, NY 10020

TOUCHSTONE and colophon are registered trademarks of Simon & Schuster, Inc.

For information regarding special discounts for bulk purchases,
please contact Simon & Schuster Special Sales at
1-800-456-6798 or business@simonandschuster.com.

Designed by Kyoko Watanabe

Manufactured in the United States of America

1   3   5   7   9   10   8   6   4   2

Library of Congress Cataloging-in-Publication Data

Bauman, Christian.
Voodoo Lounge : a novel / Christian Bauman.
p. cm
"A Touchstone book."
1. Haiti—History—American intervention, 1994–1995—Fiction.
2. Americans—Haiti—Fiction. 3. Soldiers—Fiction.
I. Title.

PS3602.A96V66 2005
813'.6—dc22

ISBN-13: 978-0-7432-7098-4
ISBN-10: 0-7432-7098-3

For Kirk Berlenbach and Tim Blaikie

"The coming of war turned out to be, somehow, intimate, like Christmas."

—Alan Furst

"It's very hard to live in Haiti and not know who cut off someone's head."

—Paul Farmer

CONTENTS

VOODOO
LOUNGE

September 20, 1994

When you go, you go for real. And there is no time more real than 3:00 A.M. Sergeants' time, it's called. Zero three hundred. Zero dark early.

On the old Army boat, the general-quarters bell rang twice for wake-up at 0300. The bell didn't matter; those who'd slept had been up for at least half an hour. Most of the thirty-four soldiers hadn't slept. In warm bunks and cold latrine stalls they'd all felt the engines throttle down at 0245, the hard rattle in the bulkheads reduced to a low buzz as the vessel went from full speed to barely making headway through the Caribbean waters.

The echo of the bell died in empty steel passageways, replaced by the hollow silence of nothing to say, nothing to talk about. Cigarettes went to lips, Zippo lids flipped back. Brown T-shirts came down over heads, camouflage BDU blouses buttoned up. The skeleton crews on night watch wiped oil from the gray sides of the diesels, raised binoculars to eyes on the bridge wings, listened to quiet static on the marine bands, made coffee.

In a cramped, two-bunk crew cabin the soldier everyone called Jersey sat in the only chair, bent over, pulling speed-laces tight on a black jungle boot, tucking ends. The door opened, Dick Wags in blue engine-room coveralls, hands in pockets. The light from the passage behind framing a tight face.

"Roomdog," Dick Wags said, with deep-voice Dick Wags drama. "Voodoo Lounge awaits."

Jersey looked up, snorted, said, "Please." The soldier tapped a Marlboro against the ashtray, bent to tie the other boot. Dick Wags was from northeast Jersey, Jersey from northwest. Dick Wags was Dick, sometimes Rick. Jersey was Jersey, except to Dick Wags; to Dick Wags, Jersey was Roomdog. Everyone's roomdog was Roomdog. It wasn't complicated.

"You done?" Dick Wags asked. "I gotta get my shit on."

"Two minutes," Jersey said, picking up the cigarette again.

"Two and two," Dick Wags said, leaving, closing the door. Boot-sole footsteps padded down the passage then were gone. "Two and two," Jersey whispered, standing, tucking brown T-shirt deep into green, camouflage BDU pants, tightening belt, reaching for BDU top. "Two and two." They had all taped silver reflective patches to the shoulders of their uniforms and the crown of their helmets yesterday. A new system, they'd been told. Easier identification from a distance. To avoid friendly fire. "Friendly fire," Jersey whispered. "Two and two."

Dick Wags was back in two and two, as Jersey stepped into the passageway. "Friendly fire, Dick Wags," Jersey said, pressing fingertips against the patch of silver tape. "Gotta watch that friendly fire."

"No friendly fire in the Voodoo Lounge, Sergeant Roomdog," Dick Wags said.

"Sergeant, yes."

They slammed knuckled fists as they passed. They were going, going for real, trying to do it right. Two sergeants—Jersey a very young buck sergeant, Dick Wags a staff sergeant—going for the first time.

The cabin door closed. Jersey made for the stairs up to the galley deck. Someone was reciting the Lord's Prayer in the head. Might be Matata, hard to tell.

Pelton filled the passage at the bottom of the stairs, M-16 rifle hanging from shoulder, forehead pressed against the bulkhead, eyes clenched tight. Jersey put a hand up to the big shoulder, squeezing past, whispered, "All good, P. All good." Pelton inched forward, head not moving, skin to metal. When Jersey made the stairs and turned to look back the thick snipe was still there, hands wrapped around the rail, face to wall.

In darkened cabins soldiers sat alone, waiting. Dressed; drumming fingertips on desktops, rubbing palms on cheeks and chins.

In the bow-thruster room, deep beneath the wave pushed by the front of the ship, another young buck sergeant, whom everyone called Scaboo, set down hand weights and picked up a towel to wipe sweat, unable to wait passively. In the soundproofed engine-room box Chief threw the breaker to switch generators. On the bridge the first mate, Mac, sat slumped in the skipper's chair, staring at the flat black of night through the glass. In the skipper's cabin, directly below the bridge, Mannino sat on the edge of the bunk in boxers and a T-shirt, vessel manifest in hand, the thirty-four names of the warrant officers and crew.

In the small crew's mess Snaggletooth and Shrug sat below the TV mounted up on the bulkhead, joysticks in hand, playing Tetris. Riddle walked in, moving to the coffee pot. "Turn that shit off." Riddle's loud, flat, Florida voice filled the mess like it filled every room Riddle entered. Snaggletooth made a noise, stood, and pushed the button to make the TV a TV again. The screen filled with segueing images of plantations, beaches, city streets teeming with black figures in cars, on foot, on bikes. Swelling symphonic music from the speakers, no words ever, just the music. The TV had been like this since yesterday afternoon. They'd lost the tail-end of the Miami NBC station the day before that, then gained a few hours of Cuban broadcasting. Now, just this: one station out of Port-au-Prince, showing the same scenes over and over, and the never-ending music. It was patriotic, Mac had said. Cedras was broadcasting this to work up Haitian nationalism and pride. The coming American invasion was no surprise, no secret D-Day. They were going for real and half the world knew it. The glory broadcast on TV proved it.

"Nobody needs that now," Riddle said, sitting at a mess table, looking at the TV. "Put in *Serpent and the Rainbow*."

Shrug pulled the Tetris cartridge from the Nintendo, swaying to compensate for the slow pitch of the boat. "Skipper came in last night, threw it overboard."

"My movie?"

"Yep," Shrug said. "Took the tape, threw it overboard."

"Shit."

"Yep."

It was 0315.

Roy stepped into the mess from the galley. Roy liked to be called the Steward. Roy had done some reading, and—Army cook or no—this was a boat, a military vessel of the United States, and that meant Roy was the Steward. It was all the cook would answer to. Roy crossed to the coffee pot, dressed in BDUs, a white cook's apron hanging from red-blotched neck. A web belt was tight around the apron and the Texan's thick waist, a 9-mm pistol in a black holster.

"Hey Steward!" Riddle called, pointing at Roy's pistol. "You think Ton Ton Macoute is coming for your chowder?"

"Fucking-A," Roy said, Texas slow, adjusting steel-framed glasses and sipping from the coffee mug. The Skipper had assigned Roy to one of the big .50-cal machine guns for battlestations because Roy had spent two years in Korea, cooking chow for an infantry battalion. "Yeah, okay, Skip," Roy had said, "but I don't know much about fifty cals." Mannino put the cook there anyway. "You know what they look like, right, Sergeant?" Mannino had a strong Long Island accent. "If I call battlestations you could probably find it on the deck, right? And pull the trigger?"

Roy had the kitchen privates, Matata and Cain, up at midnight to make chow for the 0300 wake-up. No one wanted chow, though. Just coffee. Back in the galley Roy told Matata and Cain to clean and put everything up then get dressed and ready. They didn't have designated battlestations. They were substitutes, in case someone got shot.

The ship cut through the night waters, silent and slowing. Thirty-four soldiers, wide awake with nothing to say.

At 0340 general-quarters sounded again and Mac called to prepare for battlestations. Time to stop waiting down below. Time to hurry up and wait somewhere else. Time to go.

When you go—when you go for real—you put on pounds. Even Waterborne soldiers, with no field equipment, bore some weight going in. Real-time weight. Kevlar helmet, flak vest, web belt, LBE suspenders, ammo pouches and clips, M-16 rifle slung over back. Mac had told them not to tuck their pants into their combat boots because it would be easier to swim if they fell overboard. No one bothered to point to the dead weight of their flak jacket and ask if it mattered.

A few weeks before, Jersey had picked up a dog-eared copy of *The Things They Carried* at the USO and the book—the cool parts, anyway—had become standard reading for bored quarterdeck watches in the last days before they went down range. They made up their own lists of things soldiers carry, filling in what the book left out, scribbling anonymous notes on the inside cover: CRYSTAL METH AND A CASE OF THE ASS wrote one wit. HERPES FROM SCABOO'S MOM—WE ALL CARRY THAT—a penciled line reported. Riddle, signing name to note, pointed out that Snaggletooth carried the weight of ugly for the whole detachment. Even with the patience of paper and pencil Snaggletooth wasn't quick enough to transfer the weight of anything back to Riddle. Now it didn't matter; this morning they were going for real. All of them—privates to sergeants to warrant officers alike—for the first time. All of them combat virgins. All any of them carried was gradients of fear.

There was one more signal before the scatter for individual battlestations. One more place to wait before they went to wait someplace else. Four of them crowded behind a steel hatch, forward in a tight passage on the port side, like groups were now waiting at five different hatches around the boat. Waiting for the last signal to go for real. Jersey, Temple, Scaboo, and Riddle behind this one; helmet straps tight, adjusting the pounds hanging from their bodies, waiting. It occurred to Jersey that Riddle was silent for the first time in memory, a line of sweat running down the soldier's left cheek. Jersey drew a breath, held it, let it out.

Tense, tense, feeding on the silence.

"Stupid, going to battlestations this early," Scaboo growled.

"Can't you shut up," Jersey said, spinning so quickly on Scaboo their helmets clicked together.

Scaboo brought a hand up, but PFC Temple, bigger than both of them, slipped between the two new sergeants, stepping lightly on

Scaboo's highly polished jump boot. "Not now," Temple said, and a second later the passage lights went out—their signal. Riddle reached up, undogged the hatch, and swung it open. A warm wisp of darkness came to them, sweet flowers and salt, Riddle holding the hatch open. Temple pushed through then forward into the night air. Jersey moved to follow.

"Bitch," Scaboo whispered, lips to ear, and then was gone, through the hatch and up the ladder to the deck above.

Jersey's open palm shot out, searching for the other young sergeant's head, but Scaboo was gone.

"C'mon," Riddle barked. "Fuck that."

Then Riddle was gone, scurrying up the ladder behind Scaboo. All sound was gone as well, lost to the larger wash of ocean and wind.

"Two and two," Jersey whispered to no one—furious—"and fuck you," turning to dog the hatch tight, close to hyperventilating. Concentration broken from verbal friendly fire, two quick breaths, concentration back, then moving behind Temple's shadowy form on the ship's deck, the long walk forward up the portside catwalk to the bow.

They were going, going for real, but their reality was shaky, shifting; the truth as elusive and unsteady as the deck beneath their boots on a long rolling swell. They'd had a week to prepare for one stark reality; made peace and tied themselves into its probabilities like they tied themselves into their racks to sleep through rough weather. Then it shifted, with only hours to spare.

"Ex-president Jimmy Carter has asked Mister Cedras and the Haitian army not to blow us out of the water," Mac had intoned on the loudspeaker, voice floating and alien in the dim, empty passages. "Jimmy Carter says they'll be surrendering to us instead of shooting at us." They'd heard a click they all understood to be Mac's Zippo in action on a Camel Light. "The Skipper voted for Jimmy Carter— twice." The officer exhaled. "Me, I was too young."

Nothing changed. Just more anxiety. When you finally go, you go for real. Jimmy Carter or not. You have to. And you have to hold on to that—keep it first in your head. If your cracked-leather black combat boot crosses from deckplate to soil and there is a rifle in your hand, those watching from high on hilltops or from behind thick curtains have drawn their own definition of you. It doesn't matter how you define yourself, or how a president or general defines you, what official title or task is given you and those who travel with you. All that matters is how those watching your arrival define you. They provide your definition. And they know the neighborhood better.

When you go, you go for real, because those watching you arrive may not agree with your own definition. If your cracked-leather black combat boot crosses from deckplate to soil and there is a rifle in your hand, that is definition enough.

It was two-hundred-some feet up the portside catwalk from ship's house to bow. Jersey stepped onto the steel walkway, then paused. Stopped. Pulse slowed. Breath restored. Scaboo's spit-soaked insult forgotten, even mission momentarily set aside. The soldier gripped the rail and stopped in place, helmet tight and gear hanging, fingers closing around salty, sticky steel in the humid blackness. Stars overhead, the night was full—heavy and warm. Light would crack the horizon soon, but for now they could just as well be in space as at sea. Thirty-four soldiers, floating in the void. Three points forward the port beam five tiny red lights twinkled. Straight down, the sea was an ebony void cut by a pale line of wake rushing down the vessel's side, sea wind pulled along with it; predawn oblivion.

Okay okay okay, Jersey thought. *Now we go for real.*

It had taken five days to sail from Newport News. A midnight departure from Skiff's Creek, running lights blacked-out through the Dead Fleet and into the James River, past Norfolk and the Bay Bridge-Tunnel, ten miles to sea, then due south. Five days, marked by the slow fading and gaining and fading of TV signals from Virginia and the Carolinas and Florida, intercut with bad zombie movies and war novels, engine readings and bridge watches, midnight rations, and one halfhearted rain-soaked late-afternoon battlestations drill somewhere in the Bermuda Triangle. Five days, and crossing the Windward Passage past Cuba they'd found five empty Haitian refugee rafts—bobbing silently between swells, plywood and plastic and two of them upright again, with makeshift canvas sails—the Catholics on the LSV crossing themselves as the big boat steamed between the ghost rafts, the soldiers as one scanning shadows in the whitecaps for bodies, shuddering at the deep-ocean fates of the desperate Haitians who'd stepped barefoot into midnight waters pushing these deathtraps past the waves and jumping on to huddle with their families below a matchstick mast, whispering unheard prayers for clear winds to Florida.

Five days, this run. As a crew, they'd run longer—much longer—and harder, to accomplish nothing: celestial navigation training sails around Long Island to Nantucket and Portland, a stomach-wrenching North Atlantic crossing to the U.S. Army Waterborne depot at Hythe near Southampton, a midwinter sleeper run to the Azores to pick up rusty port equipment and bring it to Livorno. Only five days, this run—just a stone's throw from their backyard—but to accomplish something real this time, sailing through death floating silent and apathetic at the gates of their arrival.

"But here we go go go," Jersey whispered to the black, sweet wind. *Two and two. Friendly fire. Battlestations. Voodoo Lounge, baby.*

The Voodoo Lounge was Jersey's destination, the machine-gun nest on the port bow. The vessel was an Army LSV, bow split in two, the center a raised mighty ramp, sixty-some feet up, thirty-some feet across, with a small line-and-anchor station on each side, each one now reinforced as a machine-gun nest. Jersey and Temple crewed the port-side bow station, and Temple called it the Voodoo Lounge. Within a day or two the whole ship was the Voodoo Lounge, but it started with Temple painting the words on the steel plate lining their battlestation on the bow. They'd stocked it yesterday with bottles of water, a few MRE bags for chow, five apples, and an extra pack of cigarettes in a Zip-Loc bag. "No smoking until the sun comes up," Mac had ordered the crew during the briefing, trying to speak infantry. "Keep five yards!" Riddle had yelled back, Mac's eyebrows raising.

Jersey inhaled deeply, pulling it all in. They were going, and they were trying their best to go for real. Dawn would break shortly. The sergeant wondered whether it was simply automatic you pissed your pants when someone shot at you, or only if you'd had to go anyway. Maybe you just shot back. Maybe nothing happened at all.

Jersey looked forward to the bow, only gray shadows defining the ship's width. It was time. Her knees hurt, her back hurt, and an ammo pouch was digging into her side, but all in all it all seemed as good as it was going to get. As ready as they could be. She tugged her rifle strap then hustled up the catwalk toward Temple and her place in the Voodoo Lounge.

PART ONE

Port-au-Prince

CHAPTER

1

Dawn came with engines half, running the north side of Île de la Gonâve. The immense aircraft carrier *Eisenhower* stood a mile off their port quarter. The white hospital ship *Comfort* with the big red cross steamed closer and closing, a few points off the starboard quarter. It described an arc, the measure between the two bigger ships; a starting point and an ending.

Through the purple of sunrise she could see mountains now, misty gray-green jungle, glowing orange points of fire and black-blue plumes of smoke and cloud rising over it all. When they cleared Île de la Gonâve it was laid out in front of them, the inside of a crescent, green and shimmering, wind thick with salt and overripe fruit again, shades of charcoal and diesel and dung. And now, faintly, noise—the sound of Haiti. A low thump with no steady rhythm, a deep-bass heartbeat working an invisible echo inside the bowl of the Port-au-Prince basin.

The kitchen private Cain crept up the catwalk to the bow with coffee in a canteen right before all this, right before the dawn. "Y'all kill 'em dead now, hear?" the skinny cook whispered, then scurried back to the house. Temple stowed the warm canteen then rolled to his side and pissed down into the open well-deck, sprinkling the tops of the unmanned trucks and Humvees lined up twenty feet below; their cargo, the port-opening package for 10th Mountain Division. Jersey, having thought this through, scrambled behind a mound of sandbags and, in the last moment before daylight made them visible to the bridge, pushed her pants down clear of hips and squatted over a Styrofoam cup. In one motion her left hand drew her BDUs back up while her right tossed the overfilled cup over the side.

"Nice," Temple said, packing his smiling jaw with a chew. "Be all you can be."

They heard Riddle's voice on the radio, asking the bridge if they were allowed to smoke yet.

Temple and Jersey spent the last hour ducked down behind the plates of sheet metal that had been painted gray and welded on the bow handrails before they'd left Virginia, peering out through the gaps as Port-au-Prince grew in their vision. They could make out buildings now, dotted colorful carpets of neighborhoods spread across the basin and rising steep up the hill. A pink cathedral stood in the center of it, and a chalky domed building. As Jersey squinted through the forward gap the main harbor slowly took form, masts of a few small boats, curve of a cement pier, a small island in the middle with palm trees and a low building. This is where they were going. She'd thought the port was somewhat removed from the city, but even at this distance it was clear the port was completely in the city, surrounded, direct in the middle of it all.

"What are the Coasties doing?" Temple asked, chewing.

The only vessel forward of them was a Coast Guard cutter, a minesweeper. The cutter had stopped, about a half-mile up. Its wake went frosty, bow coming around.

"I think they're getting out," Jersey said.

The Coast Guard would only go so far; if there was a mine dockside it was the Army's problem. The handheld radio clipped to Jersey's flak jacket squawked.

"Gentlemen, we're clear. Thirty minutes. Stand by."

The first mate's voice, from the bridge. Mac always talked like that: *Gentlemen.*

Temple gave Jersey a light shove and she rolled and sat back, resting against the forward shield.

"Hey, gentlemen, you think these things will stop a bullet?" he asked her, rapping his knuckles once against the steel plate.

"They're pretty thick, gentlemen," she said, leaning to press her face to a gap in the metal. "A bullet—yeah." Temple looked out his own gap, goggles pushed up on his helmet.

Early morning and already hot—steamy. The steel plates blocked the sea breeze. It occurred to Jersey to be thankful they weren't packing a hundred pounds and air-assaulting in today, like many were. But the hell with thankful. Sitting in direct sun, flak jacket, helmet—hot.

Their mission—the job of the boat—was straightforward: have the bow ramp down on the city's main pier at the exact moment a company of 10th Mountain infantrymen dropped from their helicopters. Deliver the ship's cargo of trucks and Humvees to the grunts. Pull back, let the other Army boats in, await further orders. Avoid getting shot.

Jersey rapped her knuckles against the steel plate again, sticky with salt and grease.

"Avoid getting shot, gentlemen," she said.

Temple looked over at her, eyebrows raised. She liked Temple. He was a surfer; stout, compact. California blond. He should have been pinned sergeant with her and Scaboo in July, but took out a stop sign near the Fort Eustis gate leaving Buck's Grill one night. Instead of up to sergeant stripes he got knocked from specialist back down to PFC.

"Scared?" he asked.

"You?"

He shook his head no, smiling.

"Maybe," he added.

"Yeah, maybe," she said.

He slugged her on the shoulder and she slugged him back. She lit a smoke and he put his face back to the gap, keeping watch forward. Their M-16 rifles lay on the deck, the big M-60 machine gun on its two stubby legs between them. When the time came, Temple would aim one point off the port bow with the M-60 and Jersey would crouch dead ahead with her M-16. They'd already agreed, days ago, that if they took an RPG hit, or something worse, and survived, they would drop the thirty feet down into the well-deck, and if one of them was too fucked up to do it on their own, the other would roll the injured one over the side and down to the steel below. Pelton and Bear, manning the M-60 nest on the starboard bow, thirty feet across the well-deck from Voodoo Lounge, had a similar plan.

Looking aft Jersey saw Snaggletooth stick his helmeted head up from behind the shield on the port bridge wing. He saw her looking up, waved once, and she lifted a hand in return. *Fucker ought to put his head down,* she thought. A few seconds later a hand grabbed his shoulder and pulled him back. That made her smile.

The handheld spoke, through static:

"United States Army LSV *Gilman,* this is Coast Guard Cutter *Richards.* We've completed our sweep. Leaving the AO to your starboard, two whistles."

"Two whistles, Coast Guard. Thank you."

Not Mac, but Mannino answering, the skipper on the radio for the first time today. The old man didn't like to talk on the radio.

"Good luck, Army."

Across the great ramp on the bow, past Pelton and Bear on the starboard machine-gun nest, Jersey watched the Coast Guard cutter hauling ass.

Static, twice, then Mannino again:

"This is USAV *Gilman,* LSV-16. We're in position."

A voice came back:

"Army LSV *Gilman,* and all Army watercraft following LSV-16, the port is yours. Refer to updated rules of engagement, keep your eyes open. Proceed at best speed."

"Goddamn, Tory," Temple said, backing off the gap, sitting down next to her. "Goddamn."

She nodded at him once. "Yep."

The handheld clicked with static as Mannino switched them out from the command frequencies and back to on-ship commo only.

"You hear that?" his voice rang out. "Don't do anything stupid. Let the grunts catch the bullets, that's what God made them for."

He clicked off.

And then, looking back, it seemed the deck of *Eisenhower* levitated off itself, a straight black line moving steadily up. It broke, twenty or more helicopters adjusting their course, taking position, waiting in the

air. This was the second time they'd seen a flight lift this morning: 10th
Mountain reported taking the Port-au-Prince airport an hour ago. The
Marines had done the same up north in Cap-Haitien.

"Who's gonna get there first, us or them?" Temple asked, watching
the choppers float from *Eisenhower.*

"Hard to tell," Jersey said. "Might be a tie. Hope so." She could see
the main port clearly now, clear enough to make out a fence beyond
the docks and warehouses, surrounding the port, a mile or so long. The
fence was dark, and Jersey blinked. It looked like it was moving.

Sun glare? she thought.

She pulled her goggles straight down so they hung around her neck.
Looked again.

The fence wasn't moving: something behind it was. The fence was
chain link, and what she saw solid and moving was a press of humanity. A thousand people? Five thousand? All of Port-au-Prince on the
fence to see America come in. To see who shot first.

"Jesus," she said. "That's a lot of people."

Temple pushed her out of the way again, glanced through the gap.
He whistled through his teeth.

"Avoid getting shot, gentlemen," he said. "You think they're
friendly?"

"I dunno. We'll be the first to find out."

The main concrete pier was empty of vessels as the LSV nosed into the
waters of the horseshoe-shaped city port. Windstorms of dirt and
debris flew a quarter-mile north and south of the warehouses lining the
pier—10th Mountain choppers dropping their chalks of troops and
dangling Humvees to the far corners of the port perimeter. But those
soldiers fanning out from the safety zones around the choppers hadn't
yet made it to the main pier where the LSV was going. The warehouses
blocked the LSV's view of the landing infantrymen, and blocked their
view of the immediate neighborhood as well.

The city's right there, though, Jersey thought. *Close enough to touch.*

For now, the LSV was alone.

"Sixty seconds," the radio blared. The deck plate beneath Jersey and

Temple started rattling as the massive gray bow ramp slowly inched down, the chain holding the ramp feeding from the locker one level below them. The links on the chain were bigger than Jersey's foot.

"Port bow!" Mac called. "Faces in the window, warehouse, ten o'clock." Temple, flat on his belly with M-60 trained through a side gap, raised his left hand in acknowledgment to the bridge and twisted the barrel down and right. Jersey, dead-ahead with M-16, couldn't see the window on the warehouse Mac was talking about. She aimed forward, rifle shifting left and right and left and right in her small field of fire. As the LSV advanced—snail's pace as they approached the pier— a section of the city fence became visible again. Whatever passed for Port-au-Prince police had cleared the port and locked the chain-link gate some time before. The press of bodies up against the fence, now less than two hundred yards from them, was huge. An immense, moving, breathing crowd, menacing and friendly at once, watching, yelling. A living thing, river of crowd, filling the boulevards and alleys from the port uphill through the city. Jersey could hear their singing and clapping, but only in waves.

"Starboard bow!" Mac called from the bridge. "Movement in the alley between warehouses. Three o'clock."

Sweat ran down her face, into her goggles, blinking, stinging. She realized she was breathing too hard, almost panting, and took a lungful of air and held it as long as she could.

Choppers dropping in and out beyond the warehouses roared like prehistoric war birds, the loudest thing Jersey had ever heard, but still there were no troops at the pier they were closing on.

They heard Mannino's growl on the radio: "Where's the fucking cavalry?"

The ramp was more than half down, the pier to portside fifteen feet and closing, the pier ahead they were setting their ramp on now less than thirty feet. She heard metal on metal in the well-deck below her, T.K. and those guys on Staff Sergeant Arnold's bosun's crew dropping the chains that held the trucks and Humvees in place, firing off their engines.

But still no one to drive them off. There was supposed to be a com-

pany of troops on the pier to retrieve the vehicles, to drive them to the
airport, but the LSV got there first. Across the pier and toward the city
the chain-link fence bulged with the weight of the Haitians pressing on
it, flags and banners waving, dirty colors floating through thick morning air. The murmur of thousands of voices drifted in between and
around the screams and roars of the engines of an arriving army.

"Twenty seconds!" Mac, on the radio. "Team One, on the ramp.
Team Two, portside pilot door. Prepare to tie off. Forward gunners,
keep an eye on that fence." The radio clicked a few times, then: "Anything approaching us on the pier not wearing Army green right now
is a target."

"Hoorah," Temple whispered, two small syllables.

Jersey leaned and looked over the bow. T.K. was on the ramp tip,
pulling his leather deck gloves on, riding the ramp down, rifle slung
across his back and nervous eye to the crowd on the other side of the
chain-link fence. As the ship nestled in the pocket, portside-to and
ramp resting on pier ahead, a Black Hawk chopper dropped like a lead
ball from the sky, slamming to a stop twenty-some feet shy of the
ground, then hovered, two lines down, ten full-gear soldiers dropping
down the ropes to the concrete in front of the LSV, not making security, just down and immediately flat-out running for T.K. and the ramp
of the boat. The dust wind of the rotors caught Jersey dead-on, her
goggles saving her eyes but her lungs taking damage from the loose,
heated dust, sending her into a coughing spasm. The chopper went
nose down, tail up, and as fast as it was there it was gone.

Jersey cleared her lungs best she could then leaned forward again.

Staff Sergeant Arnold was down on the ramp now, face to face with
a soldier from the chopper, a 10th Mountain captain. The captain
looked up in Jersey's direction, eyes locking—young, for a captain. The
blackest man Jersey had ever seen, skin a deep, rich tone that seemed to
pull in all the light around it. Sergeant Arnold was an older man, a
much lighter shade of brown, with a thin mustache. He was the LSV's
new bosun, assigned days before they sailed. Arnold's face was shining
now, under the sweat pouring from him, his helmet unsnapped and
pushed back.

"You got to clear my deck, sir," Arnold was saying to the young captain, whose eyes had remained on Jersey's for a beat, and then another, before dropping down to the sergeant before him. Arnold was swinging his left arm toward the rows of Humvees and trucks filling the LSV's well-deck. The chopper was gone but by instinct he was still yelling. "We got eight LCU boats stacked up behind us, waiting to come in." The ten soldiers who had dropped from the chopper with the captain were moving into the well-deck, throwing rucks and gear into the lead Humvees.

"I can't drive without troops, Sergeant," the captain said. "Most of my company is still sitting on the deck of *Eisenhower.*"

The captain and forward squad—dropped off without his company. Jersey, who had always imagined the Army would somehow seem smarter during war time, shook her head.

The heat in the Voodoo Lounge was brutal now, sweat pouring off her and Temple in buckets. She had seen him reach for a canteen before and drink—never taking his eye from the sight of the M-60—and she did the same now, pulling a few sips of water from a canteen, one eye down the rifle sight to the crowd in the distance, one eye on the ramp below her.

"Someone's driving this shit off here, Sir," she heard Arnold say, "and if it ain't you, then it's us."

"Not that easy, Sergeant—" the captain said, but Jersey lost his next words in the storm of another chopper.

Everyone looked to the pier, expecting the captain's lost company to drop. But this Black Hawk didn't drop and hover; it actually set down, at the half point of the hundred or so yards between the nose of the LSV and the flimsy gate holding back the ever-growing, laughing, clapping, singing population of Port-au-Prince. The rotor wash from the chopper was tremendous, sucking the breath from everyone on the bow, pushing the ship back so its lines went taut.

"What the fuck? Over," Jersey heard from the bridge on the open channel of the ship's radio. *What the fuck? Over,* indeed.

Six soldiers jumped from the open side door of the Black Hawk. Jersey noticed they had no nametags or unit insignia on their BDUs.

And no helmets. They all wore mirrored Oakley sunglasses and carried short, stocky machine guns. *Delta?* Jersey thought. *Or contractor bodyguards.* They fanned in a circle perimeter, but didn't seem particularly concerned—they sauntered. The bulge on the chain-link fence had deflated, the monster wind from the Black Hawk driving back the crowd.

Temple gave up on his assigned faces in his assigned window and scooted forward with Jersey. From around the warehouse on their port side three shiny black Chevy Suburbans came flying down the pier, screeching to a halt yards from the Black Hawk. Jersey was so startled she almost shot at them—her rifle instinctively up and over, pressure on the trigger. She barely stopped herself, adrenaline pumping so dangerously hard her head tingled, breath coming short, close to hyperventilating.

What the fuck? Over.

Looking down, saw she wasn't the only one. The young 10th Mountain captain and SSG Arnold had both dropped to a knee, pistols up. Across the pier, three of the bodyguards had also dropped to a knee, weapons trained on the captain and Arnold.

Mannino's voice came screaming out of the radio: "What in the Jesus fuck?!"

A tall soldier climbed out of the Black Hawk. Jersey recognized him. He was a three-star Army general, commander of XVIII Airborne Corps. He reached a hand up and helped out a civilian man in an open-throat shirt and sports coat and then a middle-aged woman in a blue suit and puffy hair.

"Isn't that—" Temple started.

"Yeah," Jersey finished. She wasn't sure about the guy, but the woman was easy. She was the undersecretary of somethingoranother who'd been blabbing endlessly on TV the last day they'd been able to see network TV on the way down here.

The general gave a short laugh, patting the two civilians on the back, guiding them toward one of the three Suburbans. They turned as a group and faced the chain-link fence and waved at the crowd behind it, drawing a wild cheer from the mass of people, and smiling they all got in the middle Chevy. The bodyguards hopped on the running boards of the three SUVs as they started rolling down the pier, back from where they came around the warehouse, the Black Hawk lifting then gone.

Temple put a piece of gum in his mouth.

"I take it this means our AO is safe and secure," he said, contemplatively.

Jersey heard Arnold's voice down on the ramp: "Motherfuckers almost shot me!"

Gotta watch that friendly fire, Jersey thought.

"It's a friendly neighborhood war," she said. "All the friendly neighbors gonna come down to see."

The radio crackled to life, catching Mannino up in the bridge bellowing a blue line of obscenity. Mac's voice cut in over the skipper's: "Harris, Riddle, Pelton, Scaboo—report to the bow, full gear and weapons."

"I'm already on the bow," Jersey muttered, but Mac meant the ramp and she knew it.

"Good luck, troop," Temple said, punching her arm, then crawling back over to his M-60. "I'll keep the senators and generals at bay while you're gone."

Jersey—Harris, her ID said, Sergeant Tory Harris on her ID card—slung her M-16 tight on her back, stuck a few clips in her ammo pouches, checked her pockets for cigarettes, slapped a hand down on Temple's leg, then scurried down the ladder to the catwalk.

CHAPTER

2

Down in the well-deck, Jersey slammed into Scaboo as they rounded the front of a deuce-and-a-half truck into each other. Their helmets smacked for the second time this morning, Scaboo's head jerking back. Jersey opened her mouth to yell, snapped it shut again. Eye to eye under helmet tips, two buck sergeants, Scaboo's thick brows rising over a hooked nose, panting from his run, but for once not saying anything. Jersey blinked twice then put her arms out to spin him around.

"C'mon," she said, pushing, then followed him at a jog up the well-deck, ducking between the small rumbling fleet of idling vehicles, Jersey wheezing on the thickening diesel exhaust. *It's all noise and bad air in the Voodoo Lounge,* she thought. She remembered Temple pissing down upon this well-deck at dawn and made a mental note to keep clear of the vehicles on the port side near the bow.

Up forward Staff Sergeant Arnold was working with the young 10th Mountain captain—Hall, his name was—pushing soldiers into vehicles. Captain Hall turned as he was talking, his eyes meeting Jersey's again as she came forward through the well-deck. His helmet was off, exposing a smooth-shaved head. He paused a second, midsentence, seeing her. The man was tense; it was writ on his face, lines cutting deeper on his smooth skin than age should have allowed. But he wasn't yelling. He was throwing tight, controlled orders to his sergeant and squad. It was tense but the opposite of panic, and striking because someone as tense as this young captain, someone dropped off with less than a quarter of his company, might have reason to panic. Hall finished saying whatever he'd been saying to the soldier beside him, but his eyes remained on Jersey. His gaze was locked so strong, so unexpected, she stopped short. Then he broke it, turning away, lightly pushing one of his soldiers toward a Humvee. The kid almost tripped over Sergeant Arnold, on his knees looking under a truck. The bosun cursed, scaring the kid, then looked up and saw Jersey and Scaboo. He waved them over.

"Sergeant Scabliagni—you're shotgun with Specialist Pelton. Sergeant Harris and Specialist Riddle, this other hummer's yours, babies."

"I'm driving," Riddle barked. Then, "Where are we going?"

"Airport, loudmouth," Arnold said. "You four just been drafted by the infantry. Gonna drive these two Humvees with Captain Hall's mighty squad of ten to help get these vehicles to the airport. Queen of battle, prepare for glory." He slipped a pair of leather work gloves from his cargo pocket, pulling them on to help T.K. and the deck crew break down the greasy chainlocks holding the vehicles. He was singing cadence now: *"Infantry oh in-fan-tree! Queen o battle, suck on me."*

Jersey wiped her mouth, brain clicking away. There were so many issues here, so many potential problems with her leaving the ship. She opened her mouth to say something to Arnold, she didn't know what, but something should be said, maybe—

A skinny dervish of a 10th Mountain colonel flew up the ramp, his skin an unhealthy pale, helmet in one hand and the other wagging at Jersey. She looked around quickly, unsure. The man was looking at her, but yelled at Captain Hall.

"Is that a female?" the colonel said, stopping in his tracks.

Riddle, standing right next to Jersey, let out a huge one-syllable laugh, immediately realized it was a mistake, and clamped his jaw closed over the sound. Tory Harris did not laugh, or even smile. This was not the problem she'd wanted to talk to Sergeant Arnold about, but it was related. *What am I, a fucking specimen?* she thought, furious.

Arnold and Jersey both opened their mouths—answers ready to fly—but Hall, turning, cut them both off quick.

"That's not a female, Colonel," the young captain said evenly. "That's a sergeant." He let that hang in the air a moment, then added,

"You have a replacement, Sir? Some other sergeant you'd rather have on the convoy?"

The colonel stared at Jersey and she stared the pale old man back, flat, forcing her mouth closed, jaw clenching. *Two and two and fuck you, shitheel,* she thought. The man's eyes were so red she could see them from almost ten feet away. He was old, too old even for a colonel. He was a reservist, or recalled IRR. She waited for him to say something else. Sergeant Arnold, glaring at the old colonel, coughed loudly. Finally, the colonel broke eye contact and without another word moved out back toward the bow ramp, finding other problems.

"Jackass," Hall said under his breath. He made eye contact with Jersey again, nodded, then turned toward the stern, walking aft between the vehicles.

"It's all good, Tory," Arnold said to her, checking to see if it was.

"It's all right," she said, watching Captain Hall's back as he moved through his men. She turned and faced Sergeant Arnold, rolling her eyes. He put his gloved hand on the small of her back, leaning in to whisper.

"Was just the sexy way you carry yourself in all that Kevlar and woodland-green finery, reminded the poor man how long it been since he was laid."

She snorted, shaking her head, and climbed in the Humvee with Riddle.

"Is that a *feeemale*?" Riddle cackled.

"Can you believe it?" she muttered.

Riddle was cracking himself up as he got situated in the driver's seat. "Is them titties I see? I ain't seen me no titties in so long I forgot what they look like."

"Fuck you, Riddle," she said, laughing.

"Damn, Captain, reach over and see if that soldier is smuggling titties under that BDU top—"

"Will you please shut up," she said, and he did, but only because his brain had jumped to a new subject. Next to them on the deck, T.K. and his crew were hustling to break down the chains on the last few vehicles. Riddle stuck his head out the side window.

"Can any of you fine gents tell me what this Army clusterfuck has to do with marlinespike seamanship?" he yelled.

That cracked Jersey up. From pissed to laughing in less than a minute, and laughing was a relief. She was glad to be riding with Riddle. He was loud and obnoxious but he was funny. And usually right. And it was good he was driving; she was by far the better shot.

A 10th Mountain soldier humped toward them, checking bumper numbers on the vehicles; one of Captain Hall's forward squad. He was doubled over from the weight of the ruck on his back—almost bigger than he was. He wore the big-rimmed eyeglasses they give you in basic training.

"Lordy lord," Riddle said, shaking his head. He put his head out the window again.

"Easy, Riddle," Jersey said, but Riddle was already yelling.

"Hey there, Private!"

The kid looked up, squinting.

"Where's your fucking company?"

"What?"

"Your company. The bitches that own all these trucks and hummers."

The private looked through the windshield at Riddle and Jersey, eyes bugging under those thick glasses, then shrugged.

Riddle shook his head again, laughing, then thrust his jaw forward in Drill style.

"Proper prior planning prevents piss-poor performance, Private!" he yelled.

Jersey laughed out loud at this.

Captain Hall came from nowhere, his face filling the driver's-side window inches from Riddle, his hands grabbing the frame of the door.

"Is this funny, Specialist?" he hissed into Riddle's ear. "Is there something fucking funny going on in Haiti this morning?"

Riddle locked his eyes forward, mouth stammering an apology and a *sir-sir-sir*, hands on the wheel of the Humvee. Jersey looked at Hall— ready to apologize—and saw he was yelling at Riddle but he wasn't looking at Riddle; he was looking across the front seat of the vehicle at her. And he wasn't just tense anymore, but somewhere beyond it. His face and bare skull wet, knuckles rigid tight around the door frame, he looked into Jersey's eyes and she saw he was afraid. Not locked-up afraid. But the realization of reality skipping merrily away from any semblance of plan. He was still devoid of panic, too good a soldier for that, but panic and fear don't go hand in hand. He was a new captain, twenty-six or twenty-seven, and he was yelling at Riddle but looking at her and in his eyes Jersey could see the ticking in his brain—*bastard-big-green-Army-machine-fucked-up-beyond-all-recognition . . . how could EVERYTHING go wrong less than ten minutes in-country?*—and Riddle was directly in this Captain Hall's line of fire and took it head-on for another twenty seconds. Then the man was gone, tightening his LBE straps and making for the lead Humvee, pulling his pistol from its holster. The captain's anxiety was as high as a buck private's haircut, but his shit was dialed tight and it occurred to Jersey if you had to go down range maybe it was good to be led by an officer who knew that all wasn't as it should be.

"Could be he had a point," Riddle whispered, and it was the first and last time she ever heard Riddle whisper, or concede.

Jersey pat the top of his helmet once in sympathy, then pulled a dropper bottle of CLP from her cargo pocket and squirted some of the oil into the ejection door of her M-16. Eyes down, hands working the cool metal and plastic of her weapon, she thought of the captain—his face filling the window of the Humvee, and before on the well-deck his eyes finding hers; even on the bow, in Voodoo Lounge, looking down over the edge and seeing his face looking up. *What's that about?* she thought.

The LSV's foghorn sounded loud above them. Tory clucked her tongue twice, worked the bolt of the M-16 back and forth, locked it, then closed the ejection door. Looking up, she thumbed the safety off.

They drove clear of the LSV's ramp five minutes later, sixth Humvee in line, and when they came to a stop thirty feet down the empty pier Jersey pushed her door open and put boot to concrete, just for a moment. Touching Haiti.

We're here, she thought.

Two and two and front-line view / friendly fire burns black and blue.

Jersey and Scaboo had pinned their sergeant stripes that spring, after a month in the NCO academy at Fort Knox, drilling fourteen hours a day on all things sergeant. Now her brain couldn't break free of cadences. Every other thought she had, especially when nervous, came out a cadence. It drove her nuts but she couldn't break it.

Army green and jungle boot / is it war if they don't shoot.

So far so good in the friendly fire department this morning. Two squads of Marines almost took each other out at the Cap-Haitien airport at dawn, but clear heads prevailed. *Or dumb luck,* Jersey thought— she'd come close to sending a bullet into the commanding general's Chevy Suburban just twenty minutes before. She put her fingertips to the silver tape on her helmet top and sleeve, checking to make sure it was still there.

But if they shoot and I get shot / is it war or is it not.

She looked over to see Riddle watching her. She waited for his comment but none came.

"What?" she said.

He just smiled, the same this-war-is-even-funnier-than-me smile he'd had on his face hearing the news that Jimmy Carter had saved their lives. He tapped his palm against the wheel then finally said, "You think we have time for a smoke?"

The convoy was supposed to drive into the mass of Port-au-Prince's humanity that lay held back just beyond the port fence and find the best possible route to the old international airport. A route had, of course, been planned, but before leaving the LSV Captain Hall had warned them the planned route might not be very good. He'd directed a few choice words at the map in his hand, waved it in surrender, then said, "Keep it tight out there. It'll be confusing." Now the convoy stood still on the pier, waiting behind the only visible gate in the fence between the port and the city beyond. The Haitians pressed harder on the fence with the sight of the convoy leaving the ship, young men and boys climbing the fence although not going over the top into the port.

Excited, cheering, pressing on the fence but somehow respectful, watching more than acting.

A squad of GIs arrived on foot, hustling over from some unseen muster point behind the port warehouses, and tried to figure out the best way to open the gate. "Cedras forgot to leave the key for us?" Riddle said and blew a perfect ring off the first puff of his cigarette. The squad of heavily armed soldiers at the gate didn't seem to be doing anything. The problem, it seemed, wasn't the actual opening of the gate, it was the crowd beyond. They couldn't open the gate unless the crowd moved, and the squad's lieutenant wasn't sure you could point a weapon at a Haitian. You were only allowed to shoot them now if they shot you first, and as ridiculously complete as the current rules of engagement were, they didn't specify whether you could simply point an M-16. This was far too much hair-splitting for the 10th Mountain grunts who'd been called up to clear a path for the departing convoy, but their lieutenant was having trouble getting his head around the issue. He was worried, he said; there might be a *New York Times* photographer or CNN camera in the crowd—there were occasional flashes of white faces and black plastic out there—and it might be poor public relations if the troops looked threatening. There'd been a briefing about this sort of thing.

The lieutenant's platoon sergeant, who'd ducked out of the briefing, spit a stream of tobacco juice on the ground and said, "Check it out, Sir. A few hours ago all these people were the enemy and we was gonna kill 'em if they got in the way. I know they our friends and all now, but hell I point a twenty-two at my neighbor when he's drunk and pissing on my lawn—never once created an international incident."

The lieutenant wasn't convinced, until Captain Hall half-stepped from his vehicle and yelled, "Goddammit, Lieutenant, open that fucking gate before I shoot you and open it myself!"

The crowd cheered the captain's outburst, assuming it a passionate declaration of American-Haitian unity and solidarity.

The GIs went to work with bolt cutters, the two big chain-link gates swinging in, six soldiers with weapons leveled gesturing and yelling at the Haitians to move it back. But the crowd didn't surge; the

Haitians had drawn away, creating a path just wide enough for the vehicles. They were singing now, scattered *Ouis* and *Bonjou!* and *Ki jan ou ye!* Jersey saw mostly men, some women. A lot of children. Ragged and torn clothing, taut and too-skinny faces throughout. Those not singing all seemed to be gesturing, pointing the Americans toward something, it wasn't clear what. Lots of jumping and waving and *Come! Come with me! Come see!*

Come see what? Jersey thought.

A small man with no teeth and an Adidas T-shirt jumped close to the first hummer as it inched out the gate. Jersey's fingertip tensed across the trigger, leaning forward, but the man wasn't attacking—he lifted his shirt. Raked across his dark chest and stomach were eight or nine lines, vicious scars, mole-tunnel trails across his tight, brown body.

See this, see me.

Ki sa yo fait.

See what has been done.

Oui.

The hummer in front of them moved and Riddle stepped light on the gas, staring at the little man. A woman appeared beside him then, thrust forward by the crowd, waving the stumps of her arms, both gone below the thick scar tissue of her elbows. She was speaking, a flow of impenetrable Creole, but words unnecessary.

See me. See this.

"Jesus," Riddle said. Jersey blinked through sweat running into her eyes.

This is why we're here, she thought, *this is why they sent us,* knowing she was almost certainly wrong, knowing it wasn't true, wanting to believe it anyway.

"No one said dick about crowd control for amputees when I was in boat school," Riddle muttered, his cheek twitching, staring at the woman and little man as he drove.

"You were on KP that day," Jersey said, shifting in the seat so her back was to Riddle and her face and the barrel of the M-16 were toward the side, toward the crowd. "They covered crimes against humanity in the five minutes between marlinespike and running lights."

"You'd think I was in the fucking Army," he said, but then they were approaching the gate and his left hand went out the window and slapped palms with the 10th Mountain private standing guard there and they were through, into the belly of the crowd, into the city of Port-au-Prince. They passed the man and the woman, Jersey unable to take her eyes away. The woman waved her stumps and smiled. Jersey tried to smile back and hoped it worked but she wasn't sure and then they were gone, pushing deeper into the throng of bodies and faces.

The pulse and noise and stink of the crowd and the city was all around them now. Smiles and cheers and dancing, the crowd as thick a quarter mile down the ring road of the port as it was at the main gate, the crowd so thick the soldiers could see nothing of the city, nothing of any buildings, just the road under their wheels and the press of bodies all around. *How will we know when to turn?* Jersey thought, and said to Riddle, "Keep it close." Looking through the Humvee's back window she raised a hand at Pelton and Scaboo in the hummer behind them, making sure they were still there.

They'd all been told to expect pro-Lavalas demonstrations, but this was beyond political. More a surge of life, a momentary and desperate grab for something. The convoy could barely make five miles an hour, steady but unable to break free the mass of people. After the numb fear of the spearhead arrival this morning, certain of pain and death in an invasion that never happened, Jersey wanted to smile, to laugh, joining the smiles and laughs of the crowd. A few times she almost did, her focus pulled by the warmth of the people, their joy, their celebration. But then there would be a sudden something—a shift in the crowd's temperature, a pinprick cold spot in the ocean of bodies, two eyes poking through from deeper in the ranks, making contact with hers, a flash of steel or rock below or beside. What? Unclear. Nervous. Information unclear. Hostile. *FADH, FRAPH, Ton Ton Macoute*—all words with no meaning yet to hang on them, just hostile. Ill whispers on the morning wind. *If it ain't wearing Army green, shoot it.*

. . . is it war or is it not.

Jersey kept her rifle up.

Five minutes into it, Riddle took his eyes from the road, glancing around the Humvee, and said, "Hey, Tory, there's no tactical radio in here," straining to be heard over the noise of the city.

Jersey turned to look in the back, then nodded.

"Yeah," she said. Then again: "Don't lose the convoy." She wiped her palm on her leg; she'd overoiled the bolt of the M-16, and the CLP was dripping down, slippery on her skin. Her nostrils were filled with the smell of the stuff; that, and gunmetal and diesel and, from somewhere beyond, the smell of burning rubber.

Jersey's head was moving, always moving; windshield, side window, back—like scanning the fields of fire from the bow of the LSV this morning. She watched the lead Humvees, watched the crowd, watched Riddle. Repeat. A sergeant's view: the target, the terrain, her single troop. Her gaze moved over her own reflection in the side rearview; with her goggles on she couldn't see her eyes and that was a comfort—no one else could, either.

CHAPTER

3

Across central and northern Haiti helicopters darted and trucks rolled, American soldiers with rifles dropping from vehicles onto bellies and knees to set security perimeters, then other soldiers with thick gloves pulling rolls of razored concertina wire from the backs of the trucks and forming circles of relative safety. This wasn't so much an invasion as it was cellular, specific, pockets of control in places of importance. The Haitian people stepped aside. Haitian soldiers were, so far, not to be seen.

The small convoy from the Army ship rounded a bend and started up a steep hill, deeper into Port-au-Prince, the road a washboard of potholes and gravel and concrete chunks. It was like surfacing, the crowds thin enough now to see buildings lining the road, market stalls and flimsy wood storefronts mostly, packed together and painted bright reds and blues and greens and yellows, the smell of urine and frying food—meats and sweet banana—thick in the air. The crowd here put on the same show, singing, dancing, a constant demonstration of scars and wounds and missing limbs; but lighter, the press of bodies. Easier to see through. Jersey looked harder now, to find those eyes buried in there, the malicious hiding inside the innocent, but it was gone whatever it was. Just the cripples now, Macoute survivors, the cheering, singing, walking wounded.

See us, see us all. Oui—come blancs, I show you.

The Humvee in front of them had a gunner slung up in the roof hole. As the road they were pushing up widened into more of an avenue

and they approached a small park, Jersey saw the gunner drop down
into the Humvee. Looking around, she tightened the grip on her M-16.

"What do you think?" she said, but Riddle didn't answer. He was
trying to drive and watch all at once. The 10th Mountain soldiers in the
convoy were all in commo with each other, but nobody had thought
to mix in the two Humvees driven by the Waterborne soldiers. The four
of them had no idea what was going on, just what they could see.

It seemed suddenly there was no one on the street. The hummers in
front were stopping, pulling up next to one another alongside a large
public square with a canopy of old trees and one large concrete statue
of someone on a horse. A crowd of people stood beyond the trees on
the other side of the park, but Jersey couldn't make out what they were
doing or why they were there. Captain Hall's squad of 10th Mountain
soldiers were jumping from their vehicles, only the one roof gunner—
back up at his .50 cal—staying. Riddle hit the brakes and reached
down for his M-16. Jersey already had her door open, pushing her goggles up onto her helmet as she stepped out, Pelton in the last hummer
braking next to her.

"What's the deal?" Scaboo yelled over Pelton from the shotgun seat.
"Why'd we stop?"

"Something's over there." Jersey pointed toward the trees, no idea
why they'd stopped. They weren't a combat patrol, just a convoy. In a
foreign city. *Two and two and what the fuck? Over,* she thought. She'd
wanted to see Haiti up close, but the idea of riding along with 10th
Mountain for the trip had never been appealing to her; it was less so
now. Turning around and looking back down the hill from where they
came, the deep blue-green of Port-au-Prince harbor shimmered in the
morning sun. The hill was too steep to see the port and the LSV at the
pier, but *Eisenhower* was out there, and a small flotilla of Army LCUs
lining up for port clearance. The water was far and she couldn't smell
the seabreeze. She took it as a bad omen.

"There!" Scaboo, yelling again. Jersey turned her head to follow his
arm, pointing toward an immense grandfather of a tree on the north
edge of the square. A body hanging from a thick limb, a man. Hands
tied behind his back, barefoot, blood-drenched shirt and no pants. The

rope was heavy old hemp, running a crude noose cutting deep under his chin then over the limb and down and tied off to a smaller branch near the base. Neck broken, his head completely wrong, sprung in a loose and unfixable way.

"Oh shit," Pelton said, Scaboo and Riddle crossing themselves. Jersey felt her gorge rise and fought it down. The man was black, Haitian, but pale and blue in the way of dead bodies hanging from trees. His bulging eyes had rolled up but more to the side and maybe looking for God and if they'd been standing twenty feet north his dead fish eyes would be staring at them.

The crowd on the other side of the park—and it was loud, a different loud, a Creole growl—had to know about the dead man, but wasn't under or even near him. He was forgotten for now. The Haitians were fifty feet south at the center of a grass and thin-dirt clearing. The four Waterborne soldiers couldn't see what was going on, just the backs of the 10th Mountain troops running over—they'd seen something. But behind where they'd stopped the Humvees, another mob was moving up the hill, fists in air and yelling and filling the street and closing—they knew something the soldiers didn't.

Scaboo circled on his heels and raised his rifle to a waist position. "P," he said to Pelton, "make sure Captain Hall knows there's more coming."

Pelton looked at Jersey and she nodded. She slapped Riddle's shoulder and said, "Stay with Sergeant Sca." Pelton reached through the window of the hummer to retrieve his M-16. He slapped the butt of the clip and followed Jersey.

"They hang him this morning, Tory?" he said from behind her.

Jersey flicked her eyes again to the body in the tree but there was no clue to rhyme or reason. Just an open mouth on his ash-gray strangled face.

See this, blancs—see me. See what has been done to me.

The ground beneath him was parched dead grass, and everything felt dead to her. Everything dead here, or close enough to touch it. She shuddered as she walked. One of the 10th Mountain soldiers turned, a sergeant, raising his hand at them to stop.

"Fuck that," Jersey whispered, ignoring the man. She wiped the back of her free hand across her lips, fighting nausea. They crossed the few steps to the circle of soldiers on the edge of the crowd, shouldering in to see.

There were three men on the ground, bloody but alive. Over them a squad of uniformed Haitians—police or army, Jersey didn't know. They called them FADH, she remembered; one of the whispers on the wind. *If they're in uniform, they're FADH.*

Good or bad?

Who?

FADH. Good or bad?

Yes.

It was unclear whether the three men were to be raised up in trees of their own, but one had his hands tied behind his back the same way. He groaned out loud and the soldier/cop over him brought his stick down on the man's rib cage, a spray of blood from the *thwack* of contact. Jersey drew a sharp breath, felt the crowd of Haitians do the same—cries in Creole rising, pointed. *Why don't they stop it?* she thought, then knew. The guns. Four of the soldier/cops had rifles and all of them with pistols. *Guns,* she thought, *and maybe long memories.* The uniformed FADH not directly over the men on the ground were scanning the crowd, sometimes yelling at a particular person, pointing. They knew who was there.

The stick man raised the baton again, high over head, and his victim cringed, trying to roll to the side, baring a mouthful of bloody teeth to the American soldiers and a small "Aiii" from his throat. But the stick man didn't strike this time, just held it high, teasing, laughing and taunting now, *boules grein* and *maman* and fuck *oui* o yes. He would glance at the Americans every few seconds, but didn't seem put out by their presence.

"Oh, man," the soldier next to Jersey said. He was a buck sergeant, too; young, some kind of Latin. His bloodshot eyes found hers momentarily. He opened his mouth to say something but then it all went very bad.

The stick man, baton still high, teasing, suddenly held his laugh, knees flexing and mouth tense, and with a growl his arm raised up and back to deliver a real blow—as Captain Hall's pistol went up and Jersey saw the movement from the side of her eye so flinched but didn't drop when the *crack!* of the shot sounded, dust rising in a cloud as the bullet drove into the ground halfway between the FADH and the Americans. Crowd screaming, the sergeant to her left down on a knee, rifle to cheek, all of the squad dropping or aiming from where they stood, that quick, Jersey's own left foot out and M-16 up before she realized it, a bead drawn quick and clean on the stick man's chest. The stick man's baton dropped, his hands crossed up before his face, pitiful useless defense, but the other FADH reacted the same as the American soldiers, weapons immediately up, reflexes just as quick—Jersey looking down the barrel of her rifle to see a Haitian eye looking down the barrel of his rifle and *Who dies first?*

For the second time this morning, lines of tense-triggered soldiers at point-blank range—*but this is the enemy now,* Jersey thought. *I think.*

There was a click, metal on metal, from the FADH—one small sound in chaos, but that's the sound you listen for, the power echo over all else—and the sergeant next to Jersey loosed a round into the dirt—*control, control, how does he keep such control?!?* she thought, head spinning—but the rifled Haitians had dropped their long guns and were in various stages of duck and cover with no help from duck and nowhere to cover and Jersey saw Captain Hall leveling his pistol again and a green BDU arm reaching out and pushing it down—

"Hold! Hold your fire!" the old red-eyed colonel, the one who hadn't wanted a female in the convoy, pushing Captain Hall's arm down, wrestling him momentarily for control of the pistol, the young sergeant next to Jersey shifting so just for one second his M-16 was trained on the colonel's head, taking down his captain, then down, the M-16 down, the young sergeant breathing hard—panting—all of them panting, flicking rifles and pistols and eyes and fingers back and forth and back again, everyone alive and almost dead at the same time, sweat and piss and the colonel yelling, high-pitched and almost a squeal, "Goddammit down! Weapons down! Hold your fucking fire!"

The soldiers hadn't shot anyone but the adrenaline was too high, charging through bloodstreams, and before the colonel's mouth was done the sergeant next to Jersey was on his feet, advancing steps on the FADH, the private on his left with him, the sergeant yelling at the uniformed Haitians as he crossed the distance, "Down! Get your weapons on the fucking ground!"

Each of the American soldiers stepped forward then, Pelton a step ahead of Jersey, all of them stopping where the young sergeant stopped, five feet from the closest FADH, the soldier/cops placing pistols and batons on the ground and stepping back, a few with hands in the air. They were nervous, Jersey saw. Some angry but more nervous, one with a tic above his left eye making his whole face tremble, all of them glancing from Americans to the crowd to the men on the ground to one another.

The crowd had moved in closer again, furious, spitting and yelling—but they too didn't know where this was going, nervous, unsure. They were cursing the stick man more than the others. A stone flew from the crowd and struck him in the forehead, putting him to his knees, a thick stream of blood running down his face.

Without their weapons this crowd will eat them alive, Jersey thought. Then, *Good.*

On the ground ten feet in front of her one of the three half-dead Haitians crawled into the crowd, a cheer erupting, his body disappearing. The others were too injured to move, one unconscious. One of the FADH took a step forward and yelled at the Americans, his arm up, cursing angrily in Creole. Their commander. The Americans' rules of engagement had been read out loud in the Haitian barracks this morning just as clearly as they'd been voiced on the *Eisenhower.* He was displeased at the inconvenience, and *get maman* GIs—*blancs* stay out of our business. As one, the Americans all shifted their aim on him, the slap and click of rifles moving to one target. He was caught short by that and stopped yelling, but stood his ground, face angry—the arrogant defiance of either blind courage or sure knowledge.

Captain Hall had turned on the old colonel, the two of them pulled back a few steps behind the enlisted American soldiers. They were hissing furiously at each other, arms up and gesturing. It was obvious now to Jersey they weren't from the same unit, that the colonel was just along for the ride; this conversation wouldn't even be happening if Hall belonged to the colonel. The older man was waving a piece of yellow paper in his left hand—the most recent rules of engagement, a dense and impossible document. Perhaps the Haitian FADH platoon commander understood it; no one else did. The pale colonel brandished it like a weapon. "Captain, you need to check yourself before this gets out of hand."

"Out of hand?"

The colonel lowered his voice. "There's no mandate to interfere in local actions unless the lives of your troops are in peril."

Hall opened his mouth, then snapped it shut. He looked quick at the sky, then back down, dead-eyeing the colonel straight on. He set his face, then made his lips move; short, clipped words.

"There were shots fired. At my convoy. We reacted accordingly."

The old colonel stared him straight back, wheels turning. You could see it, he was thinking so hard. Running down options, possibilities, probable outcomes, varied bad endings—trying to float Hall's lie. Jersey was impressed the colonel was even considering it.

Seconds that ran for an hour, then finally, "That's fourteen stories to get straight. In the time it takes to drive to the airport."

Hall opened his mouth but the colonel immediately cut him off.

"I mean straight. Razor straight. No deviation. You can't do it, Captain Hall. Don't martyr yourself. The man in the tree is already dead. The other three are saved."

He turned then and pointed. Jersey thought he was pointing at her, but the colonel was indicating the young sergeant next to her.

"At least one round came from that M-16. That's a missing bullet. Even without a body there'll be questions. You know that."

Hall said something Jersey didn't hear. Her eyes were flicking back and forth, from the two American officers to the now-circled cadre of FADH, all of them except their pissed-off commander with their hands at least half-raised.

Captain Hall spat on the ground. He looked at the colonel, then turned and looked at each of the American soldiers. His eyes met

Jersey's and stayed there a moment. She made no expression, continuing to shift her gaze from him to the FADH and back. When she looked again Captain Hall was nodding at his sergeant. Hall unholstered his pistol, pulling it free again, then stepped toward the FADH, gesturing.

"Back! Get back!" he yelled, then, to Jersey's surprise, continued yelling but in what sounded like French and she guessed was Creole. The Haitians looked just as surprised as she was to hear their language coming from his mouth. A long string of something, Hall waving his arm at the FADH, waving them off the two injured men still on the ground. The young Latin sergeant joined him, M-16 leveled from his waist. "Step the fuck off! Get back!"

The FADH as a group backed away, putting themselves a few feet closer to the body hanging from the tree and a few farther from the two injured men. They were now terrified—not of the Americans, but of the crowd. Their weapons remained on the ground.

Is it friendly fire if your countrymen tear you limb from limb? Jersey thought.

Two and two and front-line view / bubbling FADH in the voodoo stew.

Captain Hall pointed to the crowd, at a group of men standing toward the front. He gestured, said a few clipped words in Creole, waving them in. They nodded and ran over, grabbing the bodies of the injured Lavalas demonstrators, pulling them back into the oblivion of the crowd, a cheer rising. Small victories. Jersey was watching Hall. *He's Haitian,* she thought. Or something. His English was Brooklyn-perfect.

Jersey looked to check the anger level of the FADH, but all of them were past that now. Scared, with no weapons. Sweating, eyes flicking around, looking at this black American officer who spoke their language. Looking for escape.

The injured gone, the Latin sergeant two-finger pointed at two privates, then at the FADH's weapons on the ground. "Rizzolo, Joe Brown. Sling your rifles. Grab this shit here and put it in the Humvees."

"No," Captain Hall said, barely audible. Then, louder, "Belay that, Sergeant."

"Sir?"

"Hold." Hall put his fist up. "Return to the vehicles, Sergeant Lamas. Squad withdrawal, by the numbers."

"Sir? We can't leave their weapons—"

"What part of 'return to the vehicles' didn't you get, Sergeant?"

The young sergeant looked at his captain, eyebrows raised. Jersey watched, incredulous. Then saw the colonel, standing behind Captain Hall's shoulder, rules-of-engagement paperwork in hand. She heard Pelton, under his breath, "What the fuck."

A sunburned corporal hooked his thumb over his shoulder, indicating the crowd, a slow drawl from his thin lips. "These people gon' git fucked, we leave weapons for the troops."

But the sergeant had locked eyes with Captain Hall and like Jersey he knew the score now and already was holding his M-16 with just his right hand, pointing sharp with his fingers at his troops, coordinating the pull-back. He looked over at Jersey.

"Y'all get outta here, Sergeant Harris."

She nodded, and turned with Pelton back toward the Humvees. Suddenly it seemed there were flies everywhere, and she waved her arm, shooing them from her face.

Two by two the infantry soldiers peeled off, falling back to the vehicles. The crowd watched with curiosity at first, not sure what was happening, then in mounting collective disbelief. Shouts and murmurs, then louder, and then, as it became clear the saviors were leaving the dragon alive and armed, people began running—running for cover, down the avenue, up alleys, bellowing a warning. The FADH were in just as much disbelief to see the Americans retreat, the commander— the only one who didn't look surprised—eyeing the stack of rifles and pistols and batons like a starving man to a steak. Captain Hall, Sergeant Lamas, and the old, pale colonel stood alone in a circle in the park, then the colonel turned and jogged back toward the hummers. Hall and his sergeant stayed, and Jersey saw they were making sure the crowd was as gone as possible before they withdrew. Finally, Hall raised his pistol and pointed it at the FADH commander. Looking over her shoulder, Jersey winced. But he didn't shoot. He yelled something,

something in Creole. The FADH commander's face didn't move, didn't flinch. Captain Hall lowered his pistol and walked to the hummers. Sergeant Lamas waited a few beats, then started walking half-back-ward, covering his captain's retreat.

Captain Hall slammed an open palm down on the hood of the Humvee with the .50 cal gunner as he passed it. "Put a round in the dirt if they move toward those weapons before we're out of sight," he said.

The sergeant, right behind him, added quietly, "Only in the dirt, man. Only in the dirt."

Scaboo and Riddle, who'd stayed with the .50 cal gunner, joined Jersey and Pelton.

"We're not arresting those guys?" Scaboo asked, pointing the bar-rel of his M-16 toward the FADH.

"We're not arresting them," Jersey said.

"We're not taking their weapons?"

"We're not taking their weapons."

Scaboo blinked, twice.

Riddle barked out a laugh. "Oh that makes sense!" He crawled into the Humvee. "Why exactly are we here?" Out of sight, his rant went on: "I liked yesterday's plan better, when we were going to kill anything that moved. Can we go back to yesterday's plan?"

Jersey raised her head to the Haitian hanging from the tree. "We should cut him down," she said, but no one heard her. Everyone was scattering. She looked at her watch; they'd been on Haitian soil just over an hour. Her eyes went back to the lynching; she couldn't stop looking at him. A crow was sitting on the branch the man hung from. Jersey wondered if the crow had seen the whole thing.

Strange witness, she thought.

Strange fruit.

There were no Haitian civilians left in the park, just a few across the street, watching from a distance; none of them smiling.

Run, she thought. *Run now.*

The 10th Mountain soldiers were almost all back in their vehicles, yelling signals to one another, covering points and confirming. They were muted now, though. Sweeping their fields of fire, especially the FADH standing in the park, but watching them Jersey could see they always came back to the man in the tree.

A group of children, ten, eleven years old, were at the Humvees now, not singing, not begging, just quietly standing with the Americans. Nowhere to go. The lead Humvee was pulling slowly away, the head of the blind American snake headed for the airport. Jersey, half in the vehicle, pulled her leg back out and jogged four quick steps to them. "Tory!" Riddle yelled at her, but she ignored him. The oldest was a girl, dirt-streaked and bare feet. "Run," Jersey said to her, and then saw they were all girls. Three in shorts or pants, two in dresses, but all girls, quiet and scared. She put her hand out and grabbed the girl's shoulder. "Run now. Fast." She pointed across the street, toward an alley, away from the park. "Run, girls. Go."

The oldest looked Jersey in the face, and nodded. She clucked at her group, the little ones pulling in closer to her. She said something in Creole, looking into Jersey's eyes. "Just run. Run now," Jersey said, then turned and swung herself into the Humvee as Riddle put it down in gear and pulled out with the convoy.

The kids were moving across the street, not as fast as Jersey would have liked, looking backward as they ran, at the park, and at the Americans. There were few people on the streets now. Jersey thought they would be yelling at the Americans, but those left were silent—too late for protest. They were moving out, moving away. Behind, the soldier/cops of the FADH stood stock-still in the same place, watching—amazed—as the convoy moved down the street. Two of them stepped toward their weapons but their commander growled and they stopped. *Too bad,* Jersey thought. She dearly would've liked to have seen the kid manning the .50 cal get trigger happy.

"This is fucked, yo," Riddle said, steering.

She opened her mouth then closed it again, saying nothing.

"What're you gonna tell the skipper?"

"I don't know, Specialist Riddle," she snapped. "What do you suggest?" She pulled her goggles back down over eyes, just another faceless grunt.

She realized she was soaking wet. Under the dead weight of the flak jacket, her BDU top and T-shirt and sports bra were plastered to her chest. She opened her mouth to say something else to Riddle, and instead her left hand clenched into a fist and she slammed it down on the dashboard. She turned suddenly and leaned out the window of the Humvee, looking back. The little girls were gone. The dead Lavalas supporter hung unmoving from the tree, the crow still above him. As the convoy swept around a corner, the last view Jersey had was the FADH, at the center of the empty park, bending down to retrieve their weapons.

CHAPTER

4

Hillside neighborhoods swept by, the convoy moving at a clip now, warm air rushing in the open window. Jersey and Riddle had no tactical radio for guidance or communication, and the marine-band handheld still clipped to Jersey's flak jacket had lost signal just a few hundred yards from the boat. Pelton raised an open palm to them from his driver's seat in the Humvee behind; other than that they were alone. Riddle talked and Jersey nodded absently, rifle in her lap, and she tried hard and failed to stop thinking about how it might feel to be hauled up into a tree by a rope around your throat.

The Humvees were winding down through the city, back toward sea level, descending from poor neighborhoods into desperately poor neighborhoods. Cité Soleil, the cruelest slum in the hemisphere, the convoy forced to slow again as avenues became streets and streets became cramped blind alleys and no one could tell Jersey they weren't lost. They'd been driving too long and the route made no sense. The Captain's convoy was lost. Alert again, rifle up, she leaned out the window, gasped from the stench, raw sewage under the wheels of the hummer.

No crowd and all crowd here, individuals, faces, eyes watching from behind flimsy curtains, or filling the space between two shacks. And then, for a dark stretch, even the shacks weren't shacks, but dwellings without name, constructed in an evolutionary manner that changed with each passing storm and subsequent tidal flood. The eyes here were not just poor but hungry. Movements slower, gatherings smaller. But no less maimed and wounded than higher in the city; visible stumps and scars and once, close enough to touch as they passed, a face hollow and black and caved-in where eyes would have been, lids half enclosed in a scab of mucus.

"Dear Lord," Riddle said.

"*Grangou, grangou*"—voices from the open fronts of shacks and cramped roadside. "*Sils vouz plait, grangou,*" empty palms out, tiny children's hands and necks, skin stretched tight over round, empty bellies.

Tory Harris watched.

She wondered how many they passed carried a toxic, deeper wound than broken limbs from birth defects or work or torture. This was Haiti; that meant something. There'd even been a class, if you could call it a class, for the lower enlisted, a few days before they sailed. Hastily arranged—as all things related to this war (*is it war or is it not?*) were hastily arranged—a few direct statistics, a lot of laughs about bend-over buddies and bend-back Bettys and what passed in the blood and fluids of the unprotected. The Fort Eustis post medical officer writing on the board in the crew's mess, his clipped, blond hair so neatly parted, his tone dry as the government chalk in his hand. He reminded them about a Private Stupid who came back from Somalia with a gift from a prostitute, an evil gift in the bloodstream and a one-way ticket to an Army discharge. He'd been a stand-up guy, ol' Private Stupid, with a Bronze Star for action in Mogadishu. But you can't deploy with HIV, and if you can't deploy why bother wearing green. Bye bye, Private Stupid. Tory had sat near the door during this lecture and when she thought her fists would break from the clenching she slipped out to the passageway and then out the hatch to the deck beyond. She'd found Dick Wags on the fantail, a small can of black paint beside him on the deck, scraping rust off the ship's propane barbecue. Sitting now in the Humvee, she remembered he'd looked up at her and stopped work to smoke a cigarette with her and that's when he'd asked her—for the first time—if she knew what she was going to do. She'd told him, and he hadn't said anything. He hadn't looked surprised, though, at her decision.

Riddle droned on in her ear. *Jersey this and Jersey that and what do you think about it, Jersey? Lost, lost. Lordy, lord.* Tory kept her eyes out the window of the hummer, looking for the women among the Haitians now, wondering about them, how it was for them. It occurred to her most of them who carried it probably didn't even know their own early death flowed in their bloodstream—didn't know they had it. Just didn't know.

Tory put her wrist up and looked at her watch.

"We should just brake, fall the hell back with Scaboo and Pelton, and let these guys lose themselves down here." She put a cigarette to her lips and lit it—fuck convoy rules. They weren't allowed to shoot the soldiers they came to overthrow, and she wasn't going to shoot anyone else. Might as well smoke. "The four of us could sniff our way back to the boat faster than it's taking them to find the airport."

Riddle nodded twice without expression. "Sergeant, yes. You give the word, New Jersey. I'm on it."

She exhaled, then shook her head no.

If anyone but that captain was involved in this, she just might have. But something was going on with that guy, that Captain Hall. She didn't know what it was, but wanted to know. He was—

"Looks like the road's opening up."

She blinked. Riddle had leaned forward, squinting.

"Yeah." He swerved to avoid a scrawny chicken, almost taking out a goat instead. The front right tire of the hummer slammed hard into a pothole and if Jersey's rifle hadn't been safed it would gone off.

"Hey, that's water," Riddle said, and he was right. Centered in their vision, down the dark medieval tunnel of road, was a thin patch of the same crystal blue Jersey had seen from high on the hill, at the park. And then, as they turned a corner, the blue was replaced by chain-link fence visible about half a mile away and a warehouse and over the warehouse was the gear and spinning radar from the top of a ship's house and it was the LSV. Different angle, but back where they started.

"You'd think someone would've mapped this out, no?"

A Black Hawk sliced over them, screaming and low, its sucking wake ripping plastic and boards off the roofs of the shacks they passed, the Haitians on the street throwing themselves to the ground, arms over their heads. The chopper was there, then it was gone, echoes in their ears and debris on the ground.

"That captain up there can't be happy."

No, I don't think he is.

They turned another corner, and the LSV was gone. Two more turns and the road opened up and they were on Route Nationale One headed out of Port-au-Prince, green Air Force cargo planes circling far in the distance, descending, preparing to land.

In the hour they'd been gone into the city, the U.S. Army had arrived. Not an inch farther than the coast, it seemed—but they owned the coast. This small stretch of Route Nationale One was all racing five-ton and deuce-and-a-half trucks, hummers overstuffed with troops and gear, and a few Bradley fighting vehicles. The Bradleys, Jersey thought, were useless—she'd been to the city. The streets were too narrow. They'd never fit. Riddle laughed his barking laugh when she mentioned this.

"Chalk another for intelligence and planning."

"Airborne, baby," she said.

They were almost in an accident at the gate of the airport. The convoy was racing fast, barely time to stop, each hummer in succession almost plowing into the one before it. Rubber burned—then another wait. Static and squawking voices pouring through the humid air from tactical radios in the other idling Humvees. Riddle reached out to the dashboard and picked up an imaginary microphone. "What the fuck? Over," he said into his hand.

At the front of the column Captain Hall was negotiating entrance.

What the fuck? Over.

Hall had pulled off his helmet again, smooth skull shining in the sun, free hand back and pointing toward the city.

"Maybe they won't let us in," Jersey said, watching Hall closely through the windshield.

"We can only hope."

The gate guards were a squad of 10th Mountain light infantry, armed to the teeth and fully geared-out. They had headsets and microphones clipped to their helmets, blank expressions on their faces.

What the fuck? Over, she thought, then said, "Friendly fire."

"What?"

"Friendly fire. I'm going to shoot any gate guard who has better gear than me."

Riddle nodded, reaching for his canteen. "It's all about accessories, Tory."

The trip through the gate took them straight onto the flight line, C-130s and massive Galaxy C-5s roaring low overhead and thudding down on the runway with two-minute precision. Closer to the main group of airport buildings, choppers came in from *Eisenhower* with the same frequency, three or four at a time, dropping platoons of soldiers. And the soldiers were everywhere, thousands of them, doing nothing. Crouched on the ground, sitting and kneeling in loose formations. All of them fully dressed: helmets, flak jackets, uniform sleeves down and buttoned at the cuff.

"Why don't they take that shit off?" Riddle said, steering wide to follow the looping route of the convoy across the airport. "No sign of Charlie anywhere."

"If the Army wanted you cool, they'd've issued you a fan."

"True."

It took them an hour to find Captain Hall's lost company, squatting and sweating and cursing on a corner of the tarmac, baking under the sun. Hall's first sergeant still wasn't sure why they'd ended up in the airport instead of the seaport, but the lead chopper pilot had been from Connecticut and the Louisiana first sergeant was fairly well sure that had something to do with it.

Tory checked her watch. They'd been in-country three hours.

Jérémie

CHAPTER

5

The vessel master of the Jesus boat was a Nova Scotian named McBride. It wasn't his boat, or his Jesus. He was just skipper, paid by Pastor to do the job. An aging scarecrow of a man, tall and stalk-thin, he had short sandy hair chopped with his own scissors, massive hands and feet. Those feet, in rubber boots, splashed through puddles and chewy mud as he set out from the ship into the humidity of Jérémie to retrieve his engineer, an American, a sick addict named Davis. The Jesus boat—a 485-foot steel relic from 1914 that had been a cruise ship, a hospital for Italian casualties in World War II, mothballed, then a low-end island hopper in the Mediterranean before being drafted into the Lord's service in the mid-1980s—had been in Jérémie a month, and McBride hadn't seen Davis for the last week. He knew where he was, though.

It was only a five-minute walk from the small pier to the hovel of low buildings and huts behind the cemetery where most of the drinking was done in this town, but McBride carried his pistol, and today carried it not holstered but in his right hand where anyone could see it. Law and order were always fluid concepts in Haiti, a wise man maintained his own, and in McBride's mind the arrival of the U.S. Army this morning didn't change things at all. If anything, it complicated. He thought he might not be alone in this thinking—the road was deserted. A first. McBride kept head up, gait sure, and made for a wooden house with a second-floor balcony overlooking the larger, richer crypts in the boneyard. He paused at the door, listening to the town. Nothing. He turned his head toward the hills beyond; nothing.

Nothing at all. There was never nothing at all in Haiti. Not before today, anyway. He'd never heard nothing. He looked over his shoulder again at the nothing, then went inside.

The old woman behind the bar didn't look twice at his pistol. She pulled a glass from the shelf as he walked in, relieved for the business. There was no one else in the cramped, hot room. There'd be a lack of patrons until it was clear where things would fall with the Americans. It made a difference. Port-au-Prince might well be on fire today for all anyone here knew—probably was—and the whole of Jérémie had been quiet since sunset yesterday, holding its breath. McBride shook his head at the old woman before she could start pouring. "No, Maman," he said, then asked a question instead. He didn't speak Creole, but they understood enough of his maritime French here to get by. She pointed behind her, to another door, and the man went through it. It led to a closet of a hallway, and McBride went to the farthest of two doors. With pistol in hand he felt sinister. He shifted the pistol to his left hand, raised his right fist, and knocked twice.

"Davis!" he yelled to the wood.

There was a noise, undecipherable. Damn the man, anyway.

McBride yelled again, then turned the knob, opening the door. A wave of smoke rolled out over him, cigarettes and marijuana and something heavier, sweeter.

The hall was dark, but the room darker. Almost complete, this blackness. Limbs he could see, pale and long. And a glimmer of skin. Who or how many or of what ilk impossible to say. Then Davis's ghost-white face, blinking, floating, caught framed in a meager ray of light from the hall. His eyes were dull and heavy-lidded, unfocused and distant in his skull, the eyes of a deep cave dweller.

"Good Christ," McBride said, turning his head away. "Get it together and meet me outside. We're sailing."

Unable to stop himself, he looked again. There was the faintest glow from a weak candle in the far corner. A whisper, unidentifiable from the pitch, but not Davis.

Then, "Sailing," a voice said, and that was Davis, his face now gone.

"All right," McBride said, and pulled the door closed behind him.

* * *

The engineer Davis—his friends called him Junior, the name from when he'd been a soldier, back to basic training when he'd been the younger of two recruits named Davis—floated in the pitch-black room's cloud of smoke, lost somewhere in a fold of flesh and slick, warm wetness, the candle puffed out as the door closed. There was a large hand putting pressure on the small of his back, then a fingertip tracing the inside of his left thigh. He clamped his legs together, tight. There were rules, now; very specific rules to be followed. He'd hard-wired them in his brain, so no matter how gone he got the new rules were followed. Finding no entry between clamped thighs, the ghost hand slipped away. Junior Davis reached with his own hand to where he knew there was a bottle resting on a wood table at the head of the bed. He drew the bottle to his lips and filled his mouth with sticky rum. Swallowing, Davis reached out and placed his free hand flat against skin, pressing in and then sliding up, up, until he found a nipple, small, hard and ridged. He rolled it under his fingertips. He took another swallow from the bottle, then moved his mouth to the nipple, wetting it with his lips then placing it between his teeth. This was all right, this was in the rules. He sucked, and if there'd even briefly been a memory of McBride opening the door and ordering him out it was gone now, gone and far away. Just like the rules.

McBride let Maman fill a glass with beer for him. He took the drink to a small table near the door and sat down, prepared to wait no more than ten minutes. After that, he'd give the old woman a few gourdes or maybe a U.S. dollar and send her in to evict Davis. He kicked at the sawdust on the floor with the toe of his boot and sipped.

The beer was foamy, warm, thick with yeast. He'd developed a taste for it. The missionary boat had been here almost a month now, in this most-remote of Haitian ports, way the hell out at the end of southern Haiti's lobster claw. They'd been in Cap-Haitien before this, up north, then Jacmel, down below. Neither of which ended well. Cap-Haitien had been a quick exit, Pastor never clear why. Just a very forceful late-night waking of McBride and a clipped order to have the ship off the pier by sunrise. The departure from Jacmel, on the other hand, McBride had been involved in—a week-long negotiation to extract Davis from a cell in the basement of the *caserne* on the mountain. They should have dropped him there, but Davis had persuaded Pastor to keep him until Puerto Rico, their next call. He'd at least be on American soil, he'd pleaded. More, there was none among the hundred-odd Bible thumpers onboard qualified to take his watch in the engine room and coax the cranky old Fiat diesel to life—the real and only true reason Pastor had even put up money to get him out of the FADH's grasp, let alone keep him onboard. Of course they hadn't cleared Haitian waters before the second of the four massive cylinders that pushed the boat seized tight. They didn't make Puerto Rico. They didn't even make Port-au-Prince. They took refuge in Jérémie, the last Haitian port they hadn't been ejected out of, run from, or Jesused to death.

So far, Jérémie had been fine. But they were leaving now. The Americans had arrived, and Pastor wanted to be back in Jacmel.

The front door of the bar swung open. Two men walked in, arms entwined, both laughing. The taller of the two wore sunglasses, and McBride thought what he always did when he saw one of these guys, which was how the hell he saw anything with those glasses. But apparently they saw just fine. Or saw enough. McBride's back stiffened as they came in, but the men barely glanced at him, paid the woman for two brown bottles, and left. On the way out the door, Mr. Sunglasses threw a glance at McBride, but he never paused or broke his stride. Out the door.

Attachés. The one, anyway. Mr. Sunglasses. Almost certainly. Paid bullies. *Bullies at best,* McBride thought. Killers. Shiftless and lazy but sometimes smart and always dangerous and always on the right side of whatever argument they were in. *Macoute.* In fact if no longer by name. Ton Ton Macoute. It was why McBride carried the pistol; although the worse for him if ever he were to point it at one of them. Certainly the worse for him. He'd seen firsthand what had been done to Davis's body. He only survived his stay in the prison, McBride thought, because he was pickled.

As if the thought drew him, the door behind the bar flew open—

poor Maman there yelping in surprise—and Davis himself sailed through it, propelled by stumbling and gravity. He was dressed now, in black jeans and a half-tucked black T-shirt, and he crossed the room in three quick steps. He passed McBride without a look, and was gone outside.

Junior Davis was almost as tall as McBride. He had a sharp, pale face topped with short, curly hair. The engineer was pushing his hands through his hair now, trying to control it, weaving across the road. He looked profoundly ill. McBride followed from the bar and Davis spun on one heel to say something to him. He opened his mouth and instead said, "Oh no." He stumbled two steps from the road and vomited. McBride looked at his watch and waited. *Never again,* he thought, and wasn't sure whether he meant Davis or himself or something else entirely and then decided it didn't matter: None of it, ever again. If he could help it.

After a few moments Junior Davis pulled a wad of tissue from one of his pockets and, turning back to McBride, wiped his mouth. He looked up, his blue eyes dull and stupid. "Sorry," he said. "Okay."

"Okay?"

"Okay."

"Can you walk?"

"Of course."

"Of course nothing." McBride tapped his pistol against his thigh. "I should have left you in Jacmel."

"Yes," Junior Davis said, in perfect agreement. "You should have."

They walked slowly back toward the ship. McBride glanced behind them every time Davis coughed, nervous, jumpy at the noise. But the town was absolutely silent, empty.

"There's nothing bad in Jérémie," Junior Davis said to McBride, slurring.

"What?"

"There's nothing bad. Here."

"So you say. There were *attachés* in there. Today. In that place where you were. So what do you know."

"They're everywhere. Doesn't mean anything."

"Maybe." McBride stopped to light a cigar, then held the flame out to light the cigarette Davis had pulled from his back pocket. "Of course, there's no American soldiers out here yet. I'll bet we'll see less of that lot when your Army arrives."

Junior Davis looked at McBride through the smoke. "What makes you think the Americans have any interest in controlling *attachés*?" he finally said. He was remembering how to talk.

McBride opened his mouth, then paused. He thought a moment. "They're here to give Colonel Cedras the boot," he said.

"That doesn't really change my question, does it?"

McBride puffed his cigar, then said, "No, I suppose it doesn't."

He started walking again, Junior Davis a step behind.

Tied at the end of the narrow pier, the Jesus ship was long, thin, unbreathing. As with everything else onboard, fuel was fiercely rationed; Pastor ordered the generator off most days. The vessel looked dead. McBride and Davis slowly maneuvered the narrow, wooden gangway, McBride calling out to the watch as they went up. Unanswered; the watch, a young blond man in shorts and light-blue T-shirt, had succumbed to the sun and was sound asleep in a folding chair at the top of the gangway, thick softback Bible open on his lap. Wide awake on the deck next to him, glaring at McBride with territorial arrogance, was a large rat.

"*Hi!*" McBride yelled, quickening his step, right foot shooting out in a kick as he crested the gangway, boot tip connecting perfect with the rat's head. The watch jumped from his chair, blinking in surprise. The rat down and stunned, McBride slipped the toe of his boot under it, lifted his leg slowly, then kicked again, the rodent sailing over the rail to the water below with a fat splash.

"Keep that goddamn plank raised," McBride snapped at the watch, who still wasn't sure what had happened.

"Sir," he said, "I—"

But McBride was already gone aft, making swiftly for the outside stairs to the bridge.

"The Lord hates rats," Davis whispered to the kid as he passed him on the quarterdeck, following McBride. On his feet, the watch hoisted the rope pulley, raising the gangway off the pier a foot.

Junior Davis stumbled as he rounded aft to the fantail, slipping on something greasy, his chin nailing the steel railing as he went down. He lifted himself, vomiting again as he got his head over the rail. He let his head hang over the side a moment, then took a deep breath and wiped his mouth on his T-shirt. The noon air was still, thick as brackish water. He turned round twice, remembered, and crossed the small fantail to the stairs, up the back of the ship's house, then forward.

With no air-conditioning to cool, McBride kept the old shutters on all the bridge windows secured tight during the day. He'd fry, otherwise. No power to run even the lights meant a need to improvise. The bridge glowed red, seven or eight thick candles burning on the chart table, the radio cabinet, the throttle station. The room flickered in warmth and strange light, stopping Davis in his tracks for a second as he stepped in, confused, the scene so like a *Vodoun* hut he had to blink and look over his shoulder then look back. Even Pastor, coming round the chart table, unmistakable in cropped hair and padded safari khakis, seemed different; a second, hollow shadow face floating over skin for a second as the candlelight flickered then snapped the real Pastor into place.

"I'm late," Davis said, looking for McBride, not seeing him. He didn't like being alone with Pastor.

"You are."

"I need my engine now, Mister Davis," McBride's voice said, then there was McBride, a black hole in the glow on the port side of the bridge.

"Mister Davis," Pastor echoed.

Junior Davis nodded, and turned to leave. He stopped, and turned back.

"We can't go back to Jacmel."

"The engine, Mister Davis," Pastor said quietly. "Just the engine."

"The Army'll sink us pierside, you just barrel in there," Davis said. "If the Navy doesn't do it as we come around Point L'Abacou."

"They won't. Either." Words precise, clipped, like Pastor's hair, like all the preacher's words.

Davis looked at Pastor, and at McBride standing calm to it all. He understood, or began to.

"You have an arrangement."

Pastor didn't answer right away, then said, "There are a few blessed, uniformed American souls who carry arms in the left hand and the Bible in the right."

"I'll be damned."

"It seems likely, Mister Davis."

McBride came around the chart table, a glowing shadow moving behind the candlestick burning in the center. "I need the generator now, Mister Davis," he said. "And the engine."

Davis nodded. "It'll be all we can do to crawl back to Jacmel with that."

"It doesn't matter," Pastor said. "We've been promised assistance there."

Pastor walked the front of the bridge, opening each shutter as she went. Window by window the bridge grew brighter. She was quiet as she did this, then said, "How long?" McBride for the life of him wasn't sure what she meant. How long until Davis dropped dead? How long could they keep the vessel running, let alone afloat? If it did run, how long a sail back to Jacmel with a crippled diesel? How long until Judgment Day?

"What?" he said, at the same time she clarified: "Jacmel."

Squinting against the sudden intrusion of sunlight he glanced down at the chart although he didn't need to. "Two days," he said. "Maybe three."

"It only took us one day to get here."

"We're bound to be much slower now," he said. "Limping. No better word for it. And there'll be weather. Little doubt of that."

She came around the console to the chart table. She wet her forefinger and thumb and snuffed the candles, one by one. There was a sizzle as each went out, and a small puff of black smoke.

"There is some danger in this," McBride said. "Even if the Fiat doesn't die altogether, if we're too slow when serious weather hits she could capsize."

Pastor chewed her lip and thought about this. McBride was somewhat comforted she at least seemed to be thinking it through. He knew what her answer would be, though.

"We'll go," she said.

McBride nodded. He kept it to himself, thought it good to project caution, but he was happy to go, happy to sail. Relieved. Even crippled, it was better than sitting here, rotting on the pier like they'd been. All the brats and women running around the vessel made him crazy. The men went out to preach and the brats and women made a nuisance of themselves onboard. They all disappeared back into cabins when he got under way, though. None of them could stomach the sea. It was the only break he ever got. He'd found a stinking, crappy cloth diaper on the deck outside his own cabin the previous day; none of the women onboard were worth a damn, Pastor aside. No, he was happy to pull anchor and go.

"There's an Army vessel on its way to Jacmel," Pastor said. "They've been told to render whatever aid we need."

"They won't likely find us a new diesel engine in their parts closet," McBride said softly.

"No, they won't, Mister McBride," she said. "But maybe some light bulbs, some toilet paper."

"Light bulbs and toilet paper," he repeated.

"Yes. And whatever else you and Mister Davis can convince them to part with."

"I think it best to leave Davis out of this."

"But he might know some of them."

"My point exactly."

She chewed her lip again, thinking. Then said, "You may be right." Drumming her fingertips on the chart table, she changed the subject. "How long of a sail to Puerto Rico, Mister McBride?"

"Puerto Rico, Pastor? We can't make Puerto Rico."

She waved her hand. "Not now, I know. After we restock with whatever the Army can give us in Jacmel."

McBride shook his head. "But the thing we'd need to cross is the one thing they can't give. We need a new main. No amount of light bulbs and toilet paper will build a new main."

"I've been in touch with the mission," she said. McBride, who had skippered this ship three years and come to believe that if indeed there was a God surely no middle manager stood between Pastor and the supreme being, blinked in surprise as he always did on the few occasions when she brought up the missionary organization that owned the ship. And paid his salary. They were in Omaha, he'd learned; a fact that never failed to amuse him. "They've indicated the possibility of a complete engine overhaul, if we can make Puerto Rico."

Indicated. Possibility.

McBride chose his words with care, with as much care as he was sure the missionaries had done speaking to Pastor. "They mentioned Puerto Rico before," he said. "Last year. When they spoke of junking us."

Pastor's hand went to her throat, fluttering, an action McBride had only seen from her once or twice before. Her eyes went down to the chart table. "They were clear, Mister McBride," she said softly. "They said our work could go on. They promised, this time. An overhaul."

He nodded, unseen. What could he say? There was nothing to say. Personally, he thought if they ever tied up in Puerto Rico—or any American-controlled port—she'd be plucked from the ship as fast as the mission's lawyers could fly from Omaha, and his last task as skipper would be to strip the vessel for sale or salvage. But maybe it was true, the story they'd told her. Maybe the mission was newly flush. It was, he supposed, possible. Unlikely, but possible. And what could he say?

She'd been a nun, briefly. Twenty years or more back. A Catholic nun. And McBride could see the nun in her without much imagination. In her walk, in her voice.

"How many leave the convent because it isn't hard enough?" he'd said to Davis once, over a beer, back in that slim, brief space of time when Davis seemed to be trying and they could talk together. Davis had laughed, but there'd been something in his eye, as well. And it made no sense to McBride because it looked like envy.

She'd abandoned her orders for a man who said he was born again in Christ, a man who said he knew the true path, not all this pope nonsense, but the true path to Christ. McBride had this information because he'd asked a question once and this was the answer she'd given. Later, over time, he learned other small particles of fact, not directly but extrapolated from other things she said—that her time with the man had been brief, relatively, but she'd remained on his path though not with him; that she'd come to this boat as a volunteer, then stayed, becoming pastor a year or so later.

But only once had she ever spoken to McBride directly about herself, and it was the only time he'd ever asked. His question had been asked in bed, in the narrow rack of her cabin, and he'd been half-drunk and talking when he shouldn't have and his question had been along the line of had this—*this*—happened before. She'd waited a long time before saying anything, so long McBride thought she'd decided not to answer or maybe fallen asleep. But she did answer, eventually, her pale broad back and shoulders turned to him in the dim cabin, and her answer hadn't been an answer, just these two facts—she'd been a nun once, and had left to be a Christian with a Christian man. A few moments later she rolled back and reached for him, guiding him into her. For the second time that night she lay there while he pushed and sweated away to his drunken climax, and for the second time that night he didn't know what she got out of it, eyes closed and biting her lip, but she seemed to want him to do it, breathing hard as his strokes quickened. And a few moments after that she asked him to leave her cabin. She had invited him in, invited him to bed, then invited him to leave and never asked him back. In the three years since he never saw another man go in. It never came up again and this was a good job and it was for the best.

McBride remembered the creases in her plump body smelled like powder, baby powder, his fingers the next morning holding the smell, the smell of powder and also of dark fruit. He thought about it sometimes, late with just the thin bulkhead between them, but in the end he knew this was best.

CHAPTER

6

In the ship's house the passageways were silent. Those with the Lord taking siesta through the midday heat. No one about. *Just us three sinners,* Junior Davis thought.

He put his hand on the knob of his cabin door, one level below the bridge, paused, then changed his mind. He shuffled back down the passage, making straight for the engine room instead.

The descent down into the pit of Davis's domain was steep, reeking of salty grease water and the malfunctioning waste tank. With the generator off, the bowels of the ship were plunged into absolute darkness. Most of the caged light bulbs down here had died anyway—with no replacements—making the passage treacherous whether or not the juice flowed. But even shaky and addled he could navigate this, knew his route, slowly feeling down two levels of narrow steel stairs, then along the catwalk framing the top of the massive four-cylinder diesel. If someone stepped in front of him he'd never see them; it had occurred to Davis, making this blackout journey before, this is what it would be like to sink, to go down with the ship. Like this, just wetter.

There was a draft down here below the waterline, cool and oily air. One more short level of stairs, then a blind grope for the flashlight he kept waiting here, secured to a bulkhead. Junior Davis could hear the bilgewater, just under the deckplate, sloshing gently. If he could hear it, things were very close to being bad. He'd been off-ship almost a week, holed up mostly in the back room of the bar. He'd taught a few of the

Jesus brigade robots how to crank the generator alive and get it on-line, then down and secure at night. But they wouldn't know to check for bilgewater, or what to do about it even if they noticed. After the generator was up he'd have to get the pumps sucking, then crawl back into shaft alley to tighten the packing.

"Yes, Lord," he said, and clicked the flashlight on.

In the pale glow he caught his breath; confused for a moment, then remembering. He slapped lightly at his right cheek with his fingers, *tap tap tap tap tap*. There was an old pair of blue Army snipe coveralls hanging on a hook, and he reached for them, slipping them over his jeans and T-shirt. He snugged a tan set of ear cans over his head. Picking up a crowbar, he unclipped the flashlight from the wall and crept aft to the narrowest end of the engine room, where the generator sat. Setting the flashlight and crowbar on the deck at his feet, Davis pulled a bent cigarette from a pocket in the coveralls and lit it, taking a couple of drags. He was tired, very tired. He slapped himself across the face once—hard this time—then leaned over and pulled the generator's oil stick, wiping it on his coverall leg, then sinking it again and checking it in the flashlight glow. He spun open the water line, then the fuel. Half the top of the fuel valve had broken off weeks before, and he needed a screwdriver to get it all open.

The generator's starter battery was dead; he'd have to do this the hard way. Laying the crowbar across the nipple on the hydraulic release valve, Junior Davis paused a moment. He had to be careful here. If the hydraulic oil dumped without starting the generator on first try the accumulator would have to be pumped by hand. He was in no condition to do that. He puffed a few times on the cigarette dangling from his lips, then held his breath. Gripping the crowbar with both hands, he pushed down with all the strength he could muster. Davis heard the swoosh of the fluid and the whine of the starter and the generator coughed once then roared to life, whining, too fast, but running.

Oh thank you Jesus, he thought. *Small miracles, Lord.*

Winded, he leaned across the top of the generator and played with the throttle arm until the RPMs evened out. Then he went to the elec-

trical cabinets and threw the one mighty breaker. The last few working light bulbs in the engine room glowed, weak but steady, bringing
the space to cold, dim life around him.

"There it is," he muttered, his own voice echoing in the ear cans
above the low roar of the diesel generator. "Lord, I have made you a
place in my heart," he said, and couldn't remember right then who
sang that song. Greg Brown maybe, crusty old dirt-farm folksinging
bastard. Maybe an old Greg Brown record. Probably. Tory would
know. Tory knew all that hillbilly stuff.

"Tory, I have made you a place in my heart," he said this time, then
opened his right palm and slapped himself so hard across the face he
almost fell over. A red welt rose on his cheek. Junior Davis stood there
a moment, thinking, then opened his left palm and slapped himself,
even harder, across the other cheek. He winced as he steadied himself,
his left eye twitching and running with water.

"A place in my heart," he said, no idea he'd said it aloud. He pressed
the flat of his palm against his eye to stop the twitching, and went forward to see to the big diesel and do his presail.

The engine room had a quiet box for the watch engineer, but it was
small—like two phone booths joined together—and not very quiet.
Closing himself in the box after firing the main, Junior Davis pulled his
cans off anyway and sat on the tall wooden stool, eyeballing the gauges
he trusted, tapping a fingertip hard against the ones he didn't.

The main engine roared, but not like it could have. Of four massive
cylinders—each large enough for a big man to fit inside—only two
were working now. Davis had grown used to the sickly tapping under
the engine roar when only three of the cylinders were firing. Now it was
down to two and the metallic death rattle could be heard and felt
throughout the ship. The two cylinders alone would be enough to push
the vessel through the water—it had pushed them here—but just
barely. And only for so long. "The Lord will provide," Pastor said, and
sent a group of women into the pit every day to pray over the Fiat, to
keep it ticking along. Davis could sympathize with the Fiat; he was
pretty sure he was down to only one cylinder himself. And with or

without a group of women to pray over him, it was only a matter of time before something vital came unhitched.

"Unhitched," he muttered, and reached for the black call phone. It was cold and heavy. He dialed up the bridge. When a voice answered, Davis said, "Tell the skipper the engine's his."

Junior Davis put his head down on the gauges and closed his eyes, waiting. So much to do down here, but nothing he had to do. So he would wait. The vessel vibrating around him, watch box warm and dark, he drifted. Fifteen minutes later the engine pitch raised, reduction gear whining as the shaft began to slowly spin. Davis heard none of it, thin sleep fluttering his eyelids, the blood in his veins slow and languid as early-morning oil in a rusted old marine diesel.

In his dream he'd cut himself, navigating the engine room in the dark, slicing the skin of his arm wide open as he passed against a rusty fire-extinguisher mount. He played the beam of his flashlight down to see gray bilgewater spurting and flowing free down his arm, splashing all over the deckplates.

Port-au-Prince

CHAPTER

7

In a long, garbage-strewn room once the Port-au-Prince airport's customs office, Captain Hall did some talking to a confused clerk with a helmet two sizes too big. Jersey would have said Hall was yelling, but the officer's voice never raised. It had the same effect as yelling, just slower. The clerk said *no sir no sir no sir* for five minutes then gave up, worn down, and hooked his thumb toward an open door behind him.

"The bird out there'll be lifting off for the main port. Have your people on it, I guess." The kid wiped his nose. "Sir."

Scaboo lifted his rifle and slapped Pelton on the shoulder. "C'mon," he said. They crossed to a door where Riddle already stood, smoking. They'd been waiting almost two hours for a ride back to the boat.

Captain Hall took a step toward Jersey. His helmet was back on, chin strap unsnapped and hanging to his right shoulder. It was the loosest she'd seen him. He'd been tense when she first saw him this morning. Then, very intense. Then very, very pissed off. Now all he seemed was exhausted. She stretched her neck back, standing erect, suddenly aware, a little uneasy at how much bigger he was.

"Thank you, Sergeant Harris," he said, extending his hand. She shook it. "Thank you for being alert up there on the hill. It was . . ." His words trailed off.

"Yes," she said. "It was."

He nodded.

Not for the first time this morning, she was surprised by this man. Most infantry captains—especially the younger ones—had the bluster

and backslap of a high-school football coach. And they rarely talked
to buck sergeants, especially ones not from their branch.

He kept his eyes on hers, wide pupils making quick movements
over her face, like he was mapping it. He had an old scar below his left
eye, a small notch in his brown skin. Tory held his gaze, not sure what
he was trying to communicate. Just before it became uncomfortable he
raised his fist to his mouth and coughed. He smiled, then said quietly,
almost leaning in, "I just spent the better part of an hour trying to get
myself debriefed. No one seemed interested in receiving my report."
He looked off toward where the other three boat soldiers stood in the
doorway, on the far side of the room, smoking, waiting for Jersey and
their chopper. He lowered his eyes, then carefully looked back into hers
again. "What part of 'They're hanging people in the streets' do you
think they don't understand?"

Holding his gaze, Tory tilted her head the slightest bit, then nodded
once.

"We can—I mean—" She blinked. "I was there."

"Thanks," he said. He shrugged then; the way of things. "Thank
you, Sergeant Harris. I know where to find you, I guess."

"Biggest target in the port," she said.

He smiled, and now he pulled his helmet off again. She was struck
by how smooth his head was, and wanted to reach up and touch it,
fighting the weird urge to reach and rest her palm on his skull.

"And I'm sorry," he said. "About before. On the boat."

She pursed her lips slightly, eyebrows raised.

"That colonel," he said. "Baric. Baric is his name. He was out of
line. Completely out of line."

"I've heard worse," she said. "But thank you. For saying what you
did." He smiled again, and not knowing what else to say but wanting
to say something she added, "Sir."

Hall reached under his flak jacket into his breast pocket, drawing
out a small notebook and pen.

"Let me get your names, Sergeant Harris," he said, hooking his
thumb toward the three in the door, but never taking his eyes from
hers. His eyes were large, round, bloodshot.

Jersey took the notebook and pen from his hands, their skin touching. She scratched out their four names, ranks, and unit on the captain's pad. She handed him back the pad and he looked down at the page. "Tory," he said. "Short for something?"

"No," she said. "Just Tory."

Pad back in his pocket, he stuck out his right hand.

"Marc," he said. "Short for Marcel."

For the second time she put her hand in his, shaking. His hand was huge, warm, wrapping completely around hers.

"Marc."

"That's right."

"I'll bet your mother doesn't like Marcel shortened to Marc."

His eyebrows went up and his handshake stopped still, his hand holding hers in midair, not moving. "My mother is dead," he finally said.

"I'm so sorry."

He looked at her, holding tight to her hand, then he smiled and laughed and shook her hand again, as if they'd just clasped them together.

"Don't be sorry. I'm sorry. I mean, I'm kidding with you—"

She laughed with him, easily, and dropped her hand. Slowly.

"You're right," he said. "She never called me anything but Marcel. And my father wouldn't dare call me Marc if she was in the room."

Tory smiled.

They had nothing else to say to each other.

"Thank you again," he said, patting the pocket where he'd stashed his notebook. "And I'll be in touch."

"All right," she said.

"Thank you. Sergeant."

The chopper was almost full, room for only three more.

"Y'all new sergeants can duke it out," Riddle said, his voice raising as the chopper's rotors began spinning, "but me and P are flying the fuck home to our happy little boat." He copped a Roosevelt grin, arm going around Pelton's shoulder.

Scaboo eyeballed Jersey, paused as long as he could, then made grudging noise about staying back and waiting for the next chance. She knew he was too Italian not to offer, even if it grated him. This amused her to no end, and she let him talk a while. Then she pushed him toward the flight line.

"Tell Dick Wags where I'm at," she said. "I'll find another ride."

He didn't argue.

As the three Waterborne soldiers climbed up into the helicopter she dropped the clip from her M-16, cleared the chambered round, then slung her rifle barrel-down across her back. Before the chopper was fifteen feet off the ground she was gone, ducked around the side of the terminal building, not to the gate to look for a convoy, just gone across the airport, alone and free and moving out.

She didn't know she was looking for it until she found it. In a thin, empty alley between two low buildings she ducked through a screened doorway. Wide, tiled hall, two dead ceiling fans above, a clearly marked door to the left. Five thousand uncomfortable troops outside on the sunstroke tarmac, desperately dreaming of a place to piss, and right in here was one dark, cool, empty bathroom. She looked up and down the hall, listened, then pushed the door open and stepped in. There was a bolt on the back of the door She locked it.

Turning, she almost yelled aloud; a soldier there, a crouched, cocked troop in goggles, Jersey slamming back against the door in sudden surprise, her reflection in the full-length mirror doing the same—twin panting, head shake, lips moving around an "Ah, Christ."

She breathed out hard, clenched her jaw, said it again—"Ah, Christ"—then straightened. *What the fuck? Over.* She stared intently in the mirror, at the threat, at herself, then laughed a very shaky, fake laugh, out loud—*the ultimate friendly fire, baby; taking out your reflection.*

Jersey realized she hadn't moved. She was still crouched to strike, staring, every muscle tight, tense. A Van Morrison song came to her, one she'd never particularly liked, but now it all made sense: *You breathe in, you breathe out, you breathe in, you breathe out, youbreatheinyoubreatheoutyoubreatheinyoubreatheout . . .*

She breathed in. She breathed out.

And moved.

She crossed the three steps and looked at herself close-up. Dirty face, creased where the goggles had pinched. Raccoon eyes. Her left hand went up, fingertips touching the silver tape sewn to her right sleeve, and she mouthed the words—*friendly fire*. The mirror fogged from her breath, then cleared.

Tory Harris closed her eyes, closed them tight, and saw the man hanging from the tree, ash-strangled face looking at hers. Was he dead before they hung him? He'd had no pants. They must have beat him, like they were beating the three others. Or did they tie the noose around him alive, hands tied useless behind his back, legs kicking out in protest, three or four FADH dragging him across the dirt and grass by his neck as he gagged then hauled up into the tree and a sharp tug and Christ do you feel it when your neck snaps, do you feel that, do you hear it? Can you hear your own neck snapping? Eyes bulging, how many seconds until dead, until purple fades black and you're dead? Do you watch, do you see the men on the ground, the crow on the next branch over—

Her eyes popped open. She was panting again.

(*youbreatheinyoubreatheoutyoubreatheinyoubreatheout*)

This wasn't helping anything.

She turned away from the mirror and pulled her helmet off, setting it down. Taking the canteen from her web belt she ran the last of her water through her close, cropped hair. She was glad Riddle was back at the boat first; he would tell the story of what they'd seen. She didn't want to tell it. And she didn't want to hear anyone else tell it either.

What part of "They're hanging people in the streets" don't you understand?

Marc Hall. Marcel. A captain. Denied a debriefing.

. . . is it war or is it not?

His hand was nearly twice the size of hers. He was inches taller, not more than a year or so older, and his hand was nearly twice the size of hers. He spoke Creole like a native and his mother was dead. And he'd told her this and she didn't know why. She had a very clear thought about him, and she pushed it away as quick as it came.

There was no water in the porcelain toilet, but Jersey guessed being a member of an occupying army had its advantages, and not caring much about housekeeping was one of them. She dropped all her gear; pulling off the flak jacket was like losing ten pounds. She really didn't have to pee at all—she'd worked through probably a gallon of water this morning, but easily sweated the same.

She sat. Just sitting, for a while, in the cool, on the smooth seat. Five minutes—drifting. Breathing in, breathing out. Calming. Centering. Feeling the blood pushing through her veins. When she heard voices down the hall—unclear, then closer and pronounced, then moving away again—she stood, pulling up her BDU pants, tightening her belt. She took a long look at herself in the mirror, not sure what she was looking for, and not sure if she was seeing it. Then she gathered her gear and started the process of putting it all back on again.

She wasn't sure if it was war or is it not. She wasn't at all sure what this was they were in—and wasn't sure anyone knew yet. Whatever it was, she wanted to be in it. She'd lied to be here. Deceived. But this was what they'd all wanted, right? Or what she'd wanted, anyway. To taste it, touch it. In the face of it. All of it.

Maybe.

What part of . . .

Flak jacket back on, helmet square and strap tight, rifle barrel down across her back, she opened the door and stepped out.

Tory's ticket to freedom, her passage around ground zero of an invading army on the morning of occupation—her steps unthwarted by yells, orders, commands, or questions—came from one simple piece of cloth: the green and black 7th Group patch sewn to the left shoulder of her woodland BDUs. She knew this from experience, and used it like a weapon, keeping her left side to approaching soldiers, spinning on her jungle-boot heels to show it if questioned from behind. It wasn't a known danger to life, limb, and sanity—like maybe the lightning bolts of a Special Forces group patch or the dragon of the command group of XVIII Airborne Corps, both to be avoided for very different reasons—quite the contrary; the 7th Group patch, like 7th Group, was benign and almost completely unknown. But not much is scarier to a soldier of any rank than the unknown. To be avoided at all costs.

You might be a major and that soldier over there only a buck sergeant, but the buck sergeant might be staff NCO of a lieutenant general who outranked and maybe even disliked your brigadier general and there's a road best not even started down—not when so many soldiers with your own patch were running around in one place, ripe for the yelling at.

Likewise, on the tarmac Jersey was most comfortable around groups of soldiers with the 10th Mountain Division patch; she knew who they were, and she knew they hadn't a clue who she was. Anyone with a different patch was suspect and to be avoided.

Outside the airport's arrivals terminal was a tent, an old GP medium, sides rolled up. *That didn't take long,* she thought. A lone soldier stood inside guarding a table overflowing with plastic water bottles and flats of shiny red apples. *Perfect; what's a party without refreshments?* She stepped into the tent's shade. The soldier behind the table was young, a smart smile set on his face, specialist's teardrop insignia on his helmet and collar points.

"*Bon soir,* Sergeant," he said. "Welcome to picturesque Haiti."

"Shouldn't it be *bon jour?*"

"It might be *bon vivant.*" He shrugged and shook his head. "I don't have a clue, really."

She laughed at that. "I don't either."

He said something, but a chopper passed over their heads. They both winced, palms to ears. When it was gone he said, "Sergeant, can I interest you in one of my fine apples?"

"Yes, thanks. I'll take two."

With a bit of flair he handed her two red apples, and she put one in each cargo pocket. She took a bottle of water from his tabletop and started filling her canteen.

"It didn't take them long to get a mess crew down here," she said, carefully pouring a thin stream of water from the plastic bottle. "Although I must say, your lunch selection isn't great, Specialist."

"I'm not from the mess, Sergeant. You don't think a mess sergeant would spare one of his precious people to hand out apples and water, do you? That's what highly trained Air Assault–qualified infantrymen are for—apple duty."

"Who'd you piss off?"

"My platoon sergeant," he said. "Overslept, on Guantanamo. Two mornings ago? Three mornings ago? I don't know. Maybe yesterday. It's all kind of running together."

"So now you're apple boy."

He nodded. "Now I'm apple boy."

"Well," she said, tightening her canteen cap, "you're doing a damn fine job of it, Specialist."

"I appreciate that, Sergeant. I hope to be done with apples and back to killing fascists and communists before the sun sets."

She laughed and turned to walk. Then, remembering something, she turned back.

"How was Guantanamo?" she asked.

He tilted his head in a question.

"I was there once," she said, "but a few years ago. Did you see the new Haitian refugee camps?"

He nodded, his lips pursing. "Rough," he said. "Real rough. We just passed by, and just once. But you could tell it was rough in there. They're up on that high plain—rains a lot. Nowhere to go."

She nodded, remembering the empty refugee rafts they'd passed on the sail down—the ones who hadn't made it.

"It must be bad out there," he said, gesturing toward the city. "For them to go through all that, I mean. Just to end up in a camp. Must be really bad."

What part of "They're hanging people in the streets" don't you understand?

Jersey opened her mouth, ready to answer the question he didn't know he'd asked. Then just as quickly she closed it.

"Yes," she said. "I'll bet it is bad out there."

A group of field officers was making for the water tent. Jersey thanked the specialist again then stepped back out into the sun, squinting against white glare.

She expected to see convoys of troop-filled vehicles lining up at the gate, moving out into the city. Her pace, her pulse, had been set by the level of action early this morning—the landing, the helicopters, a locked-and-loaded violent unknown; two hours of pale worry, ten minutes of stark fear, then into the Humvees and an hour of bewildered uncertainty, all at double-time. She'd had human targets in her rifle sight this morning; she'd been a target in someone else's. But there was no smell of that here. Lots of busy, but none of it beyond the airport perimeter, or seemingly even affected by the outside world at all. There were plenty of vehicles racing importantly around the airport, but they were like tiny fish in a deep tank, zooming through the middle then bouncing off the sides, never working up a big enough head of steam to break through.

Instead, as the day went on and hot turned hotter and 10th Mountain Division continued to arrive, it looked like the troops weren't going anywhere. Not out into the city, not even erecting tents or other shelter. Just gathering in company-size formations of sitting, standing, squatting, hot, sweaty, pissed-off infantrymen. She'd never seen so many soldiers gathered in one spot. Late morning became noon became early afternoon.

Grabbing some shade under the overhang of a stucco building's tin roof, Jersey stood five or ten minutes with another female buck sergeant, a medic. A MASH unit had grabbed the small, low building as a field hospital. The sergeant said she was from L.A. She accepted a cigarette from Jersey, then glancing around quickly said, "Keep it low, though. Mister Man don't like standing around, smokin' and jokin'."

Jersey pointed out across the flight line to the growing body of troops gathered, thousands of them now. "Wouldn't be pretty if someone got a few grenades in there," she said. "Awful big target."

The medic snorted and said, "Hell—ain't gonna be pretty if it just *rains.*"

They both looked at the sky. The clear blue wasn't so clear anymore, white and gray billows rising on the horizon. Tory glanced at her watch—she was a sailor, she knew about afternoons in the tropics. "Yeah, they're gonna get wet."

"Wet and *shitty*," the medic said. She pulled a long drag on her smoke, blew a smoke ring, then shrugged big and added, "But you know what they say—it ain't *rainin'*, it ain't *trainin'*."

Jersey laughed, but thought only an office soldier with a guaranteed roof would ever say that.

Watching the troops while she finished the last drags on her cigarette, she remembered something Riddle had noticed hours before, and looked close. Every soldier on the tarmac had sleeves down to their wrists. This medic sergeant, too. Jersey was the only soldier in the airport with her sleeves rolled up above her elbows. She brought it to the attention of her new smoking buddy, and the L.A. girl's eyes widened.

"Shit. Get your sleeves down."

Jersey didn't even take time to question, just pulled her perfect rolls down, then buttoned the wrists tight.

"Come from Meade himself," the medic said, nodding her head, referring to 10th Mountain's notoriously dense commanding general. "Boot leather in the ass of a soldier with sleeves up."

"Why?" Jersey said. "It's Haiti. It's hot."

The medic just shook her head again, slow and long negative neck rolls. "Baby, it's Meade's world. You just allowed to stand in it."

Humidity rising and pressing, filling everything like it was all a hollow drum. The air heavy and hard to walk through, bodies pulled like gravity to shade, but almost no shade to be found at the airport. Only the lucky ones, medics and clerks and intel, staff officers in starched BDUs, grabbing the few structures for benefit of their computers and their paper and maybe for themselves. The grunts—and there are so many of them now, whole battalions of them—stuck, broiling and sticky on the open tarmac, steaming in their own uniforms, greased and filthy hands clutching black M-16 rifles because you're not allowed to put them down and it's too hot to hang off your shoulders and someone had the bright idea of stringing a few ponchos together to get some lean-to shade action going—*good idea, hey grab your poncho liner Jackson and . . . ah shit wait . . . no . . . someone's making them take it the fuck down anyway, some captain's telling them to take it down, what the fuck over, gonna goddamn DIE in this shit . . .*

Tory padding through them all, moving moving trying to keep on moving, dying herself in the heat but wanting to see them all and hear them, slipping between platoons and squads, the shoulder patch that says she isn't 10th Mountain clearing her way as she goes; listening, catching bits and fragments.

Canteens up, gentlemen! Up! Five minutes, time to drink!

. . . fucking water is hotter than me

shut up, bitch

. . . fucking niggers anyway, nothing but niggers in this country, why is it we always gotta save the fucking niggers?

. . . better watch what you say.

Keep that down, troop.

. . . say what I want—

—shut up!

You got a pork and rice MRE? I'll trade peanut butter.

What else?

Nothing else, you greedy bitch.

Fuck you then.

All right. M&Ms, too. Peanut butter and M&Ms for pork and rice.

All right.

Cheap bitch.

—better stand the fuck up when I'm talking to you, Private! Did you hear me you deaf-mute? Stand up!

Listen man, I dunno who you talkin' to, these ain't our people. These some fucked-up voodoo-talkin' Africa motherfuckers, ain't fucking nuthin' to do with niggaz like us.

Bitches stink, anyway.

You disrespecting your people, man.

Yo, fuck you, man. Your mama's my people, how 'bout that?

Cunt, I'll slap some sense . . .
Sergeant Rollins! How many men you got?
Ah shit, someone's digging trenches . . .
Get out.
I told you man, gotta crap somewhere.
I'll crap in your helmet and call it dessert.
Second platoon! Second platoon! Canteens up! Time to drink!
. . . drink this.
There it is.
Damn—you see the sky?
Christ, get a poncho on those ammo boxes.
Oh shit.
Sarge, we better get some plastic or something—
Sir? Sir! What are we gonna do if it—
And it rained.
The medic had been right—it was worse than hand grenades.

The raindrops were the size of bullets and felt like it. Jersey was only three steps from the hangar she'd been making for—a few quick questions, a few shrugs, then a helpful pointed finger guiding her—but three steps was all it took to be completely drenched. She laughed despite herself, happy for the momentary cool, wiping her sleeves and her rifle and her face. Turning in the open door of the hangar, the airfield was gone, a torrent of water, somewhere out there thousands of wet American soldiers.

After a half day of wandering, watching, listening, the thoughts in the back of her head moved to the front and she'd started asking questions and this hangar was where the answers brought her. One wrecked and rusting old Cessna stood tied down in the middle, all around it an office already in action, thirty or more staff troops busy at desks with computers and printers and a TV in the corner with CNN showing. Tory watched that a few minutes, not learning anything she didn't know, but fascinated at the pictures of the city she'd just been in, the crowds, close-ups of young American soldiers in helmets and goggles wordlessly guarding fences and gates. One sweeping shot of the port and a view of her LSV. The CNN anchor called it the Navy and the retired Army general with him agreed. Then a reporter, from a pink hotel in Pétionville: The day was going amazingly smooth, he said. No problems, no violence.

What part of "They're hanging people in the streets" don't you understand?

She found a PFC sitting alone at a desk, crunching numbers on a big black adding machine, and leaned down to ask him a question. He pointed her toward the back, to an office door deeper in the hangar. She walked between the desks, then through the only open door, closing it behind her. An empty office, chalkboard on the wall. A soldier's gear lay strewn across a long table.

Alone in the dark room, she found a wooden swivel chair and sat, closing her eyes. She opened her eyes again, then closed them again. A funny place to find an old wooden swivel chair; a hangar at the Port-au-Prince airport. And just when she realized she was tired, too. A funny thing, and wasn't it funny she was here, that she had sought this room out. She swiveled around, eyes closed. The rain pounded on the tin roof above her, no other sound to be heard. She sat still, just a moment, just for a moment to sit—such a long day. She must have dozed, because she dreamed—two, three feverish movements, what? who? incomprehensible—and when she woke she woke like a shot, eyes snapping open, body half rising from the chair—

—*(youbreatheinyoubreatheout)*

She sat, hard. Breathed in, breathed out. Reached into her cargo pocket, bit into one of the apples she'd grabbed from the apple boy, slowly chewing and swallowing. Thinking, not thinking. And when Marc Hall came in there was no look of surprise on his face to see her; and wasn't that interesting. More like they'd just been talking and he'd stepped out and now he was back. His BDU top was off, just brown T-shirt tucked into BDU pants. His shirt and skin were wet with rain. She stood, the apple in her hand held down at her side.

"I missed my flight."

He came within a step of her and stopped, just looking. Not knowing what else to say or if she was supposed to say anything and then thinking she'd had this all wrong and needed to say something to back out she said, "Sir."

"Please," he said, softly, and smiled.

He filled the room, Jersey thought. Blood and bone and testosterone, dark eyes and sweat. It wasn't threatening, wasn't overbearing, but it was there and big and now she knew there was no question he was looking deeper than he should and she didn't mind at all but set her half-eaten apple down on the table next to her and with nothing else to say said, "I've got to get back to port." After a few seconds of silence she added, "Sir."

"It's Marc," he said.

"I've got to get back to my boat, Marc."

He nodded once, about to say something, and the door opened, a clerk there with a sheaf of papers, they hadn't heard the knock because the rain was so loud on the roof of the hangar, and Jersey backed up as Captain Hall was backing away from her, the two of them backing away, and she thought *What the fuck are you crazy get out of here get out of this you can't do this* and she was grabbing her helmet and her rifle and he was taking the papers from the clerk and she was half out the door when he turned and said, "Sergeant Harris."

She stopped and turned around. The clerk was shuffling through the stack of paperwork, oblivious. Report in hand, Marc held her gaze.

"I have a chopper to the port in three hours, right after sunset."

She looked, and she nodded.

"Thank you."

Voices again, but harder to put a face to any one voice now, shadows creeping from lakes of puddles left by the rain as the sun eased from the sky, dark and then darker shadows and you couldn't see much of the surrounding mountains from here but what you could see was going black, with the pinpoint flicks of fires like they'd seen this morning on the sail in—*this morning. Only this morning? Last year, must be.*

Moving across the airport, all motion again, Tory pressing on, a mechanical soldier with no mission at all, two hours of nonstop walking for the sake of walking, for the sake of being here—witness to something, witness for the sunset.

Strange witness. Strange fruit.

The mood different now, post-rain, purpose creeping as if rain had slapped everyone awake.

Over here, gentlemen, over here—gather up.

. . . keep 'em tight, Corporal. Tight and formed.

Two MREs per soldier. If you haven't topped off your canteens yet you're wrong. Once we move out, it'll be forty-eight hours or more until we rotate back . . .

—the fuck you say. If you can't find our truck, then I suggest you shit me a truck, Private.

. . . through the gate at twenty-two hundred, so if sleep is something you require then find it now.

File from the left, column left!

Column left!

March!

. . . and keep your eyes peeled for those silver friendly fire tabs, fellas. You don't want to be the asshole on the cover of Newsweek *that shot up a hummer full of GIs. Your mama'll be real upset.*

Second platoon! Down range! Lock and load, you ugly bitches. We're outta here.

Deuce-and-a-half and five-ton tucks forming at the gate now, and Humvees with tall metal rods welded to the front bumpers to break any decapitating razor wire strung across roads. Vehicle lights glowing in warm puddles on the concrete, gunners swiveling their mounts.

What part of "They're hanging people in the streets" don't you understand?

Soldiers thumping chests, slamming fists down on helmet tops and closed knuckles—*hoo-fucking-rah!* and *Air-fucking-borne!*

Friendly fire, fellas, Jersey thought.

Two and two in the Voodoo Lounge / friendly fire will slow you down.

Her mind played her a picture of the face of the FADH commander from the park this morning, the lyncher, sneering arrogance and blood-splattered uniform shirt. Hummers rolled past her, headed for the gate, overflowing with soldiers and gunmetal. She willed them toward the man, willed them to find him, willed them the authority or plain good luck to take him down. Painfully.

But, of course, that wasn't the mission.

She spent the last forty minutes in the darkening arrivals terminal, bustling activity and the stink and roar of generators behind her as she stood looking out between the iron bars of an open window, smoking a cigarette. The planes were still coming, less frequently, but still coming. She saw him—Marc, Marc Hall, Marcel, Captain Hall, him—cross from the hangar then disappear again around the terminal building. She didn't move. When he came up behind her she knew he was there. His hand closed on her shoulder, face leaning down to the side of hers. She never turned, just felt him there, his skin next to her cheek, and it was done in less than twenty seconds.

"I need to find you tomorrow. If—I mean—"

"Yes."

"Are you sure?"

And now she looked up, turning her face just the slightest bit so their eyes met. "Yes."

He squeezed her shoulder, then turned, both of them, crossing the terminal floor then out back again to the chopper flight line, Tory tightening the M-16 across her back. They were the last to crawl in, crouching behind the door gunner, making space in the black crush, all senses gone, too dark to see a face or a rank on the soldiers inside, so loud from the rotor nothing could be heard at all. The tail of the chopper lifted and Tory half-spun on her heels as much as she could, looking out over the door gunner's shoulder now, and as they were pushed by the helicopter's movement Marc's hands came up—wide, strong—on her shoulders, to steady, hold her in place, and they stayed there, for the whole ride, pressing down. Once, when it could be fluid, when she thought it might look like rebalancing, her hand went up on top of his, her palm flat over the back of his hand, just that brief then gone again.

Rank could fool you, she knew. Dick Wags, a staff sergeant, was only one pay grade higher than her, only the slightest of difference in the grand scheme of things. But he was almost five years older. And here was this Marc Hall, a captain, an officer, with the rank and authority to command a company. But they could have gone to high school together.

The helicopter hovered, then swept a wide arc across the airport's perimeter, nose down and making for the safety of open water.

Pushing, pressing, buzzing hard on adrenaline all day, the inevitable energy drop came with her boots nailing the concrete, jumping short from the chopper's open door—the only passenger to hop out on this side of the port. Jersey stumbled once, recovered, got her balance back but not her energy. Turning, she looked for Marc Hall as the chopper lifted, but it was too dark to see in the open door and then the bird was gone. She circled the warehouse they'd dropped her behind, trying to find the boat.

The LSV was tied a ship's-length back from where they'd hit the pier this morning, portside-to and ramp up. The port was all activity, the water clogged with the other LSV and smaller LCUs, the pier all vehicles and soldiers, Trans Corps soldiers here, hustling and moving and yelling and directing, all of this under the wash of generator-powered floodlights. She approached the boat, dragging herself along. The gangway was up and the big steel pilot door closed. She raised her fist and banged on it once. It swung in immediately, the skipper—Mannino—standing there, preparing to leave. He was a short, round man; more a baker's body than a soldier's. He was visibly uncomfortable in the flak jacket and LBE and helmet. A chief warrant officer, he'd spent his twenty years of soldiering behind a helm, not crawling through the mud.

It seemed to take him a second to figure out who she was. He blinked once, then raised an eyebrow and said, "New Jersey."

"Skipper," she said, saluting.

He stuck his head out the pilot door, glancing up and down the pier. "No saluting, Tory. Down range."

Her cheek twitched at that.

Mannino backed up a step and motioned her through the pilot

door onto the open well-deck. When she'd left in the Humvee this morning the deck had been full of vehicles, piles of chainlocks everywhere. It was empty now, empty and swept clean. Mannino pushed his helmet back off his forehead, eyeing her. Closely, she thought.

"You all right?" he said, finally.

She nodded once, and he nodded back. New Jersey and Long Island weren't far separated, in more ways than one. Mannino tended to communicate with Tory and Dick Wags—his two Jerseys—in a series of nods, grunts, and arcing arm gestures only they understood. He put his hand to his stubbly chin now, rubbed, then dropped it to rest on the butt of his holstered pistol.

"Those guys come back, talking out their ass," he said. "Scaboo wrote some shit down, gave it to me."

She didn't say anything.

"You sure you're all right?" he asked again.

"Yeah, Skip," she said, then added, "Tired." She was, but only said it because she thought it would give him something to fix and he was looking for something to fix.

She patted her pocket for her cigarettes. He handed her one of his, lighting it for her. A first.

"So?" he said. "Did all that happen?" He reached his hand behind his head and made a hangman's-noose gesture.

She nodded, exhaling a thin stream of smoke.

"It was pretty bad."

"And that guy, that colonel—he moved you all along?"

"Rules of engagement," she said simply.

He looked at her. "You serious?" He chewed his lip, then answered himself: "Never mind. Fuckers."

Mac came from the shadows across the deck, crossing toward them, Top right behind. Both of them fully dressed out, to leave the vessel; Skip had been waiting for them. Mac was the tightest guy on the boat, screwed tighter even than Dick Wags—helmet centered, BDUs starched. Mac's was a little more cheese than substance, but not too bad. He was first mate and just thought everyone should know it. Top was Mac's opposite, in more ways than one; rounder even than the Skipper, not really an E8 first sergeant but an E7 sergeant first class filling the slot. He and Skip had gone to basic training together, back when Christ was a corporal.

"Sergeant Harris," Top said to her. His voice was higher than you'd expect for a man his size. "Welcome home."

She tried to smile around her cigarette. It was tired and weak. She didn't care for Top. His eye sometimes wandered beyond her permissible wander zone.

"You're off," he said, looking down at his watch. "It's twenty-one hundred. You've got till half-past midnight. Go get dinner and grab an hour's sleep."

"Thanks, Top," she said.

The Skipper was still looking at her. It was hard to read his face, all shadows and deep lines. He seemed about to ask something. In the end he just sighed.

"Fucking New Jersey," he said, straightening his helmet, preparing to leave. "Pain in my ass."

"Yes, Sir," she said.

"Fucking Haiti."

CHAPTER

8

There were no dreams to crack this sleep. Too deep, too far. And brief as the space between eyelids.

After two weeks at sea in a flat-bottomed ship, you come to expect the world to behave in certain ways. When the bleat of the alarm clock popped Tory's eyes open, her right arm shot out from under the thin blanket to grab the edge of the steel desk bolted down next to the rack of bunks. She held herself there, half-suspended, waiting for the roll of the ocean—then realized the bulkheads weren't rattling and the ocean wasn't going to roll. She held herself there another beat anyway, to be sure, clucked her tongue, and dropped herself back down on the mattress. She reached under the pillow and switched off the alarm. Ten minutes past midnight. A new day. Not even twenty-four hours in-country, but a new day nonetheless. She lay still in the lower bunk, blinking awake, the cabin dark and womb warm.

It was physically painful to wake after only an hour's sleep. It hurt. It hurt in the chest, and in the muscles of the legs and arms. It hurt your head, too—there's a despair to losing sleep, a second of *oh god I'll do anything,* a despair that for one moment is stronger than reason, stronger than government, stronger than love. She'd noticed it was easier to wake from quick sleep as a sergeant than it had been as a private. At the same time, it was harder at twenty-three than it had been at nineteen. She breathed through it and pinned her eyes open, waiting—forcing herself awake, waiting for the harshest pain to pass.

It wasn't completely quiet; she could feel the gentle rumble of one of the generators, deep down below in the engine room. A minute later Dick Wags's alarm clock—buried deep beneath his pillow—went off in the bunk above her head. Everyone had their own alarm, even between roommates. At any given moment on the boat someone's alarm was going off. She heard Dick Wags click the plastic switch and the cabin was silent again. She opened her ears, trying to hear anything of the port or the city, but nothing came through. Just the hum of the generator.

"Roomdog," Dick Wags said, his throat full and heavy.

"Hey."

"Good morning."

"Fuck off."

"Yeah."

They both just lay there, not moving. Tory pushed a hand under her brown T-shirt, rubbed her belly. She heard Dick Wags cough once, then the corner above her glowed red as he lit a cigarette, the click and snap of his Zippo loud in the tiny cabin.

"Roomdog," he said again, a few seconds later.

"Hey."

"You made it back."

"I made it back," she said. He'd already been asleep when she came in, an hour before.

There was the sound of him inhaling then exhaling then the smell of the smoke from his cigarette.

"Heard you got lost," he said.

"Some Army, isn't it?"

"Some Army."

There was a Zippo click and another brief red glow filled the room, then the tip of a lit cigarette hung down a few feet above Tory's face. She reached up and took it from his fingers.

"Thanks."

"Yep."

It was strangely intimate, the two of them in this cabin, the way they lived together. So close, in the dark, sharing everything they owned. Tory wondered if he noticed, if he thought about it, if he knew. She thought he did.

She sat up more, wiping an open palm across her face, then smoking the cigarette. They shared everything, but like all deployed soldiers, cigarettes didn't easily enter the equation. Cigarettes were a commodity, even between best friends, even between roomdogs. Dick Wags was notoriously stingy with his cigarettes. Him offering one up, unasked, was almost unheard of. Tory knew where his head was, where his thoughts were going; she knew the question the cigarette stood in for.

So she answered it.

"It's all fine," she said.

There was a long pause while he inhaled and exhaled, then he said, quietly, "You shouldn't have been out there. You should've said no."

"I—"

He cut her off. "You could've not gone. Without saying why."

She opened her mouth, then closed it again. She smoked instead of answering. There was no good answer, anyway. In the way he meant it, he was right. If anyone else had said that it would have been an insult, a slander. But Dick Wags wasn't anyone else, and he knew something no one else knew. He wasn't talking about *her* safety.

There was no one closer to her now than Dick Wags. She had no real family anymore. No one knew her as well as Dick Wags. After Junior Davis, definitely not. Maybe even closer than Junior Davis had been, and maybe it had always been that way and she'd just not noticed until Junior disappeared. Junior didn't matter anymore, anyway. He was as gone as the day was long. But even when they'd been together, she probably trusted Dick Wags more than she'd ever trusted Junior Davis. What had she done with Junior Davis? Been his girlfriend. Dick Wags, on the other hand, made her a sergeant. She was sure she knew which was more important.

Jersey smoked through these thoughts, not saying anything. Above her, Dick Wags yawned. He'd said what he wanted to say. He'd let it go now.

Dick Wags had parents, but they'd kicked him out; years ago, before the Army, one night when he was nineteen and came home from his shift at Jiffy Lube drunk and cursing belligerent. He didn't talk to them now. He had a fine life anyway. And a fine romance. He was married to Alicia, a young, sinewy corporal serving an office tour in the Fort Eustis transportation school. They lived across the York River way out near Gloucester, in a bungalow back in the woods. They weren't like any other Army couples Tory knew. They'd been stationed together on LSV-12 in Hawaii, and married on the PI. They skied in the Poconos and the Catskills over the winter, driving long, kamikaze hours north from Virginia on coffee-fueled four-day passes. On summer Fridays they'd been known to go down to Langley Air Force Base before dawn and wait around for free space-A flights to anywhere; London or Las Vegas, Rota or Cheyenne—didn't matter, as long as they hadn't been there before and could get back within three days. If there wasn't an easy flight by 10:00 A.M., they'd hop in Alicia's black truck and spend the day on the beach at Fort Story, Dick Wags drinking cans of Heineken and fishing the surf from the hood of the truck, Alicia in her red bikini reading mysteries and sleeping on a blanket in the sand.

Tory drove up their way a lot, past Yorktown and across the bridge. Especially in winter. Especially on gray Sundays when shadows fell long and thin around Fort Eustis, and it seemed the only souls alive were trainee privates grubbing for leaves and trash on the roadside in fresh-from-basic, unstarched uniforms. Especially on those Sundays when she'd wake up in her hard, mean little box of a barracks room with the sheets next to her long cold and Junior Davis nowhere to be found, his boots and jeans gone from the floor, his lighter and keys gone from the TV. She'd run a few miles through the frosty morning, forcing the hangover from her temples, then shower in the green-tile latrine down the hall, dressing then making coffee with the drip pot she kept on top of her mini-fridge. She'd get out to Dick Wags and Alicia's bungalow around two or three, cheese and bread and beer in a paper bag from Food Lion, letting herself in the front door to the wood-paneled hall. It always smelled of something good cooking on the stove, always the sound of a football game on TV, and there was never once when Tory got to their house without feeling she'd just interrupted them in the bedroom. Once she actually did; peeling off her boots then padding down the long hall to the kitchen, past their open bedroom door and the two of them on the high bed with the white comforter in the bright room. They hadn't heard her ring the bell and come in; Dick Wags oblivious, his back to the hall, tan body buried deep between Alicia's endless outstretched white legs, her head back on the thick, green pillow, eyes closed. Tory had stopped, stock still. Soft and low mammal sounds came from the back of Alicia's throat. Breathing quiet, fast, she raised her head then, eyes opening, right at Tory. Alicia's expression never changed, and they looked at each other, then Alicia closed her eyes again and Tory breathed and crept away to the living room and the TV and fifteen minutes later Dick Wags came in, freshly showered, wearing running shorts and a Waterborne T-shirt and saw her on the couch and said, "Roomdog! When'd you get here?"

Tory smoked quietly now in the ship's cabin, listening to her friend Dick Wags smoke in the bunk above her. She hadn't thought of that day in a long time. She tried to remember when it had been. Tail end of winter, she thought. March, maybe.

On those heels came another, much more recent memory— tonight; Marc Hall's hand coming to rest on her shoulder in the helicopter, his palm and fingers gripping, curling down, just the slightest pressure. The phantom feeling was so strong her own hand went involuntarily to her shoulder to cap his, but all she found was the thin cotton of her brown Army T-shirt.

Pétionville

CHAPTER

9

The infantry sergeant's name was Lamas. Head down, exhausted, hunched in the back of the chopper with his captain, this guy Hall. His captain right now, anyway. Hall was really S2, from battalion intelligence, standing in for their broke-dick of a company CO. Something about a sprained ankle, the week before they deployed. As if. The man rode health profiles like a fat tick rode a dog, the fucker. Some CO. Sergeant Lamas knew Marc Hall, though. From a couple years before, when the guy was platoon leader in a different battalion. He was black and bald and young as shit—couldn't be more than a year or two older than Lamas—and you just don't forget guys like that, especially officers. Especially lieutenants who maybe burn paperwork on a promotable corporal's surprise piss test after a long weekend. Word spreads. You don't forget officers like that.

The sky passed completely to night by the time the chopper spun over the port. Lamas watched carefully from the back as Captain Hall tried to help the chick sergeant out the door. And wasn't that something. Lamas held on as they lifted clear the warehouse area, arcing over the long pier and black waters beyond.

"S'fucking hot," Lamas yelled over the chopper noise as Hall crawled back and squatted next to him. Hall nodded, but Lamas could barely see the man's face.

Hall opened his mouth to yell something, then changed his mind. It was too loud in the chopper, and it didn't matter anyway. He sat,

hunched, very still, staring under the brim of his helmet at the nothing out the open door. *Watch,* he thought, and meant himself.

As a rule, Marc Hall went out of his way to pay zero attention to female
soldiers. Just SMs they were, service members, like any man. First and
foremost, Hall was still married, and the Army doesn't use words like
"still," "barely," or "sort of" in context of an officer's marriage. But, as
an officer, enlisted females were off-limits to him anyway. And most
enlisted females had grown up poorer even than he had, in broken
parts of the country that made him nervous.

And yet this small, tough woman—the airport had made no sense
to him. In the shadows of the warehouse, rain drumming the tin roof
and his gear off, alone in the back room he'd wanted to pick her up,
pick her straight up, crush her body into his, this woman he didn't
know, it made no sense.

It threw him more than he'd let on, the way she'd mentioned his
mother, even in such an offhand way. *I'll bet she doesn't like Marcel
shortened to Marc.* No, she hadn't liked it one bit; his father's laugh
rolling down the hallway to his bedtime ears: "Cass, the boy ain't some
French pastry." His mother, whose tone never seemed to go up or
down, replying simply: "He is what he is, and he is Marcel."

He is what he is, and here he was. In her land. For her people.

That's what the president said. And the ex-president. And General
Powell, ramrod straight in his new civilian suit. The predeployment
briefings were one thing: dry, military, tactical; but he'd watched on
TV, saw what the president said. They were to take down this criminal Cedras, and bring home the priest. Aristide. Jean-Bertrand, the
little priest, elected by the people. Lavalas to lead Haiti to democracy,
true democracy. *Liberté.* And eventually prosperity. Food. *Humanity.*

Here he was. One small man in a big plan, but he felt his place in it.
Knew there was a place in it, a way to lead.

"Cass," he said aloud, and it was muttering under his breath in the
loud helicopter, and he was talking to his dead mother, sure she knew
he was here.

Maybe that was it, with this woman sergeant. Tory Harris. Marc

Hall wasn't *Vodoun,* but he was Haitian, yes? Half Haitian. Could Haiti feel him? Something so strong, so powerful, so *positive,* on his arrival here. It meant something. She meant something, this sharp, tiny woman sergeant. He remembered again, her watching him argue with the colonel in the park, watching to see what he did.

Maybe, he thought, *she's here to keep me honest.* That's how he would take it.

Too dark to see, but the helicopter was over the suburb Pétionville in five minutes, up the mountainside—to little rich Haiti. Land of the casinos, once. Hotel resorts. A view of Port-au-Prince bay without too close a view of Port-au-Prince. Papa Doc's inherited playground, except he hadn't played much; more, Pétionville was his private fishbowl, and he'd emerge—*Baron Samedi,* thin-tie suit and horn-rimmed glasses— deep from his palace cellars and plunge a hand in, emerging with a wriggling, gasping fistful. The Duvalier boy after him, the Baby Doc, he'd played in Pétionville. Land of *bourgeois.* The leaders and lenders. Cedras's family now, those not in the palace. And the American reporters and camera crews, of course. All the best bars were here. The power didn't go out as much, so the ice cubes were harder. Less than twenty-four hours and Pétionville was already secure, the tightest, safest place in Haiti after the port and airport compounds. The tightest public place.

This was all very unofficial, of course; no one in the U.S. Army at colonel's rank or below ever got a phone call saying "Secure Pétionville." In a country of miserable poverty and epidemics of AIDS and TB it would be, well, uncouth to make a priority of the *bourgeois* neighborhood. No one in Washington or on the aircraft carrier *Eisenhower* or here on the ground ever signed a directive, or passed a written order. But there it was, anyway. Someone sent a company of reinforced Humvees up the hill along 101A and onward to Place St. Pierre. Someone else put a couple Bradleys across Route de Dalmas. Coincidence, certainly. It was all very accidental; form finding way from chaos, perhaps. It could be argued. Or defended. Regardless, by sunset you couldn't enter or exit Pétionville without passing an American checkpoint. If there were riots, if there was to be looting—if there were lynchings, whoever it was to be lynched—it wouldn't be in Pétionville.

The chopper set down in the parking lot of a pink hotel. The load was mostly captains and higher sergeants, up for a briefing, and they cleared instantly.

"We couldn't do this at the airport?" Sergeant Lamas muttered, hand on helmet top, running hunched over clear of the rotor wash as the chopper lifted again and was gone. He looked around as he stood, and whistled through his teeth. It was some place, all right. A torchlit pool behind the rose bush he was next to, cabanas in a row, hotel rising above them.

"This all ours now?" he said.

Hall shook his head, and it wasn't clear which way.

" 'Uphold Democracy' means 'secure the banks,' I think," Lamas said.

Hall was blinking, looking around. He'd been to Haiti four times in his life, three of them with his mother, but never to Pétionville. Small red stones crunched under his jungle boots as he turned around, taking it in. This he'd never seen. He was willing to wager he learned better Creole in the Bronx, from his mother, than anyone who grew up in this neighborhood.

The gathering of captains and sergeants had pulled apart, each in their own groups, waiting for the briefing. Sergeant Lamas walked ten or so feet down the length of the roses, discreetly lighting a cigarette. Sergeants get nervous smoking with officers around. Captain Hall followed him, pulling his ruck off his back and laying it gently on the ground.

"Land of your people, Sir," Lamas said, smoking.

"Yeah," Hall said. "Other side of the mountain," he pointed, up, "but yeah. *Oui, Rodrigo Lamas.*" He trilled the Rs off his tongue, making the sergeant laugh.

"Hey, that chick sergeant kept a cool head, today," Lamas said.

"Yeah?"

"Cool as ice, Sir." He reached under his flak jacket and fished another cigarette from his breast pocket, then lit it off the first. "I dunno. I about pissed myself."

Hall smiled at that.

"I sent that round to the dirt, then look up, y'know, to my line. And damned she ain't right there on my three, ready to smoke something." Lamas held his cigarette in his teeth. "She was probably pissin' herself too, but damn she looked tough."

"I think she is pretty tough," Hall said.

"She got an eye for you, too," Lamas said. Then added, "Sir."

"I don't know what you're talking about, Sergeant."

"Yeah. Me neither."

Lamas pushed his boot around in the red stones, watching the gathering officers and NCOs. No one seemed to be doing anything.

"Why'd they hang that guy?" he said.

"Lavalas," Hall whispered. "Aristide supporter." He didn't know why he'd whispered.

"I gotta tell you, Sir. I think that colonel was bullshit. I think we should have taken them down. Those cops or soldiers or whatever the fuck they were."

Hall didn't say anything right away. He looked at Lamas, though, holding his gaze. Finally, he said, "You're right, Sergeant. We should have taken them down. And then"—he put his hands around his neck—"we should have taken *him* down."

"I didn't like that. Leaving him there. Swinging."

"We left them all swinging."

"Who's that, Captain? Who'd we leave swinging?"

It was another soldier, behind them and quiet in the dark, Hall doing an audible about-face in the crushed stone.

It was Baric. The old colonel who'd ridden with their convoy this morning. He of the rules of engagement.

"Sir," Marc said.

"I believe the briefing is beginning, Captain," Baric said, and Lamas could have sworn he winked. He stepped past them, toward the pink hotel. His feet seemed not to make any noise, even in the stone.

* * *

The buck sergeants and staff sergeants all hung outside, smoking and laughing as the officers and higher NCOs got reamed inside for various and varied shortcomings and failures during the day's operations. When they emerged, Hall found Lamas and the two went to retrieve their rucks. The energy was gone from Hall's face.

"Your XO is taking over the company tomorrow," he said. "I'm going back to battalion staff."

"But the XO is just—"

"It's not my call."

Lamas thought about that a moment.

"This was only temporary anyway," Hall said. But Lamas knew it wasn't entirely true.

The meeting had been held in the hotel's garage and went badly. Before clearing the door completely, a one-star Hall had never even seen was in his face, chest to chest, helmet-tip to helmet-tip.

"What in the fuck did you think you were doing, Captain Hall?" the general yelled. Hall took a step back and clinked helmets that way, too; Baric, the old-man colonel, directly behind him.

"Sir—" he said, but the general cut him off, waving a piece of paper in his hand. Hall recognized the rules of engagement.

"What part of 'Do not interfere with the fucking locals' did you not understand, Captain?"

What part of "They're hanging people in the street"—

Hall was aware everything could go to shit right here. He measured his words.

"Sir, as convoy commander it was my best judgment at the time to—"

The general spun on his heels, yelling at the assembling officers. "When exactly did we start paying captains to use judgment?" The room came to an immediate hush. "Is the word 'judgment' on any of your commissions?"

"Sir, I—" Hall started, but the general had already moved on, to another captain and another fuckup, Hall's FADH conflict and lost convoy just one of eight or nine fuckups to be dealt with tonight.

*   *   *

They were by the rose bushes again, waiting for the chopper to take them out.

"You were right to stop the convoy," Lamas said. "You did the right thing, Sir."

Hall put his right index finger to his lips—quiet. He stood there a moment, smelling the warm night and Lamas's cigarette smoke and then he said, "I'm going to Jacmel. In the south. With a relief operation. Maybe I'll check in with you fellows when I get back."

"You do that, Sir," Lamas said. "You come check in with us."

Marc Hall nodded, but in the end they never did see each other again.

Port-au-Prince

CHAPTER

10

One in the morning. Zero dark early. Again. Almost two turns of the clock from their battlestations wake-up yesterday. An hour of sleep, then fifteen minutes for a quick plate of midnight chow with Dick Wags and the Steward in the crew's mess. Three sergeants, two cups of black coffee; Dick Wags and the Steward with a cheese omelet each, Jersey plain scrambled and one of the deep-fried rectangles the Army calls hash browns. On shore five thousand American grunts ate cold MREs, but on USAV *Gilman* skinny Private Cain was throwing eggs on the grill for midrats. "Keep those goddamn exhaust fans off, Sarge," the Skipper had ordered the Steward, "or we'll have all of 10th Mountain over looking for a meal." The three sergeants ate quickly, throwing plates and forks in the galley dishwasher on their way out. Roy was off to find his rack; he hadn't slept since wake-up yesterday. Dick Wags headed down toward the engine room. Tory went up the center stairs two flights, straight to the bridge. One in the morning; middle of the dark night, but a new Army day.

The ship was tied pierside, but the bridge remained blacked out as if under way; just the smallest, soft glow of orange and green from the instruments and radios. Victor Charlie sat deep down in the skipper's chair, barely visible from top of the stairs. Tory knew it was Victor Charlie from the Metallica way low on the CD player by the coffee pot. He was the ship's second mate, a newly minted warrant officer. His real name was Welsh, William Welsh, but Tory had never heard him called anything but Victor Charlie. He liked to say the day last year he'd hung up his staff sergeant stripes and been pinned the silver warrant officer bar he'd become Mister Charlie. He was a surfer, like Temple, and worked out as religiously. Raised in southern California, he was Vietnamese from refugee parents and claimed specifically North Vietnamese. "I'ma tricky chink spy," he'd say when drunk, which was often. "I'ma slit all your throats one night, you fat American fucks." He drove a Chevy truck painted red, white, and blue and was the only ship's officer who lived on the boat full-time, like a private, even when they were home at Fort Eustis. He was twenty-nine and had been married and divorced three times.

Tory crested the stairs, entering the unlit bridge.

"SergeantHarrisrequestspermissiontoenterthebridge," she mumbled.

Victor Charlie said something low and equally unintelligible in response, shuffling a pile of papers in his lap.

"Xerox!" he called out a second later, his voice cracking with lack of rest. "Xerox!" he said again. A short, bald kid in round glasses bolted from the radio room, tucking his T-shirt in. He looked suspiciously recent of sleep.

"Sir," he said, smiling at Tory as he went by, reaching his hand out to take the papers from the second mate.

"Take this shit down to Skipper's office and Xerox it. Bring the originals back to me."

Xerox grabbed the papers and hustled down below. The ship's assigned radioman, he'd been volunteered into double duty as detachment clerk. Hence the nickname.

Tory walked over to the big chair. "I'm thinking of applying for warrant officer candidate," she said, looking out the flat black of the bridge windows. "Maybe I could get some sleep then."

"Thanks for the insubordination, Sergeant Harris," the officer said. He was wearing a red 24th Battalion ball cap. He pulled it down further over his eyes, stuck up his middle finger at her, then pushed his short, muscular body a little lower in the chair. "You're first in line to walk the plank, New Jersey. As soon as I wake up."

Tory leaned forward, peering through the window. Her eyes were adjusting. It took twenty minutes to fully gain night vision, but you were 50 percent there in less than five.

From down on the ship's main deck the view was just the port; warehouses, vehicles, gray vessels tied, not much moving after midnight, even on night one of a so-called invasion. The view from high on the bridge, though, was Port-au-Prince. Hard to see so late at night in a city with the power off. But you could sense the sweep of the basin, feel it breathing there like a lumbering beast in a stand of grass. Shadows of buildings, neighborhoods. Lights on the mountainsides shifted and twinkled as only fire does. The doors to the bridge wings were propped open and the night air was heavy on a slight breeze, smoky and sweet.

Tory went to the log book on the chart table and signed in to the start of her watch then made coffee, bringing a black cup of it out the open door and onto the port bridge wing. The deck lights were out, but she could see Voodoo Lounge up on the bow. Sixteen hours ago she'd been in that nest up there, lying on the gray deckplates with the grease smears thrown from the ramp and anchor winches, sweat running from face to rifle stock.

She'd been more scared up there, coming in, than at any moment in the city yesterday. When they'd faced off against the FADH at the park and it seemed certain someone was going to get shot, that was scary but in a very controlled and mechanical way. She couldn't even really remember it. She hadn't made any decisions, just reacted—doing what training told her to do, endless, repetitive training. It was a task, just a task: *What to do when under fire.* Bladders and bowels and other unimportant things might completely fall apart, but arms and hands and fingers and eyes moved as if machined. But on the bow, up in Voodoo Lounge, with an hour or more watching the city grow, smelling it come slow, there was no task. Just watch and sit and hope you had a chance to shoot first. That was a fear that pulled at the belly, and she'd felt it before but never so acutely.

She took in a big breath, trying to blink sleep from her eyes. She sipped her coffee. Footsteps came from the stairs that ran aft of the house on the outside; Xerox, coming back up. He stood with her a minute. Xerox looked all of twelve years old.

"Nice night," she said.

"Yeah." He rubbed his head. "Good to be in port. Steady under the feet."

Of the non-Waterborne soldiers in the crew—Xerox the radioman, Doc Brewer the medic, the Steward and his two kitchen privates—only the Steward didn't mind the sailing, falling naturally into the rhythm of moving and the rhythm of sea sleep. Xerox was brand new to the ship and brand new to the Army and nothing from high school in Goshen, Indiana, or basic combat training in Fort Knox, Kentucky, had given him a head-start to living on the water.

"You been around port tonight?" she asked.

"A little bit. You gotta put all your gear on to leave the ship, though. Not worth it."

"Everything?"

"Everything. Rifle, helmet, flak jacket."

"Where's 7th Group sleeping?" she asked.

He pointed to a massive warehouse across the water on the other side of the horseshoe. "That's them," he said. He turned and hooked a thumb behind to a small island a few hundred feet off the pier. It was connected to land by a long causeway and bridge. "That's headquarters, though. The colonel and sergeant-major. And the radios."

"Nice digs," she said.

"Nice place."

From what she could see, the island had two low buildings surrounded by a breezy stand of palm trees.

Her cigarettes were in the bridge so she bummed one from Xerox.

"What's the plan tomorrow?" she asked him. As clerk, he was first to know everything.

"Skip says we're sailing."

"That was quick."

"Yeah. Taking on a load of something and going south, I think."

"Where?"

He shrugged. "Begins with a J."

"Jérémie or Jacmel," she said. She'd studied the charts for weeks and had memorized all the major and minor ports of Haiti and alternative routes of entry for each.

"Jacmel, I think." Xerox shrugged again. "Not sure." He yawned, pulling off his glasses and rubbing his eyes. "I'm going back to sleep for an hour," he said. "If you don't mind."

"Go ahead."

She ditched her smoke off the side and followed him into the bridge. He went into the radio room and closed the door.

The handheld radio on the chart table crackled.

"Bridge to ramp. Over." Snaggletooth. He was on ramp-guard duty. The forward ramp was down for the night, resting on the pier ahead of them. Tory picked up the handheld.

"This is the bridge," she said.

"Uh, bridge," he said. "Small problem. Over."

"We're listening."

"There's a small, uh, rat problem."

Victor Charlie pushed himself up in the skipper's chair a little at that, looking over to where she stood near the throttles. "What the fuck? Over," he mumbled, then stood, both of them going to the windows to look down.

"Ramp, bridge. Mister Charlie would like you to clarify. What kind of problem?"

"Rat problem," Snaggletooth said again, then the radio clicked off. Tory squinted. It was too dark to see anything but a shadow of the soldier on the bow ramp.

"What's that joker doing?" Victor Charlie said.

"Should we throw on the deck lights?" Tory said.

The radio crackled: "Sorry, over."

"Go ahead."

"I was chasing it."

"Chasing what, ramp?"

"Big fucker, bridge," Snaggletooth said, and Victor Charlie pushed his ball cap up and smacked palm to forehead, striding across the bridge toward Tory. "Big thing with only one eye, size of a dog. I keep swinging this stick at it, but it ain't too afraid. He's half up the ramp now." The radio clicked off then on again and Snaggletooth added a winded "Over."

"Raise the ramp, Sir?" Tory said.

"Can't raise the ramp," Victor Charlie said. "We're only half tied off—need it for stability." He took the handheld from her and put it to his mouth. "Hey PFC, you still there?"

"Yes, Sir. Over."

"How big a stick you got?"

"Ax handle, Sir."

"Hit the fucking thing, Private."

"It's too fast, Sir. I already tried. Runs right past me. I—" The radio clicked off. In the dark, it looked like Snaggletooth was doing a dance down on the ramp. He came back a few seconds later: "Sorry. I gotta keep moving or it'll get past me."

"We could—" Tory started but the second mate cut her off.

"Listen up, Private," he said to the radio. "How good a shot are you?"

Tory almost laughed out loud, her hand going to her mouth. *What the fuck? Over.*

"Uh, pretty good, Sir."

"Shoot the fucking thing, then." The officer reached for his cigarettes with his left hand, the right hitting the transmit key again. "How do you copy that? O-*ver.*"

There was a pause, then, "You want I should shoot the rat, Sir?"

Victor Charlie, cigarette lit, hissed through a puff of smoke into the radio. "Shoot the rat, PFC, before I shoot the rat for you and put it in your goddamn rack to sleep with!" He inhaled once then clicked the radio again. "O-*ver.*"

"Roger that," Snaggletooth said.

Victor Charlie walked over to where Tory stood, looking down on the dark well-deck. He opened his mouth to say something to her, and that's when Snaggletooth opened up, both of them ducking instinctively below the windows as the ramp blazed alive in light for one brief second, not one blast but three quick ones.

"Bitch put it on auto," Victor Charlie yelled, then grabbed the radio. "I said shoot it, PFC, not blow it up!"

There was a pause, then the radio crackled. Snaggletooth, who hadn't heard that last transmission, said simply, "Mission accomplished. Over."

"Oh shit," the officer said. Tory took three quick steps and used both hands to push up all six switches for the deck lights. Down on the bow ramp, Snaggletooth stood with his M-16 loose in one hand, a small furry mass at his feet.

"It's smoking," Tory said.

"What is?"

"The body."

Victor Charlie squinted. Sure enough, even from the height of the bridge you could see a few tendrils of smoke rising from the thing. He contemplated that, then said, "Impressive."

Xerox came from the radio room, crouching.

"Who's shooting, us or them?" he said.

"Neither, really," Tory said. She glanced over at him, and by the time she looked back the ramp was crowded with ten or more 10th Mountain MPs from the port's main gate, looking for something to shoot.

"Those boys are going to be awfully disappointed," she said.

Victor Charlie looked nervous. "Probably wasn't a good idea," he said. Tory didn't say anything. He tugged on his earlobe, then reached up and switched off all the deck lights again, throwing the ramp and well-deck back into darkness. He pulled his ball cap off and threw it on the skipper's chair, buttoning his BDU top.

"I better go down there."

"What should I say if anyone calls?" She was pointing to the marine-band radio.

"Tell 'em it was a fumigating accident," he said, grabbing his helmet. "We were protecting U.S. government property."

Victor Charlie made for the inside stairs—"Mister Welsh laying below," he yelled. "Sergeant Harris has the bridge." He mumbled to himself all the way out. "Pinhead MPs should be happy for the excitement."

He was back an hour later, having made the incident officially not happen. "The beauty of being an officer," he said, much more relaxed now, "even a warrant officer. I wave my wand and sign the log and it never happened."

"As long as you get there before a higher-ranking officer," Tory said.

"Pecking order," he said. "It's all about pecking order." He lit a cigarette and poured himself a cup of coffee. He brought all this, and the log book, to the skipper's chair and settled in again. "They got bigger fish to fry out there tonight."

There were other shots fired overnight, but fainter, scattered. Eyes would look up from the log momentarily, or head turned from fiddling with the marine-band radio. Every shot in the distance was like the beginning of a race never run; legs tensed, ready to drop body to ground. *Fight or flight,* Tory thought. But just for a second. Then on with the nervous night.

"They should've let us go to anchor," Victor Charlie said.

Five of the six Army LCUs and the one other LSV were all floating on their hooks, a good mile out in Port-au-Prince harbor. They'd dropped their loads and scattered to anchorage. No one here envied the other LSV, though, sitting out there. The CW4 who skippered it was a mean old bastard with Admiral syndrome; even at anchor the crew remained on underway watches, and after watch you were expected to do an hour of cleaning. Tory had called out there on the marine band around 0330, and talked to the bosun.

"Everyone's up," he said. "Scrubbing floors." The man sounded tired.

"The makings of friendly fire," Victor Charlie said. A shot rang out, closer than any they'd heard so far, and after she started breathing again Tory decided she'd still rather be under fire than safe at anchor, scrubbing floors.

The night crept forward.

"Are we sailing tomorrow?" she said.

"Tomorrow night, I think."

Tomorrow was already today, but in the warped world of sea shifts there was clear delineation. In conversation, tomorrow didn't start at midnight. Tomorrow started at sunrise.

"Big storm, last week," Victor Charlie said. "Half of Jacmel slid right off the mountain, into the sea."

"Jesus."

"Same tropical storm we hit before Cuba."

She nodded. The worst weather they'd hit on the sail down, one of the worst nights she'd ever been through on the boat; you couldn't do anything, couldn't move. After her bridge watch she didn't even try to sleep, went instead with Dick Wags down to the engine room because the lowest place was the steadiest place on a vessel.

"That's the one. But we caught just a corner of it. She hit southern Haiti head on."

Tory twirled the FM receiver. There was music, faint, here and there. Not from Haiti, she suspected. Words in Spanish; definitely not Haitian.

"So we're gonna load up like twenty of these boukie trucks filled with Red Cross shit and bring 'em down there."

"Why don't they drive down?"

Victor Charlie smiled and opened the log book in his lap. "Oh, New Jersey, you been in the Army a long time. Why let them drive their own trucks when we could spend time and money carrying them and make it look like we're doing good for the fine people of Haiti."

"True," she said.

"That," he said, "and actually I think the overland highway was washed out in the same storm."

It didn't matter, she knew. Both stories were likely to be true. There was never just one truth in the Army. There were layers, all of them legitimate, all of them deniable.

Victor Charlie lit a cigarette. "We're bringing a real soldier with us. From 10th Mountain." He exhaled, putting his Camel in the skipper's ashtray. "That captain, the one who led your lost convoy today."

"Captain Hall."

"Yeah. Him."

Tory looked at the floor then her hands then realized she was doing it and looked back up. Victor Charlie saw none of it. It was dark, and he had the ship's log in his lap, writing as he talked.

"Yeah," he said again, turning a page. "He's sailing with us."

"To Jacmel?"

"Yep."

She didn't answer for a minute, then said, "Doesn't he have a company? Are they all coming?"

"No and no." The second mate wet his fingertip and turned another page. "He's a battalion S2. Or something. I don't know. Or care." He picked up his smoke. "Skipper says he's like one of three soldiers incountry who speak Creole. He's supposed to keep our guests in line."

"A captain?"

Victor Charlie looked up then. "Yeah." He looked back down at the log, then looked back up. "Must have pissed someone off."

"I think I was there for that," Tory said.

"I think you're right, New Jersey," he said. "I think you were."

4:30 in the morning. The sky began to smudge purple, the sweetness of the warm breeze sharpened by charcoal smoke wafting from the city. Mannino was on the bridge now. He kicked Victor Charlie out of his chair and consumed the day's first black coffee and cigarette in grunty silence. Out on the bridge wing, Tory stood alone a moment, listening, watching. Port-au-Prince hovered on the misty predawn, white cathedral on the hill suspended in the air, floating. She looked over the rail to the pier below. A group of soldiers was standing around the pilot door. Female, all of them. They began stepping onto the vessel then, and she strained to see who was letting them on. Snaggletooth, it was. As the last female passed onto the vessel he glanced up toward the bridge. Seeing Tory, he waved once.

Rat killer, she thought, then looked back up at the cathedral.

CHAPTER

11

You'd think they'd been here a month; five rows of five cots, even spaced and dress-right-dress, perfect mosquito-net cubes over each. One of the smaller hangars at Port-au-Prince International Airport, now officers' quarters, Marc Hall returned well after midnight to find the place like this, a cot already assigned him. Second one in, two rows down, said the PFC with the clipboard outside the door.

Who knew there'd be a cot for someone just relieved of command? But then he'd not really been relieved; he'd never really had the command. It was all just shuffling and there was a new job for him tomorrow and on paper it would all look fine. He supposed he should feel grateful. It was difficult to feel grateful, though, he thought, as he unrolled his sleeping bag under the netting. It was hard to feel grateful when he'd been relieved of command.

Boots and uniform off, in shorts and T-shirt he stretched the length of the cot, staring up at the netting six inches from his face. The netting smelled of dust and desert—some 10th Mountain staff officer's legacy from Mogadishu or Baidoa, he guessed—and smelled of mildew, too, legacy of the Fort Drum quartermaster warehouse. He'd been there to in-process the post two years ago, to draw his TA-50, and the whole building smelled of it.

It was hard to feel grateful drowning in mildew. It was hard to feel anything, really. Some of it was being overwhelmed, from the day— he didn't know what to feel. Some was medication residue. It kept you midline, center; for the best, probably.

But then someone midline, center, wouldn't have saved those three men this afternoon, the three destined to join their friend in the tree. The Army was midline, center, and Marc Hall had broken out of that with his squad, into the real world, and done a real thing. He couldn't have done it from midline.

He regretted now taking the medication this evening. He hadn't, for days, because of this; since before they'd deployed to Guantanamo Bay. Since before they'd left the States. He'd thought he'd need emotion in Haiti. And he'd been proven right.

The Army's reaction had rattled him. He'd pulled the med bottle from the bottom of his ruck on the chopper flight out of Pétionville tonight, dry swallowing a tablet.

He wanted to believe it was meant to be, some part of this meant something and was meant to be. He'd legitimately saved three lives today; you couldn't sneeze at that. And now, to Jacmel. There was death and crisis in Jacmel, and he would lead the relief.

He thought about it, hand rubbing his smooth skull, eyes roaming blind the darkness of the hangar beyond his mosquito netting.

Voices, in the corner. A card table set up. Talking low, but funny how things bounced in this hangar. He thought of saying something, announcing his presence and intention of sleeping; but then why bother. Officers were no different than enlisted, no different than little kids. Everyone pumped to be here, for their own reasons. Everyone up and edgy and giddy like Christmas. Everyone talking it to death.

Marc Hall closed his eyes, trying to draw his breaths out, trying to find sleep. Or, at least, midline center.

—never seen nothing like it. The stink alone so bad I could barely stand at the gate.

Can't escape it.

Look where they put us.

It'll be better when we go out to the bush.

—ain't getting to the bush, champ. We'll sit here six months doing nothing but smelling the place, just so they can say we're here.

Dunno, man. The snake eaters ain't unpacking. They say they're going to the bush . . .

I don't see a green beret on your head, champ. Maybe they are, but I'm telling you, Division ain't moving.

Fucked up day, anyway—

Who ever heard of the Army riding an aircraft carrier?

—micromanaging's kicking my ass. I haven't made a decision since I packed lunch for my boy a month ago.

You made any decisions today, champ?

No decisions.

I got a decision for you: top or bottom?

Blow me.

—the deal with that black guy, the one who took Harrison's company in 2nd Battalion?

Harrison's a broke dick—

—but what's the deal with that black guy?

Hall.

—thought it was Call.

No, man, Hall.

That was a balls up, champ.

—had a fucking pistol to this Haitian officer's head, I heard. Right on his temple and squeezing the trigger. His sergeant had to pull him off the guy.

Hey, one less—

Watch it, champ.

Yeah.

Who gets a convoy lost, anyway? How the fuck do you get lost?

—dunno, but I'll give him that. You guys ain't been out there yet. Once you hit the city it don't make no sense. We got all turned around—

Still—

—the guy's loose, I think. That's all I know. Baric told me, the guy's loose.

Baric?

—that old bitch fullbird gives me the fucking creeps.

Yeah but if he says you're loose, then presto motherfucker you're officially loose.

Why they'd even bring Hall down?

He's fucking Haitian, champ. They need him cause he speaks boukie.

—great, I'll rub mud all over my face and start speaking some fucking voodoo chant and maybe I'll be important, too—

You gotta watch that man—

—keep it down, champ, keep it down.

Yeah.

I gotta get some sleep, gents.

Yeah.

Without opening his eyes, Marc Hall reached his arm below the cot, pushing his hand into an outside pocket of his rucksack. He found what he needed at the bottom, a prescription pill bottle. Eyes still closed, he opened it, fingering a pill. He was breathing hard, and tried to get himself under control. Finally, without opening his eyes, he popped the pill and dry swallowed. Maybe he'd get some sleep.

CHAPTER

12

The passage at the bottom of the stairs was filled with female soldiers, the ones Tory had seen from the bridge wing, coming through the pilot door. They were here for the shower. Helmets and rucks and rifles at their feet, lined up outside the latrine door, all of them from Harbormaster's office and Group headquarters.

"Hey there, Harris," one of them said, a sergeant.

It took Tory a second to place her, then she said, "What's up, Liz." The sergeant's name was Ross. They knew each other a little, through Junior Davis mostly. Liz had dated one of the Mike Boat guys from the 1098th, a PFC snipe who was wounded in Somalia and got out right after. Junior Davis had claimed not to like either of them—Liz Ross or her boyfriend. But Junior Davis didn't like anyone, and Tory had always thought Liz was all right. She had the distinction of being one of only two women in 7th Group who'd earned a Purple Heart in Mogadishu, the result of shrapnel from a midnight pipe bomb thrown over the wall from the city. "You kids been here long?" Tory said to her now.

"Flew in this afternoon—yesterday afternoon, I guess. Got to port around five or six. We've been setting up headquarters all night."

She yawned—loud. As she talked Liz was taking her hair out of the neat bun she'd had it in, shaking it out, getting ready for her shower. All the women here—and most of the female soldiers Tory knew—kept their hair like this. Women were allowed to have long hair, they just had to keep it pinned up to neck level. Tory couldn't be bothered. She'd had her hair—almost but not quite blond—cut off right before she joined the Army, and it stayed that way. Close to a guy's high-and-tight; never more than an inch on top, and shaved up the back of her neck. Junior Davis had claimed not to like it, but she didn't really believe him. "Feels like I'm sleeping with a boy," he'd say. Tory always remained silent to that.

"You guys are lifesavers," Liz said now, hooking her thumb to the latrine door. She had a handful of hair clips, and shoved them in her front pocket. "It was weeks before I had my first hot shower in Mogadishu."

Tory smiled. "Take all you want," she said. "We'll make more." Which was true.

She two-finger saluted and excused herself through the group of women. Her cabin was next to the latrine. She opened the door to the black room, closed it behind her, flicking the light switch on.

"Hey!"

"What?" She turned, not having expected Dick Wags to be in here and sleeping, ready to apologize—but it wasn't Dick Wags. Snaggletooth and Shrug were up on Dick Wags's bunk, Shrug with his face pressed to the bulkhead, Snaggletooth right behind him.

"Get the fuck out of here," she hissed.

"C'mon, Tory, we was just—"

"That's Sergeant Harris," she hissed, as loud as she could whisper. "And get out."

Shrug took a last look and jumped down, a noticeable bulge at the front of his BDU pants. Snaggletooth was red and laughing and he slid off the bunk, too, both of them slipping out the door. Tory turned off the light and climbed up onto Dick Wags's rack. A few months ago he'd tried to put in a shelf over his bunk, but misjudged where the thin part of the bulkhead was. The drill had gone right through to the shower stall, leaving a quarter-inch hole that was almost impossible to see from inside the shower. Word spread, as word does. Tory herself just never used that stall anymore, sticking to the second one in the latrine. She was the only female on the crew; it hardly mattered to her. She put her eye to the hole now, looking in at a female PFC she recognized by face but didn't know. The water was off, and the girl was drying herself with a brown Army towel in the curtained stall. Tory had never appreciated before just how completely you could see someone through the hole. *I should charge admission,* she thought. She watched for a minute as the girl toweled off, then pushed herself off the top bunk and dropped to the deck.

Lights back on, she clicked the lock on the door and began unbuttoning her uniform. It was 0500; she had four hours to get something to eat and take another nap, a longer one this time if she got to it quickly. Boots and pants still on, she pulled her brown T-shirt up and over her head, leaving just a black sports bra. She'd discovered these a year or so before, and wore nothing else now in uniform. They kept things nice and compact—no movement to slow her down or draw attention.

She looked at herself a second in the small mirror mounted on the bulkhead, turned away, then turned back, remembering how she'd scared herself in the mirror at the airport yesterday. It felt a century ago, wandering the tarmac and hangars half the day. She still wasn't completely sure why she'd done it. Not to see Marc Hall; that was a powerful impulse, but it hadn't occurred to her until later in the day. The impulse keeping her at the airport in the first place, walking and watching, had been even stronger, even more difficult to explain. She just wanted to *see.*

This is what they all wanted, most of them, whether cocky or scared or some combination—they all wanted to be here. Partly just to say they'd been here. They wanted the difference that set you apart from other soldiers—the patch on the right shoulder, to have gone for real. To be in its face. That's what she'd wanted yesterday—to be in its face. To see the machine up close. And she knew her time was limited, her time in Haiti. All their time was limited, but hers was truly limited. How tight she didn't know; a few weeks maybe. Certainly it wouldn't take more than that for it all to catch up with itself, for all the pieces to come together. She didn't know how it would come out, and she no longer really cared; but it was inevitable, she knew it.

Tory sat down in the desk chair, leaning over to untie her bootlaces. She glanced up as she did, at the peephole over Dick Wags's bunk, the portal to the naked and clueless showering next door.

I really should charge admission, she thought. Her hated cadences kicked in, from the depths of her sleep-deprived brain: *If we're all naked by morning sun / then we know the war was won.*

A fist pounded the door. "Roomdog!" It was Dick Wags. "You dressed?"

If we're all naked by morning sun . . .

"No."

"Grill's open. Breakfast. Let's go fuck up a plate of hot chow."

. . . then we know the war was won.

"Two and two, baby," she said.

Didn't we already eat breakfast? she thought. They had. At midnight. It didn't matter. It was 0500 now. Time for breakfast.

Is it war or is it not?

Almost the whole crew was up for chow; those coming on duty in BDUs, those headed for sleep—like Tory—in PT clothes: gray Army shorts and T-shirt with what they called shower shoes on their feet— plastic flip-flops. The mess window was wet with air-conditioner condensation, and through it the sky was streaked and fully light now. When T.K. opened the hatch to the deck the smell of morning poured in, warm and Haitian.

T.K. stood in the open hatchway, and Tory—handing her dirty dishes to Cain—had to will herself not to step on deck. If she stepped into the morning, she thought, she'd want to be in it and there'd be no sleep. She needed sleep. Tory made for down below, padding down the stairs, flip-flops flopping soft on her soles.

The females were gone now, showered and back to their cots in the warehouse. Liz Ross had been to Mogadishu, but Tory thought most of the privates and specialists who'd been with her had a rude awakening round the bend: There wouldn't always be a 7th Group boat in port, or a skipper willing to give away his precious ROPU water to a bunch of land troops. They were a little bit special, some of those headquarters chicks, and there was not much special about living in a warehouse for a year.

At the end of the passage, near the hatch where they'd waited for battlestations twenty-six hours before, Riddle stepped out of the cabin he shared with Pelton. He waved her over.

"Haircuts, Ms. Harris," he barked.

She put her hand to the back of her neck and rubbed. In the tiny cabin, Pelton stood like a crazed artist, bare-chested with towel round his waist, electric clippers raised high in right hand, old mustached Bear in the chair under him with head bent down.

"How's it going, P?" Tory said.

"Life is good, Sergeant," Pelton said, grasping the top of Bear's skull and putting the little clippers to the back of the thick neck. "It's a great Army day."

She thought of Pelton in the passage yesterday before battlestations, slowly losing it with face pressed to bulkhead. And then in the park, hours later—this Waterborne troop with but the barest of combat training—standing down the FADH, then wanting to lower the dead Haitian from the tree. *We've all come a long way,* she thought. *Pretty quick.* Always suspicious of time acting differently in the Army, she thought now time had ceased to exist altogether for them. *Twenty-four hours.*

Xerox and Shrug were up on the top rack, Pelton's bunk, the two of them slowly turning through the pages of *Hustler.* Temple was stretched out on Riddle's bunk, the bottom rack. Riddle, in the passage, had dropped and started a series of push-ups.

"Hey P, you crap your pants in the city yesterday?" Temple asked, in his slow Temple way.

"Yeah he did," Riddle yelled from the passage, not breaking stride with the push-ups. "Can't you smell it?"

"Bite me," Pelton said, running the clippers up the back of Bear's neck. "I did check my drawers pretty close when we got back to the boat, though."

"I couldn't take it if I crapped my pants," Temple said. "I think I'd rather they just killed me."

"You crap your pants automatically if you get shot," Xerox said, without looking up from his magazine.

"Nah, that's bullshit," Pelton said.

"That's what all the Nam books say. You lose muscle control and crap yourself."

"It's bullshit," said Temple. "What do you think, Bear?"

Bear was ancient, older than dirt—as old as Top and the Skipper—and so the final arbiter of all important questions. But Bear didn't answer. He'd fallen asleep getting his haircut.

"Hey, Bear!" Pelton reached around with his left hand and smacked him light on the cheek.

"What?"

"You're sleeping."

"Damn, Bear," Tory said. Bear was a sergeant first class, the ship's bull oiler, second only to Top on the enlisted side of life. He was Dick Wags's boss, in theory; but Dick Wags ran the show. Bear spent most of his time sleeping. He said he had Lyme disease.

"Lordy lord," Riddle said. He was still pumping out push-ups.

"You're done anyway, Bear," Pelton said, the old sergeant rising to his feet, wiping hair snippets from his shoulders.

"Did I miss anything good?" he said.

"Your life, passing you by," Riddle said, panting. He'd been doing sets of push-ups for the better part of half an hour, his arms tight and bulging.

Bear grunted, squeezing Tory's shoulder as he stepped from the room, grinning then kicking one of Riddle's hands out from under him. "Have Specialist Riddle bathed and brought to my tent," he said.

Shrug laughed out loud. "That's as wrong as two boys fucking."

Xerox, shaking his head, said, "That *is* two boys fucking, Shrugster."

Riddle rolled onto his back, lying in the middle of the passage, too winded to hand Bear a proper comeback. Bear was gone anyway, back to this own cabin, his dark den. To get some sleep.

Tory sat in the chair, hanging a towel around her shoulders. "Okay," she said, "just a—" then felt something sharp, like a pin in her neck. Pelton, barefoot, had slipped as he was laying the clippers to her neck, the sharp edge of the metal slicing her skin half an inch.

"Hey!" she said, slapping her palm to the back of her neck, half standing.

"Christ I'm sorry, Jersey. Let me see."

Tory lifted her palm, Pelton's fingers moving to her neck. "It's just a little bit—" he started to say, but she cut him off as she saw blood in her palm.

"Give me your hand," she snapped, spinning around.

"What?"

"Give me your hand." She clamped on the wrist of his free hand, the one he'd touched her neck with. It was clean; he'd touched just to the side of the small wound. Face to face with Pelton, her back was to the passage. Sitting upright now on the deck, Riddle could see a thin line of blood flowing free down her neck, under her shirt. "Talk about friendly fire," he said, but no one heard him. On the bunks, Temple, Xerox, and Shrug were all watching this, not sure what they were seeing.

"Hey, Jersey," Pelton said, but she cut him off again.

"Give me the clippers."

"Hey, let's settle down," he said. She was almost hyperventilating.

But Tory pulled the clippers from his hand, finding wet blood on the gleaming sharp edge of the metal. She wiped it quick across the front of her T-shirt, leaving a streak on the brown cotton fabric over her belly. She eyed the clippers, saw more blood, and wiped it again. She looked up at Pelton, staring him in the eye. He waited for her to say something, but she wasn't really seeing him. Finally he opened his mouth but she immediately cut him off.

"It's clean," she said.

"Yeah," Pelton answered. "Of course it is. Not a big deal, Tory."

She nodded, and dropped her eyes.

"How's this?" Pelton said, trying to reach to the back of her neck. She swatted his hand down, then grabbed her towel and clamped it against her skin back there, holding hard. She was aware suddenly of all of them, all five of them, silent and watching her.

"Sorry," she said. "I—" But she couldn't finish, and holding the towel in place ducked out of the cabin, moving quick down the passageway. Closing her own door behind her, she stood stock still, not turning on the light, but locking the door. She didn't move, her head throbbing so hard she couldn't think at all. She stood there, didn't know how long, then reached over and flicked the light switch. She pulled the towel from her neck, looking at the black stain on it. With one quick motion she rolled the ball tight and threw it, hard, against the bulkhead, picked it up and threw it again, then jammed it down to the bottom of her laundry bag. When she finally sat down she put her hands to her eyes, pressing hard. She sat like that five minutes, not moving, then killed the lights and crawled into her bunk, and— exhausted, lungs hurting, eyes unfocused—set the alarm, staring wide-awake.

CHAPTER

13

The friendliest of all fires.

Behind closed eyelids, in sleep thin and restless, they were locked and loaded face to face behind rifle sights with the FADH platoon in the park. In the corner of her vision she could see the feet of the lynched man, pale purple-brown, but there was a wind now, his feet swinging back and forth, swaying dead wood, the stink of black rot and onions on the breeze; *strange fruit.* She heard Marc Hall's yell, the crack of his pistol shot, but someone aimed wrong because Pelton was falling, on his back in the dirt, blood pumping from a hole in his throat as he grasped Tory's boots, smearing everything red and brown. *Blood! He needs blood!* a medic yelled in her ear. *Give it to him, Sergeant!* And she put the muzzle of her rifle on Pelton's forehead, watching as his eyes rolled and spun in fear, and she squeezed the trigger.

Late Morning

CHAPTER

14

"Pastor says—" The young woman's mouth kept moving, sentences flowing from thin lips, but Junior Davis's ears closed after those first two words. He nodded a few times, forced a smile when he thought it might be appropriate, but heard not a word she said and instead concentrated on stirring coffee and thinking *I wish we had real eggs.* The ship rolled, long morning-sea rolls, far and slow, everyone in the dining room eating breakfast with one hand to the edge of a table, not enough to hold tight but ready to hold on. The sun was bright through the windows, warm across the scuffed hardwood deck and reflecting off the bulkheads and Junior's eyes were two thin slits against the glare. The sun felt good, though, on his arms.

"—didn't think it could be true, but Pastor says—"

Nod, nod, weak smile, excuse me could you pass the salt, nod, smile, that *is* amazing I'm sure you're right, nod, praise Jesus.

On a normal ship he might have a wardroom or crew's galley to retreat away to, but with exactly two on the paid crew, and all in service of the Lord, he and McBride were lucky to have cabins to themselves.

"—so when Pastor told me that—"

A hundred people on this boat, and conversation never strayed far from *Pastor said this* and *Pastor said that* and *Well, Pastor told me* and *Oh, I don't know if Pastor would care for that.* He'd come on crew late winter and thought it all funny, before he'd lived in its smell awhile, and stewed in its gospel. Now he just wished they'd get some real eggs from time to time and tried not to think much else about it.

"—but like Pastor always says—"

A third of the boat was married couples—some with cabins to themselves, some not—and the midwife seemed to pull a new baby every other month or so; a few of them had to be copulating, at least occasionally. The Pastor talk was so pervasive on the boat, Junior Davis had come to assume it penetrated into procreation as well. He imagined a smack across a pale, Christian ass and a wild yell of *Who's your Pastor?* and almost spit his coffee across the table. Fist to mouth, he managed to hold it in, trying to turn his laugh into intestinal distress.

"Are you okay?" the young woman asked. Junior Davis got his breath and gave assurances and she said, "You have to watch every bite you eat in these less-fortunate countries. Like Pastor always says, the mark of good health is—"

Pastor says harder! Harder!

"—and I don't know how it is these people live like that, but once I was talking to Pastor and—"

Ohhhhh . . . pastorpastorpastorpastorpastorPASTOR!

"Could I have some more of that coffee, please?" he said, holding up his mug, and she poured it for him.

"More eggs?" she asked, holding out the bowl, and he smiled and shook his head and said no. He couldn't do it anymore, the fake eggs. Just looking at them made him ill. No one else seemed to like them either; the bowls never seemed to get lower than half-empty at breakfast these days.

They'd been getting local eggs for a while, on the barter system. Some fresh meat, too; goats and small fish. The provisions came in exchange for spiritual services: preaching, baptizing, praying. But life was supply and demand, and the American missionaries had a greater need for what the Haitians had than any desire on the part of the Haitians to be saved or preached to. When they'd first got to Haiti, round about May, this dining hall was filled every day at 2:00 P.M. with Haitians coming onboard for Pastor's daily service. And they'd leave behind all sorts of things: eggs and vegetables, small brown bottles of liquor (Pastor had these quietly poured overboard, unless Junior Davis or McBride got to them first), small weavings and idols (Pastor had these quietly burned). The room would fill, men and women and always with their babies, too, kids running up and down while Pastor did her slow, quiet thing on the small wood platform McBride had built her. Junior Davis would slip in the back of the room and watch sometimes; McBride, too—it was the only part of the vessel they kept air-conditioned, and the air cranked hard in there. Junior Davis would sit still in the back, trying to think what this old ship was like sixty years before, as a small ocean cruiser, the dining hall filled evenings with tuxedos and gowns and flirts and champagne. McBride would come in, sweating rivers from the outside heat, and sit under an air vent with hands folded in his lap. Junior Davis didn't know what McBride thought about on those air-conditioned afternoons, but he had a feeling it wasn't the sermon.

That was Cap-Haitien. By July they were in Jacmel. The heat went from oppressive to unbearable. The fuel tanks were very low. When Junior Davis remembered to sound the tanks the thin metal measuring tapes came up anemic. There seemed to be no money for fuel, either. Pastor didn't elaborate, but something had changed with the missionary organization in the States. There were a few worried, private radio messages between her and whoever was in charge; the last time, Pastor came out to the bridge and instead of having McBride arrange for a fuel purchase ordered Junior Davis to switch off the generator except for mealtimes.

That killed afternoon air-conditioning. All the good Christians seemed surprised when the Haitians immediately stopped filling the dining hall for prayer service every day, but Junior Davis had called it. Supply and demand. Pastor retreated to her cabin and stayed there a week. By the time she came out, instant eggs were a menu staple.

"Supply and demand," Junior Davis said.

"I'm sorry?" The woman had a worried look on her face.

Davis managed another smile. "Just thinking aloud," he said.

The woman nodded, chewing on her narrow lip. Around the dining hall the good Christians were finishing breakfast, bringing plates into the galley for cleaning.

"You look a little sick, Mister Davis," she said.

Junior Davis was trying to remember this precious thing's name. She'd been fluttering her eyelashes in his direction three or four weeks now, but for the life of him he couldn't hold on to her name. Gayle? Maybe. Lorraine? He thought it was Lorraine.

"I'm a little under the weather, Lorraine," he said, without the slightest trace of irony. "I haven't felt myself for quite a while."

The eyelash flutters hadn't gone unnoticed. Unacknowledged, mostly, but not unnoticed. If Junior Davis didn't know better he'd say Lorraine was trying to get to know him. In the biblical sense. The ship being what it was, you'd think this wasn't likely. But then the Lord works in mysterious ways. It didn't much matter, though. He had rules now. Strict rules. He was damaged goods, and there were rules to follow.

"More coffee?" she said, holding the plastic carafe. It was horrible stuff; weak and watery. But it was all they had.

"Thank you, Lorraine," he said, and she smiled sweetly, filling his cup. People seemed to want to take care of him. It had always been so. He hadn't checked a mirror but was fairly sure what he looked like this morning, and couldn't imagine anyone on the ship seemed more in need of care than him.

That, and nothing set the Jesus girls' hearts to beating like a convert. Although, with all that fluttering, he wasn't sure conversion was where Lorraine's head was at.

"Good morning, Mister Davis." McBride slid a chair out from the table and lowered himself into it, across from his engineer. Junior Davis lifted coffee mug in greeting, a thin expression on his face. The vessel master was unshaven and tired, forearms dark with grease, gray T-shirt and jeans looking like they could get up and walk on their own. He'd been awake all night, and would remain up—and almost constantly on the bridge—until next they saw port. Davis was the sole engineer, but there was only so much you could do under way in the pit. He had volunteers down there to keep an eye on the gauges, and run for him if something happened, but not much was needed beyond that. McBride, on the other hand, was the only real able seaman left on the ship. It hadn't always been so; when he'd taken the job there'd been a crew of three under him. Clean, praying, Godly men, and not a one over twenty-four, but two from tug families and one a maritime academy graduate, all able to stand a solo bridge watch. They'd drifted off, his crew, as God grew heavier on the boat and the ship sailed less. Now it was just him, against all maritime regulations and common sense. But what could you do. It was calm enough now; he had a few onboard he'd trained in fundamentals, and one of them was on the bridge so McBride could slip away for a cup of coffee and talk with Davis.

McBride nodded at the girl sitting next to Davis—he couldn't remember her name. "Morning, Miss," he said. "If you don't mind, I need a moment alone with himself." He cocked his head at Davis, winked at her. She apologized and stood, walking over to a table on the other side of the dining hall, joining a group of women finishing their breakfast. McBride's eye followed as she went; too skinny for his taste, but a fine ass under those shorts. She'd do well to steer clear of Davis, but it was obvious from watching that's where she was headed.

"You know the rules, Davis," McBride said. "Not unless you plan on marrying her, and even then not until you do."

Davis gazed up at the ceiling. "There's lots of rules," he said, "from lots of directions. And I follow them all."

"I'm just saying—"

"Don't get fucking preachy with me, McBride."

"Watch your mouth," the older man hissed.

Junior Davis looked down into his coffee and didn't say anything.

McBride eyed him, then sighed and reached for the carafe, filling the mug he'd brought to the table. He took a sip, then said, "Forget it."

"Yeah." Davis looked up and shrugged.

They sat and drank their coffee in silence, watching the women at the far table. Lorraine looked over her shoulder, saw them staring, and put her eyes quickly back to her own group.

McBride sipped from his cup, leaned back in his chair. "You come on here 'cause you knew we were going to Haiti," he said.

Davis nodded. "I didn't make a secret of it."

"No, and nothing wrong with it. But I think you wanted to go to Haiti because you had a good idea your Army wouldn't be far behind."

The engineer raised his eyebrows. "I came to Haiti," he said, "to drink."

"Indeed. And a good job you've done of it, too, my friend."

Davis laughed despite himself, and said, "I was always a good soldier, Skipper. I get a mission and I see it through."

McBride chuckled with him, then stopped. He didn't say anything for a moment, then asked, "What's driving you, Davis?"

Junior Davis opened his mouth to answer, then closed it. He shrugged again. McBride grunted, crossed his arms over his chest. There was no way in. No way at all. Davis was killing himself and he'd likely take his reasons to the grave.

"Listen," McBride said. "There's going to be an American boat in Jacmel. An Army boat."

Davis looked up. "Mike Boats?"

"No. A ship. An L something."

"LCU."

"Maybe." McBride pushed a hand down into his front pocket and pulled out a folded piece of paper, a fax. He glanced over it then said, "No, an LSV." Davis kept his face poker-straight. There were three LSVs in the active-duty Army; it didn't necessarily mean anything. McBride raised his eyes to Davis, and spoke slowly, not unkindly: "I can't have trouble in Jacmel," he said, and Davis nodded. "Am I wrong in thinking you didn't leave the service on the best possible terms?"

"No," Davis said quietly. "You're not wrong."

"And am I wrong in thinking some people on this Army ship might be familiar with you?"

"It's possible."

McBride leaned forward. "It's desperate for us, here," he said. "I know you don't care about Pastor, or these people, but it's my job. And they deserve a break. She deserves a break."

Davis nodded, staring at his lap.

"Look," McBride said, "I'm gonna leave it up to you. You know what's at stake for us. You act as you see fit, but I'm thinking you try to stay out of sight."

Davis nodded again, unable to look up. It didn't mean anything, he thought. The odds were so against it. Yes, once he'd had thoughts along these lines—it *was* why he'd joined this ship. It *was* what he'd been thinking. In a drunken, vague, hazy way, but still.

But not now. There was no redemption and he knew it. Too far gone. He'd set out for it, but he wasn't here—on this ship, in Haiti—as a way back in now. He was here to check out.

"I won't be any trouble," he said, then finally looked up, looking McBride in the eye. "I'll be no trouble."

McBride nodded. "Okay." He stood to leave. Davis pointed at the fax paper in his hand and said, "Can I see that?" McBride put it on the table, then turned and walked from the dining hall, sea legs braced in the long rolls of the morning ocean.

Junior Davis reached out and touched the paper, drumming his fingers on it. He looked up and saw Lorraine smiling at him from across the room, and he smiled back. *Oh, Lorraine, Lorraine,* he thought. He picked up the paper. It was a simple fax, providing ETA information for Jacmel and a friendly skipper-to-skipper greeting. There was a typed sign-off: CW3 JOHN MANNINO, US ARMY, TC, COMMANDING. The vessel designation was below that: UNITED STATES ARMY VESSEL *KENNETH E. GILMAN* LSV-16.

Tory, I have made you a place in my heart.

Davis's right hand was tapping feverishly against his leg. Noticing, he gripped his thigh, squeezing as hard as he could.

Tory, I have—

Like a shot, his hand went up then stopped short before making contact with his face, remembering where he was, all the motion and energy in his body going suddenly to his feet instead, both of them tapping uncontrollably.

—made you a place in my heart.

Right-hand fingers on his left forearm, he pinched, hard, then again, then again, fingernails digging. The fax crumpled under the pressure in his left hand, and when he pinched this time he drew blood, surface capillaries popping like grapes. When Lorraine came up behind him he was so startled he almost hit her, jumping to his feet, then falling back into his chair, mumbling apologies.

"You're bleeding," she said, reaching out for his arm. He pulled back, not letting her touch, grabbing a napkin from the table and pressing it against his arm.

"You're bleeding," she said again, but still he kept his arm away.

He said, "I have a bandage in my cabin, Lorraine. But I'm a little unsteady. Would you help me there?"

CHAPTER

15

The lieutenant in charge of the 10th Mountain soldiers guarding the port had requisitioned himself an open-air brick hut, set back from the actual wire and—hopefully—out of grenade-throwing range. The lieutenant was the same one, Tory realized, who'd had trouble opening the port's main gate yesterday. His name was Vine. Lieutenant Vine had been to the airport earlier this morning and carried somewhat harder news than port gossip.

"Biggest thing so far I guess was the Marines, up to Cap-Haitien."

"Hit?" Tory said.

"No, or not bad anyhow. They all walked away. Killed like eight or nine FADH, though. Right at their own police station. Blew 'em away."

"No shit."

"Yeah, no shit." He shook his head, then said again, "Killed 'em." Like he was trying to get his head wrapped around it.

"What were they doing, Sir?" She was thinking of the FADH yesterday, in the park. The lynching.

He shrugged. "Don't know." Vine took a drag off his cigarette. He looked out beyond the brick wall as he smoked, watching the crowd—shifting and moving around the port fence in the thick heat. "FADH's bad business, though, I think," he said. "Not quite sure what the deal is there."

Tory remembered her question about the FADH.

Good or bad?

Yes.

"They're hanging people in the streets," she said.

The lieutenant nodded and flicked his cigarette butt over the bricks. "All's I know is someone needs to uncork head from ass on this issue. No one knows who it is we're fighting."

"Yes, Sir."

Tory walked up to the wire to wait with Pelton and Riddle. The air smelled of burning rubber again; not as thick as yesterday, but there all the same, tendrils of odor heavy on a light breeze.

The little buses zooming around Port-au-Prince's narrow streets were called *tap-taps.* Some were actual buses, some ancient, modified VW and Volvo vans. The Haitians said it fast, two quick consonants—*tap-tap.*

"Stupid name," Pelton said.

Riddle shook his head. "Nah, bro. Makes sense. It's a definition." He put his hands up, pantomiming. "Bus hits tourist—*tap!* Tourist hits ground—*tap!*"

Pelton laughed. Tory, deep behind combat goggles this afternoon, didn't react. She hadn't slept well and wasn't talkative.

"*Tap-tap,* Sergeant Harris," Riddle said. Tory heard, but didn't answer. She kept stealing glances at Pelton, when she thought he wasn't watching. It was disorienting, next to him; her dream of firing a shot into his head still vivid, his mute, pleading eyes and the spray of blood and tissue.

The three were waiting for a *tap-tap* of ten men hired to accompany the Haitian lorries already driven up the LSV's ramp and secured to deck. The trucks were filled with food, medicine, drums of water and fuel, blankets, light construction material—all from the Red Cross. For Jacmel, hit by the storm.

"Here it comes," Tory said, ditching her cigarette. Over the heads of the crowd gathered outside the gate they could see an old van, painted bright stripes of blue and red and orange, dirty Red Cross flag flapping from a makeshift antenna. The vehicle was packed with a group of Haitian men in clean, white shirts, one in a Chicago Bulls ball cap.

"That's it," she said to the corporal in charge of the gate detail. "The Red Cross guys."

The corporal gave his helmet a push back. "We need to go ahead and get some kind of ID from them," he drawled. He didn't like this chick sergeant, standing at his gate.

"I'm gonna go out on a limb here, Corporal," Tory said, "and guess that they left their library cards at home."

The kid twitched his jaw but didn't say anything.

Tory took the corporal through the gate with her to speak to the driver. Rifle in right hand, she ran her left quickly across her LBE suspenders and web belt as they walked out, making sure everything was tight, prepared to push through a crush of people. But the crowd parted with the gate opening, giving them room. The *tap-tap* driver was an older man, crinkled around the eyes and mouth. He spoke perfect accented English and gave the corporal repeated assurances of their legitimacy, convincing him in the end. Tory stayed quiet, then pointed to where the LSV sat berthed, across port. They could see the lower radar turning lazily, and a group of soldiers on the bridge wing. Too far to see who they were.

"You drive there and wait, Sir," she said through the window to the van driver. "We'll follow on foot and meet you."

"*Oui,*" he said, smiling large, and she smiled back and patted the man's arm. All the men in the van waved as the vehicle rolled past, into the gate, and she raised an arm in return.

The crowd moved in on Tory and the corporal, pressing forward in a slow, warm wave of flesh. The kid looked nervous for a second. He tried talking as he backstepped away.

"Okay, then," he said, and "Afternoon, ma'am," and "All right, little fella," and then the Haitians were shaking his hand and touching his arm—*Bonjou!* and *Welcome, welcome!* and *Yes America!*—and Tory noticed he was trying to keep the muzzle of his rifle pointed to the ground and she wondered if he knew what a nice guy he'd suddenly turned into.

"Hey," she called out, amused, but he didn't hear and then she was doing the same talking, "Pleased to meet you, Sir," and "Hey there, girl," and stepping back and stepping back and then she stopped and stepped forward, one straight step forward, arm extended, and gripped the outstretched hand of a young woman, a girl with dark, duty-smooth skin. "Hello," Tory said, and the young woman shook her hand vigorously and laughed and spoke so fast Tory caught none of it, even the parts in English, but both smiled and they shook hands and Tory just said, "Hello," and then again, "Hello."

Gate buttoned and everyone back in place, the corporal made it a point to shake hands with the chick sergeant before she turned and followed the van and her two guys back toward the boat they said wasn't the Navy. The corporal's name was Miller and he was smiling now—whistling, actually, when Lieutenant Vine came back—his head in a different place about all this.

"I dunno, Sir," he said. "I guess they're just like regular people."

The officer looked out at the crowd. He was eating an apple. He swallowed, then said, "Women? Or Haitians?"

But Corporal Miller had turned and didn't hear the lieutenant's question.

The LSV's cavern of an engine room gleamed with fresh coats of white and haze gray on the bulkheads and polished deckplating you could eat from. The bilge was wiped clean, by hand, weekly. Under bright fluorescent lights, Dick Wags and Scaboo went through the presails for the mains, spinning valves for water, fuel, oil. Both in coveralls, and Dick Wags had a sunburn from sitting out on the fantail most of the morning, smoking cigarettes and watching the Army settle in to the port. Scaboo gave a thumbs-up to Chief, sitting in the box, and the two massive locomotive engines whined then roared to life. Dick Wags tapped Scaboo on the shoulder, pointing forward, and the younger sergeant nodded then climbed the long stairs topside to go presail the bow-thruster engine. The ship was ready to move.

The deck crew was up, the whole platoon, regular shift or not, in coveralls and gloves on the well-deck or in uniform and sunglasses on the bridge. T.K. guided the Red Cross van into the slot they'd saved for it, right inside the ramp. Behind him, Arnold walked the two rows of lorries, checking tension on the chains locking the vehicles in place. He'd never seen such a load on an Army vessel; rusted-out old trucks painted twenty different ways, the drivers all sitting up in their cabs because they'd been told by Victor Charlie not to move—*and I mean don't even lift your leg to fart!*—until someone briefed them on where exactly they were allowed to go on the vessel—*and that's probably fucking nowhere!* "Don't yell at the boukies, you fucking chink," Skip had said to Victor Charlie, and Arnold just about lost it on that one, tears popping. "What are you laughing at, Staff Sergeant Arnold?" Victor Charlie had growled. "You're as boukie as the Haitians." Arnold rubbed his palm on the officer's head, unable to stop laughing. "Yes, Sir," he said, "but better boukie than chink, right?"

In the dry-goods storeroom off the galley the Steward checked on a plastic vat filled with fermenting juice and fruit. It smelled godawful—*like a jar of kimchee set in the sun,* he thought—but what it would eventually produce could be mixed with Coke and *What the fuck,* Roy decided, *we run out of real booze this'll start tasting better overnight.* Dick Wags and New Jersey had the biggest stash onboard—of the enlisted anyway—jealously guarded and shared with few. But the two bottles of Jack and two bottles of tequila under the bottom drawer of their cabin desk was already a third gone, and they were less than two weeks out of home, one day in-country. The ship might hit Roosevelt Roads in Puerto Rico for fuel sometime in the next few weeks, but maybe not. That's why Roy had started the brewing process. Just in case. When you go, you go for real.

There were ten soldiers at the gate. They'd been on it five hours, and the yawns were starting to go around.

A PFC named Wheeler stood next to Corporal Miller and said, "Who knew this would be boring?"

"There's just no goddamn war here," Miller said. "There's no war."

PFC Wheeler—who played bass in a Dead cover band at the Fort

Drum USO's talent nights—mimed grabbing a microphone and said, "Can I get a little more war in the monitors, please?"

The crowd on the other side of the fence was pushing less but no smaller. Lively and moving about, people talking to one another, letting newcomers and children up front for a good view of the *blancs* in their helmets and green camouflage. Every few minutes a great cheer would go up, the Americans catching shades: *Aristide! Lavalas!* was the hands-down winner, with *Clinton!* (or just plain *Beee-ill!*) in close second.

Drums showed up, drummers scattered through the crowd, the people moving and chanting in rhythm now. The air temperature pegged well beyond anything Corporal Miller had ever felt before, every move he made slow and heavy like he was under water. He pushed the goggles off his eyes and up on his helmet, splashed his face from a canteen. Out in the street they were stomping now, dancing, some of the women spinning like tops.

Boy, I'd like a nice iced tea, Miller thought, and stepped back away from the gate so he could smoke a cigarette.

On the ramp, Tory and Pelton stood under the burning sun, watching as T.K. and Arnold secured chain locks on the Red Cross van. The Haitians were all out of their vehicles now, gathered in the shade of the tunnel under the house at the aft end of the well-deck. Riddle had run up to his cabin to grab some money, and he came back now, trotting across the well-deck, Temple right behind. Some boys were selling wood carvings and other trinkety things through a gap in the fence a few hundred yards south, past a massive mound of rusted scrap metal and useless ship's parts.

"Y'all set?" Riddle said, winded and puffing.

"You're gonna be in Haiti a year," Tory said.

"Early bird gets the worm, New Jersey."

"Don't miss the boat," she said, and Riddle winked, him and Temple and Pelton jumping to the concrete and moving down the pier.

Tory turned to take a last look at the port before walking up the ramp and then there was Marc Hall, coming at the LSV from around the warehouses. He raised a hand when he saw it was her, and she waved back, taking a step toward him then stopping herself.

"Sergeant Harris," he said, stepping on the ramp, a smile on his face. It was what she needed, that smile, and she gave it back to him.

"Sir," she said, and the habit was ingrained to raise her right arm in a salute but this was a combat zone—down range—and you don't salute down range and her arm went straight out instead and he grasped her hand with both hands and leaning in close he said, "It's good to see you."

CHAPTER

16

The crowd around the port fence pressed again, moving with the rhythm of the drums but heavy and thick as the afternoon air. Tight and close, feet padded and arms waved. Naked and half-naked children zoomed throughout, through and around legs, over and under boxes, chasing and racing in circles. The noise was louder, distinct cries ringing out, singing, yells of liberation and yells of curiosity and mostly it seemed yelling for the sake of yelling. Corporal Miller stopped hearing it, mostly; he didn't know what they were saying anyway, beyond the realization that the yells weren't threatening to him. He stood behind the gate with his squad, too hot for anyone to talk now, moving slowly or not at all if possible. Watching, watching, eyes back and forth across the sea of bodies.

There was a scream then, sharp, and he didn't hear it because he'd tuned it all out, and he didn't hear the next one either. But the crowd changed, like a pocket of cold in a warm lake, turning attention from him to something behind, and that's what did it: realizing suddenly he wasn't looking at anyone's face anymore, just seeing their backs, and that snapped him out like snapping sober from a daydream.

"What's—" he said to PFC Wheeler next to him, and then the air was sliced by a real scream, a woman's scream, high and horrible, from somewhere beyond what the soldiers could see.

As if by invisible order, the rifles in the hands of the American soldiers all steadied, brought down from high port arms or up from low relaxed at-ease. Lieutenant Vine rushed from the hut, crossing the few steps to the gate, and his presence, the look on his face, was a second invisible command, all the squad pushing down the thumbs of their right hands, pushing their M-16s off safe.

Marc Hall turned, hearing something, but couldn't see the gate from the ramp of the LSV or the crowd on the other side. Tory thought for a second he was drawing away from her, then she heard it, too—a scream, then another, then a yell.

"That was—" he said but was cut off midsentence by the blast of the ship's foghorn, a long and low note, then Top's voice on the loudspeaker: "All ashore going ashore. Deck parties to stations."

Marc Hall took a step forward on the ramp, one foot planted on the pier, looking in the direction of the port gate they couldn't see.

"No time," Tory said. She cocked her head toward the well-deck. "Ramp's going up."

"That was screaming," he said.

"I think so."

He looked up, straight up, to the bow over their heads. The portside line and anchor station. Voodoo Lounge.

"Can you get me up there?" he said.

"C'mon."

She turned and crossed the ramp in five quick steps, Marc Hall right behind. There was a fixed ladder inside the well-deck, and as she climbed up she could hear the winch turning for the ramp chains and felt the vessel shift slightly as the foot of the ramp lifted from the pier.

The crowd parted in almost a straight line, bodies pushing back against the fence on either side of the gate, those closest to the road running away. There were two gray Jeeps out there, a group of Haitian men in caps and uniform standing around and looking at something, all of them with heavy riot sticks in their hands.

"Who the hell is that?" Corporal Miller said. Lieutenant Vine came up behind him. He drew his pistol from its holster.

"Police—sort of," he said. "Beaucoup bad."

The crowd shifted again and then they could see where the screams came from, both men's shoulders jerking back as they realized what they were seeing. Out by the road four or five FADH troops were taking turns plunging into the crowd with their riot sticks flailing, swinging high, connecting with heads and necks and chests, dropping people around them, writhing, bloody and moaning. The people had turned away from the Americans at the port, turned toward the FADH, and the Haitian troops were taunting them, pointing at individuals they recognized or pretended to recognize, yelling then laughing then yelling again and every now and then reaching forward and grabbing someone by the collar or hair and dragging them into their ranks, pushing them away or smacking them down. Miller saw a young man, a teenager, crying and running to a woman on the ground, bending to her, and as he bent a stick came swinging down and cracked across his lower back, dropping him across her.

"Hey!" Miller yelled, involuntarily, pointing at what he'd seen, then turning and yelling again, "Hey!" He couldn't get his mouth to form any other words.

The ten American soldiers in Miller's squad were all on the gate and fence now, pressed as tight to it as the Haitians on the other side had been. Out in the street, one of the FADH leaning against a Jeep, watching, noticed the Americans. He nudged the man next to him and pointed, and both of them broke into big grins. The bigger of the two raised his arm then in a greeting toward the American soldiers, letting it hang in the air a few moments, then waving from the wrist, still smiling, still lounging against the Jeep—one professional to another, *Yes, don't mind us.* He yelled something then, at the Americans, and Corporal Miller could have sworn he said "Crowd control."

On the pier, Riddle, Pelton, and Temple were flat-out running back to the boat, T.K. standing in the pilot door, waving them on. They fell into the well-deck, pulling off their gear and dispersing to duty stations, T.K. securing the pilot door behind them.

Forward, Scaboo came through the hatch from the bow-thruster room, wiping sweat from brow on the sleeve of his coveralls, dogging the hatch down tight. He turned to walk aft across the well-deck back to the engine room then saw a soldier above him on the ladder—Hall, the black captain from yesterday, with Tory Harris above, pulling herself onto the catwalk. Scaboo gripped the rungs and followed them up.

"Open the gate! Open the fucking gate!" Miller was yelling to no one in particular. Turning around, looking for the lieutenant, he saw PFC Wheeler with rifle up, aiming, muzzle through the wire of the fence. Miller smacked his arm down. "You can't shoot from here!" he ordered, then started pointing positions for Wheeler and the rest of the squad. "Let's get this fucking gate open," he said.

Out at the Jeep, the FADH commander watched all this without moving, shifting his eyes back and forth from his officers working through the crowd to watching the Americans in the port. He hadn't moved when he saw one of the Americans level his rifle through the fence, and he didn't move now. When Miller's gaze passed in his direction, he waved again, pleasantly.

Miller was looking in every direction at once. The lieutenant had completely disappeared. "Jesus H. Chr—" he said, then Vine came running from the hut. He'd ducked back in to get the handheld radio, and had it now to his ear as he ran.

All right, Miller thought, *now we're in fucking business.* He was a corporal—he couldn't make a move like this without an officer, but his officer had arrived. He pointed at Wheeler and then at the still-closed gate. "Let's go, man," he said. He looked down to check that he had a round chambered then stepped forward as Wheeler fumbled with the latches on the gate. Miller drilled a stare at the FADH commander, then—without turning his head away—said to the lieutenant behind him, "I'm thinking Sir we'll move through and forward and get him to—"

Vine closed his fingers on Corporal Miller's shoulder, cutting him off. "Hold it, Miller."

The corporal swiveled his head quick.

"We can't go out there," the lieutenant said.

Miller didn't get it. "There's no time to wait for another squad, Sir," he said, thinking Vine was worried about numbers. Miller sure as hell wasn't worried about numbers; he had ten M-16 rifles—fuck up a pack of stick-swinging boukie goons. "Price and Lopez can cover from here, me and Wheeler'll take 'em down. We can't wait, Sir." As he spoke a FADH officer used both hands to bring his stick down directly on the head of a man who'd just gone to his knees. Amazingly, the man remained upright, almost hovering, certainly unconscious or perhaps dead but perfectly balanced. Eyes rolled up in his head, he swayed, once, twice, then the FADH officer kicked the man's chest with his foot, knocking his body over.

Miller took a step closer to the gate but Vine's hand was still on his shoulder.

"Hold it, PFC!" Vine yelled at Wheeler, pushing on the gate latches. Vine gripped Miller's shoulder harder, pulling him back. "We can't go out there—at all." His left hand held the radio and he raised it now, showing Miller. "First Sergeant Marcus and the CO are coming now, with Reeder's squad, but the order is from God himself." The division commander. "We don't interfere."

"Interfere?"

Miller looked away from the lieutenant, back out through the gate, to the crowd beyond. Those closest to the fence were turning now, yelling in Creole at the Americans, begging, crying. PFC Wheeler stood there, waiting for an explanation, or an order. Vine gave him one.

"Step off from the gate, PFC."

On the LSV's bow, in Voodoo Lounge, Marc Hall pulled a handheld radio from deep in his rucksack, turned it on, and switched around until he found the frequency he was looking for. Tory kept her eyes on the crowd beyond the port fence, mostly visible from where they stood. She could see two Jeeps, and two FADH officers leaning against them nonchalantly. She wished for binoculars to see if one of them had been in the park for the lynching yesterday, but the bow equipment box was empty. She looked up again in time to see the stick crack down on the man on his knees. A voice behind her said, "Christ." It was Scaboo, in his engine-room coveralls, cresting the stairs up to Voodoo Lounge in time to see the same sight. Marc Hall glanced over, recognizing him from the convoy yesterday, and nodded absently. He'd just turned up the radio as loud as it would go, so all three of them heard the order as it was given, the transmission from airport to port, the request for verification from the lieutenant on the gate, and then the order repeated again. Hall gripped the rails of the bow, fists tight as he could get them. Scaboo said simply, "Oh man," and Tory said nothing at all. Behind them the ramp banged as it came to rest in place, fully up, and the foghorn sounded again, right over their heads, the officer and two sergeants almost jumping from their skin with the surprise of it, the air blast drowning out the military chatter from the radio, drowning out what they could hear of the pain and fear and anger of the crowd, drowning it all out.

There was a distance now, between the FADH and what remained of the crowd, those unable or unwilling to run away. A gap of feet and a gap of purpose. Twelve men with sticks could do only so much harm to a crowd of a thousand—could breach the crowd only so far—before being swallowed. Farther incursion was absolutely possible but required guns, and shooting now would cross the gap of purpose: Somewhere out there was a camera crew, or a photographer; the Americans suffered a ridiculous self-imposed impotence, but perhaps not so in the face of obvious massacre.

Elsewhere, throughout the day—in Cité Soleil, in Cap-Haitien— crowds swarmed over former *attachés* and the occasional single, unarmed FADH officer and took their revenge. In some places the *attachés* were pulled from the jaws by American soldiers or Marines at the very last second, eyes wide in fear and bodies shaking violently from the nearness of death, shoved down in the back of a Humvee or five-ton truck for the trip out of their neighborhood. Bleeding profusely from knife sticks and duller wounds, they rolled to fetal positions in the backs of the vehicles, their ordered American saviors wordlessly planted over them, plastic gloves to keep off the blood and plastic faces to show the world. Not a one among them could figure why they were saving these men but they'd been told to so they pulled on their gloves and pulled them to safety. When the occasional *attaché* started babbling Creole thanks and assurances of political and moral purity as they were swept from their place of intended destruction the blank-faced soldier keeping a weapon on the crowds around the retreating vehicle would stare at the man without comment—eyes and thoughts hidden far beneath wide, silvered goggles—or sometimes utter a simple, "How 'bout you shut the fuck up."

And at the port, the Americans stood caged, staring through their fence and locked gate, the organized FADH demonstrating to the people of Port-au-Prince exactly who was in charge, exactly what American liberation was worth and how far it could go, reminding the good citizens of who would still be there when the *blancs* inevitably left the country.

The FADH commander got into his Jeep, lit a cigarette, and with a twist of his fist signaled his men to fall back. Sticks raised, they backed to the Jeeps, climbed on, and the two vehicles began rolling down the avenue, slowly, the men pointing out faces in the crowd as they passed, one of the troops singing. A group of women moved from the mass of people, sobbing, cries of *doktè!* and pleas to absent saviors, the women lifting the bodies left lying in the street, to get them to a clinic, hoping the clinics were open today.

But most of the crowd wasn't watching the wounded, or even watching the pull-back of the FADH. They'd turned, turned back to their original focus here: the American soldiers behind the port fence. But no cheering now, or yelling; no dancing. The people stood, mostly mute, mostly numb, looking at the faces under helmets with the powerful rifles in their hands, realizing the score, and as they stared at their liberators the soldiers dropped their eyes, trying to find something else to look at, anything else, turning away, wishing they were anywhere but right here right now.

It was tricky, their position: 274-foot ship head-in to a corner berth in the horseshoe of the port. The soldiers on deck crew dropped and pulled the starboard bowline, then the line midship. Mannino had them leave the starboard aft line as a pivot point and engaged the bow-thruster to slowly kick the nose around. Aft line dropped, alternating small taps on the twin screws and the bow-thruster nudged the LSV the rest of the way, center port, facing out.

The vessel pushed through dirty water, steaming down the long concrete pier, past the harbormaster office on the small island, past the few small rust buckets unable to move under their own power, soon to be towed. In exile at the end of the pier were seven Army Mike Boats from the 1098th, lonely and tied together. Tory had remained on the port bow in Voodoo Lounge when Scaboo showed Marc Hall the way into the ship's house and up to the bridge to see the Skipper. She sat on a bit, watching as they slid past the Mikes, watching the guys clean their boats up, searching for faces, realizing she was looking for Junior Davis's face—force of habit. Junior Davis hadn't set foot on a Mike Boat, or worn a uniform, in almost a year.

Past the Mike Boats lay open water, wide channel to the first anchor buoy. In the time it took the LSV to steam clear of the pier a fresh squad of soldiers was brought to the port gate to relieve Lieutenant Vine's men, who'd stood their posts most of the day. In the street, the injured had been carried off, and the word was none had died. The man who'd taken a direct crack on the skull was said to be unconscious, his left side twitching like a rabbit, but he wasn't dead. Not yet, anyway. The living are not as interesting as the dead—even the bleeding, unconscious, twitching living—and when the reporters descended from their perch up in the bars and hotels in Pétionville they poked around but didn't stay long. There were small pools of blood here and there, but they would be gone, too, in the evening rain.

Past the anchor buoy, the LSV corrected course for the shipping channel. Its wake frosted white with the order of all-ahead full, twin screws pushing the ship out and away from Port-au-Prince.

PART TWO

Under Way

CHAPTER

17

The rolling of the old ship increased in equal measure with the draining of light from the sky, as if the two were connected, heavy Caribbean sun pressing flat the natural swells and waves until its strength sapped and the ocean current pushed up and through as dusk advanced. It certainly felt that way. The missionary ship rode relatively calm most of the day, against all hope, from their departure out of Jérémie and through the long day beyond. The clouds settled thick across the sky late in the afternoon, wind blowing noticeably stronger approaching sundown. With the total loss of light the ship began rocking, taking hits broadside as it trawled ever so slowly on its crippled main.

There was a kid standing bridge watch with McBride. He'd be on the helm soon, if this weather increased. But for now the autohelm was holding steady and the boy stood forward with McBride, eyes out the dark, wet bridge window, both hands wrapped around the bar to steady against rolls. He was college-aged, this boy, raising a question in McBride's mind—it was September. But McBride had long ago ceased asking personal questions of those who passed through this boat—and more often than not they did just pass through, not many staying aboard more than a couple months, with a few notable exceptions. Early on he'd been curious and asked a lot of questions but discovered the answers were invariably depressing, sometimes extraordinarily depressing, and now he tended not to ask. Instead, he was telling this boy about the green flash, rarest of Earth events, visible only to sailors and then just a handful of times in the course of a life. Not possible on a night like tonight, of course. One needed an absolute absence of clouds, not even a wisp. No atmospheric moisture, and no wind. A completely dry, flat counterpart to the sea.

"At sunset, at the very point where the sun passes under the horizon, it will flash—bright green, very intense. Just for a second."

"Green?"

"Green."

"Amazing."

"Indeed. Nothing more beautiful."

The boy nodded, thought, then said, "The eye of God."

"What's that?"

"It's like the eye of God."

McBride grimaced. "I don't think—" he said but was cut off by a large roll to port, out of sequence, catching them both by surprise, the boy losing his grip and falling into the vessel master. He clung to the rail with one hand and held the boy up with the other. "Steady," he whispered, righting the two of them. It was now too dark to clearly see the boy's face, but McBride guessed he was scared.

"That," the older man said, "was the *hand* of God."

Pastor had laid below an hour before, to sleep. She was back now, in her thick khakis, working her way slowly across the bridge as if climbing a ladder—one hand out with each step, grabbing something solid and pulling herself along.

"Mister McBride," she said, breathlessly. "How long will this last?"

"Easily all night. Can't tell beyond that." The map from the weather fax had been vague. They rolled starboard and McBride shifted his knees, Pastor gripping tight to the chart table. The kid had wedged himself into the forward corner of the bridge. "Young man," McBride said, "stand to the helm."

Pastor managed the last few steps and stood next to him now, a tight grip on the bar running across the front of the bridge. "We've never rolled so badly before," she said. "Even in worse weather, yes?" She was scared.

"No, you're right. It's like I warned—" and he paused as they pitched hard to port "—I have very little control over the ship. We have almost no power to maneuver."

McBride was scared, too, but a vague and detached fear. He found this interesting. He should be scared—they had no business out here. And in a clinical way he knew he was afraid. But it was the same as knowing someone else was afraid; some other person he was observing.

They rolled starboard and it was a long roll, deep, seeming without end. Pastor lost her grip, shuffling sideways across the deck, whispering, "Dear God." Balance regained, she said, "We can't survive this."

"We can," McBride said. "As long as it gets no worse."

Pastor was flustered, and he felt for the old girl. She had an iron will, this one. Faith, he guessed. Perhaps stubbornness. But the last few days had shown her just flustered.

"This was a mistake," she said. "Put her in, Mister McBride."

He shook his head. "There's nowhere to put her in. We go on or we turn back, but no other options. There's no other deep-water ports."

She nodded, and stood silent a few moments. Finally, she said, "They're frightened, down below. I'll go see to them."

"Good," he said. "It will make it easier for them. To see you." McBride turned then, to the kid. He was standing at the helm console, holding on to the sides. "Take her off auto, young man," McBride said. "Hold tight and listen up for my orders." They'd been running fairly close to shore through the daylight. Crippled as they were, McBride hadn't wanted to lose sight of land. It was a comfort, he thought, to everyone on the ship. But it didn't matter now, and he might get some relief in deeper waters. "I'm taking her out farther," he said, "and we'll see what happens."

Pastor was halfway back across the bridge, and she nodded without turning, holding tight with each step. She stopped at the stairs, and turned then. "You'll get us through this, yes, Mister McBride?"

He nodded but didn't answer. One of the few times she put something directly into his hands was one of the few times he felt for sure the outcome would have little to do with him.

* * *

In the narrow passage below the stairs Pastor rounded the corner and literally ran smack into someone, both of them thrown to the deck as the ship rolled.

"Oh God I'm so sorry," the voice said, then, "Pastor! I was coming to find you."

Pastor squinted in the dim passage. It was a young woman, a silly girl named Lorraine. "It's all right," she said, irritated, barely holding dinner down. She put her hand up to the railing but couldn't seem to raise herself from her sitting position. "Help me, Lorraine," she said, and the girl reached down to pull her up.

"It *is* Lorraine, yes?" she said, grunting as she was pulled to her feet.

The girl ignored the question. "It's Mister Davis," she said. "He's sick, ma'am. Real sick."

"We're all sick, Lorraine," Pastor said through clenched teeth, holding tight as the ship rolled deep. "It's unavoidable in this weather—"

"No, really sick. He's passed out, I can't wake him. He took something, I think. Pills. A lot of them."

The older woman tightened her jaw. "Where is he?"

"We were in his cabin, Pastor. He's in his cabin."

"What were you—"

"I'm sorry, Pastor, I'm so sorry! But please, he's so sick."

CHAPTER

18

Captain Hall merited a solo cabin on the officer's deck below the bridge but, walking a ship's tour with Mac, found the top bunk in Bear's cabin unused. "Good enough," he said, and heaved his ruck up onto the bed. "I'll get you a blanket and pillow," Mac offered, relieved not to be pushed from his own digs. The first mate turned to Xerox, shadowing the two officers, and said, "Get the captain a blanket and pillow." The bald-headed private scurried down the passage to the linen locker, one hand on the rail as the ship moved with the ocean.

The crew calmed under way, decompressed. They knew what to do out here. No colonels, no sergeants-major. No unanswered questions, no ambiguous missions, no mindless rules of engagement. Instead, a sensible world, logical rules. The ship moved, and you tried not to do too much. Out here, sundown and sunup might pass unnoticed even if you stepped outside, because it simply didn't much matter. Under way was a different reality—four hours on, eight hours off, four on, eight off, four on, eight off. Every day, twenty-four seven.

On the bridge: a warrant officer, an NCO, and a specialist or PFC on the helm. And Xerox; always Xerox. A similar shift in the engine room. A constant rotation though the three cooks in the galley, a meal always available. On the officer's deck, Skipper at the ship's computer, usually playing Doom. Across the passage, door propped open, Chief in blue coveralls at his small desk, buried in overflowing parts catalogs and equipment manuals, somewhere in a never-ending cycle of inventory.

Passages quiet, under way; from the moment they left a pier someone was always sleeping, or trying to. The hushed stop-start waterfall of a sea shower, the faraway bleat of someone's pillow-buried alarm, quiet chatter of a postwatch card game—cigarettes and cocktails behind a closed cabin door. These were the only underway noises, all muted even more by the ever-present hum of the diesel mains and the generators. The hum made the ship's air dead, words becoming weighty things that would pass your lips then drop to the floor before arriving at another's ears. Half of most conversations consisted of "What?" and there wasn't much to talk about anyway so why bother talking at all.

Give me a cigarette.

What?

Give me a smoke.

Get your own.

But I'm sitting here, man.

What?

Never mind.

On the shelves in each enlisted cabin, strapped down for sea with bungee cords, each soldier's flak jacket, helmet, M-16 rifle. As they hit open water, Top had ordered all weapons and ammo to be turned in and secured in the small-arms locker down below. Skip had countermanded the order, yelling as he made for the stairs off the bridge. "Am I the only one who remembers we're supposed to be at war? This *is* the Army, right?" He passed the medic, coming up the stairs. "We are at war, right, Doc?"

"Sure, Skip. Whatever you say."

"Skipper," Marc Hall said, rapping his knuckles on the open door of the ship's office. Mannino, leaned back in his desk chair, computer joystick in hand, came as close to jumping as his squat body would allow before Hall waved him off. "It's your ship," the captain said.

Feet on the floor, leaning forward, Mannino said, "What can I do for you, Sir?" He set the joystick on the desk and picked up a pen, tapping it, not sure what to do with his hands.

"I'm going to head down to the deck, talk to the drivers—the Red Cross men. We'll need to set some guidelines for the trip."

Mannino thought a moment, tapping, then said, "Is it all right for them to sleep in their trucks? In the cabs?"

"I think they'd be most comfortable."

"Yeah, okay. Good. Run of the ship, but only outside, only on deck. We'll feed 'em three times a day—someone'll come lead 'em in for chow. And the shitter, too, I guess."

"Thank you, Skipper," Hall said.

Mannino nodded. As the captain turned, he said, "Spent any time at sea, Sir?"

Hall stopped, turned back, and said, "No."

"It'll be rough tonight, once we're out in it. This is a flat-bottom boat, she always rolls, but we'll have weather tonight, too. Get settled in quick. Might be tough to get around later."

"All right." Hall turned to go again, but Mannino wasn't done.

"Most guys tie themselves into their bunks. You might want to think about it, Sir. If you don't want to wake up on the deck. "

Hall laughed, and said, "Really?"

"Really." Mannino made a twisting motion with his hands. "A loose wrap of Ranger cord'll do the trick."

"How's it going to be for the men on deck in the trucks?"

"Rough. Wet if they walk around. But just tonight. Tomorrow should be fine."

Down on deck Hall had the Haitian truck drivers and Red Cross clerks gather aft and spelled it out for them. He was slowly learning he didn't speak Creole as well as he'd thought, but he managed to get through it okay.

"Attention bois moue," he said—mind the wet deck, especially in this weather. Already the ship was rolling deeper, farther, a fine mist spraying even this far back every time the bow crashed down into a trough. Their questions were about food, meals, and Hall's answers were good. Even in the dark he could see smiles, feel them relax. *But hold tight tonight, fellows,* he said. *After the meal, back to your trucks. If you must vomit, do it on the deck. It will wash away.*

They laughed and talked between themselves and Marc said a few more things then someone spoke from the back of the group, *"Ki pays ou sorti!?"*—What are you, anyhow?

I don't understand.

What are you? American?

Yes. American. My mother—she was Haitian.

His mother! His mother! Good boy.

Laughs all around.

Your mothers, too, right fellows? We all have Haitian mothers.

And they laughed even louder that he could laugh with them.

Hall turned to go and one yelled—*Wait!*

"*Oui?*"

"*Pouqui ca ou la*"—So, why are you here?

What's that?

"Why, Sir, are you here?" the man asked again, in English.

Marc could find no words to answer, in Creole or English.

The cabin door was propped open, Tory in the desk chair with a Jack and Pepsi cocktail in her big ceramic Waterborne mug. Dick Wags sat on the lower bunk—her bunk—tucking the bottoms of blue coveralls into his combat boots. He was coming on watch; it would be eight hours before Tory started hers. The cocktail was to force sleep, her first real sleep since they entered Haitian waters. She was wearing gray Army shorts and a T-shirt, her feet up on the desk. Her feet were raw, hard, the bottoms and sides like cracked stone. Tory took secret pride in her feet; she walked barefoot in the summer, on sidewalks and pavements, no pain.

"Rough sailing tonight, Roomdog," Dick Wags said.

"I always sleep better, though." She took a large swallow of her drink. "Unless it gets really bad."

Boots tightened, Dick Wags stood, checking himself in the mirror, then lighting a cigarette. "If you want—" he started to say, but was interrupted by Bear, filling their doorway.

"Sergeants, I'd like to introduce you," he said, and Marc Hall stepped up behind him. Tory stood, in one move setting her drink down and plucking the cigarette from Dick Wags's hand, taking a puff, trying to mask any hint of the Jack Daniels on her breath. She liked Bear but didn't know him well.

"Captain Hall, this is Staff Sergeant Wagman, my assistant bull engineer, and Sergeant Harris, the bridge quartermaster."

Marc put his hand out, finding Dick Wags's first. "Pleased to meet you, Sergeant."

"Sir."

Tory took another puff, stepping forward to take Marc's hand.

"Sergeant Harris and I already know each other," he said. "We had quite a day yesterday."

Bear looked confused, but didn't say anything. He was often confused, and generally kept it to himself.

"That's great," he said, no idea. "Captain Hall's getting settled in for the night. I showed him where the shower is, and the importance of the male/female sign on the door. He's bunking with me."

"Sir," Tory said, their hands still locked together.

Tory walked Dick Wags out, getting a drink at the water fountain by the stairs. She walked slowly back to her cabin, closing the door behind and standing still a moment, hand on the knob. She pushed her fingertip against the button, the lock giving a slow click as it set. She put her right hand up and switched off the light, the dark of the cabin instant and complete.

It was one step to the desk chair, and she stepped it, pulling the chair out, turning it around, then sitting. From the other side of the thin bulkhead she heard the latrine flush. Passing her hand across the desk top she found a pack of cigarettes, pulled one out, and lit it with her Zippo.

There was a knock at the door. She didn't move.

"Jersey?" It was Roy. A knock again. "Hey. New Jersey?"

The doorknob rattled. He'd come down for a cocktail. Tory smoked, silent. The Steward's footsteps trailed off down the passage. Next door she heard the sound of the shower spray on the steel stall.

There was light now, a little. From under the door. She could see her feet. And light when she took a drag on her cigarette; the cherry bloom, Junior Davis used to call the warm quick-burn glow. She took a drag now, lingering, the tip burning red and filling the room for the briefest second. Then she exhaled, resting the cigarette in the ashtray on the desk.

She stood. One step to the bunks, and she stepped it. Then one step up, her left foot on the mini ladder, her arms pulling, and she swung herself up onto Dick Wags's rack, clicked the small bulkhead reading light on, then swung herself around: belly on the green Army blanket, her feet on his pillow. The sound of the shower in her ears, she scooched forward and pressed her right eye to the hole.

Junior Davis's naked body was the first Tory ever examined in great detail, and she went at it with a small obsession in the first months of their relationship. Meeting Junior, being with Junior, fell like a last step in an unplanned process that began with signing her Army enlistment papers almost two years before. Tory clung to Junior with a fierceness she didn't understand, learned who he was with her eyes and fingers. Their first night together, in a roadside motel on the strip leaving Virginia Beach, she got up out of bed and turned on the overhead light. She liked—needed—to *see*. He was pale, tall and tough as a piece of rope, with more scars than she thought a twenty-five-year old should have. She traced them and knew them like she knew the little veins on her own ankles or the freckles on her forearms.

Junior would shower in the middle of the night, walking the second-floor hallway of her dormitory barracks with just a brown Army towel wrapped low around his waist, using his copy of the key to open the door when he got back to her room. (They rarely used his room, three buildings over, because he had a roomdog, a crew-mate of hers; Scabliagni, whom everyone called Scaboo.) Tory kept a purple lava lamp in the corner, and after his shower Junior Davis would stand framed in the doorway, glowing in liquid light, then stretching up with both arms to grab the door jamb and do a pull-up—Tory, curled in the bed with blanket to chin, watching.

"Stop it, New Jersey," he'd say sometimes, crossing the room to put his hand in front of her eyes. "You're making me nervous."

But he wasn't nervous and she knew it. He liked to be watched. He liked to be liked, and liked to be noticed. Which was fine; Tory liked to watch.

It was comfortable. Not like seventeen, eighteen; high school and the long, dry summer before she left New Jersey for good, fumbling in dark places with her gray-eyed boyfriend under the stands at the stock-car track in Flemington, night air all grease and fries, rushed hands pushing up under shirts and down into tight, unbuttoned jeans, lips and tongues kept locked together so no chance to stop or change your mind. Tory always tried to pull back from the never-ending kiss, break her lips away and just watch for a minute, just breathe, the roar of stock engines making everyone deaf to everything. She'd known him in high school but only to look at, a memory of passing in the hallway and the parking lot. Wayne his name was, Wayne Apgar, cousin of the family who owned the bar in Croton. He worked part-time on a pit crew, and was nineteen, one year older. He took her under the stands three different Saturday nights, with a blanket from the trunk of his car, red and black squares. Wayne Apgar's face smelled of fuel, the smooth skin on his chest deeper, musky. He was the first one she put her hands on and explored by touch. She came very close with him, very close; short, quick breaths. He didn't like it when he noticed she was watching him work, and on the third night, wool blanket itchy and rough beneath them, he rolled her over so she couldn't watch, his chest on her upper back, his one hand gripping tight to her long hair, the last boy who would ever have his hands in that hair, just two weeks before she shaved it down to barely an inch and got on a Greyhound to Fort Leonard Wood.

Junior Davis was dark-eyed in his own way, and baby-faced in the sunlight, but he was no kid. Twenty-four when they met, he was slow, languid—their nights together rolling out with no end. They would lock her barracks-room door at nine or ten o'clock on a Friday night, the little fridge tight with cans of Rolling Rock, a fresh pack of cigarettes and bottle of Jack Daniels on the desktop. Junior Davis liked to fuck in the heat, thermostat cranked so they'd sweat; she'd raise the window and stand by it when they'd finish something, icy breeze pushing goose bumps across her breasts and belly, her back and legs still red from the warmth of the room and the blankets. She liked the openness of leaning there like that, on the cracked winter windowsill of her barracks room, raw and tired.

"That's a control thing," Junior told her, eyes half-closed, smoking his own cigarette on the bed.

"What is?"

"Standing there naked like that. It's exerting control. Something in your past makes you need to exert control."

The corners of her mouth raised, amused, and she smoked and shivered and said, "Maybe I just like being naked in the window."

Junior liked to talk, and would, under the blanket, wrapping long limbs around her and telling long stories then talking would turn to touching and touching was exquisite and then he couldn't talk because he'd pushed her onto her back and spread her thighs and his mouth was busy. Even then she looked at him, down the length of her body, over her breasts and to where his hands lay flat on her belly, the top of his head framed by her thighs, and she'd stare until the point where she couldn't anymore and had to stretch her neck out and lay her head back, teeth bared and eyes squeezed closed. They moved, it seemed to Tory, across the room without walking or memory, realizing you're on the old couch then on the bed then sometime much later blowing cigarette smoke out the gap in the cracked window, Junior kissing her neck as she smoked.

She went on the pill because he didn't like to wear anything—he went in smooth, and it did matter, she thought, it mattered in the feel, and more it mattered in the mind. What she liked most of all, what made her growl, was to push him down on the couch and crawl on top, kissing his face and mouth, kneeling over his lap, drifting her bottom back and forth, teasing him, grazing but not letting him in, then slow, slow, a centimeter at a time, pushing herself down, hands flat on his chest and knees in his sides, riding at her own lazy, determined speed, her own time, riding. *It matters,* she thought. This time, with him. It mattered. The music loud in her ears, Junior underneath. The music was all Tory's on those winter nights, endless in the CD changer as the night ground on, all her guitar players, all her old men, and when she was done, eyes squeezed and her chest flush and trembling—when she'd gotten everything from him she could—she'd pull herself off, open and empty, padding naked across the floor, taking a pull from her beer as she reached down in the darkness to turn up the volume for "Life by the Drop."

They were drunk together. Their long rolling nights—Junior Davis finally curled asleep under the sheet as Tory watched the sky purple with Sunday dawn—and their short evenings, too. Everyone had a beer in the car between port and barracks at the end of the day, and a beer to shower. If they all went out to eat there was a pitcher and Riddle would refill it then T.K. and so on. If Junior Davis came over after there was a beer open before the door closed. Whether they fell asleep on the couch watching the ten o'clock news or passed the weeknight boredom naked in bed, there was the same nice buzz, the same low cloud in the brain.

They were drunk alone, too. Tory mixed vodka and frozen lemonade over the summer when Junior Davis was out with the Mike Boats, drinking when she watched TV or read a paperback out on the lawn before the sun went down then maybe some eight ball on the pool table in the dayroom. Her barracks neighbor, a loud pool-shark parts clerk PFC named Candy Phelps, stuck to Diet Coke and tequila and walked around the barracks most evenings in cut-off sweats and flip flops hefting a glass stein filled with ice and the syrup-sweet drink.

Enough so it wasn't drunk anymore, just the general state of being. But that's how it was in the green machine, in the dorm barracks or the cheap off-post apartments down Warwick and Jefferson avenues; after your first year, then two, you slipped into it, slipped through, one day after the next, hot summer rolling to cold winter rolling to hot summer. Tuesday was just as good a night to kill a twelve as a Thursday or Friday. Easy, with the TV or a card game and what else were you going to do? No tax on beer at the Class 6, and what else were you going to do? It was just raising the bar on what drunk was; drunk wasn't drunk anymore, civilian drunk—that was every day. True drunk now was really fucking drunk. True drunk was what you did on an August Saturday afternoon in Mac's backyard with Victor Charlie

using an oar to mix up a batch of Purple Jesus Juice in a kid's plastic
bathtub and Doc and the Steward burning up a mess of chicken on the
grill, then heading out to Bucks or the Crystal around eight with
Junior and Dick Wags and Alicia to raise hell and waking up next
morning with no idea where you'd gone after that or how you'd got
home to the barracks or to the boat. That was drunk, true drunk. It was
social and about as subtle as an old steel hammer.

When Tory and Junior Davis were drunk together just the two of
them it was different, low and slow and constant, never rushed. It was
a steady killing of bottles and an endless burning cigarette. It was
instant fights, sharp tempers, small objects flying across the room and
slamming into the wall and sometimes each other. It was quick make-
ups, fierce apologies. It was Tory busting out laughing, slamming her
forehead into his chest so hard he yelled. It was hands all over each
other, going down on him as he drove her truck cross-post to make the
Class 6 before it closed; Junior Davis following her down the sterile
store aisles, his wide hands up under her shirt, palms cupping her small
breasts hard through the lace of her bra.

Their drunk was a lot like their relationship in that way; it matched
their relationship, followed the same track. Same as when you're drunk
and you don't notice things have started to change, or you think maybe
you see a change and you don't know why or how long it's been that
way and you shake your head to clear it but you're drunk now and
nothing is very clear.

Tory pulled away from the pinhole, leaning back on Dick Wags's rack,
thinking. She ran a hand over her hair, lips pursed.

Not sure why anymore, she leaned back in, putting her eye to the
hole. She'd been watching him, watching his body in the shower,
intent, but Marc was gone, nothing there, everything black.

Tory pulled back again, blinked, then switched, putting her left eye
to the hole. And that's when Marc Hall pulled his eye back, stepping
away from the bulkhead in the shower. He lifted his heels, pushing
himself up a bit on his toes, and put his mouth to the pinhole.

"Hello," he whispered.

CHAPTER

19

"Get me some water."

"Pastor, I—"

"Quiet. Not now." She pointed to the door of the small latrine connected to Davis's dark cabin and Lorraine nodded then struggled to her feet. The ship was rocking so violently now even these few small steps were difficult, requiring split-second planning: where to put feet, hands, when to time each step. Pastor sat near the head of the bed, wedged, one sneakered foot on deck and one foot against the bulkhead, braced against the rolling.

Davis lay unconscious on his back under a thin blanket, eyes closed, face gray and breathing shallow. He probably wouldn't die now, but Pastor was only guessing on that one. He would have died. She'd seen the pill bottle of what he'd taken when she'd come into the cabin, said, "Help me now, girl," then grabbed the unconscious Davis under the arms and pulled him into the latrine. She'd flipped him over, hands locked together around his waist, and started pumping him until he vomited into the shower stall. Lorraine had sobbed through all this, hysterical, but Pastor was too busy to even yell at her to shut up.

Pastor put fingers to Davis's wrist again, checking his pulse. His skin was cold. She'd known the risk, taking him on. McBride said it had been a mistake, and he blamed himself—he'd made the hire. But it hadn't been a mistake, at least not then. The ship wouldn't be running now, if not for Davis. Perhaps taking him back, after his run-in with the junta's thugs in Jacmel, had been the mistake.

But then, could something be a gift from God on one day and a curse on another?

"Thank you, Lord," Pastor whispered.

She resented this, though. No question. She felt shallow, equating a man's demon sufferings with intrusion and inconvenience on her part. But that's exactly what she felt. This was an intrusion—on her flock, on her ship, on the future of her mission—and she resented it. It wasn't just inconvenience, either. His presence, dead or alive, could be dangerous.

Lorraine cried behind the closed door of the small latrine. The girl's bra lay in a tangle of blanket near the foot of the bed; she'd forgotten it in her haste to dress. Pastor pulled it out, staring blankly at the latrine door, running the smooth fabric between her fingers. She turned her head, looking at Davis again. She reached out with her free hand and felt his forehead, running her palm across it, then gently down his cheek. His breathing was growing more labored, and she wondered if he was waking or dying.

This man is a disease, she thought.

Pastor rolled the girl's bra up in her right hand and shoved it under Davis's mattress, just to be done with it.

Junior Davis spent six years in uniform, two of them as sergeant. He was sharp. Sharp, shined, creased. Lazy, slouched, slow-talking and quiet in jeans and a T-shirt, he transformed in uniform, starched backbone and chin up, fingers locked in perpetual sergeant's fists, the best snipe on 1098th's Mike Boats. He could fix them, sail them, shoot from them. He'd told New Jersey a story, though, how he'd been a pissy mess to start. Every private is a pissy mess to a certain degree, but Junior Davis pushed the envelope.

Already bitter about the judge's order forcing his Army enlistment, they'd thrown Junior Davis in 1098th's maintenance platoon right out of boat school and solidified his resentment. He had a dirtbag of a barracks roomdog everyone called Penguin, and basically Junior didn't give a fuck. He'd wanted to give a fuck, he told Tory, but it was hard when the Army crapped green on him right off the bat like that. So he stayed drunk with Penguin, showed up to formations in wrinkled and greasy BDUs, never shined his boots, never cut his hair. No one in the company's line platoons knew who he was, and he didn't give a fuck for any of them. His dirtbag roomdog, the only companion he had, got knocked from specialist to PFC and then straight down to E1 buck private, once for a hot urine test, once for insubordination. Junior Davis woke up one morning, newly promoted to an E2's mosquito wings, and realized he outranked the four-year veteran who shared his barracks room and lonely life. That night they did a line of crank to celebrate this achievement, then used the hallway pay phone to call the civilian girlfriend they shared, a chick from down near Poquoson; Penguin called her Sweaty Betty. With the lights off in the barracks room and someone else supplying the high, she wasn't picky about how many soldiers sandwiched into the narrow bed with her.

Three months into this the platoon leader for Maintenance—a first-dot warrant officer almost as slovenly as the rest of them—was booted and replaced with a CW2 named Valentine. This chief was from the LSV attached to 24th ID in Hawaii, and he looked like it. He fired the fat platoon sergeant and proceeded to ram his highly polished jump boot up every lazy ass he could find, starting at the top of the platoon and working down. On day four of his tenure he called Junior Davis into the VSO at Third Port and put him at attention before his desk.

"Why the fuck are you in Maintenance Platoon?" he asked.

"No idea, Sir."

"New private like you should be out on the boats."

"If you say so, Sir."

"Don't you want to be on the boats, Davis?"

Junior shrugged. "Not sure, Sir."

"Not sure? What the fuck," Valentine said. "Why the hell are you here, then, soldier? Sailing is life. Life is sailing. Waterfuckingborne. You want to spend a four-year enlistment in a maintenance shed?"

Davis shrugged again. "Never really thought about it, Sir."

Valentine nodded. He shuffled some papers around on his desk, then said, "I inspected your barracks room this morning. You and that fat fuck you live with—Penguin."

Oh shit, Junior Davis thought.

"He's toast," Valentine said. "Well, he was already toast, but he's done for good now. Ate up. No waiting. You know why?"

Junior Davis shook his head no, but he knew. There'd been a collection of baggies under the bottom panel of Penguin's wall locker.

Valentine knew he knew, but didn't pursue it.

"There were a lot of books on top of your wall locker," he said instead. "Paperbacks. Those yours?"

Not knowing whether it was right or wrong, Junior Davis nodded yes.

"More books in your room than in the rest of the barracks combined," Valentine said. "You must be pretty smart. You think you're smart, Private Davis?"

Davis shrugged. Then nodded. Yes.

"Yeah, well fuck that. But I'll take your word for it. Those books are why you're here right now and not getting a piss test up at the company with your friend the Penguin."

Davis opened his mouth to speak but Valentine held up his hand.

"Shut up, Private. Don't say a fucking word."

"Sir, yes Sir."

"You look like shit, Davis," he said.

"Sir, yes Sir."

"You're stinking up my platoon and you look like shit. Do you know that?"

"Sir, yes Sir."

"You're stupid because you could be cakewalking this bitch. You could have your beer and your pussy and whatever else you been fucking around with up in the barracks and nobody would pay you the slightest attention if you'd just starch your fucking uniform." Valentine leaned back. "People been riding your ass, Davis?"

"Sir, yes Sir."

"I'll bet." He shook his head. "Stupid. You're stupid. This is the Army, Davis. It ain't rocket science. It's 50 percent showing up on time and 45 percent looking good when you get there." He shrugged. "If you look good, no one'll blink at you twice, Private."

"I hadn't thought about it that way, Sir."

"Well start thinking. And get your goddamn uniforms to the dry cleaners at the PX."

"I don't have a car, Sir."

Warrant officers are sergeants at heart. Sergeants who get saluted. You have to attain sergeant's rank before applying for warrant officer school, and even twenty-year warrants retain a sergeant's bearing. Valentine proved it now by looking at Davis as only a sergeant can, neck extended and locked, eyes wide, incredulous at the idiocy set before him.

"You don't have a car," he said quietly.

"Sir, no Sir."

"How far is it from the barracks to the PX, Private?"

"About a mile, Sir."

"About a mile."

"Sir, yes Sir."

Valentine looked down at his desk. "So do you think, Private Davis, that a motivated soldier like yourself, a highly trained and professional communist killer, could walk a mile, once maybe twice a week, in a trade-off for being able to drink your beer and read your fucking books and be left alone?"

"I think I could do that, Sir."

It was decision time, and Junior Davis made his decision. He was a quick study. Penguin was gone by the time he got back to his barracks room, as if he'd never been there, never to be seen again. Davis cleaned the room—sanitized it, Army style, on his hands and knees, with a sponge and buckets of hot water and bleach. He walked the mile to the PX that night with his green laundry bag over his shoulder and paid the Korean woman twenty dollars extra for instant service; he stepped into the Class 6 while he waited, his last few dollars for the month going to a case of Bud cans and few packs of generic smokes. An hour later he was walking the mile back to the barracks, beer and starched uniforms in hand. It was a Friday night, and he spent it polishing his combat boots and low quarters. Monday morning everything on him including his dog tags was shined to a high buff. His new squad leader and coxswain put him on the boats that afternoon, throwing line at dock bits until he could loop one without touching metal.

All this had been news to Tory back then. The Junior Davis she met when she was a private looked like he'd been in starch all his life. It was one of the reasons she latched onto him. He dressed and acted, actually, a lot like her new squad leader, a sergeant named Wagman, just in from Hawaii. They had the same bark, the same standards. It wasn't a surprise then when she learned Dick Wags was also a product of the Chief Valentine school of soldier reform, and although Dick Wags and Junior Davis were never really close, they had that between them and admired it in each other. The Valentine cult, Tory called it, the society of overachieving, hard-driving, massively alcoholic soldiers—but she said it with a smile. Once, over beers with Dick Wags in the backyard of Valentine himself, Junior said, "We're survivors of the Valentine prescription. But my New Jersey here is a Valentine self-medicator."

And that was true enough.

CHAPTER

20

Lorraine hung to the small metal sink in Davis's cabin latrine, staring in the silvered mirror secured to the bulkhead, wiping her eyes. The ship rolled and she rolled with it, her face moving in and out of view. She filled a plastic cup with stale ship's water from the tap and choked it down. Rubbing the back of her wrist across her mouth, she watched herself float in the mirror. Pastor's assumption wasn't entirely correct. Close, but not completely correct.

Lorraine had been up to the room twice today. First, just briefly, not even inside, this morning, she'd helped him back from the dining hall. Davis had been very quiet on the walk up—he was always quiet, the boy was like a stone—and at the door he'd said, "Thank you, Lorraine." When she stepped in behind him, he'd said it again, "Thank you, Lorraine," but stood there in the doorway, holding tight to his bleeding arm, like he didn't want her to come in. "Listen, I better get some rest," he'd said.

"You sure you're all right?"

"Right as rain, Lorraine," he said, and she giggled. She'd reached out and grabbed his hand then, squeezing it, but he was already half backing through his door and then the door was closed.

She'd had to work through the midday. Today was the galley, washing dishes. There were a bunch of girls in there today, all of them talking and passing the time, and Lorraine tried not to think about things too much. She showered after her shift. What with rationing they were only supposed to shower every three days, and short ones at that, but she snuck in anyway. None of her three roommates were back in the cabin, a nice change. It was hard to find any privacy on this ship. She powdered herself all over, luxuriating in a moment's aloneness and the infrequent state of nakedness. She dressed in clean shorts and her last clean T-shirt, a purple one they'd sent from church back home in Indiana, to let her know they were thinking of her out here on the high seas.

This was the first she'd worn the shirt. A terseness had crept into the last few letters she'd sent home, and recently she'd stopped writing altogether. When the T-shirt had arrived from the pastor's wife—in a package wrapped in brown paper bag, with a pound of stale brownies in foil—she'd shoved it in her drawer without a glance. Being out here was a mistake. Maybe this worked for some, this kind of life and service, but this was a mistake for her. She'd been out here three months and couldn't do it much longer. Her pastor at home had talked her into it, talked her into joining the ship mission, when she'd lost her boyfriend and her job. Her boyfriend—Frank—was a member of Lorraine's congregation; so was his wife. He was also Lorraine's boss, branch manager of the bank she'd been a teller at since graduating high school. It was complicated.

A few weeks after he'd been transferred to Lorraine's branch Frank started staying late, to help her close, even though it wasn't his job to do that; he was allowed to go at five. He'd stand very close as they counted bills and closed-out drawers. He smelled good, she thought, with a thick chest and clean-shaven face. He never tried to take her out and ply her with drinks. It just was what it was, no pretending to be anything else. The first time had been on the old couch in the break room, with the burnt-coffee smell and the yellow refrigerator. She thought it was kind of cute when she realized he'd had it planned, fretted over, mapped out: "Lorraine, maybe if you don't have to rush right out the door tonight . . ." It was cute. She put him out of his misery by kissing him, somewhat taken aback then at how ravenous he became. Like a switch thrown. Hands shaking, kneeling on the couch between her parted legs, he'd been so nervous he didn't even get the condom rolled on all the way. But she'd put her arms around him, held him, not letting him feel bad, and they'd tried again with slightly better success.

Frank got bolder as time went by. They never took it out of the bank, and never, ever during business hours, but they seldom went back to the break room again after closing. This was fine with Lorraine; the old couch was itchy, and she had to eat her lunch in there. It was hard talking to the girls with the thoughts of that stuff just steps away from their table. Besides, she thought he looked stronger, more like himself, standing, holding her upright in a corner of his office. A few times he made her stand at the closed drive-through window and pretend to be with a customer—*Good evening, Mister Montgomery! Do you want that all in twenties?*—while he knelt before her under the counter. Once he wanted to be the banker at the window, and she knelt under the counter, his ultraclean smell filling her mouth. He had a smooth, pale penis that tasted like detergent. They had sex in the bank every day after closing, five days a week, for three months. There were only two breaks; once he took two days off to have a wart removed from the side of his foot, and once he took a week's vacation with his wife and two daughters to Disney in Florida. Lorraine had never really been completely comfortable with things—his office, for instance, was covered with family photos— but while he was in Florida was the worst. In the bank she could pretend a different reality, that it was just the two of them, but a man doesn't go to Disney alone and the weight of his kids became too much for her to bear, the thought of seeing his wife in her trim, fancy pink stuff on Sunday mornings at church too much. She told it all to her pastor, the whole story spilling out through tears after Thursday-night Young Women's Bible Study. The pastor came by the bank on Friday morning with a leaflet for the missionary ship. She was young, she was directionless, she needed a change. That's what he said. When Frank came back to work on Monday—his pale skin reddened from the Orlando sun, neck peeling—Lorraine resigned with a simple explanation: "We can't anymore, Frank. It's not right." She went through the door promptly at five, leaving him to close alone. He came by her apartment that night. He'd never been there, and she'd never seen him in anything but a suit; he looked funny to her in chinos and a green polo. "How am I going to make it without you?" he pleaded, standing in the doorway, trying to push his way in. "You can't come in, Frank," she said. "It would be a mistake. It's all been a mistake." She was trying to close the door but he was persistent. Finally she took her keys and walked him out to his silver Buick. She wouldn't get in, but she let him kiss her, standing by the trunk in the dark parking lot, his whole body so desperate. She pulled his rock-hard detergent-fresh dick out and with a couple quick strokes finished him off, poor Frank apologizing for the mess and then crying.

It wasn't until later, alone in her apartment with the TV on, that she thought his sobbed sorrys might be for the whole mess, the whole thing, not just the stickiness that hit her shirt tonight. And then she felt even worse and did some crying of her own because Frank wasn't a bad man, any more than she was a bad woman, it's just how it was and they were weak, she thought, like most people they were weak, and like her pastor said at this point in her life she needed some time to cool off and get straight with God and with herself.

"And what a fantastic opportunity!" the pastor had said, those massive teeth of his framing the laugh. "Floating in the Caribbean sun! Wish I could go along."

There'd been no answer to her knock. She'd thought about it a moment, then turned the knob and eased the door open. The cabin was almost completely dark, her eyes still narrowed from the afternoon sun. She heard him before she saw him; "Is dat you, Santee Claus?"

Lorraine giggled. No one else on this ship would have said something like that.

Davis was on his back in bed, sheet up around his chest, leaning against a pillow. She could smell the alcohol immediately, a heavy fume thick in the air. There was another smell, too, under the alcohol. She couldn't tell what it was. He saw her eye go to the bottle sticking out from the top drawer of the night table next to him. "Care for a drink?" he said, and patted his hand on the mattress next to him.

She took a step toward him, next to the bed, then said, "I'd better not. They could send me home."

"Would that be so bad?" he said.

She giggled again. "No."

He pulled the bottle up and put it to his lips, taking a swig.

"What is it?"

"Rum."

He patted the mattress again, and this time she sat down. "Maybe one sip," she said. He wiped the top of the bottle with the edge of the sheet and handed it to her. She took a big swallow and grimaced, eyes going wide. She held it, then swallowed hard. "Strong!"

"Lorraine, Lorraine," he said.

She took another swig and handed off the bottle, lying back flat on the bed, across his legs.

"Oh this boat." she said. She closed her eyes then opened them, focusing on the ceiling. "I don't know. I'm trying hard, I really am. But . . ." Her right hand had come to rest on the sheet over his stomach. She gripped the sheet in her fist, pulling it in a ball, then smoothed it out. Davis took a drink from the bottle, then said, "Don't let it get you down, Lorraine."

She turned her head to look up at him, and smiled. Her fingers were moving in circles now on the sheet over his belly. "You're a sly one, Mister Chief Engineer," she said, then swung her legs onto the bed and crawled up on him, chest to chest, nose to nose. "Hey there," she said, and he laughed.

"I'm gonna spill the bottle."

"Roll over, you."

"This is not Godly, Lorraine."

"I'm just tending to the sick."

He chuckled, reaching to set the bottle back in the open drawer, Lorraine pushing up off him a bit so he could roll over.

"I don't know what you're going to do back there," he said. "I'll have you know, I'm a virtuous man."

She smacked his shoulder, laughing. "You're bad."

She pulled the sheet to his waist. He was leaner even than she'd imagined, her fingers moving over muscle and bone and a series of long, pencil-thin scars on his sides.

"What's this?" she asked, tracing the raised scar.

"That's life, Lorraine," he said.

She pushed her finger down to a lower scar, the smoothness gone from his skin. It felt like a scab. She pushed harder and he flinched. Although Pastor had never said anything to the missionaries, everyone on the boat knew Junior Davis had been arrested, and that he was the reason they'd been delayed in Jacmel.

"Did they do this to you in that place?" she said. Davis didn't answer.

Lorraine massaged from his neck to his lower back then up again, listening to his silence in the cramped cabin, the slow creaking sway of the ship. She rolled him over again, lowering her face down, pressing her lips against his. His mouth yielded just the slightest bit, a rough softness, face cold and eyes opening. Davis put the open palm of each hand on the sides of her face, holding her in place, then pushing her head up a few inches. They looked at each other but he didn't talk, this guy never seemed to talk, but it didn't make her nervous now like it had before. He put his hands down on the bed and sat up.

She'd been thinking he was naked under the sheet, but he pulled it back to reveal a pair of gray Army shorts. No mistaking what was underneath, though, and as he pushed himself up he did nothing to hide it; an unself-consciousness she'd never seen before.

She lay down flat on her belly, arms up around her head, burrowing into his pillow. It smelled of him, smelled of maleness. She snuggled her face deeper into the fabric. Behind her, Junior Davis crawled up on her, pushed up tight between her legs, tight against her. He sat there a minute, left hand braced against her lower back, reached for the bottle and took a healthy swig. Done, he leaned forward, until his face was in her hair. "You know," he whispered, "this will work out much better for you without a shirt."

"You're bad," she said, softly, then reached down and lifted her purple church T-shirt up and over her head, unsnapping her bra and pulling it free. Davis had his hands around her waist as she did it, sitting upright, keeping himself pressed hard into her clothed ass. Her arms around her head, she pushed herself back against him.

He was thorough. No piece of skin on her back and neck untouched. He would pause every few minutes, one hand in place on her body, the other reaching for the bottle. She had her head facing to the right of the bed, and even in the dim light could see the bottle level decreasing rapidly. He finally finished the bottle, reaching way low to a drawer under the bed, producing another. She'd never seen anyone consume so much alcohol in a short period of time. And he'd been up here all day, as far as she knew; she wondered how much he'd drunk beforehand.

It didn't seem to affect his hands. He molded his calloused fingers into her, pressing, pushing, hard then soft then hard. His hands slipped down onto the fabric of her shorts, squeezing, drawing lines, then finally reaching around her thin waist to pop the button, fingers grasping the tops of the shorts and panties together and easing them down and then off. He reached up to press on her back as she tried to roll, tried to sit up. Lorraine put her head back down and his fingertips went to her inner thighs, tracing and circling, brushing lightly past and against her. She moaned, and he paused, to take a drink, then pushed her legs farther apart. She thought she knew what he'd do next and she pressed her chest into the mattress, lifting her bottom a little. But it was his fingers that went down, circling again then moving across her soft center, zeroing and picking up speed. She lifted higher, letting his fingers in, her breathing shallow now and quick, eyes closed tight.

If she could have seen him, she might not have relaxed. If she could have seen his face, she might have run from the cabin.

Late, late on a Sunday night, lights off, Tory's breathing soft in her chilly barracks room. Maybe she's sleeping and maybe she's not. Jeans down and T-shirt off then under the covers with her. He'd rather be on the couch, even better his own room, but he's been gone all weekend and there are already going to be angry questions—there'll be so many more if she wakes up and he's not in bed. It's better, he's found, easier, to explain away missing time if he wakes up next to her.

He's tired, so tired, a tired he didn't even know you could have. This is different from an Army tired, a workout tired. This is something altogether strange; a chemical imbalance in his muscles, and in his brain. So tired.

Tory's back is to him, shirt off, in just a pair of his boxers. He tries not to move. His head is spinning, whipping, but he tries not to move, not to breathe, not to wake her. He's so tired.

Her hand reaches back, fingers finding him, moving across his side and stomach.

He holds his breath.

"Junior," she says.

He can't answer any questions, can't do it. So tired.

"Junior."

He can't answer. He pushes her hand from his belly down to his crotch. He wasn't hard—furthest from it—but it's a good soldier. He pushes against her, hands going around her, sliding up to her breasts. Tory has perfect breasts, he thinks, a perfect handful, firm. Not like the loose flesh he'd found his lips on earlier this evening.

"Junior."

No questions, he can't. He's got both arms around her, and it's about survival now, he's in survival mode.

He nuzzles her neck, biting, his teeth grazing rough then lips to her ear. "Fuck me," he whispers.

"Junior—"

"Fuck me," insistent now. He pulls her tight, pressing hard against her bottom.

She wrenches away and rolls over, pushing him on his back, crawling onto him. Her face goes down in his, and even in the dark he can see her nose wrinkling, nostrils flaring.

Oh sweetie that ain't gonna work, he thinks. *You can't smell what I been doing.*

He circles his big open palms around her ribs, pulling her down, kissing her. She pulls her head up, though, and grabs a handful of his short, brown hair.

"Where have you been, Junior?"

He's pushed himself under the fabric of the old floppy boxers she's wearing, and he's pushing, pushing, insistent.

"Junior—" she says, but he thrusts then, hard, holding her waist in place, tight, forcing up inside her. She yells—screams almost—and punches his chest, slamming her closed fist down on his sternum, and then she hits him again, but he's thrust twice now, three times, four, spreading the wet, and her head goes down and she lays her palms flat on his chest, lifting herself and then dropping, and now she's fucking him, like he wanted, head down and growling she's fucking him and she's crying. "I love you," she says, panting, thrusting, and she says it again and then she smacks him, open palm, across the face. She loves him, loves all of him, and she wants to kill him, hurt him, make him feel it, feel it like she feels it. She's slamming down on him, determined to fuck him harder than he's ever been fucked, wanting to break him, break his cock, crying and moaning, and she makes a fist and punches him in the chest, then again, and when she hits him the third time he comes, deep inside her, yelling out loud.

Fingers in Lorraine, thrusting and circling, she's silent and silent and silent then tenses then gasps, a quick audible breath and long moan, her body going rigid around his hand, contracting. He holds her there, on his knees behind her as she comes in waves, and—purely clinical now, on the job—thinks about wetting a free finger and jamming it quick up her smaller, tighter hole, wonders about her reaction, but then it's too late, she's done, he can feel it—her body collapsing into the mattress.

He's done, too. This took too long, he's exhausted, lost interest, drunk and bored and sick and just wants to sleep. *Now I can, though,* he thinks, *now I can sleep. Just a few minutes.*

But Lorraine's button just got pushed. She turns, mouth all over him, cheeks and chin and forehead, trying to find his mouth as he ducks and moves.

"You liked that?" he says, low and laughing, but he's somewhat disgusted, trying to keep his mouth away, her tongue going everywhere.

Her hands are on him now, pushing under his shorts, finding him limp, shrunk. She laughs. "We'll fix that."

Davis cringes, pulls back, but she's got her hands yanking down his shorts.

"Lorraine," he says, trying to push her away. "It's okay. I'm fine, tired."

"I'll fix it," she says, panting.

"It's okay, I don't feel great, really."

And now her mouth is on him, taking all of him in her mouth, not seeing, not seeing the look on his face, and as his skin enters her mouth he grabs her hair and pulls her off, a yell from his throat, "No!" and he's off the bed and in the latrine, door slammed closed behind him.

He's in the latrine five minutes. When he comes out he's in sweat pants and a black T-shirt. He thought she'd be gone, but she's not. Lorraine is curled up on the bed, face buried in her arms. He sits next to her, touching her arm, and she shrugs his hand off.

"I'm sorry," he says. "It's not you."

"I don't understand," he hears, her voice from deep in the sheets.

Davis lies down, stretching out. *This won't take long,* he thinks. *It won't be long now.*

Junior closes his eyes. A minute goes by. "I don't understand," her voice again. He'd forgotten she was here. "I thought . . ." and her voice trails off.

"I'm sick," he says, not sure who he's talking to. "I'm pretty sick. There's rules." *Christ,* he thinks, *how much did I drink?* then remembers the pills, the handful of good ones he just swallowed.

How many did I take?

You took 'em all.

Yeah?

Yeah.

That's probably not safe.

Nope.

Well, I was saving them.

Yeah.

Junior Davis hears a voice again, sort of floaty, ". . . I just thought . . ." There's a hand on his back, moving in circles, kind of nice. He likes that, pushes into it.

"Oh, I like that," he says, not sure if he did or not.

Who's back there?

New Jersey, I think.

Yeah? I dunno. I thought she was mad.

I think it's New Jersey.

All right.

A hand on his chin, rough, yanking his head. He opens his eyes.

You're not New Jersey.

". . . drank too much. Oh, honey, you did."

She's probably right. He doesn't feel well. Maybe he did drink too much. She doesn't look unsympathetic, though, whoever she is. Doesn't look mad. Maybe she drank some, too.

She's smacking his cheek now, and he has to open his eyes again.

Hey, cut that out.

She's not looking at him now, she's looking across the room, shaking her head. She looks sad.

What's wrong with her?

She's bummin'. Doesn't like the Jesus freaks anymore.

Oh.

". . . use your shower, Sweetie."

Where'd she go?

Who?

That chick.

Which one.

You know. Skinny chick with the fat pussy. Chick with the smack.

Huh. Dunno.

He opened his eyes or thought he did but he wasn't sure so closed them again. He rolled over, pretty sure he did that. The air was warmer, down here in the blanket. Thick in his lungs, thick.

Junior.

What?

Junior, where have you been?

I, uh—

All the time. You're gone all the time now.

Was with Scaboo. Went drinking with fucking Scaboo.

He hasn't seen you.

Yeah?

Wasn't any use lying about it. They all knew now. She knew.

Downtown, Jersey. Took a few trips down range.

What do you mean? What—

There's that hand! Shaking his chin again. The fuck . . .

Who ARE YOU?

"Honey, these yours? Did you take these? All these?" Rattling something, in his face.

Damn.

Yeah, that's mine.

In his face. Crying, why's she crying? It's all good, really, not like—

Hold on, hold on.

Slap her, slap her, man! She'll come back.

I can't—

Slap her, man! She's going out, fuck, she's—

Gimme that, hold it here, right here man hold it here steady yeah tie it off

Too much, too much, she went over

No, more more

can't be here I can't be here can't be found here they'll put me out

His face slapped, hard.

"No!"

Junior? That's your name? C'mere. Don't worry about that.

Yeah, no, we—look, I can't be here, I tried but she's gone out there and I can't—

No, c'mere, lay down baby

Hands, those hands, long fingers, those rough hands everywhere. Hands better than, well, better than anything better than all of it, chemical, mineral, animal, melts in your mouth not in your hands

damn, Junior, you ARE a soldier, aren't you? Isn't that the strongest one ever. Damn that's sweet. Junior.

Who's

I'm

Yeah

yeah, now, c'mere—oh

you kids want—?

yeah, yeah

tie it, tie it off

put your finger there

there

yeah

CHAPTER

21

It was easy enough to avoid him; Tory knew the ship, Marc did not.

She fled her cabin. The door lock was no protection. He might knock. She was sure he would. If he knocked, she'd answer. She was sure of that, too. And sure in those two things, if nothing else, she fled. Grabbed a uniform and bolted, completely off the portside cabin level. Up and over, through the silent, rolling house of the ship, dropping stairs two at a time to the starboard crew's quarters, Tory trying to remember watch schedules, who might reasonably be awake in the middle of the night. She went to the last cabin forward, knocked. Temple was on watch, the door swung open to T.K., kicked back in the desk chair, writing a letter.

"What's shakin'?" he said, slow. He looked stoned.

"You stoned?" she asked.

"No such luck," he said. "Just tired. How about you, New Jersey?"

"Marijuana and other intoxicants are illegal." She stepped in, closed the door behind.

"Indeed they are, Sergeant Harris. Indeed."

"I gotta change," she said, holding up the uniform and boots she was cradling in her arms.

"Your cabin slipped into the sea, I presume?"

"Something like that."

He smiled, then put his feet to the floor, turning the chair so his back was to her. "Change away," he said, and leaned over his letter.

Tory dug her cigarettes from the boot she'd shoved them in, lit one, took a few puffs, then set it in T.K.'s ashtray on the desk. She stripped to her underwear, slipped her dog tags over her head, pulled a brown T-shirt and her BDUs on, smoked a few more puffs, then sat on the edge of T.K.'s bunk to pull her boots onto her feet. Tied and tight, she stood.

"Thanks, Lenny," she said, patting his shoulder. She called him Lenny. Neither of them could remember why. "I'll be back for this later," she said, placing her flip-flops and folded sweats on his desk.

"You're gonna give me a reputation," he called after her, eyeing the sports bra on top of the pile, and was back at his letter before the cabin door swung shut.

Tory took the outside stairs to the bridge. She found Xerox sleeping hard on the cot he'd lashed to the cabinet and bulkhead in the darkened radio room. She set the alarm on her wristwatch, closed the radio room door, and curled up in a corner on the deck beside him, wedged tight against the rolling sea. She slept four hours, the longest stretch of sleep she'd had since arriving in Haiti.

The ship pitched hard all night. Not the worst this crew had sailed, but deep and painful rolls. Private Cain made sandwiches for mid-rats but the crew's mess stood empty. No one could eat, just coffee and cigarettes. It was always worse at night—you couldn't go on deck and find the horizon, fixing your brain. The crew dug in the way they knew how, at work on watch or trying to find somewhere low and flat and sleeping through it.

Skipper sent a soldier to the well-deck every thirty minutes, checking the Haitian drivers. They'd all been sick but were sleeping now, mostly, or quiet and uncomplaining anyway, curled in the cabs of their trucks, the vehicles soaking wet and salt-sticky from the constant sea spray. Cain put on his poncho and brought down a big box of sandwiches and apples shortly after midnight. The Haitians climbed from their trucks, groggy, shivering in the cold of the storm and carefully gripping the sides of the trucks as they worked their way aft on the deck. They divided up the food and stowed it away in pockets and bags for later. "That's good stuff, made it myself," Cain yelled over the wind in the black wet of the well-deck as he passed out the grub. He smiled and shook hands with the men then managed to make it to an aft scupper before throwing up the bacon sandwich he'd forced himself to eat. Feeling somewhat better he slipped and struggled back across deck to the house, then returned up to his galley where he vomited again and every twenty minutes for the rest of his watch.

The weather cleared with sunrise, seas calming, clouds thinning then vanished by full light. The birds found them, terns and gulls following and circling, diving into the wake. On bridge watch at dawn Tory watched the last of it, ship's blunt nose diving, long pause, slap, and a torrent of wave crashing as far up as the top of the massive ramp, sixty feet high, spraying all the way back over the well-deck and sprinkling the bridge windows. It was spectacular, a thing you never got used to, grew jaded with, could ignore. Crushing fists of water, relentless, making you very small and very aware. Very awake. Very alive.

Tory gripped the rail at the bridge windows, holding on, watching the sea, bridge crew with her, the quiet hum of radios and radar. The morning was not so much light breaking as darkness receding, blackness fading to pale gray, white foam washing over the bow. Tory with her feet flat on the deck, riding it.

After watch she felt charged, moving quickly down below, skipping breakfast. Dick Wags would be going on watch soon. They put on sweats and went forward to the bow-thruster room, lifting weights. They didn't talk as they worked out, and she tried to gauge his mood. Then decided she didn't care. Coming up on deck after, the early morning air was salty and thick, a weighty humid, but clear in smell, good pulled up in the lungs. She felt powerful, sweat running and muscles tight. They hadn't worked out in more than a week, since leaving Virginia. She felt new this morning. She stretched her back muscles and felt powerful.

Back in the cabin, Dick Wags grabbed a towel and his leather shaving bag and went to the shower. Tory clipped the cabin door open, stretched some more, then stepped into the passage, dropping for push-ups. She breathed through her mouth, back straight and head up, forcing out a set. Done, she let herself collapse, then rolled over, knees up and arms crossed for a set of sit-ups. Her belly burned and she closed her eyes, pushing through it. Done, she rolled over for push-ups again, face to face with Marc Hall, in the push-up position on the deck in front of her.

"Good morning," he said, smiling.

She tensed every muscle to stop herself from jumping in surprise. Then she smiled back. "Is the captain looking to lead PT?"

Hall bounced on his palms. "The captain was taught that sergeants are the guardians of fitness. I place this Army property into your care."

Oh, fuck you, she thought. "We'll just count silently."

Tory nodded once, and they began, together, four inches between their faces, arms flexing with the push-ups. Well into her workout already, Tory sweat freely, dripping from face and chest to the deck. She watched his shaved skull, glistening. They didn't blink, and when she realized neither of them had blinked she laughed, collapsing on the deck, twenty-some push-ups into it. He stopped, too, lowering himself slowly to rest on the deck. He said, "The sergeant is too easily distracted."

"The captain is too easily amused."

They both rolled over, a set of sit-ups, and these she counted off, quietly. *One, two, three, one—one, two, three, two—one, two, three, three.* Sliding on the smooth deck with their sit-ups, they banged heads, laughing again, both resting. Staring at the ceiling, he reached back with his right hand and found her short hair, moist with sweat and very soft, and then she stopped laughing, quiet, and his palm found her forehead, and her cheek. Tory lay very still, as if by not moving all would cease to move. She could see his hand, his skin, from the corner of her eye. She raised her own hand then, to place her hand on the back of his, bringing her arm up as the latrine door opened loud right behind them, Marc Hall sitting up quickly, grabbing his knees and pulling himself up.

Dick Wags stepped out, shower done.

"Careful of PT with Sergeant Harris, Sir," he said. "She'll smoke you like a cheap cigar."

Marc grabbed the rail over his head and pulled himself straight up, standing. He nodded at the other man. "I'll bet." Dick Wags stood there a moment, fresh cigarette tight between his lips, towel around his waist. His skin was red, water-beaded. He had a snake and dagger from the old Jungle Warfare School in Panama tattooed on his left arm, a sunset and palm tree on his right, and DICK in fancy swirled letters on his chest. "That's a bold statement," Hall said, pointing at the chest tattoo.

"It's not a statement," Tory said, still prone on the deck. "It's a definition."

Hall laughed and Dick Wags said, "I just like everyone to know where I stand." He winked, then backed into the cabin. "Excuse me, Sir," he said, "I go on watch in ten minutes." He closed the door behind him.

They were alone in the tight passage. Marc Hall reached his hand down to Tory. She gripped it and he pulled her up, face to face. Her eyes moved over him, thoughts moving, spinning. She wanted to devour him.

You breathe in, you breathe out, youbreatheinyoubreathe—

"This can't—" she finally said, but he'd already started talking.

"I have to go down to the deck, to see how my drivers are," he said. "They had a rough night of it. Would you like to meet them?"

His voice had the slightest sing-song quality to it, which she never would have placed forty-eight hours before but now knew was distinctly Haitian. Not an accent; his accent was pure New York. It was a lilt in the way he spoke. "Would you like to meet them?" carried with it, "Of course you would"; not an arrogant assumption, but an assumed delight—aren't we all delighted? She watched his eyes. He still wasn't blinking. *Maybe he doesn't blink.*

"Yes," she said. "I'd like to meet them."

Tory held his gaze, then looked down. His eyes followed. She was looking at their hands. Marc still had his hand wrapped around hers, from pulling her up. They looked back up at each other, then he let her fingers go.

"I'll just be a minute," he said, grabbing his shaving kit from where he'd dropped it on the deck, and disappeared into the latrine, leaving

Tory alone in the passageway. She wiped a hand across her face, gripped the rail that ran the length of the passage, then lightly tapped her forehead against the bulkhead a few times. She dropped and started knocking out push-ups again.

Tory had dropped for her first Army push-up during basic training at Fort Leonard Wood in Missouri. The main exercise of punishment and torture there, though, had been the leg-lift, not the push-up. It was a sex-segregated training company—most were then—and the women's standard for the push-up was much lower than for men. Almost non-existent, really. Most of Tory's platoon couldn't do a handful of real Army push-ups, so getting dropped for them was mostly pointless. The four platoon drill sergeants—starched and looming, three of them men—had the platoon do "girl push-ups," knees on the ground. Since those weren't particularly tough, when pain was required the drills would drop them for leg-lifts—flat on your back, heels held four inches up. Then the drill would call the cadence and the trainees would alternate scissoring their legs then spreading them back and forth. There was a drill sergeant named Hoya and when he had the platoon alone they all knew he was looking up their shorts during the leg-lifts. Army PT shorts were loose, and they did a lot of leg-lifts for Drill Sergeant Hoya. They all knew it but there was nothing they could do. Tory's bunkmate—battle buddy, they were supposed to call them— was a small, hard girl from Oakland, California, named Martins. She'd glance up from their leg-lifts, muttering so only Tory could hear, "I swear the pig's holding his crotch up there. Sick fuck." A quiet girl named Smith from first squad stopped wearing anything under her shorts. In a platoon of thirty, living close together like they did, everyone knew everything, especially a personal detail like that—Smith's bunkmate saw her leaving an item out while getting dressed, same thing next day, then the bunkmate whispered it to someone in the chow line. Then everyone knew.

"That girl's a dim bulb," Martins said. "She's gonna get it."

Tory couldn't tell if the statement was a threat or sympathetic, and didn't really care. The upside of dim, pale, mousy Smith spreading her legs was Hoya didn't pay much attention to the rest of the platoon during leg-lifts anymore. Allowing leeway for sham.

"Sham-a-lam-a-ding-dong," Martins would whisper, one leg raised, one resting comfortably on the ground, Hoya yelling out cadence but eyes burning a hole between Smith's legs.

"I don't know what he's looking at, anyway," Martins clucked. "You seen that girl in the shower?"

Tory shook her head no, blowing fast, painful breaths through her lips. She was one of only three or four in the platoon still doing the exercise for real.

Martins, staring up at the sky, switched legs in her sham leg-lifts and made a sound Tory had gotten to know well these past few weeks, a grunting sigh Martins used to express wonderment, amusement, or disgust with the Caucasian race—Tory included. "Girl needs a weedwhacker, Tory," she said. "I don't know how that pig Hoya can see the forest for the trees down there."

Evidently he saw enough. Within a few days of Smith deciding to fall out for PT sans undergarments, she stopped falling out for PT altogether. "Drill Sergeant Hoya wants me to take some paperwork to battalion," she mumbled to her battle buddy, head down, then slipped down the back stairs from the second floor of the barracks. "Ain't that some shit," Martins said, shivering out on the parade field. The other trainees stopped talking to Smith, even her own battle buddy, but it didn't mean much in an atmosphere where no one was supposed to talk to anyone else anyway, for any reason, at any time.

Tory Harris paid little attention to Drill Sergeant Hoya, except to stay out of his way. She'd only had to deal with him personally once, called to the desk one night to give a progress report on a cleaning detail, standing at attention while his eyes crawled over her chest. She'd stood through it, about-faced, and tried not to think about it after. The other two male drill sergeants never betrayed their drill mask, never let an emotion through—other than anger or disgust, both professional and acceptable for a drill sergeant. If their minds went the way of Hoya's, you'd never know it.

The drill who mattered, the only drill who mattered to Tory, was

Drill Sergeant Chase—"My first name is Drill, my middle name is Sergeant, my last name is Chase. You will address me, at all times, with my full, God-given, Pentagon-approved, Army-issue name."

The woman was short, five feet if she was lucky. There were trainee privates in the platoon who towered over her. Tory was a few inches taller. She never realized it, though, until after graduation, when her platoon picture arrived in the mail. She was in the first row, standing at attention directly next to Chase, and clearly taller. If you'd have asked, though, she would never have guessed. She would have bet money the woman was taller, taller than all of them. That's how she carried herself, that's how she got in your face.

Tory Harris had never seen anything like her. Chase's skin was dark, darker than Martins's, hair as tight and close as it could get, a round, shaved cut. She looked, Tory thought, like a warrior. Not how the Army liked to throw around the word, but for real. A dangerous African warrior. Someone who could maybe kill her own dinner and eat it raw. She was small, but strength in miniature; round jaw, a long and muscled neck, large hands outsized for her body with fingers that shot out, pointing, signaling attention, jabbing painfully into folds of sloppy uniforms or loose, undisciplined flesh.

"Hey there, female," she'd yell, those fingers grabbing and pulling at an untucked T-shirt on a sweaty, panting trainee in PT formation. "Your exhaustion does not justify disgracing my Army. Tuck it in or take it off."

"I believe that woman could kick all their asses," Martins whispered once when all four drills stood together in a line before formation. Tory thought, more precisely, Chase looked like a woman who would die trying. You rose to her standard or fell to her wrath. She suffered neither fools, malingerers, nor individualists—all of them crimes against her and her Army.

She'd exploded all over Tory late on the first day of basic training, the first and last time she approached Chase. "Drill Sergeant, may I—" the rest of the question drowned in Chase's fury: "I? *I*? Did you say I? There is NO goddamn *I* in my Army!" Her nose almost touching Tory's eye, hissing in her ear: "Are you a dirty individualist, Private Harris?"

The word rolled from her tongue like a Slinkee down the stairs, syllables popping, *in-di-vid-u-al-ist* dripping with a poison Tory identified with *communist* or *child molester.* It required a whole new way of thinking, a whole new way of looking at the world.

The first few days of basic training, Drill Sergeant Hoya or Drill Sergeant Roland had led PT. They'd taught the standards for the official Army female push-up—knees on the ground—and that's what got done. Not so much because no woman could do a man's push-up—many of them could—but because uniformity reigned supreme in the Army. The first morning Drill Sergeant Chase took the platoon out they all did push-ups as taught, but Tory happened to glance up from the cold, wet grass to see Chase doing real push-ups. She hadn't called for it, and didn't expect it from her trainees—couldn't, actually. Uniformity. But she was doing it, doing it for real. When they stood back to attention Tory really looked at her for the first time, at this little soldier with the square shoulders.

"That's a bad, bad woman," Martins said.

"Yeah," Tory whispered. "Yes she is."

Tory began doing real push-ups, too. It wasn't easy. Nothing in basic training is easy, but this was brutal. Her arms, after all, were getting worked out in other ways. This was a harder exercise, and on top of everything else they were doing. First time she could only do five before collapsing to her knees, barely able to keep up then with the girl push-ups. So she began doing them at night, in sets of five.

"You're sick," Martins told her, then sighed and dropped from her bunk to knock them out best she could with her battle buddy.

Tory tried her best to keep an eye on Chase during PT, watching what she would do, watching her form. She was a machine; oiled, calibrated, muscle movements precise and perfect.

Alone with a mop in the latrine one night during week four, Tory paused in front of the mirror. She still surprised herself in mirrors, not used to no hair. Blond stubble, the only female trainee who'd shaved down her head. She looked over her face, raised her chin. She pushed up the sleeve of her T-shirt, curled her arm to make a muscle. Felt it with her other hand, then tensed and made it harder. Then jumped,

as Chase's long, black fingers curled around her bicep, the drill
sergeant's face appearing next to her own in the mirror.

"Don't think for a minute I don't see everything," she whispered,
squeezing. "Them push-ups of yours are paying off, Private Harris."
Then she was gone.

It was only the second time Chase spoke to her directly, and there
was only one other occasion in the entire eight weeks. It was week
eight, two days before graduation, the platoon working all night in the
barracks bay cleaning and buffing. Some of the privates had asked Drill
Sergeant Chase about a ritual they'd heard of, the drill sergeant deciding who among them would be the future drill sergeant.

"Yeah, I know your game, I know who it is," she said. A girl named
Guerrin looked up, nodding her head. She was platoon leader, ranked
highest in all things physical and mental. She'd been a sprinter in high
school, and shot a perfect score on the M-16 range, the only one in
the platoon. But Chase didn't look at her. Nor did she name any of the
girls in the top three. She named the private ranked fourth in the platoon of forty.

"Six, seven years from now, Harris, you gonna make some trainee's
life miserable," Chase said, smiling so her teeth showed. Tory, polishing boots on the other side of the bay, heard her name. "What?" she
said, but Chase had already turned, bending to inspect the brass on a
private's uniform. Tory meant to talk to her the next day, their last day
as trainees, the only day you could reasonably do something like that—
ask a drill sergeant a civil question. But it didn't go like that. That night
Drill Sergeant Hoya and Private Smith were caught, CID busting them
in action in an unused barracks office. Chase woke the platoon at
0300, standing the trainees into formation in the frigid night. No one
ever saw Hoya; the MPs whisked him out the building quick. Tory
caught a glimpse of Smith, head down in jeans and a baggy, purple
sweater. She wasn't in handcuffs—as they heard Hoya had been—and
was put in a white van, not an MP car. The MPs finally left, the battalion commander and sergeant-major finally left, the company commander and first sergeant. When they were all gone, Drill Sergeant
Chase emerged from the building, standing on the stairs a moment in

the orange of the street light affixed to the side of the barracks, then walking down slow to the hardstand and facing her platoon, breath from her mouth in frozen puffs. Tory remembered a strange thought, one that came back to her occasionally over the years, in other situations: *No one left,* she thought. *Just me and the Army.* It was terrifying.

"Y'all disgust me," Chase said.

If any of them had thought about what might happen next, it wasn't this. She smoked them, absolutely smoked them. They used muscles in their body they didn't know they had, on their backs and on their knees and over and over and around the building and back through the 4:00 A.M. mud and "God be my witness, we're gonna keep running and pushing right through until this time tomorrow," Chase yelled at one point.

She didn't, though. She stopped them as the sky lightened in the east, pale thin-cigar clouds pulling over the parade ground, the dawn of their graduation day. She put them at attention, girls bouncing off one another in exhaustion and confusion, a few weeping. Chase stood silent a moment, her previously perfect, starched BDUs filthy with the same mud smeared over her platoon, sweat running from her face, steam rising from her damp head.

"How could you do it?" she asked them. "Is there a one of you, even one, who didn't know what was going on?"

No one answered. Chase spit on the ground.

"That stupid girl," she said, and her chin went up, tensed. "But I'll tell you now, ain't one among you this morning who's not stupider, and weaker, than that poor girl. She was only one human being. You had the strength of twenty-nine." Chase was stalking the front of the platoon now, pacing, as out of breath as they were. She never, not once in eight weeks, ordered them to do something she didn't do herself. Even the punishments. "Let me tell you something, Privates," she said finally, louder now, her usual bark restored. "Friendly fire don't just happen in war."

Chase left them there, at attention, shivering and filthy, slamming the barracks door behind her. When she emerged again—an hour later—she was clean, showered, in a fresh uniform.

"Platoon, right *face!*" she called. "Forward, *march!*" And off to chow.

Marc Hall was clean-shaven when he emerged from the latrine, gray PT jacket pulled on, wiping his neck and face with a brown Army towel, running it over his smooth skull. Tory was still on the deck, pumping out push-ups.

"At ease, Sergeant," he whispered. She looked at him but wasn't smiling.

"I'm almost done," she said, and made him wait while she did ten more.

Junior Davis was so manic himself in soldiering he didn't think much of Tory's drive, or if he did never said anything. Not at first, not in their first year together. They weren't in the same company, they never ran together on weekends (even though they both almost always ran at least once over a weekend). Junior encouraged her to stand for the promotion boards and do it early, but he didn't coach her; that was all Dick Wags inspecting her uniform and quizzing her—*What's the muzzle velocity of the M-16 rifle? Recite the creed of the noncommissioned officer. How many techniques for sighting a compass are there and what are they called?*

Junior Davis took unabashed pride in having an ass-kick of a girlfriend but distanced himself from the process. It wasn't until late, very late for them, that he seemed to watch her, watch what she was about beyond him.

The first they ever ran together was after a very bad time. So bad as to be almost beyond repair. For months he'd been building to it, disappearing, gone a day then days at a time, gone from her and also gone actual AWOL once although he talked his way out of it. And then he talked his way back into her truck and back into her room and she shouldn't have been surprised because she loved him—there it was, she did. The next morning, a Sunday, she made coffee early and suited up and then he was next to her and said, "I'm coming, too." He smiled. "Gotta show you how it's done."

It was the first time she knew how far gone he really was. The disappearances hadn't actually done it for her. Somehow she'd gotten past that. But this was hard to get past. He couldn't make the run. Less than a mile, and he was heaved over, hacking, desperately pulling air into his lungs.

That night in bed was the first he asked about her, her future, in a way not directly connected to him.

"What is it you want?" he said. His palm was flat against her belly, head on her chest. Her fingers moved across the stubble of his high-and-tight and the smooth skin of his neck.

"I don't know," she said. Then, "This."

His palm lifted and he slapped it down—wrong answer.

"I don't know," she said, and her fingers on his hair stopped moving. She was quiet a minute, then said, "Well—I'm doing it. What I want."

"Doing what?"

"You know," and then she growled, a good Army growl. *"Grrrrrr."*

"Hoo-rah," he said, quietly.

"Yeah. Exactly. Hoo-rah. *Grrrrr."* And then she raised her voice, head lifting from pillow, and did it for real, echoing loud in the little cinder-block barracks room, Junior Davis feeling the vibration from her chest—*"GRRRRRRRRR."*

Junior Davis said, "Pretty good."

"Yeah," she said. "It is."

"And that's what you want."

"Yeah."

"You're already there."

"I'm getting there."

"You're there. You kick ass."

"Yes," she said, her fingers moving across his head again. "I do."

"So," he said. "Why?" His head was still on her chest, his face still not visible to her. "Why are you here?"

"What do you mean?" she said. "That's stupid, Junior. Why are any of us here?"

"Maybe," he said, "but I think you're gonna stay."

Silence.

"Aren't you?"

She nodded, then said, "Yeah."

"*Grrrr,*" he whispered.

"*Grrrrr.*"

His open palm moved across her belly, then counted ribs until it annoyed her and she swatted his hand away. Still he kept his head down, face averted. Hand back on her belly, he let it sit a few moments, then slid it up to her breast, cupping it. This she let stay. After a while she reached with her free arm to the night table and pulled a Marlboro from the pack there. She lit it, and smoked that way, on her back, Junior Davis half-curled up and softly caressing her. She was leaving in a week, for school at Fort Knox, sergeant's school. When she graduated a month from now she'd have the same three hard stripes as Junior Davis. It was, in the end, the reason she'd taken him back this weekend. It was selfish, her first purely selfish act in their relationship: she'd be at Fort Knox a month and didn't want any distractions. Junior, drifting about at home, would be a distraction. But now, she thought, now she could concentrate.

Junior had asked why she was here but it was hard to pin. And why she was here and why she stayed were two very different things. Both with Junior and with the Army.

She knew people who'd enlisted for a specific, known reason. But not many. And of them, half she didn't believe. In the small percentage left, there were a few good reasons—Dick Wags and Junior Davis, for instance. Starched and shining now, but both came in the same way: a judge's order. Army or jail. Green uniform or orange. Tree suit or jumpsuit.

On the boat, Cain the kitchen private was nineteen, had a wife and two kids in a town east of nowhere in east Texas. Pelton was the same, nineteen, from northern Oregon, subtract one kid and add diabetes to the wife. These two, Tory thought, were born with enlistment papers in hand.

Only once could she remember the subject coming up, one night, a group of them out drinking late, telling horror stories from basic training that didn't seem so bad now, then a few predator recruiter stories. Scaboo, who rarely drank and was the only sober head among them that night, announced he'd sought out the recruiter. He was in the U.S. Army for one reason and one reason only: to serve like his grandfather before him, to defend the country, defend freedom. This was a while back, when he'd been a PFC. Junior Davis, just pinned sergeant, had reached across the table and smacked his young, Italian roomdog on the side of the head. Hard.

"Fuck you," Davis mumbled. "You think your cock is bigger than ours? You're here 'cause you were too lazy or stupid to get into college. Same as everyone."

Tory remembered the guys at the table laughing. Except Scaboo. And Junior, of course. He hadn't laughed. He'd no tolerance for poster patriotism. Anyone who gave a reason like that for enlisting was either lying or, as he said, stupider than dirt.

"Remember before the Gulf?" he said. "Did you watch TV? Wasn't a black face to be found calling for war." He pointed to Matata, still a buck private then. "Or Spanish. Am I right, Don Pablo?"

"Right as rain, white man," Matata said, nodding. "Nothing in Saudi got nothing to do with nothing."

"Exactly." Junior Davis was slurring now, his face gone red. But he wasn't done. "Until I see a gunship with an Iraqi flag off the coast of Maine, one thing we're *not* doing here is defending freedom." He took a drag on his cigarette, then poked his finger at Scaboo. "My little roomdog, you're a hired gun. Nothing noble about it." He spread his arms. "*We're* noble, mind you. We're the goods." He slammed his palm down on the table. It was impossible to tell whether he was serious or mocking. Tory wondered whether Junior knew it himself. He hit the table again. "We're American *soldiers*." He hissed the word, drawing it out. The group was silent now, drunk and holding its breath. "But don't think what we *do* is noble. You're drawing a paycheck, is all. Taking a bullet." He stubbed out his smoke on a cold piece of pizza. "You're an offensive tool of the United States government. You ain't *defending* nothing."

Scaboo opened his mouth to say something, and Tory tensed

because she knew he was going to argue and Junior was drunk and if Scaboo argued more likely than not Junior would be across the table punching. Without looking up Scaboo said, "I think—" but Riddle slammed his fist down on the table and cut him off. "I'm defending something, Junior," he said. All heads turned toward him, a sneer rising on Junior's lips. Riddle leaned across the table, right in Davis's face, and said, "I'm defending my God-given right to pork your Mom."

And that was the end of that.

Another thing Tory hadn't missed: they'd gotten to talking about Somalia later. Junior Davis openly questioned why the Army and Marines were there. This was tricky; there was a Waterborne unit, the 710th Provisional, en route. Some of their own. But Junior questioned the whole mission. And she knew he meant it. But because she was his girlfriend, she also knew he'd begged—literally begged—to be on the deployment, and when his name wasn't on the list, he'd gone to see the battalion sergeant-major to plead his case. He didn't think the Army should be there, but he was furious he hadn't been sent. Heartbroken, really. And she knew he didn't see this as a contradiction.

Tory, if he'd asked, would have told him she didn't see it as a contradiction either.

She'd made her reenlistment decision over the last weekend he'd been gone. Her first enlistment was running out. It was a simple choice: let it expire, or re-up and be a sergeant. It was automatic, she'd already been accepted into school, top of the battalion list. She made the decision with Dick Wags and Alicia over beer and soup at their place, but it wasn't really a decision and she knew it and they knew it, too.

Junior Davis seemed surprised. "I thought you were getting out," he said. "I didn't know you wanted this." And she thought he meant *Why would you want this?*

And she said simply, "You never asked," and meant *How could you not know?*

And she wondered about Junior. Especially since his growing silence after being left off the Somalia deployment roster. Lately when she watched him—when he was there to watch—she thought of Lucy Harris, her grandmother. Lucy and old Dean, who might or might not have been Tory's grandfather, had raised her, from four years old. When Tory was around twelve or thirteen, Lucy started going soft with Alzheimer's. She'd had it years, but it seemed to stay more annoying than bad—forgetting who was on the other end of the phone, or why she'd gone upstairs. Her doctor wasn't even sure it was really Alzheimer's, maybe just old age. But no, she'd had it. It was Dean, his presence, keeping her together, and Tory read it was that way sometimes. The old woman burned extra strength to keep it together while her husband was around, all energy diverted to the brain to keep those synapses firing. When he died there was no longer a reason. She slipped quickly, from making Tory's breakfast every day to not knowing who she was in six months. She went into a coma just shy of a year from old Dean's death, and died a month later, on Tory's sixteenth birthday.

It made her think of starched, squared-away Junior Davis, so recently popping at the seams. And she wondered who or what he'd been white-knuckle holding it together for, and why, and she wanted to think it was her. But maybe it wasn't enough. It was like his steam was running out. He'd been pushing all his energy to one thing—going to war—for so long, and like old Lucy he was starting to shut down.

Tory stood, brushing the dust off her hands. She'd worked out to exhaustion, muscles limp in her arms, pushing so hard after such a long break. Marc Hall leaned against the bulkhead, still there, watching her, waiting. "I think I should shower," she said. "I'll meet you on deck?"

Dick Wags walked out then, raising a hand, wordless down the passage on his way to engine-room watch. Tory grabbed her stuff from the cabin and when she stepped out again the passage was empty. She knocked on the latrine door, flipped the sign to FEMALE, locked it behind her. She went to the far shower stall and it felt funny, knobs on the wrong side; she never used this one.

Marc Hall pulled his cabin door closed, stepped back in to the empty passage. He was clicking his teeth and not noticing. He knocked lightly on the cabin door next to the latrine, though he'd seen Staff Sergeant Wagman leave for watch and Tory go into the latrine. Still, he knocked anyway, soft, just to be sure. Then twisted the knob and stepped in. He climbed to the top bunk, found the hole in the bulk-head. It wasn't hard to find, a small hole but right there. He put his eye to the hole.

She was slick and smooth, four small line tattoos on the back of her shoulders, lean and muscles tight. Her dog tags, encased in plastic silencers, hung from their chain backward, between her shoulder blades. A long, raised purple scar ran the front of her left thigh. She circled and soaped, then stretched her neck, face direct in the spray of water, eyes closed tight.

See me, she thought, though he would have no way of knowing. *This is the me I want you to see.*

Tory never looked up, never opened her eyes, and when she reached for a towel, water off, Marc slipped from the cabin, down the passage to the forward hatch, outside to the deck.

CHAPTER

22

Tory towel-dried slow, dressed quick, then went back next door to her cabin just to drop her shower gear and get a pack of cigarettes. Stepping back out of the cabin she was almost knocked to the deck by Riddle, running flat out down the passage. She was too surprised to say anything, and by the time she thought to he was already gone, out the forward hatch to the catwalk outside, gray metal slamming behind him. A few seconds later Temple came around the corner from the bottom of the stairs, running much slower but obviously following Riddle.

"What's he doing?" she said.

"Staying awake," Temple huffed, stopping to jog in place in front of her.

Tory raised her eyebrows.

"Poor guy's been up all night, but caught himself dozing a few minutes ago—took off like a bat out of hell from the mess. Victor Charlie told me to follow, make sure he doesn't trip and go in the drink."

Tory remained silent, not sure what to say besides the obvious. Finally, Temple said, "You didn't hear what happened."

"No, I don't think so."

"He got hit in the face. With powder."

"Powder?"

"Powder. When we were at the fence in Port-au-Prince, buying shit. This old woman comes up close, throws a handful of yellow powder right into Riddle's face."

"Powder."

"Powder! Voodoo powder, Jersey—you know? Like in the movie?"

"You have got to be kidding me."

"Kidding you?" Temple was turning red, either from running in place or frustration, it wasn't obvious which. "What? What could it be? We're in Haiti, some old lady is throwing powder at us—what else can it be?"

She shrugged.

"So we gotta keep him awake."

"Who? Riddle?"

"Yeah. If he sleeps, he's done for." Temple smacked his hands together. "Pow! Zombie time."

"Zombie—"

"That's how it works. When you fall asleep you don't wake up, then you look dead, and Pow! You're a fucking zombie."

Tory nodded. Temple was almost purple now.

"A fucking zombie!" he said again.

She pointed forward, toward the hatch. "You better go get him," she said.

"Yeah," and he was gone.

The Haitian drivers weren't in the well-deck. Marc had led them all to the fantail—in a line, up the steep staircases through the house—so they could see the horizon and feel the breeze. The shoreline of their country lay a mile off the port side, a thin green line hovering in the morning sea haze. There was no way of telling from looking which part of Haiti it was, just certain knowledge they were far from home.

There was a picnic table lashed to the aft anchor winch, and Matata had laid out hotel pans filled with scrambled eggs and ham, the ever-present Army apples, and a jug of instant orange juice. The Haitian men sat cross-legged on the damp and sticky deck, faces turned to the morning sun, paper plates of breakfast in their laps. Marc was sitting on the picnic bench and when Tory came out on deck she sat beside him, immediately uncomfortable. Young white woman with black boys at her feet. She looked at Marc, thinking it might help that a black man sat with her. It didn't. She stood, walked to the rail, lit a cigarette. When she looked back Marc, too, had his face raised to the sun. She sat next to him again.

"This man," Marc said, pointing to the driver closest to them, "is from Cange, in the Central Plain. His name is Jean. He's never been to Jacmel. But he has a cousin there, whom he hasn't seen in ten years. They were close once, he says. So he's excited."

"Hello, Jean," Tory said.

The man smiled, unable to talk, his mouth stuffed with food. He was not an old man, but older. She imagined it would be difficult to pinpoint someone's age in Haiti. He wore green shorts and plastic flip-flops, his thin shirt off and around his neck. His throat bulged when he swallowed, skin tight and stretched.

"Are they all from so far away?"

"No," Marc said. He pointed to a boy across the deck, the youngest of them, maybe a teenager. "He is, though. He's from Gonaives. He's the farthest I think. He left Gonaives because a church group in Port-au-Prince sponsored him to go to their school. He says he gets good marks. Now he works with the Red Cross when they have room for him. But he's young, so he doesn't get much of the work. He's here free, no pay. They filled the slots, but he wanted to come anyway." He waved at the boy, who waved back. "To ride on the ship."

"We'll pay him," she said.

"I already have." He turned and filled his plastic cup with more of the orange bug juice. "Gonaives is my mother's hometown. I've been there. She left when she was fifteen, went to Port-au-Prince. Then came to the States when she was nineteen."

"How?"

"My father," Marc said simply. He laughed then. "I guess I am the Haitian who has come farthest today." He said it again in Creole just loud enough for Jean to hear and the older man laughed with the Army captain, nodding. He sputtered a string of syllables through his scrambled eggs and Marc nodded vigorously—*Oui! Oui!* Tory asked what the man had said and Marc whispered, "I've no idea."

She smiled at that. Across deck, two of the men had finished their meal and produced a ball of thin line and a hook. They baited it with a piece of ham, tossing it out then tying it off to the rail.

"Will they catch anything?" Marc asked.

"Maybe. If they bait it so the ham doesn't pop off in our wake, they might. It's been known to happen." She rested her arms on her knees, watching them fish. "Are they fishermen, or just well-prepared?" she asked.

Marc shrugged. "Definitions are fluid in Haiti," he said. "Especially these days, as desperate as everything is. Most of the men here are from Port-au-Prince, or near. These are all very lucky men. To have these jobs. Where some of them come from . . ." He shook his head. "You couldn't imagine. The conditions, and disease."

Tory was watching the men by the rail with their fishing line. The boy, the teenager from Gonaives, had walked over to look. He kept his distance, though, she noticed. A few feet removed from the other two.

Without taking her eyes from them, she said quietly, "How many have HIV?"

Marc tilted his head. "In Haiti? God. A million. It's one of the—"

"No, here. These men."

He shrugged, curious. "I would have no way of knowing."

"No, of course not," she said, shaking her head, looking at him. "Dumb question. Never mind."

Jean stood now, carefully folding his empty paper plate and pushing it into the garbage bag tied to the end of the picnic table. He moved his hand over the apples, picked one, and pushed it down into his shorts pocket, winking at Tory. Then he, too, wandered over to the fishing line. The apple rolled like a strange tumor in his pocket as he walked.

"This is like a vacation for them," Tory said, and Marc nodded yes. Jean waved his arm at one of the men, saying something, and the fellow began pulling the line in to check.

"It is inevitable, I guess," Marc said.

"What?"

"That one of them has HIV. At least one. Maybe two? Not all— God, I don't think. But some. Someone here has it. Probably more than one."

The line had no fish, no bait either. The boy ran over and took another piece of ham. Jean was speaking sharply to the two men; it was clear he wanted to bait it this time. On the deck, a few of the other men were watching all this, some still eating, a few talking quietly. One man had curled into a ball and was sleeping.

"Haiti is bad enough for HIV, but these men would be even higher risk," Marc said.

"Why?"

He waved his hand in the general direction of the well-deck, the trucks. "Drivers," he said. "They pick it up, spread it to the next town."

"Prostitutes?"

"Sure. And wives. And girlfriends."

Jean had folded the thin ham carefully, somehow running the hook through five or six times it looked like. He nodded at one of the younger men, and the line was tossed back in the water.

"Let it go out!" Tory yelled, hand cupped around her mouth, then said to Marc, "Tell them to let all the line out, way past the prop wash. There won't be anything alive in there, they have to get it back farther."

Marc spoke but they couldn't hear over the noise of the ship so he got up and walked over, telling them what the female sergeant had said. The men looked at her then did as she advised, thin line spinning out from the rough brown hand, until just enough was left to tie to the rail.

Maybe it's him, she thought, carefully watching the owner of the line. Then she looked at his friend. *Or him.* The boy walked by then, to get an apple, and the thought it might be him was too much and Tory dug into her front pocket for her cigarettes, lighting one, her hand shaking just a little bit.

Marc was back, smiling at her, his face and round scalp glowing in the sun. *He really is beautiful,* she thought. He looked as if he was about to say something, but sat next to her wordless, looking at her, then back at the men.

Tory smoked, her anxiety slipping a little. She ran her palm over her short hair.

"Do you think they know?" she said.

"What? Does who know what?"

"The ones who have it," she said. "Do you think they know they have it?"

Marc put his hand to his face, wiping his dry lips and cheeks. He raised his eyebrows and sighed. It was all the answer he could give.

Jean laughed then, across the deck, the boy running over, a few of the men standing up.

"Poisson!" he shouted. *"Agwé apportez pour nous!"* His bait had worked.

Agwé delivers. The spirit of the sea provides.

CHAPTER

23

They survived the night. Barely, but—it seemed—intact. The worst hit around 0300. The worst for McBride, anyway. That's when whatever illusions he'd had stripped away like deck salt in rain. There was always a moment, he thought; sometimes the moment came too late. It came at three in the morning for McBride, on the bridge. It wasn't too late, it turned out, but you never know at the time. At 0300 the lights went out. Just a few seconds, not much more than a flicker, really. But in such a storm, with the battering they were taking, it was enough. His hands began shaking and he couldn't stop the shaking, even holding them tightly together. *All these people,* was all he could think. *All these people.*

If ever he'd needed Davis, it was tonight. Davis's strange talent lay with precisely a night like this: damage control, fixing on the fly, rerouting and reworking and forcing the last possible bit of life out of an engine, pump, generator. But Davis was of no use now, his own possibilities run cold. He might, actually, be dead. If so, McBride thought, they'd survive that, too.

As it is at sea, the morning was as if the night had not happened, all things calm, still. The ship lay adrift—full stop while she was checked nose to tail—exhausted, spent; from the night, from the pile of years. The bulkheads and seams were as the crew onboard: limp and worn, pulling for breath. Somewhat surprised, even, to see this new sunrise.

By 0600, the weather was completely done, the decks of the old ship steady and unmoving. On bunks, huddled in corners, flat on the floor in the small prayer room or one of the two children's class-rooms—wherever they found themselves overnight—the missionaries fell into listless sleep, drained and wasted, unable to move. Pastor her-self was on the deck in a corner of the little ones' classroom, legs out in front, two boys curled with their heads in her lap. They'd fallen asleep at dawn as she stroked their hair, now all the twelve or so adults and children in the room asleep, all except Pastor, sitting in her cor-ner, hands still running over the boys' heads. She stared straight ahead, lips moving silently, until her eyelids fell and she, too, drifted off.

Colgan and Johnson, the biggest men on the boat—both of them divorced, recovering alcoholics, who'd come to the ship to stay clean and pay their social debts—found McBride on the bridge. His young helmsman was curled up snoring on the deck; the skipper had told him to lie down and close his eyes and he'd kick him if he needed him. McBride had opened the door to the starboard bridge wing and was standing in it, hands hanging on to the old stained wood of the frame, the polished brass of the rail. He polished the bridge brass himself because he had no one to do it for him and he thought it was right it should be done. Colgan came up the stairs first, Johnson behind him, and when he got to McBride he embraced him, clamping his arms around him. "God bless you, Skipper," he whispered.

Johnson could keep an eye on the silent bridge. McBride took Col-gan down below to the pit. It was a disaster. The bilges had filled in the storm, the violence of the ship's rocking throwing oily seawater over everything. McBride showed Colgan how to operate the bilge pumps and what to keep an eye on as the piping shuddered and thumped the sludge through and up and over the side. McBride stayed almost thirty minutes, carefully circling the engine room with a flashlight, checking what he knew to check, hoping what he didn't know wouldn't sink them. The incredible thing was the Fiat, the old dying Fiat; still run-ning. *Thank you,* McBride thought. *Just take us to port, girl. And you and I shall both retire there.* Colgan had found Davis's rag bin and was wiping down the sides of the main. McBride patted him once on the shoulder, took a last look around, then climbed out.

At the top of the stairs, in the dark, empty passage near the dry-goods store, McBride broke down. Brief and controlled, but here it overcame him and he allowed it, for a moment, shoulders shaking, hand white around the rail. It passed, then, and he pulled himself together, deep breaths and head up. If asked a day before had he ever in his years at sea faced death he would have said, "Many times." This morning he knew it wasn't true, not like this; just once was the true answer: tonight. He'd seen the black tunnel open for them, the opposite and elusive cousin of the sailor's green flash.

McBride found Pastor, boys in her lap, asleep in the kindergarten. He moved the boys, lifting them and laying them next to their parents still curled on the deck. Pastor had opened her eyes halfway, watching him, and when he'd moved the second boy he came back to her, taking her hand, and whispered, "C'mon now, Miss. To bed with you."

She stood, stiff, leaning on his arm, and allowed him to guide her through the door and down the passage.

In the cabin of the ship's engineer two exhausted souls lay at rest on the thin bed. Junior Davis, tied down by Pastor to weather the night, asleep on his back; he'd yet to wake, clothesline still loosely wrapped around him. Lorraine lay next to him, curled under Davis's thin blanket, because she refused to go back to her own cabin.

Jacmel

CHAPTER

24

The boy who fetches water for the chickens is first awake in the Place d'Armes, an hour before sunlight hits the square. His tiny sister wakes with him but she is blind so will stay, still and quiet, in the wooden packing crate they've camped in next to the big statue. She sits as far back as she can get in the box, chin on bare knees and arms wrapped round her legs, silver-white eyes wide and unblinking.

The boy goes for water from the big barrel he knows behind Hotel de la Place and is back with his buckets in fifteen minutes. He delivers to the two old chicken men—also up before light—who tend their small roosts in a corner of the iron market. They pass him a few coins and he stands there, silent and unmoving. One old chicken man shoos a hand and yells at him to go away and then the boy speaks, eyes to the ground, reminding him he wasn't paid at all the night before, nor the previous morning nor the night before that. The one old man grumbles but the other old man is already reaching into his pants—he says *give me those back* and the boy passes him the coins and the old man gives him instead a *gourde* note. The old men begin to bicker but the boy is already gone, running back to his sister, empty buckets bouncing off his legs.

In the Place it is not yet dawn and none move about but you can tell most are awake or waking, the breathing of the square different, the air lighter. Eyes open but bodies curled under carts or market stalls, not willing to move yet, a few more moments of silence before day. Someone must be up for there is smoke, black and greasy, pungent burning wood and dung. The chickens cluck and peck and a dog barks and then that's it, morning is here, still dark but morning is here, bodies emerge stretching and yawning *bonjou*.

Down and up cramped, colonial streets, a small group of men cross Jacmel's three steep hillsides. They pass beneath hanging balconies encircled with wrought-iron and vines, past crumbling plaster walls and high gates, the morning smell of smoke then flowers then smoke again. Up and out early, the men are all important—they live in town, in houses. There are six men. Two of them own suits and wear them this morning, black with thin ties. The others have no suit, but dress well. One is old, but the rest are not, middle-aged and well-fed. They walk slow, so the old one among them won't get winded. Slow, but with a walk of nervous purpose—walking forward but looking back sometimes, and around, to see if any watch; it's early, but in Haiti someone is always watching.

A small squad of American soldiers arrived late yesterday, overland in two Humvees, fewer than ten of them, moving into a club not far from Place d'Armes. A FADH officer was seen to arrive not long after, and FRAPH goons. No one could say how they were received by the Americans, warmly or sent packing; they all left with the same stone look. But these town men gathered to talk and it was decided they should go as a group, also to meet the Americans soldiers, to tell them how it is here, and in the caserne on the mountain, before the *attachés* could work their snake charms on the *blancs*. The men walk quietly, not remarkable in any way, just a group of men, well-dressed for a work day, perhaps, but that is all. They were brave, though. Five others had not gone with them, afraid.

You are fools, to upset the cart.

No, we have a chance, one chance.

The Americans will be gone and then where will you be?

But Aristide will be back.

Who cares? The Americans will be gone, and where will you be?

We have a chance . . .

Two of their sons were in the caserne, and this had swayed the old man, and the old man swayed the other three. The old man had been in that prison himself, a guest of Papa Doc for five years. It was almost unheard of that one could be in such a place five years and emerge alive. But he'd done it, and then lived on twenty years—another fairly remarkable feat.

The men cross the Place, unavoidably in the open now, drawing courage from one another, heads up. They angle toward the club and the American detachment.

The club had been part of an American chain—Hard Rock Café. Effectively closed by the embargo, along with most of Haiti's limping, empty resorts, it sat unused almost from the day it opened, the faded outline of the name still visible on the building's stucco façade.

An American Green Beret master sergeant stood behind the iron bars of the gate, watching the sky lighten, listening to the songbirds in the thick, drooping trees above. He wore his flak vest but not his helmet. He'd been inside Kuwait and Iraq as a staff sergeant, then Somalia as a sergeant first class. His forty-eight hours in Port-au-Prince had prepared him for similar surroundings, but southern Haiti was different. Lush. Even here, in town. All green and sweet smelling. A small red bird landed on the gate, hopping, then another. The master sergeant pulled out a fat cigar, cut the tip, lit it.

Half the men inside were sleeping, the others poking around. They wouldn't be staying—Special Forces teams were required to pay rent on whatever property they appropriated. But Master Sergeant Rice had slammed the brakes when he'd seen the place yesterday, walking back to the second Humvee to confer with the team's captain.

"Hard Rock Café, sir," he pointed out. "What more can I say, really?"

The men all agreed, captain included. There were opportunities for pictures here, and souvenirs. They were the only American forces for fifty miles, and who could pass this up?

"What self-respecting GI wouldn't have bivouacked under a bar for a night or two passing through Paris?" the master sergeant said.

"I'm not sure it's a clear parallel, Sergeant Rice," the captain said, "but what the hell. As long as we found the door open—we're just securing American property in a dangerous foreign country."

Master Sergeant Rice had trotted around the corner, pulled his

9-mm from the holster, and blown off the gate padlock then the dead-bolt on the club's heavy front door.

"Damn," he said to himself. "Imagine that. Door's wide open."

The club was mostly picked clean—packed up by the owners, prob-ably, and whatever left looted by the caretaker—but it didn't dampen the team's feeling of good luck. Most of the Special Forces ODAs in-country were sucking hind tit under General Meade's bloated thumb at the Port-au-Prince airport, or out in the boonies, scrounging for a dry place to sleep and watching their backs. But here sat the 909th, play-ing eight ball at the Hard Rock Café on their third day in Haiti.

The main wall around the dining room was still covered with frames bolted in place, copies of gold records mostly. There was a Fender Stratocaster bolted to the wall, a signature scrawled across it. A bull of a Hawaiian sergeant squinted until he could read the signature. "Eddie Van Halen," he said to the team medic next to him. "No shit." He had a lump of tobacco under his lip, and spit on the floor, con-templating. "You think Eddie Van Halen was here, Doc?"

"What do you think, Mickey?" the medic said.

The team's captain was named Greg Nellis. He was African-American, one of very few black soldiers in Special Forces. Two of his men didn't like him much. He knew it. He didn't like them, either. It didn't get in the way. He got along with Master Sergeant Rice, and let him run the men. When they went up on the roof of the Hard Rock that night to fire up the prick radio and report in he told the battalion TOC they were hunkered down for the evening in an old hotel, and yes they'd paid the owner—no, he couldn't see the name of the place, and *oops!* there goes the signal, I'll call you in the morning. When he got off the line Rice told him one of the men had found a case of gin down in the basement.

Nellis grimaced and said, "Christ, we just got here."

Rice shrugged. The captain had a point. "But," he said, "it's awful hard to look at free booze and not drink some of it."

An equally good point.

Nellis thought about it a moment. Then he said, "Draw straws. Three of them can stand down for the night and have cocktails. We take the bottles when we leave, and rotate drinking parties every few nights."

"You're an officer and a gentleman, Sir," Master Sergeant Rice had said, then left the captain alone on the roof.

Rice found a uniformed Haitian waiting for him downstairs, a grizzled pot-belly who said he was a major, the first of what would be a steady stream of visitors through the early evening, until the Americans finally locked the gate. Rice thought they were creepy—the FADH and whatever else they called themselves, some in uniform, some not. Creepy. They smiled big behind sunglasses and grabbed their crotches, talking loud and not seeming to care if Rice couldn't understand a word they said.

And now, next morning, enjoying his cigar behind the gate, Rice saw the day's first group approaching. These looked different, though. Scared, for one thing. They completely lacked the swagger and arrogance of the official visitors from yesterday. Older, too, these men.

This'll be interesting, Rice thought, grinding his cigar out under his boot, turning to go inside to wake Captain Nellis. The officer could deal with the visitors while Rice took a few men in a Humvee to scout a permanent place to billet. Battalion said to prepare for a year in Haiti. They might not be able to stay at the Hard Rock Café, but Rice had no intention of being uncomfortable. He was getting too old for that shit.

The air warmed as the sun filled the sky over Jacmel. The boy and his blind sister sat outside their crate, the newsprint pages of *La Nouveliste* spread on the ground under them. They ate the few beans he'd bought with the *gourde* from the old chicken men. He clucked at her from time to time, reaching over once to wipe her chin. She swiped at him with her hand when he did, waving him away. Then he reached and wiped her chin again.

They were refugees twice. First to the small shanty camp outside Jacmel, last year when their maman died. Then last week the shanties and the *SIDA* hospital beside—and, it seemed, everything on that part of the mountain—slid to the sea in the hurricane, the whole world north of Jacmel flowing in mud to the ocean. The boy and his sister were lucky;

they'd been caught in a flow and he'd barely gotten them out. Many whom they'd known had gone to the water. Whether they died in the mud and trauma on the way down or drowned later, the outcome was the same. The undertow was vicious in *Baye Jacmel*; in a hurricane, no chance. If there were bodies they weren't to be seen again in this world.

Maybe they made it to Miami, the boy thought. Everyone talked about Miami like it was heaven, golden heaven. Maybe his neighbors floated off to Miami.

That was a happy thought.

After the storm, drenched and alone, the boy got his sister into town. He found the crate near the Place d'Armes, and turned it so wind didn't push the rain in. Perfect. Home.

Now, eating breakfast, he clucked at his sister again. They must hurry, he said to her. A woman had told him that Americans were coming today, in a ship. She said he'd want to be up front, first in line when the Americans walked down the pier. Surely, they'd have food to share. Something.

Standing, he looked at their wooden crate. He hated to leave it unguarded. There was nothing in it—they had no belongings, only the two plastic buckets that provided his livelihood—but the crate itself was shelter, hard to come by. Hard won and easily lost. The opportunity to see the Americans come in was too great to miss, though, and he had to take his sister. Her wide, blind eyes were their ticket. The woman this morning had told him so, had explained it all to him.

Come on, let's go, he said. He put his arms around her, rubbing up and down until she giggled. He kissed the top of her head, then hand in hand they left their crate and the *marché* behind, stacked empty buckets swinging in his free hand, winding down through Jacmel to the port below.

The ships rose as two dots on the horizon, far down the long, sheltered bay. One overtook the other, and within an hour was clearly identifiable to any by its gray as a military vessel. The other ship was blue, dark blue, and moved it seemed not at all, except when you looked from time to time it was clearer in vision so must have moved.

There was one narrow pier, concrete, pointing out into the water, a single finger beckoning. It filled quickly, a mass of people so solid some fell into the water, pushed by accident and then by joke. Mostly it was laughs, and the swimmers were pulled back up. The gray ship, small for the American military, was huge for Jacmel. It grew, funny looking with its massive raised ramp. The ramp slowly began descending, allowing the people on the pier to see inside the ship's open well-deck: Haitian trucks, Red Cross, overfilled. When the people realized the ship was headed for the black-sand beach, the pier emptied, swift as a draining sink, everyone moving to the shoreline. An American Humvee with two soldiers pulled up, the captain and master sergeant from the Special Forces detachment, watching the ship's progress.

The crew stood battlestations, but the loosest possible definition of the word. In Voodoo Lounge, on the port bow, Sergeant Tory Harris and PFC Brian Temple sat on two deck bits, weapons locked and loaded but safed and loose in their grips. They were up here less for security than just it was a good place to watch. Tory had a pair of binoculars around her neck; she raised them to her eyes.

"What do you see, Jersey?"

"Heaven."

If riding into Port-au-Prince had been creeping into the belly of something urban—shadowed and smog-filled—Jacmel rose in their view distinctly Caribbean, tropical and overgrown, Old World. The town clung to its hills like Port-au-Prince, a cathedral rising in the center, but the comparison ended there. Spanish tile and thatch roof sat on pink and tan plaster, bright blues and yellows dotted throughout, and the brown-red of old brick.

Tory pulled the leash over her head and handed the binoculars to Temple. He let his rifle hang on its strap around his neck and put the glasses to his face with both hands. He whistled a happy note.

"You think they got breadfruit here?"

"I don't know," she said. "What's breadfruit?"

He lowered the binocs. "From that movie—*Mutiny on the Bounty.*"

"It was a book."

"Whatever. Place looked like this. They spent the whole flick eating breadfruit. I always thought it looked good."

"On my honor as an NCO, I'll try to find you some breadfruit."

"Yum," he said, raising the glasses again. Then yelled, "Mistah *Chris*-tian!"

Tory took a long swig from her canteen. The bay here was not at all like the Port-au-Prince basin. It was narrow, long—hills and jungle rising sharp to the north, a low, clear peninsula to the south. There were ranch houses with satellite dishes there, new-looking iron gates and swimming pools—Mac had told them it was Colombian drug lords, Cuban smugglers, Duvalierists, all hunkered down for the American occupation, nervous on their private coast.

"Nice neighborhood," Temple said. "Doesn't seem too devastated to me."

Tory was looking for why they were here, and now she found it. It hadn't been obvious, she realized, because why they were here looked like nothing—there was nothing there anymore, which is why they were here. It was a swath of brown, cut into the hillside just north of town, a wide mudslide that had taken everything in its path and dumped it into the sea.

"There," she said, touching Temple's arm and pointing, taking the binoculars from him.

On the starboard quarterdeck the Steward stood at the mounted .50-cal machine gun, binoculars up, sweeping the beach. Victor Charlie came through the hatch from the wardroom, late for battlestations. He reached and tried to grab the binoculars from the Steward's hand. "Gimme that," he said.

"Wait a minute," Roy said, holding tight.

Victor Charlie was hung over and his head hurt. "*Now*, Sergeant," he said, pulling harder.

Roy took a step back, not giving up the binoculars. "Goddamn it, wait!" he said, a wounded look on his face. "Who's fucking this chicken, anyway? I'm the machine-gun NCO."

Victor Charlie looked at him, prepared to yell, then couldn't be bothered. He waved him off, turning and lighting a cigarette instead. "It wouldn't kill you to say *Sir*," he mumbled.

"Yes, Sir," the Steward said, eyeing the beach again.

"Worthless cook."

Riddle sat on the deck behind the .50 cal, leaning against the bulkhead, his helmet to one side. Eyes drooping, then closing, he snored, loudly. Victor Charlie leaned over, putting his lips an inch from Riddle's ear, then yelled: *"Wake up!"*

Riddle jumped and grabbed his helmet, mumbling incoherently.

Victor Charlie smoked, watching him. After a couple of puffs he said, "How long you been awake now, Riddle?"

"I dunno," he said. "Two three days. Since Port-au-Prince."

"Damn, Riddle," the Steward said, turning and handing the binoculars to Victor Charlie. "You're screwed. A zombie for sure."

"You done screwed the pooch, man," Victor Charlie said. "Kissed the baby. Shot the president. Fucked the monkey—"

"Shut up, man!" Riddle yelled, almost crying. "Just shut the fuck up!"

Victor Charlie turned his head so Riddle couldn't see him smile. "That's 'Shut up, *Sir*,' asshole."

Ramp most of the way down, the LSV stood off the beach like a gaping mouth. The Haitian drivers had all turned their trucks on, waiting to drive. The well-deck quickly filled with sooty diesel exhaust and the bosun ran from door to door yelling at the drivers to turn their engines off again. The men sat in the cabs of their trucks, eating Army apples and waving at their countrymen on the beach.

The ship approached, slow, then pulled back. The skipper moved the nose five degrees, tried again, then had to pull back. There was a sandbar offshore, too high even with the peak tide, he couldn't get the tip of the ramp on dry ground. Their Humvee might have done it, maybe, but these Haitian trucks wouldn't have made it two feet before sinking then cementing in place, yards offshore. On the bridge, Mannino paced, chain-smoking, anxious and muttering to himself.

The crowd gathered to watch had settled in the shade under a line of trees, most of them sitting now, enjoying the show. A cheer would go up as the ship pushed forward, then excitement belayed as the vessel rose on the sand and pulled off to try again. The men in the crowd chattered and pointed, quarterbacking the skipper's moves and decisions, each with a solid idea of how best it should be done. Up on the bridge, Mannino received none of their telepathic messages, just a headache, growing behind his temples.

An hour into it, the Special Forces master sergeant picked up the radio in the detachment's Humvee and answered the ship's call. They talked back and forth awhile. The ship's skipper asked a question and Rice squinted into the sun, looking over the single, long concrete pier jutting straight out into the small bay. "I dunno, Sir," he said into the microphone, "looks stable enough to me."

There were a few seconds of silence, then Mannino's voice came back through the speaker: "Why don't you put that Humvee of yours on the end of it and find out?"

Rice looked at Captain Nellis, and both men shrugged. Nellis stepped out of the vehicle—no reason why both of them should take a swim this morning—and Rice drove off the beach, up and around then back to the pier. He eyeballed it, shrugged again, then slowly drove down its length, stopping at the very end. He sat there a minute, then picked up the microphone.

"Affirmative on stability."

The trucks left the ship single file, off the ramp and down the pier into the cheering crowd. The ship sat like an extension, straight off, the skipper using tiny corrections in the main engines and bow-thruster to hold the nose absolutely steady while the Red Cross trucks moved. Fairly sure there would be no invasion against the ship from the starboard quarterdeck, Victor Charlie left Roy at their battlestation and walked forward. He lit a cigarette and watched the maneuver, looking up at Mannino pacing the bridge wing. "He's really good," Victor Charlie said aloud, to no one. The Army didn't teach things like this.

The ship's Humvee had remained shackled in an aft corner of the well-deck since they'd loaded in Fort Eustis. It was released now and fired off, pulling up behind the line of disembarking trucks. Inside, Pelton and Riddle sat alone, Pelton at the wheel.

"How long's it supposed to take to get to this place?" Riddle asked. He was pale, unhealthy looking.

"Don't know, man," Pelton said, packing a line of dip behind his lip. "Hard to tell from the map. An hour or so, I guess."

Riddle sighed, then removed his helmet and curled up on himself in the front seat. "I can't take it anymore, P. I gotta sleep."

"Hey, whatever you think is best, man. It's your funeral."

"Don't let them bury me," Riddle said, and was asleep before the Humvee cleared the ship's ramp.

The lorry first in line to leave the ship was loaded with grain bags. Marc Hall pointed to it, picking the vehicle with the largest promise of comfort on what might be a long, bumpy ride to the hospital and the camp beyond. Tory crossed the well-deck forward to where he waited. He climbed up the back, then reached down for her rucksack and weapon.

"I'm surprised they even issue rucksacks to boat soldiers," he said as she scrambled forward and settled in next to him, midtruck on a stack of the grain bags.

"Me, too," she said. She pointed to the truck cab's rear window before them, an illustrated picture pasted in it. "Who's that?"

"Samedi," he said. "The real Samedi. Papa Doc tried to be Samedi, too. Baron Samedi. Who knows, maybe he was. My mother had this same picture, inside a kitchen cabinet."

"So your mother believed in Voodoo?"

"*Vodoun*—yes. Of course."

"You wear a cross, though." She'd seen it when he was showering, hanging between his dog tags—she spoke evenly, but felt her cheeks blush as she realized the implication. If Marc realized, made the connection, he didn't show it.

"Yes," he said. "I was raised Catholic. The two are not mutually exclusive."

She looked at him, a question.

"They're hand in hand, in Haiti. The Catholic Church, the real

church, in Rome, would say it isn't so, it couldn't be so." He sipped
from his open canteen, wetting his lips. "But Rome is a long way from
Gonaives." He smiled.

Tory turned, squinting through the bright sun back over the well-
deck to the ship's house. She gazed up, Mac and the skipper on the
bridge wing, both looking down at them. She raised a hand and Skipper
raised a hand back. It was not a coincidence she was the sergeant picked
to join Captain Hall on the relief run. There was another ship entering
port behind them, a civilian missionary ship. Skip had taken her aside to
tell her. "I don't know who's onboard now," he'd said, but they both
had a good idea—they both knew who had been onboard. She'd said
simply, "It doesn't matter. I would have volunteered to go anyway." If
Dick Wags had seen her leave he might have said something to her, but
she never saw him—an absence so conspicuous she wondered if it was
intentional: If he didn't see her go, he couldn't say anything.

Tory faced front again. The truck fired its rattling old diesel, belch-
ing fumes, and pulled forward slowly. The two Special Forces soldiers
had kept the crowd off the pier, so there was a straight, empty shot off
the ship to solid land. Tory held her breath a little as the truck's tires
began to roll—but the pier held.

The crowd didn't roar like in Port-au-Prince, but the people cheered
as the relief trucks rolled toward them, off the pier then onto the small,
unpaved road winding from the harbor up into Jacmel. The cheer could
barely be heard over the whine of the truck's diesel engine. Marc Hall
leaned in to ask her a question and she couldn't hear that, either.

"What?" she said, waving at the people they passed, feeling slightly
absurd and glorious all at once up here on the back of this truck, sun
beaming on her face. She felt like a GI, like a hero, like she was needed.
It was a good feeling. Especially after Port-au-Prince. A good feeling.

Marc put his mouth next to her ear. "I said, 'And what religion are
you?'"

"None, really," she said. "Why?"

Marc didn't answer at first, then leaned over to her again. "Because,"
he said, "I noticed you *don't* wear a cross with your dog tags."

CHAPTER

25

Dick Wags waited for Scaboo in the crew's mess, standing alone with a cup of coffee, staring out the window. The younger sergeant stuck his head in, and the two left the ship by the gangway, the first time the gangway had been lowered since they were in Haiti. After the truck roll-off, Mannino had put the ship starboard-side-to, directly across the pier from where the ragged blue missionary ship tied off portside-to. The two sergeants stopped to salute the flag and the quarterdeck, one at a time, then quick about-faced and headed down the stairs. Also for the first time in Haiti, the two wore soft caps instead of helmets. Dick Wags had his rifle slung across his back barrel-down, but neither had their flak jacket or LBE suspenders and pistol belt. Scaboo kept shrugging his shoulders as they walked down the gangway; he felt naked and strange leaving the ship without the extra weight.

On the pier they both lit cigarettes. The *Agape*'s gangway was steps away, but they took a minute. The pier was empty, T.K. and Temple and a deckie named Carver standing guard at the end of it. T.K. had his helmet off, acoustic guitar strapped around his neck, murdering what sounded to Dick Wags like a Bob Marley song, a gaggle of Haitian children gathered around him dancing and clapping. Scaboo walked across the pier, smoking, looking up and down the length of the *Agape*. No one was visible on deck above them, but they could hear people, the sounds of early dinner maybe, silverware and chatter. The sides of the ship were pitted and rough under the faded blue paint, tired old steel, but not too bad with rust around the waterline.

"Don't look as terrible as I thought it might," Scaboo said.

"No, not from here. We'll see about inside."

Dick Wags had been on her once, five or six years before. The old ship steamed out of Norfolk docks, just down the James from Newport News and Fort Eustis, and Junior Davis was not the first Army maritime engineer to sail her. The *Agape*—and her now-retired sister ship, long since sold for scrap—had a reputation; turnover was high in the engine room, and questions kept to a minimum, if asked at all. The contract skippers tended to like Army engineers because they weren't too specialized like the Navy trained them. They could do more, in the engine room and on the bridge, too, if needed. More than one Waterborne snipe had found a bunk and small paycheck from the missionary ships after a quick—and, often, forced—exit from military service. When Dick Wags had still been a PFC he'd made a midnight drive down to Norfolk one night with Chief Valentine, a drunken dischargee in the backseat of the Chief's Buick. The man had been a sergeant first class six days before—the ACE on one of the new LCU-2000s—and a married man with a passel of kids. Now he was a civilian via punching an officer, and on his way to divorced via the private he'd been sleeping with. They sat in a diner off Ocean Avenue most of the night, sobering him up with coffee, then made for the wharf at sunrise. Dick Wags hadn't seen much of the ship then, but what he remembered was unlit, dirty, and smelled like a church basement. He'd helped the sarge carry his two duffels up to a small cabin in the ship's house, then left him there, sitting on the bare bunk under a framed Jesus bolted to the bulkhead—a man in shock.

Dick Wags smoked on the pier now, remembering how silent Chief Valentine had been as they drove away, and how he'd finally said, "We take care of our own, Rick. Best we can, anyway."

That was true, Dick Wags thought now; both parts of it. They did take care of their own, but there was a limit, too. There was a limit both to what you could do—as in the case of the sarge they'd packed off, and who knew what happened to him after that—and there was also a limit to what someone earned, what they deserved. Junior Davis case in point. Dick Wags and Scaboo might have different thoughts on the subject. Scaboo was loyal like a hound to his former roomdog. Dick Wags had an alternative perspective.

Scaboo took a last look at *Agape*'s waterline, then flicked his cigarette into the bay. "You think he's still onboard?" he said.

"I don't know."

Dick Wags tossed his own cigarette, then started up the missionary ship's gangway. They passed a sandwich-board sign at the bottom, a chalkboard notice: SERVICE FOR THE LORD, 9 AM TOMORROW! SOLDIERS AND HAITIANS ALIKE ALL WELCOME! There was a man at the head of the gangway. Tall, grizzled, he'd not been visible from the pier. His eyes set thin into the sun, lines carved deep on his face.

"Staff Sergeant Wagman, United States Army," Dick Wags said quietly, stopping two steps below. "Permission to come aboard, Sir."

McBride stuck out his hand, shaking with both soldiers. "C'mon in, then," he said, turning and walking toward a hatch into the house. "I'm tired as hell and it's too hot out here."

The doors were propped open on the bridge of the LSV, a warm, sweet breeze pushing through from starboard to port. Mannino had changed into a pair of cut-off cammies and a gray T-shirt, sitting in his skipper's chair with feet up on the forward rail. He'd left a cigarette burning unattended in the ashtray and was rifling through a stack of envelopes, resting them on his belly. A resupply chopper had stocked the Special Forces soldiers shortly before the LSV made port. Among the load was a locked mail sack Master Sergeant Rice had tossed through the pilot door at Xerox after the ship tied off. They hadn't been in-country long enough to get personal mail yet, but the ship had been either under way or locked down for twenty-some days now—command and battalion communication had backed up.

Items not in sealed envelopes were almost sure to be irrelevant: notice of change in dining-hall hours for Fort Eustis permanent party, notice of increased random breathalyzer checks by the MPs at the post gate, monthly schedule for the movie theater—all of it routed to every unit whether they were home or in Istanbul. Most of the envelopes Mannino knew the contents before opening, even if he didn't know who it pertained to. A thin white envelope with a Texas return address stamped AAFES would be bad news: a soldier who hadn't paid his DPP credit bill at the PX. Mannino pulled the form out: Holan, the youngest private on the boat, a trainee in Dick Wags's engine room. Two grand in debt, the money spent on Nintendo, cigarettes, *Hustler,* clothes, and CDs—no payment made in two months. Young Holan, Mannino knew, also had a shiny new Jeep, recipient of all his money.

"Top," Mannino said, waving the paper in the air.

"Sir?" Top was standing just outside the door on the bridge wing, nursing a mug of tea.

"Where's Holan?"

Top looked at his watch. "Engine room."

Mannino held out the paperwork to him. "Go fuck him up."

"Check." Top glanced at the paperwork and headed down below.

There wasn't much more. Battalion promotion scores, but Jersey and Scaboo had just been pinned sergeant and he wouldn't be able to pin any new hard stripes for quite a while. One interoffice envelope contained a memo from the 7th Group XO: an individual packing list for possible deployment to Haiti; that merited a chuckle from Mannino and a break to take a few puffs from his forgotten cigarette. One item he saved for last because he didn't know what it was. Thick, from the Office of Personnel, stamped as a copy of material sent to battalion command. This merited another smirk: the battalion commander was sitting in a warehouse in Port-au-Prince right now; Mannino doubted the colonel would be getting to his mail any time soon. The skipper finished his cigarette, taking a moment to look through the bridge window at Jacmel before him. They were scheduled to be here forty-eight hours, but Mannino was already thinking up reasons why they needed to stay longer. He opened the thick envelope.

It took him a few passes to figure out what he was reading, mostly because half the forms were medical and he'd never seen them before. The last few he knew, though—notices of change of deployment status and a blank authorization form for early discharge. He shuffled the papers and read them all again, in a different order this time, hoping a different read might elicit a different outcome. It did not. Mannino set all the paperwork carefully in his lap and lit another cigarette. It sat burning between the fingers of his right hand while he massaged his forehead with the fingers of his left. He read all the papers again.

When Top returned to the bridge ten minutes later Mannino was in the same position, staring out the bridge window. A slow talker, Top reported in: "Private Holan is appropriately scared. He's going to—"

Mannino cut him off.

"Sergeant Harris went with the Red Cross?"

Top nodded. "Yes, Sir."

Mannino bit his lip, thinking. Top stepped over to the skipper's chair. He glanced down at the paperwork, but the warrant officer pushed it all together and flipped it face down in his lap.

"Where's Dick Wags?" Mannino said. "Still with the Jesus freaks?"

Top nodded.

"All right," Mannino said.

"Should I—"

Mannino stood, holding his hand up at his sort-of first sergeant. "I'll take care of it," he said.

Scaboo left Dick Wags and McBride at a table in the dining hall, the two hunched over a wish list of parts and supplies. The quick tour of the boat this old skipper McBride gave them made the Army's generosity seem sort of pointless. *Agape* needed a lot of light bulbs, and the LSV could easily give them up, but as far as Scaboo could tell all it would accomplish was showing more brightly everything broken. He slipped away from the table and wandered the ship alone, slowly, opening hatches and peering around corners.

There were a lot of damn people on this boat. He didn't know how they did it. He'd once sailed a training cruise on a Navy oiler and thought he'd pass out from the crush of bodies; this was a lot like that, except it smelled bad, too. In places, anyway. An unwashed stink. Smell of dirty clothes and sharp breath and he tried to breathe through his mouth so it wasn't overwhelming. The church people seemed nice enough, everyone friendly and talkative, but there was a serious shortage of personal space on here, and quite obviously a shortage of potable water and soap. Scaboo was fastidious in his personal hygiene. This ship made him anxious.

He walked the length forward on the galley deck, went down one and came back aft. The ship had weathered a hard ride the night before, and there was a cabin-fever energy in the closed, stale air. Little kids zoomed through and around his legs, up and down passages, bouncing off bulkheads and one another. His uniform drew stares and he was glad to be visibly unarmed. Most at least smiled at him. A few stopped him to talk briefly. He was nervous, waiting for a *Praise Jesus!* but there was none. One older man was from Queens and that gave them something to talk about, though the man hadn't been in fifteen years. Scaboo heard a lot of Southern accents. A mom yelling after running kids had a drawl on her mom voice, although Scaboo noticed it seemed to slip away when she talked quietly.

"You can take these guys outside, you know," Scaboo said to her, pointing at the backs of the band of boys tearing down the passage. "It's pretty nice. There's a beach."

The woman smiled and shrugged and that was the end of that.

He worked his way topside again. He thought he'd like to see the bridge—McBride's sort-of tour had been all below decks, mostly engine room. Avoiding the dining hall, Scaboo picked his way up through and into the house and the direction he thought he ought to be going. This being an old cruise ship, the bridge would be forward.

An old brass plate on a door said Chapel and he turned the knob, looking in. A small empty room, no bigger than a cabin, with a large wooden cross. He'd seen where they did real church up in the dining hall; this must be the original ship's chapel. Scaboo let the door close behind him and went to a knee, crossing himself. He slipped into one of the four benches bolted to the deck. Doing it made him think he was certainly the only Catholic on this ship—not counting Dick Wags, who hadn't seen the inside of a church in ten years. He didn't know what to do, sitting here, so he said the Lord's Prayer, leaning against the bench in front of him, hands wrapped together. He sat another silent moment, then kneeled and crossed himself again and left the room.

It was quiet up here, no kids—no people at all. McBride hadn't been joking about the light bulbs: there were none working. Not in the passages up here, anyway. Everything dark, just slivers of daylight poking in from outside.

Scaboo climbed another narrow steel staircase. The passage here ran across-ship, the old officer's deck. He put his hands in his pockets then took them out again. It was there, a white index card taped to the cabin door in front of him: DAVIS.

Well.

They hadn't really said anything in the engine room, just asked if the ship's engineer needed to talk about supplies. They didn't ask by name. McBride hadn't volunteered the information, either, just said the ship's engineer was quite sick. He'd written a list, though, and McBride pulled a piece of paper from deep in a pocket and handed it to Dick Wags, who glanced at it then passed it to Scaboo. Hydraulic oil, if possible; a fifty-pound can of heavy grease; rubber sheets for making gaskets—all clearly in Junior Davis's logbook handwriting.

Scaboo stepped across the passage, raised his fist to the door, hesitated, lowered his arm, then quick raised it again and rapped twice. No response, though he thought he heard something. He knocked again. A voice, but unclear. He reached down and turned the knob, easing the door open.

The cabin was dark, curtain pulled across the round hatch window, one dim overhead light and deep shadows. Davis was in bed, sitting up, a sweatshirt on him.

"Roomdog," Davis said, and it was too dark to see if he was smiling or not. The voice was almost a croak but unmistakably Junior; the body, on the other hand, seemed much thinner than Scaboo remembered.

Davis caught him looking. "Lost some weight."

"Yeah."

It was all Scaboo could think of to say.

"Come on in."

Scaboo closed the door behind him and as he did the cabin's other door opened, from the small head. A woman walked through, wet hair slicked back and a towel wrapped around her. She jumped, startled, seeing Scaboo, but made no noise. Junior nodded toward her.

"Roomdog, this is Lorraine, from the shower. Lorraine, this is Roomdog from the Army."

Not knowing what else to do, Scaboo put his hand out. "Sergeant Scabliagni," he said, voice cracking with nerves. He blinked. "Steve, I mean. Steve Scabliagni."

Lorraine's left hand clutched tight to the towel near her neck. She looked at Scaboo's hand, saying nothing, and just when he'd decided to drop it she took his hand in hers, shaking once.

"Hi," she said.

CHAPTER

26

A strange-looking pair of soldiers they were, tall black officer and small female sergeant, sitting high atop bags of grain on the back of the lorry—a slow and mostly uphill climb, nestled in the cradle of burlap around them, riding in bright afternoon sunlight. The two talked almost the whole way, absolutely alone in their world, any last pretenses dropped.

"Jacmel is the city of Carnivale, sort of like Mardi Gras."

"Do they throw beads?"

"They throw a lot of things. It's famous for masks."

"Masks?"

"Big," he said, and used his big hands to show. "Papier-mâché, oversized. Exaggerated." He held his hands even wider, making a clown face, making her laugh. "Good for hiding anything you don't want to show."

People lined the road along their route, waving and sometimes singing as the convoy passed. Not thick crowds like Port-au-Prince, even as they drove through town. But a lot of people, a steady line, children running and calling out and curious men. The drivers of the lorries waved with all their might, enjoying their role in the parade. Tory waved to the children.

"What's under your mask, Tory Harris?"

She watched a little boy running along the side of the road, desperately trying to keep up with the convoy. They passed him finally, and Tory looked at Marc. "Scratch the sergeant and all you'll find is more sergeant."

The city they climbed up through and around was completely unlike Port-au-Prince and unlike anything Tory had seen. She'd been to New Orleans once, on leave with Junior Davis, and there was a comparison to be made there, but Jacmel felt more intense. French colonial, close and narrow, bright Caribbean colors and, in places, what were clearly bullet holes splayed along a plaster wall or up a wooden shutter. There were actual plants here, trees, flowers, and an absence of the smog found in the dead Port-au-Prince basin.

"Like paradise," Marc said.

She nodded.

"Papa Doc almost killed it. Tried to kill it."

"Kill what?"

Marc waved his arm. "All of it. The city."

"Why?"

"They didn't vote for him. He was insulted."

"That was a long time ago?"

Marc shrugged. "Not that long."

Tory almost said something about the people here, how they looked not as poor, not as ragged. Then, as they climbed from the city, the buildings became less solid and the clothes less substantial. It was a change, a marked change, like moving through layers of water—all the same ocean, but different pressure, different temperature. And as they left the city the general goodwill directed at them increased fivefold, from happy curiosity to an almost hysterical relief. Here is where the wild cheers came, and some tears. As if emotion was in direct proportion to quality and quantity of clothing.

"These people lost their homes."

"It must be a fairly regular thing," she said, the maritime quartermaster speaking. "They're smack in the middle of hurricane country."

Marc nodded. "Yes, I guess you're right," he said, somewhat clipped. He seemed not to like her observation. He seemed sad, and it was unclear whether he was sad for the Haitians or sad she'd made such an obvious remark. Tory got angry for a second, watching his face, watching him watch Jacmel go by. She reached for her canteen and took a drink and it had passed by then, whatever it was, and she was sure it was nothing anyway, her imagination, her nerves. For one split, irrational second she wanted to tell him everything, tell him how it was with her, tell him everything Dick Wags knew, make this man her new confessor. She opened her mouth but smiled instead of speaking, smiled through it, and when he looked over at her she was waving at a group of women, smiling but wistful, unknown and strange. They were rounding a sharp corner where for one moment the other trucks and the single Humvee behind weren't visible. Marc reached over and took her free hand, held it tightly, squeezed. She looked at him, squeezing back, and she raised his hand and kissed it, pressing her lips to his warm skin, bowing her head slightly but keeping her eyes locked on his, pleased at the reversal.

The convoy moved, curved and bouncing, up and across the bowl around *Baye Jacmel.* In the rear, the LSV's single Humvee followed, Specialist Pelton at the wheel. He'd thought to grab a bag of hard candies from the galley, and he reached into it as he drove, grabbing a few pieces now and then and tossing them at groups of kids as he passed. He tapped the top of the gearshift as he drove. Next to him, curled, Riddle slept—still breathing, still alive.

They split an orange, Marc Hall stripping the fruit in one long peel, digging his fingertips in and ripping it in half. Tory never ate oranges anymore—an unconscious aversion to all things uniform-staining—but she liked them. She popped her half straight into her mouth, squeezing teeth down slow.

"That's a lot of orange," he said, sectioning his half.

She smiled around her mouthful, chewed carefully, swallowed, then said, "You're married."

He said nothing for a moment, then held up his hands, wiggling his bare fingers. She waited, and he said, "Yes."

"All officers are married," she said.

He nodded. It wasn't quite true, but it was an Army fact.

"Is your wife Haitian?"

"Soon-to-be-ex wife. No."

Tory wiped her orangey hands across her leg. She didn't care, but had been curious about what he'd say.

"And you?" he asked.

"I'm not married," she said.

"Ever come close?"

She shook her head no, then said, "Maybe." Her legs were falling asleep, tingling, sitting in the same position so long. She stretched them best she could from her cradle in the burlap grain bags. Then she said, "Yes, sort of. Not really, but sort of. Something like it, anyway. You know us enlisted, not all get-out formal like you officers." She half-smiled. "All shackin'-up and doublewide trailers for us."

"Was he in the Army?"

"Yes. Not now, but then." She reached for her cigarettes, pulling one out. Marc Hall took the pack from her hands, getting one for himself. She hadn't seen him smoke before. She lit them both, watching him. Marc smoked like an ex-smoker, comfortable but not unconscious. It made her self-conscious, and she mostly let her cigarette burn down between her fingers. "He's here, actually," she said.

"Who?"

"My ex."

Marc Hall's eyebrows went up and he said, "You seem to have a strange attraction to Haitian men, Sergeant Harris."

Tory laughed out loud.

"He's not Haitian—he's Philadelphian. Irish Catholic."

Marc laughed with her, and before he could ask she answered: "He's an engineer. On the mission ship." She hooked her thumb over her shoulder, in the general direction of Jacmel Bay.

"Oh, you mean he's *here,* in Jacmel," Marc said.

"Funny world, isn't it?"

Marc smoked, not answering.

"He has a small problem with sobriety," Tory said. "Sobriety, moderation—fidelity. Fidelity he can't quite get his hands on."

"I'm sorry."

She shrugged.

The feeling she'd had before came back, the desire to talk. She bit her lip. Her cigarette had burned unsmoked, but she took a big drag from it now.

"He, uh—he did a lot of . . . You know, to be honest I don't really know. His best friend dimed him out. Trying to help, or something. A real arrow, that guy. A little naive. You met him, on the boat. Sergeant Scabliagni."

Marc nodded.

"Scaboo dropped the dime on him, and battalion pissed him. Surprise piss test. Junior came up hot for—" Tory laughed, bitter. "Everything, from what I understand. Pretty near everything, really."

"Did you know?"

"No. Yes. You know?"

She flicked her cigarette over the side of the truck.

"Yeah, I didn't know everything. Not nearly. Not even close. I knew he was in trouble, but . . . not like it turned out."

"He got put out?"

"It was bad."

"He got put out and you left him."

"No, actually. He got put out and left me."

The trucks followed a long, straight road. The road was brown, sodden dirt and still thick mud in places, from the storm. Out here there was vegetation, green and low then higher and sometimes curving over the road, swaths of grasses and wide leaves. The road finally curved down into a short, shallow valley and then up again to a high place, a flat plain with no trees. They could see now where the mudslides had run, carrying buildings and people off the mountain into the bay.

Tory hadn't looked back once the truck cleared the ramp of the LSV, hadn't looked back and beyond to where she knew the mission boat was limping into Jacmel's small harbor. She didn't know for sure if Junior Davis was still on that ship but believed it to be true. Dead was a possibility, too, of course. Junior could be dead. But Tory didn't feel he was dead and if he wasn't dead he was on the ship. Junior tended to stick to things, one foot planted on a home base. She'd been his home base for two years. She'd thought she'd been his home; but no, she'd been his home base.

Tory didn't look back when the truck rolled off the LSV, didn't look back at the mission boat beyond, because looking at the ship was maybe a first step in something. Maybe not, but maybe. *Hey, there's Junior's boat and hey there's someone who must know Junior now and hey there's Junior. Did I mention, Marc, that I shoot Expert? Really. Sure. Let me get into the unsupported prone position here. Watch this.*

Or worse. There's worse.

Hi, Junior.

Hi, Tory.

How's things?

Good, you?

Good.

Great.

Whatcha up to?

Not much, you?

Not much.

I miss you, New Jersey.

Really? You do?

Yeah. Want to make out?

Okay.

Tory had nothing to say to Junior Davis. Nothing and everything. Everything is impossible—you can't say everything, so everything is better off reduced to nothing.

CHAPTER

27

McBride climbed to the bridge, looking for Pastor. She'd taken a radio call from the home mission while he was with Staff Sergeant Wagman. He wanted to hear what they'd said. More, he wanted to tell her what the Army sergeant had promised, how generous the military ship was, the parts and supplies they'd been offered. It wasn't enough, but he knew it would cheer her, this small stuff. He rounded the corner at the top of the stairs, squinting into the sunlight gleaming across his bridge. The space stood empty, dust motes floating in the brightness. He turned and went below to her cabin.

McBride was weary in step and in the slow plod of his thoughts. As a skipper he needed to be quick on his feet, nimble. He felt neither now, just exhausted, tired past where he could easily push through it, press on. No matter, he thought; he would sleep soon enough. Secure the ship for the day, receive the supplies from the Army, maybe check in with Davis—then rest. Undisturbed, long sleep. He almost salivated at the thought of it.

Pastor's cabin door stood open and he stuck his head in. She sat on the edge of her bed, a white piece of paper in her left hand. She wasn't looking at the paper, just holding it, staring at a space on the bulkhead. Her eyes rose to McBride's as he stepped in.

"Well," he said, "we're set. They're—"

She put a hand up, stopping him.

"It doesn't matter," she said.

"Well, it's not an engine, but it's a start. We can camp out here a bit, a month or more. Establish a church schedule. Davis and I can work on the main, see what comes of it."

She looked at him blankly. "Davis is a half-dead addict. And we don't have a month." Her face seemed to shiver. She waved the paper in her hand. It was a notebook page, McBride saw, scrawled on in her handwriting. "They're coming for us, Paul."

"Coming for us?"

"A tug. A commercial tugboat from Miami. It's already through the Windward Passage. They're discontinuing the international mission. They've sold the ship, for scrap."

So, he thought. *Here it is, after all.*

"What of us?"

"Stay on the ship, for the tow to Puerto Rico."

"They can't leave all these people stranded in Puerto Rico."

"They've made some arrangement, with another maritime mission. They say everyone will be in the States by Christmas at the latest."

"They've got it all figured out."

"They do," she said. "They do."

She moved her eyes to the deck, hovering over nothing.

"I insisted and they agreed to pay you, and Davis if he wants it. To strip the ship in Puerto Rico. And they'll fly you both home from there. Or to New York, at least."

"I'll do no such thing," he said quietly.

"Don't be a fool, Paul. You're not a young man and it's an easy paycheck. Through January, I'd guess."

McBride said nothing, felt he couldn't. She was pale, paler than normal. She looked sick, he thought. Physically sick. He wanted more than anything to embrace her, to put his arms around her and hold her and reassure and comfort her. But she was sitting, just sitting there forlorn on her bed, and it was awkward.

Finally, he just said, "You did the best you could."

She raised her eyes again, her doughy face soft and fragile. "I need to be alone, Paul," she said.

She hadn't called him Paul in two years, and here she'd done it three times in five minutes. It came on him again, the almost overwhelming need to embrace her. Instead, he turned and stepped out wordlessly, pulling her door closed behind him. He stood alone in the passage, holding the rail outside her door, listening to the distant sounds of the ship around him and the deep silence from her cabin.

CHAPTER

28

Lorraine was gone, slipped sideways past Scaboo through the cabin door to get breakfast. Junior Davis hadn't moved from the bed, nor offered a seat to Scaboo. So the young sergeant stood, soft cap in hands at the foot of the bed, feeling like a kid calling on a sick older relative. He supposed he was, in a way.

The two stayed like that, silent and unmoving, almost two minutes. Finally, Junior said, "Say something, Roomdog."

"I don't know what to say."

"You're the one who came in here. I figured you had something to say."

"I, uh—" Scaboo shook his head. "Maybe I better go."

"Sure, whatever. Come, go." Junior waved his arm in the air. "You lack direction." It was meant to be a joke but neither of them laughed.

"You don't look good, Junior," Scaboo said. "Is there a doctor on here? Are you sick?"

Junior stared at him, unblinking. Then he said, "No, there's no doctor on here. And yes, I'm sick." He let that hang in the air.

Scaboo forced a smile. He regretted his next sentence as soon as it came out of his mouth. "I thought you might get clean on here."

"What the fuck is it to you? *Get clean,*" Davis sneered. "Fuck you."

"Hey man, I just—"

"No, fuck you. You just what? You just come to finish me off? Come to drive another stake through me?"

Scaboo put his soft cap on. Very quietly he mumbled, "I gotta go."

He turned to leave and Junior said, "I'm sick, Steve. Pretty sick."

Scaboo turned around again, and Junior told him how it really was. There was another wide silence, then Scaboo said, "Are you on medicine?"

"No."

"You gotta get on something, Junior. You'll die."

"Not so sure I'm not dead already."

Junior Davis hadn't made it to his final Army physical. This wasn't hard to do; when the government puts you out the only thing they're concerned with is property, namely theirs, namely that it's returned. Leaving the Army naturally is a half-year process of meetings and workshops and physicals. Leaving unnaturally takes only a day. Junior had the vague notion that this day was his bottom, absolute bottom—drunk in the passenger seat of Scaboo's Jeep, making the rounds of Fort Eustis to clear his hand receipts and turn in gear, Scaboo in the end walking most of the stuff in, obtaining the signatures.

The bottom, though—if there is such a thing—and the physical—if you could call it that—came two weeks later, in the Newport News city jail. The quick trip to jail came after being pulled from the back of an idling Pontiac downtown at 2:00 A.M., windows steamed and tailpipe puffing in the frosty night. The police asked the red-faced suit in the Pontiac if he had a wife then sent him home to her. Junior was handcuffed. The physical, such as it was, came because Junior passed out in the back of the police van. His blood was drawn in the emergency room, as he slept it off on a restrained gurney.

He was out of jail in a few days. A nurse came with papers he had to sign before they'd release him. She asked if he'd known and he said yes just to bypass the prepared script. He hadn't known, though. He hadn't. Somehow he'd thought—if he thought at all—he was bulletproof. He was a soldier, a fucking good soldier, a one-out-of-ten soldier. His uniform was bulletproof. His skin, his veins, all of it bulletproof.

"A fucking good soldier," he mumbled, watching the back of the nurse grow smaller as she walked down the cellblock.

A fucking good soldier.

And a good fucking soldier.

Ha! *That* was funny.

A good fucking soldier—and a good fuck.

"A good fuck," he said. He ran his open palms across his eyes, push-ing the water clear, then making a fist and wringing it into his forehead, driving himself back to collapse on the cell cot.

He'd convinced Tory to meet him at a diner on Ocean Avenue in Norfolk six hours before he sailed with the missionaries.

"Why'd you pick that ship?" she said. The missionaries were going to Haiti. And on this cold, rain-soaked spring morning the word across Fort Eustis was that 7th Group would be in Haiti by Columbus Day. "You could have picked a different ship," she said.

It wasn't really true, but he didn't want to argue.

"Listen," he said. He reached for her hand but she pulled it back, off the table, both hands in her lap.

"This doesn't have to be this hard," he said. She didn't answer.

In the end, he had to just tell her.

"It doesn't mean anything," he added, almost frantic. "Doesn't mean *anything*. It's just a chance, is all. You should get checked because there's a chance, but I'm sure . . . I mean, a chance doesn't mean any-thing."

Tory sat stone-faced because it wasn't a chance and they both knew it. There was no chance about it. She felt it as soon as he said it, felt it in her, the truth of it and aliveness of it. She sat, stone-faced, because she was bulletproof, too, in other ways, and she sat and deflected the bul-lets for another three minutes then stood without a word and left a ten on the table and walked out of the diner, into the rain. He tried to fol-low her out and she turned without looking him in the eye and told him to sit back down. Alone in the cab of her truck she checked her watch: 0800—she'd skipped PT and morning formation to come down here, but the LSV was sailing at noon, to spend the afternoon shooting .50 cal a mile off the Virginia Beach coast. They were preparing for war. No one else in the country knew it, but they knew it. She was a new sergeant and her ship was sailing to war and she intended to be on it.

* * *

On the back of the lorry, on the way to the camp, Marc asked, "Did you love him?"

She didn't answer, but she nodded, almost imperceptibly.

"I trusted him," she said finally. She was looking at her hands. "Even if a part of me never really trusted *him*, I—" She thought for a moment, squinting into the bright, afternoon sun. "It's a funny thing. I adored him, truly. But I never trusted him in jeans. I trusted him in uniform, though. Because that's where his true love was. And that was something I understood. Or, I thought so."

"He wasn't the first soldier to fool around on his girlfriend," Marc said, as gently as he could.

Tory smiled. "It's a little deeper than that, Marc." And that's as much as she would tell him.

CHAPTER

29

The hospital sat on a small plain, a collection of low buildings gathered inside a stucco wall. The poor arrived with minor and major wounds, gangrenous cuts, missing limbs, to deliver babies or cure them; most patients in this hospital, though, suffered AIDS or TB or both. It was why the hospital had been built, on charity money and medicine from the States and the UK. Beyond it a sprawling camp of sorts had grown—permanent, semipermanent, and completely temporary structures pushing away toward the forest, filling all the available empty land. There were people from other parts of Haiti living here now, travelers to the hospital, in small stone houses they'd built with no quick intention of leaving, and people living with not more than a newspaper between themselves and the elements. And all manner of dwellings and poverty in between.

"It was much more solid, before," the woman said to Tory, gesturing with a narrow hand across the field from where they stood, looking out the hospital gate. Her name was Brinia Avril. She was a doctor, a young Haitian in a white lab coat. She had large, silver hoop earrings dangling to a sharp jaw line, sharp cheeks. "The camp is here because the hospital is here. And we've tried very hard to keep it sanitary, keep it safe. A month ago, I would have told you it was."

The tropical storm had loosened the surrounding mountains and brought the mud. The mud had taken out a quarter of the hospital, knocking flat a lower wall and sweeping away two small administrative and storage buildings inside. The storm destroyed a third or half the camp outside the hospital walls.

"How many died?" Tory asked, but Brinia Avril shook her head again.

"I'm not sure how many were there alive, you know? So it's almost impossible to say how many died. It's more like, you're used to seeing certain people, certain faces, during the week, coming and going, feeding a sick relative in the ward, doing laundry, whatever. And one day you remember you haven't seen that face in a while and then you know, 'Yes, that's another dead.' "

There was a small, clean hut where Captain Hall would live for the few days it would take to supervise the distribution of the Red Cross materials. He disappeared into it to stow his gear.

"I'm staying, too," Tory told Pelton. "At least through tomorrow. Come back with a Humvee tomorrow and get me." Pelton raised his eyebrows but said nothing.

Riddle walked toward them, camera in hand. He was snapping pictures of everything, talking to everyone—whether or not he understood them. Not speaking Creole was no impediment to Riddle; constant conversation was necessary for him—actual communication wasn't neccessary. He'd found friends, a small boy and smaller girl who must be his sister. The girl was blind, and held tight to her brother's hand. The boy and his sister had been given a ride on one of the Red Cross lorries. They'd followed Riddle and Pelton for the last hour, walking everywhere with them.

"You got a name?" Riddle asked for the fifth time, but the boy didn't understand.

"Ti garcon Qui jen ou relais?" the doctor asked.

"Henri," said the boy.

"You got to stop following me, Henry," Riddle said, "or I'll marry your sister and take all your money."

"Henri!" the boy said.

"Right."

Tory explained Riddle's near-zombification to Brinia Avril and the doctor burst out laughing.

"The *coup poudre!*" she said to him. "You thought you fell to the *coup poudre!*"

"What's that?"

"*Zombi* powder," she said, exaggerating and rolling her accent.

"That's it exactly."

"Yes, except there is no such thing. It was a misunderstanding, that's all."

Riddle shook his head. "No, it was real," he said. "I could *feel* it. Working in me." He pounded his chest. "Only my strength of will and total powers of concentration kept it at bay."

Pelton smacked him on the back of the helmet, walking past on his way to the Humvee. "You mean you talked it to death."

Riddle stared after him, wounded. Then he thought about it, and slowly began to nod. "That's it!" he said, snapping his fingers, Pelton already out of earshot. "Dude, you're right. That's what I did! I talked the zombie right out of me."

No one was listening. They'd all walked away, except Henri and his sister. Riddle stooped down, talking directly to him. "I talked the zombie out, Henry," he said. "I cured the voodoo curse. The great mystery of Haiti—solved, Henry. By me."

"Henri!"

"Exactly."

Across the hospital's open yard, Pelton fired off the hummer's engine. Tory wanted her two soldiers back on the boat before sunset, and already the afternoon shadows were long. They'd make the distance much faster without the convoy, but had to leave now.

"Riddle!" Pelton called.

"Gotta go, Henry," Riddle said, shaking the boy's hand, then taking one of the girl's hands and clasping it. "Y'all keep it real. *Vive le Haiti.*"

"Henri!" The boy stamped his foot.

"Variety is the spice of life, Henry," Riddle said, pocketing his camera. "Expand that vocabulary, son."

The hut was empty when Tory entered it, but Marc's rucksack lay on one of the two cots, a spray of belongings across the cot from where Marc had been digging through his stuff. A notebook and papers, his flashlight, open shaving kit. Tory dropped her own ruck on the other cot, and her helmet. She unclipped her web belt and pulled off her flak jacket, folding it back together and laying it flat. She drank from one of her canteens and ran a few drops of water through her short hair. There was a small, green lizard on the hut wall over her cot and she watched to see if it would move but it didn't. Outside she heard a baby crying, and a woman talking to another woman in Creole. It would be sundown soon; Tory hoped for some coolness in the air. Her belly rumbled, and she remembered how long it had been since chow.

She stepped over to Marc's cot and without bending over used the fingers of her right hand to open farther the already-open shaving kit. She pulled out his razor and held it to her nose, sniffing. It didn't smell of him. It didn't smell of anything. She dropped it back in. She looked again. There were two pill bottles, brown prescription bottles. She pulled them out, one at a time, reading the labels then placing them carefully back in the bag. She pursed her lips and zipped the bag, remembered it had been open and unzipped it again. She picked up her rifle from where she'd propped it in the corner, checked the safety, put her soft cap on, and left the hut. Evening was near and though it wasn't cooler yet, it felt cooler just from the late-day stillness of the yard and promise of night.

Tory saw Brinia Avril through a window and entered the building. It was a long white room with tables and equipment. A silver clock hung on the far wall, another green lizard perched beside it.

"Your lab?" Tory asked.

"Yes, that's right."

The doctor was on a stool, alone in the room, her lab coat off. She wore blue jeans and light blue T-shirt.

Tory looked around a minute then said, "Can I walk through?" She nodded in the direction of the far door and the ward behind it.

"Yes." Brinia Avril smiled. "Do you need that?"

She meant the rifle slung across Tory's back.

"I'm sorry."

Brinia Avril shrugged.

The ward was darker than the outside and quiet, those in the beds seemed to be sleeping. Ten beds lined each wall, a narrow walk down the middle. Four ceiling fans turned lazily overhead. Almost all the lights were off.

"Most nap after dinner." Brinia Avril had come up behind. "Those who can eat dinner." Tory hadn't heard her coming but wasn't startled.

"What's the—"

"AIDS," the doctor answered, not needing to hear the question. "In the last year, two years, we treat HIV early and aggressively. As much as possible, anyway. The medicine flows more freely down here than before, somewhat. Relative." Tory moved slowly down the ward, Brinia Avril right behind, almost whispering in her ear. "Still, it is inevitable some will slip through the cracks of treatment. Others will eventually just stop responding to treatment. Then HIV becomes AIDS."

As her eyes adjusted, Tory began to see the emaciation of the bodies in the beds, then realized they were all women. And they weren't all asleep. Eyes followed the two as they walked, silent eyes. Tory wished to be rid of her rifle, rid of her uniform. She wished dearly she could strip it all off. She was, she realized, a scary, unknown presence in this quiet place. She was a disturbance, an imposition on tranquility.

"The tragedy—" Brinia Avril said, then stopped herself and started again. "One of the tragedies is that in the States, HIV is not quite the death sentence it once was."

"Retrovirals," Tory whispered, staring at the blank-faced women they padded past.

"Among other things, yes. The key is you must be quick and stay the course."

"The course?"

"The course of treatment."

"The course of treatment is forever."

Brinia Avril nodded. "In this case, in HIV, yes."

They were at the far end of the ward now, standing by a nurses' desk. "How many Haitians can afford a course of treatment for HIV?"

"None."

CHAPTER

30

Junior Davis made a peanut butter sandwich standing at the stainless-steel counter in the empty galley. The missionaries made their own bread onboard, graveled with seeds and grain and sliced thick. The peanut butter was from shiny, label-less cans, gritty and you had to mix in the oil and though he hadn't liked it at first he'd developed a taste for it since. He took a bite from his sandwich, spit it out. He drank from a glass of water. All was quiet, twilight tonight moving down through the vessel like a magic spell, ship's company dropping and falling with exhaustion.

Back in his cabin he found Lorraine deep asleep under a blanket, breathing gently. He realized the stack of stuff on his one chair was a pile of her clothes and belongings; evidently, she'd moved in. Junior stayed as quiet as he could, finding what he needed by touch. He stripped naked, washed, and shaved himself in the small head, then pulled on a clean black T-shirt and pair of coveralls. He found his engineer boots under the chair, grabbed his cigarettes, and closed the door quietly behind him.

He worked alone in the engine room almost two hours before another soul disturbed him. He was very tired and very weak and no getting around it, with the ironic, uneasy chemical feeling you get after the chemicals have left your body. His brain moved slow but he was clear-headed; clear-headed and completely sober for the first time in quite a long time. He didn't imagine he'd remain sober, it didn't seem likely or even desirable, but he was for now and thought he'd better keep it up a bit.

There was so much to do.

Again with the bilgewater, he thought, wondering about the Jesus crew he'd trained and why they hadn't taken care of this then wondering if he'd actually trained anyone to do this and thinking probably he hadn't so it was his fault after all. He started the bilge pumps and stood a moment, listening to them *thump, thump, thump.*

He unlocked his toolbox, dug around for a three-quarter-inch and one-inch socket and took a pile of wrenches, sticking them all down in his deep coverall pockets, and worked his way around the engine room. Anything belt-driven was bound to be loose and still running on nothing but luck, he knew. It had been so long since he'd checked. He did forty-five minutes of nothing but bolt cranking. Belts, filter cases, the packing gland on the shaft. Little in the world vibrated like an old ship's engine room; truly it was remarkable everything was still intact.

He wondered about that.

Lord, did you make us a place in your heart?

Maybe Pastor was on to something.

Junior worked steadily, sweat dripping.

It was McBride who finally came down, two hours later. He'd searched the boat for his engineer, and was somewhat surprised to find him in the engine room. The old skipper had caught a few hours' sleep. Not enough, but a start. His hands shook a little, much like Junior's. Different reasons for it, but they were a team. Junior lit a cigarette and joined him in the small watch box. With the main down and just the generator running it would be possible to talk in there if they talked loud. McBride took a cigarette out of Junior's pack and lit it with his own Zippo. Davis tapped the dials on the electric control panel, his back to the skipper.

"Sorry about all that," he said.

"Turned over a leaf, have you?"

"No. You'll probably need to get yourself a new engineer." He turned and looked McBride in the eye, so the man might know there was at least a little substance behind his words. "I'll make sure she hums until then," he said. "I owe you that much, and I can do it."

McBride coughed. He never smoked cigarettes anymore. He

stubbed the thing out in the old piston cap Davis used as an ashtray then told him Pastor's news, the fate of them all.

Junior sat down on his stool.

"You didn't know this was coming, then?"

"No," McBride said. "Well, you know." He shrugged. "I guess somewhere in me I knew. Knew it more than she did. But she didn't want to believe it so I kept my mind clear of it, too."

"What will she do?"

"What do you mean?"

"Did she say what she'd do?"

"No. She'll ride her ship to the end, for one. I'm sure."

Junior wondered if McBride envisioned her riding the mast, cross in hand and held high. A crusader. And him not even religious. It was funny if it wasn't so awful.

Mannino didn't say anything about it for a while, mostly because he didn't know how to. This was the drawback to a warrant officer's roots as a sergeant—these were all your friends. And Mannino never did a very good job pretending it was any other way.

Friends or not—drunken, singing bar-closers onshore aside—onboard drinking was strictly segregated. It was courtesy, and caution, back and forth. The Skipper minded his business as long as he knew a level head ruled the crew's quarters. And the NCOs kept it close to the vest and out of obvious sight as protection to their warrant officers.

When Mannino called down below to Dick Wags and told him to come topside and bring a bottle, though, it clearly wasn't time to argue or deny. Dick Wags checked his uniform, opened the desk drawer, reached into the empty space below the drawer, and drew out a bottle of Jack Daniels. He put it in a laundry bag along with two cans of Pepsi and went to report in.

In the Skipper's quarters, Dick Wags started talking about the missionary ship. "I got someone collecting up some stuff in boxes—"

"Shut up. Close the door and sit down."

Mannino had a tin of good Italian anchovies and a plastic container of calamata olives. He laid them on his desk with some crackers and a couple of forks and two glasses. Dick Wags didn't say anything, just asked Mannino if he wanted it straight or with a Pepsi, filled both glasses with Pepsi, and added a few shots of Jack. They raised their glasses and drank.

"Absent friends," Mannino toasted.

"Absent friends."

"So tell me about your friend."

"Who do you mean, Skip?"

"New Jersey."

"What do you need to know?"

Mannino didn't say anything.

"She's turned into a fine NCO," Dick Wags said, and ate a handful of olives because he was nervous and didn't want to say more.

"I got a problem here, Sergeant Wagman."

Dick Wags chewed his olives.

"I got a feeling you know a little bit about my problem."

The staff sergeant shrugged.

"I'll be honest—if you do know, it's a serious fucking ding on you, Sergeant."

Dick Wags put his drink down and lit a cigarette. He noticed then the paperwork on the desk next to the ashtray and picked it up. He read through it. Mannino lit a smoke of his own, drained his glass, then said, "I guess I just need to know if you'd thought through the implications of it all, of her being here, or her being out there."

Dick Wags let the paperwork drop and sat back in his chair. Mannino leaned forward. "There's a phrase, Sergeant," he said. "A label. It's called 'a danger to yourself and others.' Heard it?"

Dick Wags nodded, then finally spoke. "Look, she—" and then his voice cracked. "Ah, Christ," he said.

"You knew?"

"Yeah. I knew."

"Anyone else know?"

Dick Wags shook his head. "No one," he said, defeated, sad. The top sheet on the stack of paperwork was Tory's deployment physical, just catching up with them.

"She found out on her own?"

"Yeah. She paid for her own test."

Mannino ran a hand over his head, then hooked his thumb behind him, in the general direction of the pier.

"This came from our boy next door?"

"That's right."

"Shit."

Dick Wags nodded.

"How long did she think she could—"

"Not long, Skip," Dick Wags said. "That's the only reason I went along with it. She knew it was borrowed time."

"She wanted to make the sail."

"She's worked very hard to be here, Sir."

Mannino lit a new cigarette off the first. "Did you see Davis when you were next door?"

"No. Scaboo did."

"What'd he say about him?"

"Nothing. Nothing at all. Said he'd changed. Looked bad."

"I'll bet." Mannino thought about it, then said, "You can hold all those supplies, anyway. There's a tug coming to pull that ship to the scrap yard."

"Do they know that?"

"They do now."

The two smoked in silence for a minute. Dick Wags poured them a second round, and they drank it. Mannino rubbed his head again. He tapped the ash from his smoke and said, "Problem is if something happens, to her or someone else, if someone gets wounded—"

"I'll go out tonight and bring her in. Let me do it."

Mannino picked up the paperwork and tapped it on his knee. "You know what, let her finish out there. When's she coming back? Tomorrow?"

Dick Wags nodded.

"If I send you out there, everyone's gonna know it, and think something stupid. She's earned better than that."

"Yes, Sir."

"They're going to fly her out of here, though, Dick. No way around it. That paperwork is already in Port-au-Prince. Sooner or later they're going to come looking for her." Mannino rubbed his chin. "Medical disability, I guess is what they do. Or let her keep her rank and put her in an office."

"I don't think that's much comfort to her."

"No," the Skipper said. "I suppose it isn't."

Junior Davis stepped out on deck to see the moon but found just a pale circle shimmering on a gray cloud. No stars, just black. He walked aft on the main deck, the night sweet and moist, a light breeze in his curly hair. He still wasn't used to having hair, and never remembered to comb it. He stopped at the head of the gangway. No one around. He walked the steps down to the pier.

The Army ship's gangway was just feet from him. There was a quarterdeck watch up there, Junior could see a dark form, but couldn't tell who it was or even if he knew the soldier. It didn't matter; he certainly didn't want to see anyone.

He walked down the pier toward the beach. There was a small, stone house not far from the end of the pier. A group of American soldiers had moved into it. Special Forces, they must be, Junior thought. They'd moved in this morning. He'd also heard their previous digs had been the Hard Rock Café. He didn't know if he believed the story, but it was a good story.

One of them stood outside guarding the place, a big Hawaiian called Mickey. The rest of the team was inside the house, four of them at a large wooden table playing pinochle.

"Hey, come on, sailor," Master Sergeant Rice said to Davis, knowing about him only what he'd told them—that he was American, the engineer of the missionary ship down the pier. "Take a break from the Lord and play some cards." Someone had scrawled on the wall with spray paint: 909TH HAITIAN VACATION: THE VOODOO LOUNGE.

Voodoo Lounge, Junior thought. *That's pretty funny.*

Big Mickey was leaning in the doorway, his rifle over his shoulder. "I already checked, he says he ain't got a bottle."

Rice motioned Davis over to the empty chair next to him. "You meet someone new, and all you want to know is can he get us some booze?"

"Fucking-A," Mickey said, and sauntered his big frame back to his post.

"How long you going to be here in the Voodoo Lounge?" Davis asked.

"Duration, I guess," Rice said, accepting one of Junior's cigarettes. "Long as it takes."

"Long as it takes to do what?"

"Good question."

"It's a nice place, Jacmel. You could've done worse."

"Guess so. You've been here before?"

Davis nodded. He wasn't sure why he'd said it was a nice place. It was a nice place, mostly, but he hadn't had such a nice time here. Rice asked and Davis told him; an abbreviated version, anyway.

"How long were you in there?"

"Couple weeks."

"No shit. How was it?"

Davis said "Pretty bad" and left it at that. He couldn't think of a better way of putting it.

Rice got up and went to a door in the corner and knocked on it. The door opened and a face appeared. A thin, well-groomed African-American captain in a neat, creased uniform.

"Hey, Sir, this guy here's been in the hoosegow up on the mountain. Recently. For a couple of weeks." He hooked his thumb at Davis.

"Really?" Captain Nellis said. He stepped out into the room, looking at Davis. "Would you mind telling me about it?"

Davis shook his head. He didn't mind. Would they mind giving up an MRE? He'd been eating powdered eggs and peanut butter for weeks now.

"Come on in here with me," Nellis said. "Sergeant Rice, bring a notebook, will you?"

CHAPTER

31

Tory walked alone through the hospital grounds, small pebbles in the yard crunching under the soles of her boots and bats zipping past her ears. Inside the wall all was quiet. Outside the wall she could hear voices, singing, diesel engines; the sounds of night and the weak glow of lights in the darkness.

She saw Marc through the iron bars of the gate. She almost called to him, then didn't, watching instead. He was under a set of generator lights set up around the Red Cross trucks. His rifle he'd slung barrel down over his back, but all his other gear he'd taken off, helmet and flak vest and LBE. He'd been helping them unload and working with the director of the hospital, taking notes on what else was needed, and on where best this stuff should go. His smooth, bald head shone under the white light, and he laughed as he worked, his whole face filling with it in the same manner as all the Haitian men around him; full-body laughing, not a surplus of movement, but a sense that one's whole body was invested in the emotion. She smiled to see him this way, and when finally she did call to him and he turned to see her his face grew even brighter and his eyes gleamed like a cat and she knew it was a trick of the generator lights against the night but she liked it anyway. She recognized old Jean, one of the truck drivers from the boat, standing next to him, and Jean clamped his hand down on Marc's shoulder and whispered in the captain's ear and both men laughed as Marc raised a hand and waved her over.

"Sergeant Harris!" he called, his arm around Jean. "Our friend Jean was just telling me a joke."

"And what was the joke, Captain Hall?"

Marc's smile grew even wider, and he said, "Once again, I've absolutely no idea."

"Your Creole may be more lacking than you thought."

"Either mine or his."

Marc picked up his gear from the ground. "Have you eaten?" he said.

"No."

"Let's go lock this stuff up then find something to eat."

The hospital director—a pale, thin, very tall Frenchman everyone called Pip—had an office with no windows, a solid door, and a solid lock. The two soldiers kept their weapons on their backs but locked everything else in his office.

"If the Dominicans invade tonight," Marc said, "we're done for." He had a special kind of handheld radio he'd brought from Port-au-Prince, and he clipped it to his rifle strap.

Dinner was in a long, low thatch-roof building with no walls, directly outside the hospital gate. Marc and Tory sat on stools at a high table, the only ones eating, but a small party gathered to watch them. Four women worked the open-air kitchen and they shooed people away but only to the boundaries of the building's wooden support beams. The effect, then, was of being alone at a huge table with floating eyes in the shadows twinkling and hovering.

"Eating as spectator sport," she whispered.

"Quite romantic." The lighting came only from candles and lanterns, warm red light flickering off the wood and thatch. Absent the crowd staring at them, it was, Tory admitted, intimate.

Dinner was served on tin camp plates. Thick black beans and fried plantains first, all sweet and smooth in the mouth, the plantains brown with their sugar. One of the kitchen ladies came saying something neither of them understood. She left two cups of water. Marc put his hand on Tory's arm. "Don't drink that." He motioned to a boy in the crowd watching them, a teenager, said *"Apprens bier pour moin,"* and passed him a few dollars. The boy was back as they were finishing their beans, two brown bottles of Red Stripe in his hands.

"Warm," Marc said. "But safer than the water."

Tory looked at him over her empty plate as he popped the caps off and wiped the tops clean with his uniform sleeve. "Likely story," she said to him. "I think you're just trying to get me liquored up."

"A positive side-effect of keeping you safe from bacteria."

They raised their bottles and clinked them in a toast.

"Absent friends."

"Yes."

The oldest of the kitchen women motioned them over, and they took their plates into the cooking area. There were five or so unlit burners attached to a string of small propane tanks, and a large open-air fire a few steps away from the hut with a pot hanging over. The woman, though, went to another pit, this one just coals in a ring of stones. She prodded at the edge of the coals with a stick, uncovering something. She reached down and gingerly grabbed two blackened husks from the hole there, turning and dropping them quick on the soldiers' plates, whistling and blowing on her fingers where she'd almost burned them. It took Tory a moment to realize what she was looking at.

"Lobster?"

"Yes!"

Marc thanked the woman profusely, a string of Creole gratitudes.

"There's no claws."

"No," he said, guiding her back to their seats. "This is rock lobster. No claws. You throw them in the coals, burn 'em, pull 'em out."

He picked up a big knife from the table and slammed the wooden handle down on the smoking carcass on her plate, cracking the burnt shell. He peeled it open with his fingers, revealing the clean, pink, cooked flesh of the tail. He wiggled it out and held it for her. She took a bite from his fingers, the meat soft and just a bit chewy.

"Hot!" she whispered, fanning her mouth. "Fantastic." She took a long pull from her bottle of Red Stripe, the beer warm and perfect.

Marc cracked open the tail of his lobster and began to eat.

"You know what the fishermen call these in Maine?" she said, speaking around a new mouthful of food. She held up the shell, wiggling the head at him. "Bugs," she said. "Sea bugs."

When they finished Tory washed the lobster from her hands and cheeks at a basin set in the far corner, careful to keep the water from her mouth. Marc took their plates and paid the women with a few dollars, washing his hands, too, then guiding her out of the hut and through the crowd of watchers.

"Bonswa. Bon nuit, messieurs," he said as the passed through. *"Bon nuit, s'ami. Dormi bien." Good night, friends. Sleep well.*

Tory assumed they'd be followed, but they weren't. Not overtly, anyway. The show was over, it was late, life went on. American soldiers were interesting, but only to a point, she guessed. Marc guided her—one step behind, a hand soft on her back here and there to show her when to turn—around a series of small dwellings, deeper into the camp. They passed into an area completely unlit, only the silvered, clouded moon to define walls of huts, curves of a face. Marc's hand closed on Tory's, holding it, and he stepped up beside her. His hand was big, smooth around hers, and she squeezed it. She stopped, keeping hold of his hand, and turned into him, pressing her face into his chest. She felt his other hand in her hair, and she breathed deep, pressing harder. She looked up then, his face ghostly in the moonlight. Their lips passed, barely touching, her face going to his neck. She squeezed tighter on his hand, wrapping her other arm around him, pulling him close, feeling herself pulled in by him, holding each other tight and close, his skin warm against her cheeks and lips.

"This is fraternization of the worst kind," he whispered.

"Good."

He put his lips against hers then, and she savored it a moment, a brief moment, not thinking just feeling, all the nerves there alive and receiving his lips, soft and full and his face in hers. She dropped her head then, back into his chest, feeling him pressing harder against her, his hand flat between her shoulder blades and holding her there. The rain came, just a few drops on a breeze, then stopped again, the air moist and thick.

"Walk with me," he said, letting her body go, keeping hold of her hand. And in that way they walked, hand in hand, Marc leading deeper into the warren past sleeping families and heated conversations alike,

from shadows through fire-lit clearings and sometimes lanterns hanging from hooks on poles. Small fires burned here and there and they
stopped at a few, men around the fires offering a bottle. They always
said no but felt warmed by the offer, and would stand or sit a few minutes, Tory listening to the singsong talk and Marc's attempts to dupli-
cate it, join it. They held hands openly or he put his arm around her
if they were sitting because it didn't matter here, nothing to hide here,
no one to keep a secret from. She smoked cigarettes as they sat by the
fires and when they walked she stopped him when she felt like it and
put her face in his neck and once her hands flat on his chest as he stood
there.

At one fire, later, Marc asked a question and an older man answered,
his tongue dancing between toothless gums, pointing out toward the
edge of the field and pointing at Tory then again into the distance. Marc
thanked him and walked to where he'd been pointing, through an area
where the tents and huts thinned and toward a line of woods and thin
jungle.

"There are so many fires."

"It's special, tonight, they say. Many of the people are celebrating."

Tory had a hard time imagining anything for them to celebrate.

"A man died this morning, a worker in the hospital. Everyone loved
him, everyone knew him."

"They're celebrating? Like a wake?"

"Yes, and that he went *mort bon Dieu*—by God. He was old and
died natural."

"Rather than in the storm."

"Yes, or by soldiers or Ton Ton Macoute." He said the last words
very quietly.

She could see the light of another fire now, through the branches.
And drums, she was sure of it—the low sounds of the camp at night
had solidified into something distinct, a rhythm of drums. They
stepped into the woods, dark growing darker except for the bright lick
of flame. They could see people then, forms and shadows and then
someone moving around the fire. Tory and Marc moved into the
group, no one seeming to notice or care about their presence. She saw

three drummers now, under a roof of braided leaves, and a woman dancing around the fire. She was what all the people watched, this woman, leaping and spinning and bending over, hands on knees, then leaping again. She was nineteen or twenty maybe, this dancer, with a long red skirt and her breasts bared, full and heavy on her chest as she danced and twirled. Marc's hand tightened around Tory's. He nodded to where a man sat, wrapped in white, near the drummer.

"The *houngan*," Marc whispered. "Like a priest. This is his *houn-four*."

Tory heard him but could not take her eyes from the woman. The dance was entrancing, the woman magnificent. She must have been dancing for some time—the muscles of her arms and back and legs shaped and trembling, cut and moving with the effort, a sheen of wet across her body, a slick second skin of sweat. She didn't pant, exactly, but breathed short, quick breaths through open lips. Her eyes closed sometimes, head back as she moved. Other times she would seem to pick someone to stare at, her bare feet planted wide in one place as she moved from the waist, her eyes locking into one of the onlookers. She screamed suddenly, high-pitched and almost desperate, throwing herself backward and to her hands. She leapt, landing on her feet in front of where the two soldiers stood, and her eyes locked with Tory's.

Tory stumbled back, startled.

The woman was swaying now, back and forth, slow, her arms rising over her head, drawing herself out and up, her breasts rising, her chin lifting, but still her eyes fixed on Tory's.

She said something, a stream of syllables, and Tory didn't know if it was Creole and if she was saying it to Tory or part of the dance and Tory said *I hear you* but didn't know if she said it out loud or only in her head and then the woman showed her teeth, a tiger's smile, and was gone around the fire.

Tory showed her teeth then, too, showed them to the fire and whatever Haitian god was watching all this, pulling on Marc's hand, pulling him away, back through the wet leaves and to the field where it was raining now, slow but for real, everyone asleep as they moved through the camp. Tory led, tiger teeth bared, rainwater streaming down their faces, through the gate of the hospital, to the director's office to retrieve the gear. They didn't look at each other in there, just got what was theirs and left, to their clean hut with the two cots.

The rain on the thatch roof was soft static on a radio, and the noise, she thought, was good, like the noise in her head, soft and muted but more than a little insistent.

She climbed on him where he stood, like a tomboy girl climbing a tree, his back straight and strong as she moved over his limbs and wrapped her two hands around the skin of his skull and moved her mouth over the top of his head, his ears and neck.

His hands found her breasts then, rough through her wet uniform top, and he made a noise, Tory whispering, "I saw you watching her, watching her chest as she moved," and Marc answered, "I wasn't the only one watching." She clung to him fiercely, letting his hands move. His mouth came to hers, and again she let it rest for just a moment then drew her head away. "This has to go how I say," she said.

"Yes."

"Promise me."

"I promise."

"I'll dance for you then, Marcel."

He lay her flat on his cot, undressing himself then undressing her, one article at a time, slow with his hands. He folded her up into himself, their bodies entwining skin to skin, warmth to warmth. She let him move over her, allowing his fingers here and then there, but holding his head away as he ducked low, pushing him away as she teased it out, or he thought that's what she was doing. Then his back was on the cot and she wrapped her legs around him and held herself there, held herself close, so close, but not quite and it was agony, delicious agony, but then just agony and she moved up and off and grabbed his hand.

And then it was all hands and fingers, open and closed palms, the two of them touching and holding and sliding across the other's body. "This," she said, her thighs holding his hand in place. She reached down for him and held him tight and felt the blood under his hard skin and when it was his time he raised off the cot, voice loud and fingers gripping her so it hurt. And when he was done he pushed the fingers of one hand through her soft hair and the other hand moved slow and even and she called his name as she came, "Marc," she said, "oh, man." She curled in his arms and the blood pumped in her temples, blood pushing through her veins so she could feel it, almost hear it, her hands on his heart and her own blood still thumping through her body.

Tory was so aware of her blood, so attuned. It infuriated her, this over-awareness, but she was powerless before it. She could feel blood well from a small cut on her finger, the weight of collected drops and liquid smell of copper. And under her skin, running in veins and capillaries and the fluids of her body, always the knowledge of it close to the surface, so thin the skin trapping and holding it, an easily pierced envelope embracing the poison warmth.

She felt it. She felt it pound in her head, behind her eyes; she felt it between her legs.

This awareness was immediate, from the moment Tory left Junior Davis sitting in a Norfolk diner. She hadn't known for sure yet, but the physical inventory was immediate, every particle of skin and fluid needing to be accounted for and not a molecule to be carelessly lost or passed on. She'd gone to a clinic, in jeans and a T-shirt, a private clinic where she paid cash and used a different name. The thin needle slipped into her skin, sliced the protective envelope, and she'd winced at the stick and weird pull and more from anxiety, the possibility of a drop falling, an unaccounted-for drip sliding where it did not belong.

The awareness was immediate, the careful-stepping and full inventory immediate—it was the soldierly thing to do, full and precise control, dress-right-dress, all corners tucked and tight all weapons locked and loaded all units stand-to until information is complete, until situation is understood. But though awareness was immediate, belief was not. Odds were not good, and she knew it. The logic was quite clear about how this would almost certainly go. But still, belief wasn't there. Or, rather, belief was there, but it was disbelief. You just didn't work

this hard, struggle so long, to have it end this way. It just wasn't supposed to happen this way. It was baffling, ridiculous.

She'd gone back to the clinic three days later, and collected an envelope and left without opening it, leaving a counselor sitting in a small
room. However this was going to go, she'd not talk to a stranger about
it. She held the envelope all afternoon, then most of the night. She
watched TV and drank vodka and orange juice and smoked cigarettes
and not until the eleven-o'clock news was half over—just before the
weather report, the chubby baby-faced weatherman—did she finally
reach for the envelope and begin to open it—*Ladies and Gentlemen I'd
like to thank the Academy and my maker the Lord Jesus Christ and I can't
believe this I can't just can't believe this and who knew how far this New
Jersey girl could go and*—

The paperwork was clear and simple to understand. She was
positive.

Tory drove from Fort Eustis in a blind rush at midnight, blowing
through three red lights on the highway up to the York River bridge
and Gloucester beyond. She pushed her headlights off for the long,
unpaved driveway through the woods, then popped her little truck
into neutral and killed the engine at the last clearing. Dick Wags's Jeep
was gone, but Alicia's pickup was in front of the little house, and Tory
let hers stop next to it.

There were no lights on, and she let herself in, quietly, feeling her
way to the living room, to the couch, and she stood there, just stood
there, for at least two minutes, staring in the dark, at the dark, stark
silent in the middle of the room, and it wasn't until then she started
crying—almost a full hour past reading the news—but crying now,
then sobbing, doubled over in a wail of grief, *oh God,* she cried, *oh God,*
helpless in despair, helpless on the floor, all sense of time and place
gone and nothing but sorrow and loss and fear, real fear, deep and solid
in her muscles and pounding in her veins, all the poison blood, pounding death through her veins. Alicia came from the bedroom and came
without a word, kneeling on the floor and wrapping her arms around
Tory's shaking body, pulling her head down to her breast, holding her
tight there, her fingers in Tory's short, soft hair. She said not a word

because she thought she knew what was the matter. She thought she knew, but she was wrong—it was worse. Much worse. It didn't matter though because her silence was right. Tory didn't stop crying, but she slowed, then quieted, and after five minutes Alicia stood, drawing Tory along. Arms still wrapped tight she half-carried her to the bedroom. With no light and no sound Alicia pulled Tory's sweater off, and her jeans, and laid her on the bed where she curled into a tight S and Alicia came in behind her pulling the comforter over them and wrapped her arms around her again and listened to her cry. Tory was still crying when Alicia fell asleep, and many hours later they were both asleep, and when Alicia awoke Tory was still curled, sleeping now, and the room was bright and white with morning and Alicia could hear Dick Wags in the kitchen, home from overnight battalion CQ duty, the smell of strong coffee in the crisp early air.

They were entwined under a thin hospital blanket in the humid night, Marc asleep and Tory listening to him sleep. Her grief had bubbled up, briefly, earlier—threatening, its head poking close, and she'd trembled in its path. Then, just like that, gone. Gone and gone, leaving her as a vessel neither full nor empty, just being, just her. And, tonight anyway, she thought, it was enough to just touch, enough to be skin to skin again, to feel this warmth.

And then they were both asleep, eyelids quivering and breathing deep and slow. Exhausted, sleeping hard. So hard that when the hospital director banged on their door at 1:00 A.M. neither woke immediately, it took six, seven, eight hard bangs with his fist and then a panicked yell—"Captain! Captain Hall!"—before Marc's eyes popped open, then Tory's, confused and rolling from the cot.

CHAPTER

32

Alone in her cabin, Pastor passed hands over the items on her desk and the books secured in their sea shelves. She'd brought none of these books onboard herself; all inherited, here when she arrived. She had read them all, or pretty close to all. They were church books, mostly. She could barely remember them now, though she knew by reading the titles she'd read them. The ones she did remember were from the small collection of mysteries she'd found pressed flat behind the main stack. Dorothy Sayers and Agatha Christie, mostly. Those she'd enjoyed immensely, and remembered all of them. She moved her open palm over their spines.

She was having a hard time finding a toehold for any of her five years on this ship. She felt quite useless. As if she'd been asleep, her body standing here five years mechanically performing monkey tasks.

Yet she'd fought with such desperation to stay.

"Perhaps," she said aloud, "because there is nothing else." She wasn't aware she'd spoken out loud.

Master Sergeant Rice took the radio call from Port-au-Prince. He had Big Mickey wake Captain Nellis, then left the room as the officer took the microphone. It was a colonel on the line, an old guy named Baric they'd all met on Guantanamo the week before. A spook, the old guy was. A uniformed spook, but a spook nonetheless.

"And a pissed-off spook, too, from the sounds of him," Rice said to Mickey, mixing himself a cup of cold instant coffee.

The captain was in the office a long time. When he came out he said, "Someone go down to the mission boat and requisition that sailor who was just here—Davis. We're gonna need his services."

Mickey put his helmet on and headed for the door. Captain Nellis was looking over the notes he'd made during the conversation.

"Did you meet that 10th Mountain captain who rode in on the LSV?"

"The guy with the Red Cross?"

"Yeah, him. Hall, Marcel Hall."

"Just passed a few words," Sergeant Rice said. "He seemed all right. A little intense, maybe."

"I guess he is. He just called JTF in Port-au-Prince to say he was headed out to liberate the old prison."

"Alone?"

"Alone."

Rice didn't know what to say to that. Finally, he just said, "It's one in the morning."

"It sure is," Nellis said.

CHAPTER

33

Three men had arrived at the hospital in the dark of midnight, two of them carrying the third, who'd been shot in the belly. He was bad—the belly is a painful, dangerous place to be shot—but Brinia Avril thought he would probably live so somewhat lucky. Another man had been shot tonight, in town, and had not lived. A fifth hadn't been shot at all; he'd been beaten then shoved into the back of a police Jeep, a cloth sack pushed down over his head. The Jeep disappeared out of town, but everyone knew where it was going.

"And these men," Captain Hall had said, "you're sure they were in uniform?"

"Yes, yes, in uniform. They did not hide it." This old man was wringing his hands, in grief. It was his grandson who'd been taken.

"And these two who were shot—the shooters were also in uniform?"

The other man answered this time, shaking his head. "No one saw them."

The man wringing his hands wailed now, a long moan of grief like Tory had never heard. Her skin crawled to hear it. This man was one of those who'd mustered courage and gone to see the Special Forces soldiers in Jacmel. Retribution for that act had, it seemed now, been quite swift.

Marc made a sudden decision. "We'll go out there and get him released," he said. "Now. Before they kill him."

The hospital director raised his eyebrows. "It would perhaps be wise to wait until morning—"

"No, now," Marc said. "It has to be now. This is flagrant human-rights abuse."

Tory spoke for the first time, quietly. "There's no way the rules of engagement cover this." She didn't disagree with the idea of going out there, but felt it had to be said.

Marc didn't hear her, or pretended he didn't. "Why in the hell are we in Haiti?" he said. He grabbed his radio from the table and went outside to call, answering his own question for himself.

The back of the lorry was wet, a fine mist of rain soaking them. Tory clutched her rifle, half-kneeling in the back as the truck barreled down a blind road, bumping and bouncing them to nausea.

There is something wrong here, she thought. *This doesn't feel right.*

She tried to watch Marc's face, to measure what he might be thinking, but it was too dark to see.

The fact that she'd been asleep—not just asleep, but naked, in another's arms—thirty minutes before didn't throw her much. Anyone with ten seconds in the Army wouldn't blink at a perspective shift like that. There was something else about this not right. It was Marc, but she was trying not to think that. That was not a comfortable road of thought to go down right now.

She'd wanted to get the ship's Humvee.

"Not necessary, and too long to get here," Marc had said. "Jean will drive us in his truck. I want to strike while this is hot—and while that boy might still be alive."

Then she'd mentioned the possibility of a few more soldiers, from the boat. To show up with a full squad.

He'd been kneeling on the floor of the hut at the time, checking his gear. Without looking up he said, "A squad of Transportation Corps soldiers? What kind of good are they going to be to me?"

She'd said nothing to that.

He'd stood then, pulling on his flak vest. "This is just an inquiry," he said. "I just want to know what they have to say. And unless they give me some fast and perfect answers, they'll find a U.S. Army division sitting on their doorstep tomorrow morning."

Tory doubted that, but said nothing.

Marc told her then he didn't want her to go with him. She'd simply answered no, and stepped out of the hut to wait.

And now this truck raced through the rain at what surely was a suicidal speed for Haiti's roads, and Tory wondered about the intelligence of racing off to battle in a broken-down Red Cross lorry. Marc said they weren't racing off to battle, they were making a simple inquiry. She wasn't sure she believed that, either.

In the end, Marc had simply knocked on the door. It was a big door, massive wood planks, and when he realized his knocks were ineffective he kicked the thing. Hard and repeatedly. Tory stood six or so yards behind him, nervous and watching. Her feeling that this was wrong, fool headed, completely filled her now and she tried to push it down but it wouldn't go.

Oh Christ this is a bad way to check out, she thought and tightened her hand around the pistol grip of her rifle. *No one left, just me and the Army.*

It was a stone caserne, an old prison with high walls out in what felt like the middle of nowhere. The rain had stopped and a thick white mist stood a foot off the ground. A distinct itch developed between Tory's shoulder blades and she turned around in place once then twice.

The door opened a crack. Marc said something but she couldn't hear what. He put his shoulder to the door then, and his foot pushed into the opening. Tory tensed, raising her rifle. The door swung fully open and Marc's rifle went up, too.

There was a head in Tory's rifle sight, a head with a peaked cap, and she fought an overwhelming urge to pull the trigger.

Breathe, she ordered herself. *Breathe!*

Marc took a step in. "Where's the warden? Who's in command?"

You breathe in, you breathe out.

"Who the fuck is in command here?"

youbreatheinyoubreatheout

Peaked cap raised his hands; partially, anyway.

"Hey," he said. "Hey hey." He was smiling, laughing a little—we're all friends here, all professionals. *Comrades in arms, baby—hey hey.* He motioned with his hands and Marc let the barrel of his rifle drop a few inches. Tory's didn't move, and she imagined his grinning head exploding in her rifle sight.

"Hey hey hey."

Marc kept his voice calm, even. "I want to know the whereabouts and condition of Ben Narcisse. And I want to see the commander of this detachment. Wake him, if necessary."

"Hey," the Haitian officer said again, smiling wider.

"*Now!*" Marc said.

The Haitian officer took a step back and Tory took two steps forward. She could see three other uniformed men now, seemingly unarmed, lounging behind the officer. Marc raised his rifle again and this irritated the Haitian. He froze his smile and spit on the ground, just inches from Marc's boot. Marc ignored this and spoke evenly: "I want to see the commander—"

"I am the commander, *Captain*. And I am a major." He pointed to the rank on his shoulder boards. "Some respect, *sils vouz plait*."

"Respect? I demand you—"

"Don't tell me! I know you, *neg pa*. I know your Army better than you do." The man's eyes flicked in the direction of Tory. He had to have seen them drive up in the Red Cross truck. *We're doomed,* she thought. The major was ignoring Marc's raised rifle now, as if he knew the American wouldn't fire. He took a step toward him. "Where did you learn to soldier, *Captain*? Some college parade ground, in New York City?" he spit again. "I went to Fort Benning! I studied under real officers, real soldiers. I am more of an American soldier than you are."

Tory heard a noise, diesel engine. She turned to see two pair of headlights coming through the mist, the unmistakable set and width of hummer lights.

Marc was staring at the Haitian major. Very low, so Tory almost didn't know he was speaking, he rattled off two quick sentences in Creole. The Humvees pulled to a stop behind her, their engines loud. The major laughed and answered Marc, but in English, not Creole. "You need to pick your loyalty, Captain. You are not Haitian."

Three Special Forces soldiers flanked her then, quickly passing, one of them an officer with a pistol. "Captain Hall!" he said, and Marc turned.

"There is a man in here," Marc said. "Ben Narcisse, abducted from Jacmel tonight—"

"Shut the fuck up, Captain." Nellis was clearly pissed off. Pistol still up but not pointing at anything in particular, he put himself directly behind Marc and began whispering in his ear. Master Sergeant Rice approached Tory from the side.

"I'd feel a lot happier if you'd hang that M-16 from your shoulder, trooper," he said. She let the barrel of her rifle drop, a wave of relief washing over her, then disgust at the relief. She safed the weapon, slung it on her shoulder.

"Anyone else out here I should know about?"

She shook her head. "Just us."

Rice squinted, taking a step toward her.

"Holy Christ, you're a wo—" he said then stopped himself.

In the doorway of the prison, Nellis talked alone to Hall then to the Haitian major. He spun on his heels, walking back over to Rice.

"They're gonna give us this guy and in return we're all going to leave."

Rice nodded, then shrugged. "Good."

Captain Nellis pointed at one of the two Humvees his team had come in. "Go talk again to our sailor friend there and make sure we know how this place is laid out. Hall is insisting we take a quick walk around in there."

Tory could see the shadow of someone sitting in the backseat of the Humvee. Rice said, "Should we just bring him in?"

"No, this is already too weird and complicated."

Tory took a step to the hummer, to get a better look at the passenger. Rice went to the vehicle's window, though, blocking her view. She walked to the prison door, where Marc and Captain Nellis waited. The major was speaking to one of his men. He turned then to Nellis. "He'll be up in five minutes. I'm sure this is all a misunderstanding."

"I'm sure it is," Nellis said.

"I want to look around," Marc said, and took a step in.

"Restrain yourself, Captain," Nellis said, and Marc spun on his heels then, coming face to face with the other captain.

"What do you think this is, exactly, Captain Nellis?" Marc hissed. "This isn't some paper exercise or snake-eater training course. People died tonight, human beings, this man is responsible"—he jabbed his finger in the major's direction—"and we would be criminally negligent to ignore it."

Nellis ground his jaw and said nothing, just holding Marc's gaze. Finally he spoke, but so low Tory barely heard him, and she stood just a foot away. "I'm not sure what's in your head right now, Captain Hall, but criminal negligence is the least of your troubles. You do know that, right?" He shifted his gaze then, looking for Master Sergeant Rice, who'd just returned from the Humvees. "C'mon, Sergeant Rice," he said. "Let's go get this guy and get out of here."

Tory let the master sergeant and two other Special Forces soldiers pass, following Marc and Nellis into the prison. No one had told her to join them, but no one had told her to stay put, either. She pulled the rifle off her shoulder and held it loose in her hands, turning to follow the men into the prison. A flash caught her eye as she turned, some-one lighting a cigarette in the back of one of the Humvees, the flame flickering on a pale-skinned face. She had a quick, momentary flash—somewhere between memory and déjà-vu—and paused for a second, then turned and stepped into the courtyard of the prison.

Junior Davis's impulse to throw open the back door of the Humvee and wave to Tory, call her name, rush over, was difficult to control. It was the impulse of seeing an old friend, a good, good friend you haven't seen for a long time. There's no thought involved, just action: "Hey!"

But he fought it. And stayed put.

He wasn't completely surprised at seeing her. He knew from listen-ing to the SF boys talk that at least one soldier from the LSV had joined the 10th Mountain captain. Logic said it was an NCO, and Davis knew that if offered the chance Tory would have jumped on it.

Still, it was one thing to know he might see her. It was something else entirely to arrive at the old stone prison in the middle of the Haitian night and realize the soldier in the headlights with rifle aimed to shoot was Tory Harris, his New Jersey.

She looked strong, he thought. It was a stupid, simple thought, but nothing else fit. She just looked . . . strong. Her stance, posture, her movements precise and exact. He watched her talking to Rice, saw her laugh and knew from where he sat that it was forced but also knew no one but him would know it.

And the one thought more than anything else: *I didn't kill her. Oh God I didn't kill her.*

Just that she was here, in Haiti, was all the proof he needed. It was a feeling beyond anything he'd ever felt, the word *relief* not even approaching, something more, something in his soul.

He couldn't have hoped for this. Hadn't hoped, actually. Something like hope stirred somewhere inside him—he wouldn't have come to Haiti, otherwise—but he'd never really believed. It was too impossible, there was no way he *hadn't* infected her.

But, obviously, he hadn't. She couldn't be here, otherwise. No soldier deployed without the mandatory HIV test. The battlefield blood supply had to be pure. Here stood Tory—ergo, Tory was clean.

Junior's fingers went to the door handle again, actually touching it this time before withdrawing his hand. He lit a cigarette, instead, and saw her face move in the direction of his, their eyes locking although he knew she couldn't see him. Then, she was gone. Stepped into the prison and out of sight.

One of the front doors of the Humvee opened and a soldier's face appeared, Big Mickey. "Must be creepy, huh? Back here?"

Junior nodded. Actually, he felt nothing. Nothing at all. His time here, what he'd suffered inside, all of it was unimportant and hard to even remember now. But he nodded at Big Mickey and said, "Yeah— I'll be happy to be gone," and laughed a little and Mickey laughed, too, then was gone.

Junior Davis sat back in his seat; alone in the dark, alone in Haiti.

I didn't kill her. If nothing else, there is that. She's not infected. I didn't kill her.

CHAPTER

34

She had to remove herself from the blood chain. She knew it, had always known it, had ignored it. She regretted being so selfish, to risk infecting another just so she could *see*. So she could *do*.

There are, she thought, other things to *see*. Other things to *do*. She'd not believed it so before, convinced nothing but oblivion awaited. One of the reasons, perhaps, she'd not begun any course of treatment. Why? Why bother? For what? The Army wouldn't have her. Not as a worthwhile active, deployable soldier anyway.

The hospital today changed that, changed how she saw it. She didn't quite know why, but it was unmistakable. She had changed. She shouldn't even be here right now, should not have come, should go wait in the back of one of those Humvees.

These thoughts all passed through her head as she made the step through the old door into the open-air prison courtyard. There was a hesitation in her step, then it was gone, then she was gone—inside.

On the LSV, Dick Wags left the Skipper's office. He went down below and woke Pelton, telling him to get dressed and suited up for driving into town and beyond.

"Damn, what time is it?"

"Never mind."

Ten minutes later, walking down the pier to where they'd parked the ship's Humvee by the SF house, Dick Wags said, "Whatever happens, don't ask any questions, and nothing gets repeated."

"Sergeant, yes."

Tory didn't know if Captain Nellis's anger at Marc had been bluster or real or both, but either way he was silent now. A still, wordless silent only shock can bring. He walked in front, Rice a step behind, Marc a step behind him. Tory followed Marc.

They didn't go far into the prison. They didn't really expect trouble—hurting them in some way now would be suicide. Still, it was the middle of the night, their numbers were few. So they didn't go far. But they didn't have to go far. They circled the open-air courtyard, the far end lined with cells. Then moved cautiously down one narrow passage, until Nellis decided it was too narrow and backed them up.

Master Sergeant Rice was first to vomit, and Captain Nellis followed almost immediately. Tory held out, gagging, trying hard to think of who might be sent to clean it up, then could hold it no longer and leaned over where she stood. Marc Hall was the only one of them who did not throw up. His skin went cold and he felt as if his blood had chilled, but he refused—refused—to allow himself to vomit.

"There's a big courtyard, and open-air group cells around it. Four of them, I think. Maybe five. I spent most of my time there."

Sitting at the table in the cottage hours before, Junior squinted his eyes, trying hard to be precise. He was a soldier, or had been. Precision was important.

"Five, yeah five," he said. "Four in the back and one on the side."

Rice scratched away with a pen, trying to get this all down. Junior took a drag off his cigarette, exhaling into the already smoky, thick air around them.

"They shove twenty, thirty bodies into those courtyard cells."

"How big are the cells?"

"Ten by ten, maybe."

Rice stopped writing. "Can't be right. You can't fit twenty people in a ten by ten."

Junior shook his head. "Sure you can."

The stink was first, then the realization of what the stink was. Excrement, people standing in it, sitting in it, sleeping in it.

"Oh Jesus," Rice said, and that's when he lost it.

"In each cell there's a big barrel for shitting, and if it gets emptied you're okay. But sometimes they forget, or sometimes they just don't want to. Then it stagnates, then it overflows." Junior paused, then said, "It's awful hard to get used to."

Nellis pulled a small flashlight off his belt, clicked it on and moved the beam around one of the cells. Tory followed the light, trying to count. She'd never seen people so closely packed together. What was skin, what was scab, blood, shit, hair, scalp. For a second she thought they were all dead and really hoped so in a way, but then someone moved and hope fled. She hung her M-16 over her shoulder and pulled her helmet off her head. It was a reflexive action, the only sign of pity available to her.

"And who's in there? Who's locked up?"

"Not much rhyme or reason, not that I could tell. Some got slammed in and were out in a day. Others told me they'd been in there two years and I had no reason not to believe them. They were certainly skinny and sick enough."

"What're we talking, murderers here?"

"None that I met. Couple of petty thieves, I guess. Bunch of kids—boys, mostly. But, you know, most people in there, I don't think there was much of a real reason. Wrong place at wrong time."

"Political, then."

"Sort of. But who the fuck talks politics when you know this will be the outcome? The real political prisoners were just shot, I think. Or dragged out and machetied in the street. That's what the *attachés* are for, *Macoute* or whatever they call themselves now. *Loup garou,* right? They just shoot dissenters. No, most who got jailed, I think it was money. Nothing much to do with politics. Lock 'em up till their folk can pay to get 'em out. It's a system."

"And you?"

"That's it, really. I passed out drunk in the town square one night. Woke up in a cell, sleeping in someone else's shit. They held me until the mission could come up with enough bread to get me out."

"How long?"

"Almost three weeks. They kept raising the price."

What was worst, somehow, to Tory, was the silence. No pleas, no begging, no cries. Just small moans and sighs and snores, the sounds of bodies moving against one another, the sound of wet and slick.

On Marc Hall's face, a brick wall, jaw set and unmoving. Tory couldn't look in the cells anymore so she looked at him, looking for his reaction. He turned once and their eyes met but he would give nothing in his gaze, nothing on what he was thinking. Neither disgust at what they'd found, nor satisfaction at being right. Marc looked into Tory's eyes for one brief moment then turned away. Tory clicked on her own little flashlight, panning it around.

"What's down there?" She pointed at a stone passage.

Sergeant Rice shook his head. "C'mon, it's too fucking narrow. No way we're going in there."

"There's a downstairs?"

"Yeah."

"And?"

Junior shrugged. "I went down twice. First time, they took me out of the main cell and I'm thinking, 'Great, I'm out of here.' I'd only been in a day, and they had no reason to hold me, so I'm thinking this is one big inconvenience. Then we passed right by the main door, right by the office, and go down this narrow, stone stairwell. I thought they were taking me down to shoot me."

Davis lit another cigarette, and smoked it in silence a few moments.

"Second time they took me down, few days later, I begged them to shoot me."

He stood up then and lifted his shirt.

The Haitian major had declined to accompany them on their tour. His men had found Ben Narcisse and brought him outside, where Big Mickey half-carried him over to the Humvees. The Haitian major stayed a step outside the gate, smoking a cigarette.

The Americans, inside—the clean Americans—had seen enough. They walked back across the courtyard to the main gate. As they walked Marc accelerated. Nellis was half-looking behind him at the cells and Rice was looking at his feet and only Tory saw Marc pick up his pace, reverse the rifle in his hands. She opened her mouth but nothing came out. By the time he reached the door Marc Hall was almost running, rifle held high. He stepped through the door and slammed the butt of the rifle into the major's head, sending the man's peaked hat and cigarette flying, a spray of blood and teeth chasing.

Slumped on the ground, unconscious, Marc stood over the major, reversed his rifle again, and put the barrel against the officer's forehead.

"Marc!" she yelled, and stopped in her tracks. It had happened so fast Nellis hadn't seen it, only how it was now, with Hall poised above the Haitian major.

"Captain Hall," he yelled, trying to keep his voice even. He gripped tight the pistol in his hand and stepped quickly forward. "Captain—Marc. Marc, right? Marc, don't do it, man. Don't pull that trigger."

Marc didn't look up, didn't move or even twitch, didn't say anything. He was staring at the major below him, his only thought that he was disappointed he'd knocked him out.

"There are lines and then there are lines," Nellis said. "This is a line you don't want to cross, Marc." He was only two steps away. "Drop the clip from that rifle, Captain. Drop the clip and then drop the rifle."

Marc finally spoke then. He didn't look up, just talked quietly. "You can't order me to do anything. We're the same rank."

"That ain't true, Captain. You have to know I was sent up here tonight to take you into custody."

Marc looked at him then.

"Captain Hall, I'm giving you a direct, lawful order to drop that weapon and surrender yourself."

"Here's the thing I never understood," Junior said. He took a long drink of water from the cup Rice had offered him, then leaned forward, laying his arms across the table. "There were times when the cells would be opened, for cleaning or whatever. And sometimes they'd stand around and guard, and sometimes they wouldn't."

"What do you mean?"

"I mean, there were twenty-five unshackled men in the courtyard, with maybe one guard or no guards and the door wide open."

Rice shrugged. "They knew there was probably a guy with a rifle outside. Wasn't worth it."

"I don't know, man, I don't know. You haven't seen it yet, you don't know how bad it was. And twenty against one, even if that one has a rifle—those are pretty good odds."

"So, why didn't you ever take them? Did you ever cut and run?"

Junior snorted. "Fuck no. I was too scared."

Voodoo Lounge

CHAPTER

35

Jean drove his old truck back to the hospital much slower than the trip out, for which Tory was profoundly grateful. Also, in the front seat, the bumping was less noticeable. She rocked back and forth, her elbow and forearm occasionally grazing the brown, leathery skin of Jean's arm. They didn't speak the same language, and for that, too, she was profoundly grateful. The ride was silent. Through the windshield the clouds parted and a hazy moon lit the road ahead.

She was so tired. She'd nodded off a few times in the truck, but sleep would have to wait. She had a lot to take care of if she was going to pull this off. A lot to take care of, then she could sleep. Later, much later. She would sleep then, deep and undisturbed. Sleep and sleep and—

Her head slammed into the dashboard of the truck. She'd dozed again. Jean offered her a banana.

He'd asked her, when they'd started, "The *Capitaine* . . . he, uh . . . ?" and through a series of hand gestures and translation guesses she figured he was asking if Marc would be joining him.

"No," she said. "*Non.*" Shaking her head. "Just me. *Moi.*" He'd smiled sadly and with no more questions started his truck.

Dawn was coming. She could see the outlines of trees now. They were close to the hospital. She ate her banana. When they got to the hospital Tory thanked the older man and tried to hand him a ten-dollar bill. He refused it and gave her another banana, which she accepted. She walked through the hospital gate in the dim gray of early dawn, no one about, alone in the stone yard.

There'd been no goodbye with Marc tonight. There'd never been a goodbye with Junior either. He'd left her, and the one time she saw him again—at the diner in Norfolk, when he told her what he'd done to her—she'd seen no trace of the Junior Davis she loved, and she left him. She had no intention of seeing him now. If she hadn't been sure on that before, she was now. And as tender as she felt for Marc this morning, she wondered the same simple but not simple question about him that she did about Junior: In the end, what is there to talk about?

Tory sat on Marc's cot. Then she stretched out on it. She could smell him. She curled up, burying her nose in his poncho liner and the blanket. There was some crying to do and now is when she did it, her face pressed into the poncho liner, pulling in his smell and warmth, the feel of his smooth skin and hands. She slept, briefly, then she woke, a headache fierce behind her eyeballs. She rolled off the cot to the floor, breathed through it a few minutes. Then she kneeled in the corner, cleaning her equipment best she could, taking it all apart, fitting her LBE and ammo pouches and everything into her rucksack, tying the helmet to it, trying to make it as easy as possible for whoever would have to carry it and turn it in.

And that's where Dick Wags found her, on the bare floor, using her toothbrush to clean the bolt of her M-16 rifle. She looked up, genuinely pleased to see it was him.

"Hello, Roomdog," she said.

"I came in before but you were sleeping, so I went to get some chow."

"They take care of you here?"

He nodded. "Yes. Me and Pelton. He's waiting in the hummer."

"Have a seat," she said. "I'm just cleaning up here."

He sat on Marc's cot and asked if he could smoke then lit one for himself and one for her. She was putting her rifle back together now.

"You have to shoot that thing last night?" he asked.

"No. Just cleaning it."

Tory gathered up all the cleaning gear into its little bag and shoved it back in the butt stock compartment.

"I'm really sorry, Rick," she said.

"You should be," he said. Then, "You have nothing to be sorry for."

"I do, though. Especially with you," she said. "Discharge and other death sentences aren't an excuse for bad manners, are they?" She grunted. "That was a bad place to put you in."

"No one held a gun to my head."

She looked at him then. "No, no one did, I guess. Thank you."

He took a drag off his cigarette, trying to keep his face clear. She did the same.

Tory handed him her rifle. Thinking something else, he stood and slung it over his shoulder. Then she picked up her rucksack and handed that to him, too. "Little bit lazy this morning, huh?" he said.

She smiled. "I'm not going back, buddy."

"What do you mean?"

"I'm not going back." She began unbuttoning her uniform top. "I don't know if I died going off the side of the road in that fucked-up Haitian truck or what exactly happened, but I'm sure it wasn't pretty." She pulled her top off, placed it on the rucksack in his arms. She reached down then and lifted her T-shirt up and over her head, putting that on the pile, too.

"What are you talking about, Tory."

She pulled her sports bra off—onto the pile it went. She sat on her cot and began unlacing her boots.

"I can't go back, Rick. I can't face anyone, don't want to face anyone, and there's nothing for me there anyway. What is there? Bullshit or discharge or both. Skipper will know that soon enough."

"He knows."

Boots and socks off, she began to unbutton her pants.

"Well, you know. They can use me here, and I can use them. So I'm just not going back."

"You can't do that."

"Sure I can."

"They'll want a body."

"Yeah, but only a little, especially when there's no family back home bothering them for it." She pulled her pants off, folded them carefully into a square, and placed it on the pile in Dick Wags's arms. She

hooked her thumbs in the elastic of her underwear. "Mostly, all the
Army cares about is property. And I'm giving it all back." She pulled
her underwear off, folded it neatly, and put it on the pile. She stood
there, looking him dead in the eye. "What—you seeing something you
haven't seen before, Rick?"

"Does this make you feel better," he said. She thought he might be
mad. That was okay. She was mad, too.

"Yes," she said. Tory reached up and laid her open palm on his
cheek, holding it there a moment. "Yes, it does make me feel better."
She stepped around him then and grabbed the poncho liner from
Marc's cot, wrapping it around herself. "This was Captain Hall's, so I
don't feel any personal responsibility in returning it."

"It's a grand gesture, Tory, but you can't do this."

"I'm doing it. Get that straight. I'm doing it. I'm not going back."

"What the fuck are we going tell them?" he said.

"I don't know. You and Mannino are pretty bright. I'm sure you'll
think of something. But I'll be gone about two seconds after you are,
and I'm going to stay gone for a while, until I know no one's coming
back to get me."

He wasn't even listening anymore, just staring at the floor. When he
looked back up at her he said, "I don't think it's a good way to go out,
Tory. This is not how you want to go out." She said nothing to that,
just held his eyes. Finally, he said, "You've got to get on a treatment
program, whatever you call it. Can they do that for you here?"

She shrugged, then nodded.

Then she walked over and hugged him, as best she could, with the
gear and clothes piled in his arms and the poncho liner around her
body. She hugged him, held him tight with all her gear between them,
and then he turned and walked out the door.

Wrapped in the poncho liner she found the cot again, and then it
was time to cry again and she did a little of that. *This is ridiculous,* she
thought. *I don't cry.*

Tory lay for five minutes, regret growing stronger and stronger in
her until finally she jumped up and stuck her head out of the hut and
called after him but he was gone, long gone, the Humvee gone.

Brinia Avril came to the hut later, waking her from sleep, and when she saw Tory's condition she left again and returned with a simple red and blue dress. Tory slipped it over her head, smoothing it out. She couldn't remember the last time she'd been in a dress.

"We'll have to get you some sandals," the doctor said, pointing at Tory's feet. "You can't walk around like that. You'll get a tapeworm."

Tory ate and then slept and it was later, much later in the day, when the hospital director knocked on her door. She opened it. In his arms was her gear. All of it. Rucksack, helmet, clothes, boots, rifle. He held it out to her.

"I was out, all day. In the camp. This was on my desk. Yours?"

She nodded and thanked him, taking it all from him. There was a note in the front pocket of her uniform pants, in Dick Wags's scrawl. It read: *You may need this more than you think. If not, bury it. See you around, either way. Your friend.*

Jacmel, Morning

CHAPTER

36

McBride stood on the pier at the bottom of his ship's gangway. The skippers of the two commercial tugs were waiting for him, but he'd insisted on checking one more time. Finally, he realized he wasn't going to find her onboard. His radio buzzed.

"We can't wait anymore, Skipper," the radio said.

"Piss off," he answered without pressing the button. He looked down the pier, into the glare of morning. There were palm trees down there, on the black sand beach, and maybe she'd gone there to read and had fallen asleep. Except, he'd gone down and looked. Twice.

"Where are you?" he said, and then before he could change his mind raised the radio to his lips and said, "Okay then. Let's go."

He walked up the gangway stairs. As he stepped onto the deck he looked across the pier to the Army LSV, to the skipper there standing, leaning on a rail. The man raised a hand, and McBride raised a hand back.

"Good luck," Mannino yelled, and McBride nodded and stepped inside the house of his ship.

The morning outside was bright but the blind drawn and the cabin dark. They'd slept like the dead, then woke, then slept again.

Lorraine hadn't said anything to him yet. Nothing. Just moved her stuff in without a word. It was so odd, so strange, he said nothing in return and didn't question it. If she wants to be here, Junior Davis thought, I won't stand in her way. It wasn't until after they'd slept the first time, in that dreamy, dozy place in between naps, that she spoke. They'd ended up with their arms around each other, and made no move to unwrap on waking. It was warm. When she did speak, she had one simple question.

"What is it that you have," she asked.

He told her.

"I thought so," she said. She kissed his chest, and they both went back to sleep. He woke later, alone, and slipped from the bed. He pushed the shade aside a little, and saw they were under way. The silent passage of a towed ship, a dead ship. He could see the mast of one of the commercial tugs, and the clouds and sky beyond. In his desk he found an unopened bottle of whiskey. *Our last sail*, he thought. *What better reason for a toast.*

Junior Davis crawled back into bed with the bottle and an empty glass and poured himself a drink.

CHAPTER

37

When you go, you go for real. It's just not worth doing any other way.

The soldier walked with helmet off, hanging it on one of the canteens strapped to the back of her web belt. She'd retrieved her soft cap from her cargo pocket, shook it out and put it on, pulling the curved brim low, two fingers off her nose. Her rucksack straps were tight, the load on her back and shoulders almost imperceptible. She held her rifle at an easy port arms with both hands, the reversed strap around her neck taking most of the weight.

In this way, on her terms, the soldier everyone called New Jersey stepped along the road from the hospital through jungle then lighter woods and walked out. Going for real.

She'd left the boat—two days before—in her old, original-issue black combat boots. The soft leather was dust-covered now, small sprays of dried mud on the sides and road dirt across the toes. It pleased her, to look down on them, moving forward on the march—working boots, stepping out.

Her mind clicked to sergeants' cadences.

Left, left, your military left

She watched her dusty boots.

Your mama was home when you left! You're right!
Your sister was home when you left! You're right!
Your mama your sister your uncle your aunt! / Aren't you glad you left?
You're right!

It was good to move, good to walk. She breathed deep the thick tropical air.

I wanna be an Airborne Ranger / I wanna life of sex and danger

She kept eyes front, looking neither left nor right, stepping it out.

Hey there soldier, you forgot to duck / was it friendly fire or just bad luck?

She remembered then the silver friendly fire tabs they'd taped to the sleeves of their uniforms and the tops of their helmets. She stopped walking, pausing only long enough to rip them off, crumple them in her hand, and throw them to the side of the road. *Worthless,* she thought. *Bad omens.* Then she walked on.

It was her last road march, and she stepped it out with purpose.

A mile from the hospital little Henri and his tagalong sister with her wide silver eyes appeared from the bushes. He waved and Tory waved back then he fell into step with her, pulling his little sister along. She stopped and tried to tell him to go back, back to the hospital, but he was having none of it. He found a long stick on the side of the road and laid it over his shoulder like a proper soldier and kept her pace for more than an hour. The two disappeared as Tory neared Jacmel, then were back—as if they'd never been gone—as she walked down a cobblestone street near an old hotel. She was passing people regularly now, her uniform and weapon drawing stares.

Around the next bend was a woman, a white woman, and Tory stopped abruptly—the sight so strange, so out of place. She realized the woman, too, had stopped abruptly, with probably very similar thoughts about the female soldier who'd just come into her view. They stood, twenty feet apart, staring at each other.

The woman was small, Tory's height almost exactly, but round. Her hair, too, was round, an almost bowl cut and straight across the forehead. She wore a long khaki skirt and blouse, sturdy black shoes, and what looked like an old sea bag—but white, knit cloth—over her shoulders. She carried a walking stick, and even from twenty feet Tory could see the older woman was suffering from the heat. Sweat tracks lined the soft creases of her face, dark stains visible on her blouse.

The boy ducked behind Tory, pulling his sister with him.

Down the road, the woman was breathing hard, unused to walking.

Tory wanted to say something but felt herself tongue-tied. She opened her mouth to yell hello and what came out was, "I'm an American."

"So I gathered," the woman said.

Tory smiled, feeling stupid. "The uniform."

"The uniform." The woman answered her smile, strained as it was through heat exhaustion.

Surprise over, the two women approached each other.

"I'm sorry," Tory said, "you looked out of place."

"I was about to say the same. I've seen soldiers before, but a single woman and two children is a funny patrol."

"I guess it is." Tory's left hand dropped to the girl's head.

"Perhaps there should be more patrols like yours."

"This is kind of an accident," Tory said. "But maybe you're right." She removed one of her canteens then and offered it to the woman, who thanked her and drank deeply. Tory realized suddenly she'd offered this woman water without a second thought but hadn't even considered the two Haitian children, walking with her for more than an hour now. She removed her helmet from where it hung on her second canteen, pulled the canteen free from her belt and unscrewed the top, then handed it to the boy. He put it into his sister's hands, whispering to her then watching as she drank.

Tory slung her helmet off one of her ammo pouches and turned back to the older woman, who seemed to be catching her breath.

"My name is Sergeant Harris."

Pastor held out her hand, shaking. "It is a happy pleasure to meet you, Sergeant. Thank you." She held the canteen out but Tory indicated she should drink more. The older woman raised the green plastic to her lips, swallowed, then said, "I may be lost." She laughed. "Actually, no, not lost. Lost would indicate I'd any idea today where I was going. But I didn't, and don't. So, not so much lost as—"

"Where are you going?" Tory said, but Pastor continued without answering.

"I've lost my ship, you see," she said.

"Lost it?"

"Well, it's left and I wasn't on it."

"Are you with the missionaries?"

"Yes," Pastor said, "I was," and didn't elaborate further. "I think, though, I might be of more use here."

"I don't know enough around here to know of any churches," Tory said.

"No, I'm not looking for a church. But I understand there's a hospital here, an AIDS hospital, somewhere on the mountain?"

Tory blinked, looking at the woman. Finally she said, "I know the place. They suffered quite a bit of damage in the last tropical storm. Mudslides."

"That's what I heard," Pastor said. "I thought I might be of help."

Tory started to say something but Pastor cut her off. "I grew up on a farm," she said. "I'm not much afraid of mud."

"There's no shortage of mud there."

"I have no shortage of time."

Tory looked away then, turning around completely, facing the other way, away from the woman, biting her lip hard. She stood there a moment. Then, without turning back around, unbuttoned a rear pocket and pulled out her wallet. She found a five-dollar bill, put the wallet away, and crouched down to the boy. She held the bill in front of his face and—talking slow, using her hands to make sure he understood—told him what she wanted him to do. She pointed and talked and pointed again, the boy nodding. When she was sure it was clear, she gave the boy the money, stood, and turned back to the older woman.

"These two will take you there, to the hospital," she said. "Their names are Henri and Christina."

"Bless you," Pastor said, almost more of a question than a statement, curious and wondering at the strangeness of it all.

Tory said, "Hold the blessing until this little guy actually gets you there."

Pastor looked down at the two children. "The girl is blind?" she said.

"I think so, yes. And I think they're orphaned."

"Well," Pastor said, then said it again: "Well."

The older woman held the canteen out but Tory shook her head. "Keep it," she said. "And theirs, too. I don't need them. I'm almost home." And this was true; she could see the gray antennas of the LSV's bridge through the trees. One more hill to go down and she'd be there.

"Thank you," Pastor said.

"I have to go," Tory said, raised her arm in goodbye, and walked on. When she looked up again a few minutes later she could see the whole ship, aft to bow, ass to Voodoo Lounge—her starting point and now her destination. An arc turned on itself. After such a walk she had a moment of regret, pure and true, just like yesterday but reversed. After such a walk Tory thought maybe she'd like to just keep on walking. But, then, maybe she'd walked far enough. For now, anyway.

When you go—when you finally go—you go for real. It's not always so clear, though, how or when you should leave, or what happens in between. There's a decision there, and she'd made hers. She was going out now, but going out the way she'd come in.

AUTHOR'S NOTE

The United States military entered Haiti on the morning of September 20, 1994, a planned violent invasion that in the last hours beforehand became instead a mostly unresisted occupation; America's second occupation of Haiti in the twentieth century, a much shorter and less sadistic stay than the earlier visit (1915–1934). This novel is set against the backdrop of these days and based in part on events that unfolded in this oddest of little wars, but remains entirely a work of fiction.

The words of Paul Farmer in the epigraph are from Tracy Kidder's biography of him, *Mountains Beyond Mountains*. The Alan Furst quote is from his novel *The World at Night*. Van Morrison's song "Beside You" is from his album *Astral Weeks*. Greg Brown's song "Lord, I Have Made You a Place in My Heart (But I Don't Reckon You're Gonna Come)" is from his album *The Poet Game*. "Life By the Drop" is the only acoustic recording Stevie Ray Vaughn ever made; it's on his posthumous *The Sky Is Crying*.

The writing of this novel began with scribbles in the ports of Cap-Haitien, Jacmel, and Guantanamo Bay in late 1994, six years before I had any idea what I was writing. The bulk of the novel ended up being written—eight years and much other writing later—in Bucks County, Pennsylvania. Thanks to Chuck Miles for building a solid room for me to work in there, and Kristina Bauman for sharing her occasional home with my notes, maps, and books. Thanks most of all to Brenda, Krissy, and Fiona for being here. I'm breathing now—better late than never.

313

Another thank you to Brenda for editorial reality checks and the push for perfection.

I remain indebted to Diana Finch *(agentus extremus)* and Amanda Patten *(editrix)*—thank you. Many thanks to the real Kevin Riddle, whose perfect name I borrowed for this book. Many thanks also, for many different reasons, to Pierre and Emily Henry, Matt Walker *(et tu, Zombi?)*, Kimberly Brissenden, Chris Hedges, Trish Todd, Nick DiGiovanni, Margaret Harris, Barry Raine, Bill Wright, Neal Pollack, Dick Wertime, Joel Turnipseed, Foster Winans, Martha Wexler, Connie Sharar, and Brian Wheeler.

—C.B.

STONEHAM-ET-TEWKESBURY, QUEBEC
FEBRUARY 2005

Voodoo Lounge

1. Both the natural environment and the political climate of Haiti are described throughout the novel. How does the contrast between the two contribute to the story? Are there any aspects of the natural world in Haiti that reflect the characters?

2. Discuss Tory's character. What motivates her to join the Army? Do you think she is a good soldier? Why or why not? Why do you think she chooses, unlike the other female soldiers in the book, to cut her hair short? How does Tory differ from the civilian women in the novel, such as Lorraine and Pastor?

3. How is the dynamic between male and female soldiers explored within the novel? Discuss the relationship between Tory and her fellow male soldiers, in particular Dick Wags. Examine the sexual energy between Tory and Marc Hall. What is it that draws them to each other, and do you think the war-zone setting has an effect on their attraction?

4. Discuss the incident in basic training that happened between Drill Sergeant Hoya and the trainee from Tory's platoon named Smith. What effect does this have on Tory and the other female soldiers? What do you think of the platoon's ostracism of Smith? What do you think of Drill Sergeant Chase's reaction to it?

5. Bauman describes Tory's relationship with Junior Davis this way:

> "Their drunk was a lot like their relationship in that way; it matched their relationship, followed the same track. Same as when you're drunk and you don't notice things have started to change, or you think maybe you see a change and you don't know why or how long it's been that way and you shake your head to clear it but you're drunk now and nothing is very clear."

What does this passage illustrate about their relationship? How much of an impact do you think their alcohol use had on their overall relationship and its eventual demise?

6. Marc Hall is a unique character, an American officer of Haitian descent deployed to occupy Haiti. Do you think there is an inherent conflict in that, and if so, how does he deal with it? Do you think his misinterpretation of the American mission in Haiti is inevitable, given his ancestry, or simply naive? The novel hints at divorce and a problem with depression; how do these affect Hall's interpretations and actions?

7. Discuss Pastor's character. Do you think she is in love with McBride, or has she simply come to rely on him? What motivates her to continue with her maritime ministry? Why do you think she chooses to stay in Haiti at the end of the novel?

8. *He took a drag on his cigarette, then poked his finger at Scaboo. "My little roomdog, you're a hired gun. Nothing noble about it." He spread his arms. "We're noble, mind you. We're the goods . . . We're American soldiers." He hissed the word, drawing it out. The group was silent now, drunk and holding its breath. "But don't think what we do is noble. You're drawing a paycheck, is all. Taking a bullet." He stubbed out his smoke on a cold piece of pizza. "You're an offensive tool of the United States government. You ain't defending nothing."*

   Do you agree with this statement made by Junior Davis? Why or why not? Do you think it is a sentiment felt by others in novel? What does this say about Junior Davis? He was referring to the Gulf War; do you think this sentiment is applicable to current events in Iraq?

9. Why did Captain Hall make the decision to rescue Ben Narcisse from the Haitian prison? What effect did witnessing the horrible conditions in the Haitian prison and the families gathered at the HIV hospital have on Tory's final decisions?

10. How do both Junior Davis and Tory individually deal with their HIV infection? What do you think of Tory's delay in telling anyone of her condition? Was it justified? Does Junior Davis's mistaken impression that he didn't infect Tory change him in any way? Why do you think Lorraine chooses to stay with Junior Davis?

11. Why do you think the book is titled *Voodoo Lounge*? What does that part of the ship symbolize?

Q & A with Christian Bauman

1. *There's a great tradition in literature of tragic or doomed love stories set in wartime. What is it about war that affects relationships?*

   War heightens all emotions. It bares nerves. It's like a high or a sexual rush; you'll do heroic or horrible things in wartime you'd never do sober, and wake up afterward unable to remember your motivations. This holds true on or off the battlefield—think occupied Paris in World War II, or lower Manhattan in the weeks immediately following 9/11. In a nationalistic sense war stirs anger and revenge and gives a sense of purpose to those who are otherwise powerless—something that never fails to be exploited by those who want to wage a war. For soldiers and others intimately involved in the war there can be other complex and seemingly contradictory emotions, all of them heightened: desperation, power, fear, strength, hate, desire. Wartime romance is dangerous. And for those with such real knowledge that it could all be gone tomorrow, connecting with another human being is imperative.

2. *Why did you choose to shield the gender of Tory Harris in the novel's opening?*

   Voodoo Lounge is a novel of transitions, in the characters and place, as well as in the narrative. The biggest narrative transition is how Tory is slowly revealed through the book, from soldier to human being. It occurred to me that if I was opening with a sketch of a soldier, it would make no difference whether the soldier was male or female. Her gender means very little to her situation at the beginning (although it means everything to her decisions in the end). Once I wrote Tory's opening description in these terms, it then became important to me to strip overt references to everyone's gender in the opening, for the sake of equality. We're all just soldiers going in; who we really are comes out later.

3. *Is there any particular character in this novel that you identify with the most? If so, why?*

I didn't plan this, but Tory and Junior are, I think, the yin and yang extremes of my personality. Not their actions, but their take on the world. Writing them was like pulling apart two halves of a whole to see what's inside, see what makes it tick.

4. *How much of this novel is based upon your experiences while serving in Haiti?*

I witnessed the opening minutes and hours of the Haiti invasion from the bow of the Army ship *LSV-1*. After the first few days, though, most of my time in-country was passed in relative comfort and safety, under way from port to port on the ship. It gave us a perspective most of the ground soldiers never had. We saw different parts of the country, and were able to freely and casually interact with the Haitians—especially in Jacmel—in a way not allowed to most of the Marines and 10th Mountain Division soldiers. My Haitian experience was an interesting juxtaposition to my deployment to Somalia two years before: We went to Haiti expecting violent urban combat in Port-au-Prince, and at the last minute entered and held the country mostly unopposed. Somalia, on the other hand, we deployed to expecting a non-violent, humanitarian mission. That unraveled rather quickly.

Printed in the United States
By Bookmasters